MW01633542

THE PIONEER WEST

THE PIONEER WEST

NARRATIVES OF THE WESTWARD MARCH OF EMPIRE

SELECTED AND EDITED BY
JOSEPH LEWIS FRENCH

WITH A FOREWORD BY
HAMLIN GARLAND

INDIAN HEAD BOOKS
New York

This edition published by Indian Head Books,
a division of Barnes & Noble, Inc.

1995 Indian Head Books

ISBN 1-56619-697-3

Printed and bound in the United States of America

M 9 8 7 6 5 4 3 2 1

Westward the course of empire takes its way;
  The four first acts already past,
A fifth shall close the drama with the day:
  Time's noblest offspring is the last.

Bishop Berkeley.

VITAL PAGES IN AMERICAN HISTORY

THE history of America is the story of trail-makers, pioneers in every sense of the word. Our forefathers had trails to make in new fields of government, of invention and in city building, but before all, smoothing the way for all, came the men and women who explored and ploughed and planted the wilderness. Their story will grow in interest as the years pass. Their deeds have already taken on something of the dim quality of heroic myths. They form the most distinctive of our contributions to history and poetry.

Many of the most stark and stirring of these chronicles of the border have passed out of print and are now inaccessible even to the painstaking student. It is from among these almost forgotten, yet vital records that Mr. French has selected the chapters of his book of narratives of the PIONEER WEST. I am personally grateful to him for rescuing for me several of these chronicles of which I had heard but which I had not been able to read until they came to me in this volume. I perceive in this collection another link in the lengthening chain of our traditional story. The Great War has thrown the events of our early settlement suddenly into remote distance. It is as if an extra half-century had been abruptly interposed, and this added perspective has given us a new and keener interest in the beginnings of our nation.

No one who has spent a recent summer in Europe can fail to perceive the change of sentiment which has come, since the war, to the peoples of the Old World. To them America is admittedly the dominating economic force of to-day. No well-informed European writer or speaker now pretends to patronize the United States as a young and unformed colony. The foundation stages of American history have acquired new value in the minds of many English and French readers, and such students this book which Mr. French has built up of scattered and neglected chronicles will stimulate to wider research. I commend it to all Americans who have neither time nor opportunity to read in their entirety the volumes from which these notable and representative chapters have been lifted. Broadly chronological in arrangement, they suggest a panorama of the rigorous Westward march of the hunters, woodsmen, planters and gold-miners who were chief actors of the century which ended with the outbreak of the Spanish War in 1898.

With regard to the inclusion of a section from one of my own books I can only say that when approached for a grant of copyright I suggested something to offset the many chapters of life in the mining camps and on the trail, something which should tell of the homely methods of settling the plains. Beyond this suggestion, I did not care to go. The excerpt which the editor has used is a leaf out of my personal experiences in Brown and MacPherson counties in Dakota, in the spring of 1883, and is a faithful picture of the life we led while holding down our homestead claims.

HAMLIN GARLAND.

PREFACE

Oh, that glorious West! The magic and the memory of it! How it thrilled us in our boyhood, how it held us in our youth, how the dream of it filled our young pulsing manhood, till there was none other! "O, to be in England now that April's there!" once sang Browning, but the song in the heart of young America, forty years ago and more, was the great glorious, boundless West! I crossed the bare Kansas and Colorado plains in the month of March, 1880, — when the Great West was still a vision, yet largely a dream; when scarce small clumps of buffalo could still be seen from the car windows. I shook hands at the bar of the St. James Hotel in Denver with Buffalo Bill and Texas Jack in full buckskin regalia, — still to be seen and known in their habit as they lived.

Yet it was the dawning of a new day for the West and all men knew it. The old order passeth, and so it was here; a new West was coming in, and the great pioneer heroes of an earlier day shook hands with the derby-hatted tenderfoot from the East and tilted glasses in friendly companionship. But the old West — the great, the never-to-be-forgotten epic of our newer civilization — still lingered; and happy, yes, a hero of sorts was he of the East who still sniffed the footprints. Railroads were still largely a dream; the Union Pacific had cut the boundless wastes of the great desert and made travel to California an actuality; but a second great transcontinental iron path was still largely a possibility. The footprints of the pioneers were everywhere; echoes of the pathfinder were yet in the air; gold and silver were being found every day in the wilderness of the Rockies; new camps — reachable only by the primitive stagecoach, whose final departure in an older realm had been magniloquently signed over by old Sir Walter — were springing up overnight; Leadville had a population of thirty thousand and not a score of streets named; Buena Vista, at eleven thousand feet above sea level, was a dream of the gods! Away to the South were Silver Cliff and Rosita, with their hitherto uncombed rocks pouring out fortunes. Ouray was an acknowledged bonanza; and into the Gunnison country poured a steady stream of prairie-wagons over mountain trails that the Indian himself did not know. The plains held unlimited resources in the golden imagination of the pioneer! Was there ever such a dream as his — of sheep and cattle by the thousands — such flocks as Abraham never dreamed of; and away to the South, boundless, unconceived-of possibilities, an absolute Eldorado! Such was the great, the Golden West — to make no concrete mention of California — when the compiler of these pages first felt the urge and the surge toward it. Horace Greeley's pæan was in the air: "Go West, young man." And most of us did; and whether fortune or its reverse came, there is not a man of us in whom the red blood flows still that can ever forget that splendid scene. If to the survivor, as to the more or less belated traveler, some echo of it lives in these pages, he has done his work faithfully.

This, then, is an outdoor book. The breath of the prairie, the mountain, the desert, the lake, the sea blows through its pages. It describes for the most part an outdoor life, — a life that in its main aspects and features is the most stirring and eventful chapter in the history of any new civilization. All the elements of romance were crowded into the making of our great West; not a single one is lacking. It was the last great scene in the history of world-pioneering, and contains episodes, like the discovery of gold in California, that are epic. The tale in its infinite variety has been told by many writers; some of whom have passed into oblivion, but have left us living pages; others of them belong to our best literary tradition; a few are among our immortals. It is impossible in a volume of this size to give more than a vivid glance at the scope and importance of this vast literature. The compiler has endeavored to convey an impression of the general scene inspired by the men who were themselves its living actors. " All of which I saw, and part of which I was " has been his motto in gathering his material. He has therefore some hope that he has presented, at least in degree, a living picture of a great drama, now vanished forever, and which undoubtedly can never be paralleled in the annals of world civilization.

JOSEPH LEWIS FRENCH

CONTENTS

	PAGE
VITAL PAGES IN AMERICAN HISTORY	vii
PREFACE	ix
THE UNBROKEN WILD (1804)	1
From Lewis and Clark's Journals	
JIM BECKWOURTH'S NARRATIVE (1824)	15
From "Autobiography of James P. Beckwourth"	
THE PATHFINDER: IN THE HIGH ROCKIES (1842), *By John C. Frémont*	37
From Frémont's Journal of the First Expedition	
THE WILDERNESS HUNTER (1845), *By J. B. Ruxton*	56
From "Adventures in Mexico and the Rocky Mountains"	
AT FORT LARAMIE (1846), *By Francis Parkman*	72
From "The Oregon Trail"	
GOLD! GOLD! SUTTER'S FORT (1848-1849), *By Charles Pettigrew*	86
From the *Caledonian*	
A FRONTIER DUEL (1848), *By Emerson Hough*	115
From "The Covered Wagon"	
EL DORADO, *By Bayard Taylor*	124
From "Eldorado"	
FRÉMONT'S GREAT RIDE (1849), *By Frederick S. Dellenbaugh*	158
From "Frémont and '49"	
THE LUCK OF ROARING CAMP, *By Bret Harte*	161
From "The Luck of Roaring Camp and Other Sketches"	

Contents

PAGE

THE CITY OF THE SAINTS, *By Sir Richard Burton* . . 174
From "The City of the Saints and Across the Rocky Mountains to California"

ON THE COMSTOCK (1860), *By J. Ross Browne* . . . 202
From "A Peep at Washoe" and "Washoe Revisited"

ALDER GULCH (1863), *By Nathaniel P. Langford* . . 231
From "Vigilante Days and Ways"

CHEYENNES AND SIOUX (1867), *By General George A. Custer* 245
From "My Life on the Plains"

THE PONY EXPRESS, *By Mark Twain* 268
From "Roughing It"

SLADE, *By Mark Twain* 270
From "Roughing It"

GENERAL SHERIDAN HUNTS THE BUFFALO, *By De B. R. Keim* 284
From "On the Border with Sheridan's Troopers"

AT TUCSON (1870), *By Capt. John G. Bourke* . . . 296
From "On the Border with Cook"

TOLD AT TRINIDAD (1879), *By A. A. Hayes, Jr.* . . . 310
From "New Colorado and the Santa Fé Trail"

SPECIMEN JONES, *By Owen Wister* 319
From "Red Men and White"

THE LAND OF THE STRADDLE-BUG—DAKOTA (1883), *By Hamlin Garland* 343
From "The Moccasin Ranch"

OLD EPHRAIM THE GRIZZLY, *By Theodore Roosevelt* . 357
From "Hunting Trips of a Ranchman"

THE VANISHED SCENE, *By Hal G. Evarts* 378
From "The Passing of the Old West"

THE PIONEER WEST

THE UNBROKEN WILD

LEWIS AND CLARK

1804

Reprinted from Lewis and Clark's Journals.   July 22, 1804.

OUR camp is by observation in latitude 41° 3′ 11″.[1]
Immediately behind it is a plain about five miles wide, one
half covered with wood, the other dry and elevated.   The
low grounds on the south near the junction of the two
rivers are rich but subject to be overflowed.   Farther
up the banks are higher and opposite our camp the first
hills approach the river, and are covered with timber such
as oak, walnut and elm.   The immediate country is watered
by the Papillon (Butterfly) Creek, of about 18 yards
wide and three miles from the Platte; on the north are high
open plains and prairies and at nine miles from the Platte
the Moscheto Creek and two or three small willow islands.
We stayed here several days during which we dried our
provisions, made new oars, and prepared our despatches
and maps of the country we passed for the President of the
United States to whom we intend to send them by a
pirogue from this place.   The hunters have found game
scarce in this neighborhood; they have seen deer, turkeys
and grouse; we have also an abundance of ripe grapes, and
one of our men caught a white catfish, the eyes of which

[1] Platte and Missouri Rivers. The expedition started May 14th.

were small and its tail resembling that of a dolphin. **The** present season is that in which the Indians go out into the prairies to hunt the buffalo; but as we discovered some hunters' tracks, and observed the plains on fire in the direction of their villages, we hoped that they might have returned to gather the green Indian corn, and therefore despatched two men to the Pawnee villages with a present of tobacco and an invitation to the chief to visit us. They returned in two days. Their first course was through an open prairie to the south. They then reached a small beautiful river called the Elkhorn or Corne de Ceri. (These natural features have brush names in some instances.) About 100 yards wide with clear water and a gravelly channel. It empties a little below the Pawnee village into the Platte which they crossed and came to the village, about forty-five miles from our camp. They found no Indians though there were fresh tracks of a small party. The Ottoes were once a powerful nation and live about 20 miles above the Platte on the south bank of the Missouri. Being reduced they migrated to the neighborhood of the Pawnees under whose protection they now live. Their village is on the south side of the Platte about 30 miles from its mouth; and their number is 200 including about 30 families of Missouri Indians who are incorporated with them.

Five leagues above them on the same side of the river, resides the nation of Pawnees. This people were among the most numerous of the Missouri Indians, but have been gradually broken and dispersed and even within the past ten years have undergone some sensible changes. They now consist of four bands; the first of about 500 men, to whom of late years have been added a second band called the Republican Pawnees from their having lived on the Republican branch of the River Kanzas — they amount to nearly 250 men. The third are the Pawnees Loups or Wolf Pawnees, who live on the Wolf fork of the Platte, about 90 miles from the principal village and number 280 men. The fourth band originally resided on the Kanzas and Arkansaw but in their wars with the Osages they were so often defeated that they at last retired to their present home on the Red River where they form a tribe of 400 men. All these tribes live in villages and subsist chiefly on corn; but during the intervals of farming rove the plains in quest of buffalo.

Beyond them on the river and westward of the Black Mountains are the Kaninaviesch consisting of about 400 men. They are supposed to have been originally Pawnees — but they have degenerated and now no longer live in villages but rove the plains. Still farther to the westward are several tribes who wander and hunt to the sources of the River Platte and thence to Rock Mountain. Of these tribes little is known more than the names and the numbers, as first the Straitan or Kite Indians, a small tribe of one hundred men. They have acquired the name of Kites from their flying; that is their being always on horseback; and the smallness of their numbers is to be attributed to their extreme ferocity; they are the most warlike of all the western Indians; they never yield in battle; they never spare their enemies; and the retaliation of this barbarity has almost extinguished the nation. Then come the Wetapahato and Kiowa tribes associated together and amounting to two hundred men; the Castahana of three hundred men, to which are to be added the Cataka, seventy-five men, and the Dotami. These wandering tribes are conjectured to be the remnants of the great Padouca nation who occupied the country between the upper parts of the River Platte and the River Kanzas. They were visited by Bourgemont in 1724, and then lived on the Kanzas River. The Seats which he described as their residences are now occupied by the Kanzas nation; and of the Padoucas there does not now exist even the name.

It being vital to the success of further progress to hold

council with the Indians messengers were sent with presents and a few days afterwards: in the afternoon the party arrived with the Indians consisting of Little Thief and Big Horse, together with six other chiefs and a French interpreter. We met them under a shade and after they had finished a repast we supplied them we inquired into the origin of the late war between their tribe and the Mahas, which they related with great frankness. * * * The evening was closed by a dance; and the next day the chiefs and warriors being assembled at ten o'clock we explained the speech we had already sent from the Council Bluffs [1] and renewed its advices. They all replied in turn and the presents were then distributed. We gave large medals to Big Horse and Little Thief, and a small medal to a third chief. We also gave a kind of certificate or letter of acknowledgment to five of the warriors expressive of our favor and their good intentions. One of them dissatisfied returned us the certificate, but the chief fearful of our being offended begged it might be restored to him; this we declined and rebuked them severely for having in view mere traffic instead of peace with their neighbors. This displeased them at first, but at length all petitioned that it should be given to the warrior who came forward and made an apology. We then handed it to the chief to be given to the most worthy among them and he bestowed it on the same warrior whose name was Great Blue Eyes. After a more substantial present of small articles and tobacco the council was ended with a dram to the Indians. In the evening we exhibited different objects of curiosity and particularly the air-gun which gave them great surprise. Those people are almost naked, having no covering except a sort of breech cloth around the middle with a loose blanket or buffalo-robe painted, thrown over them. This delegation was from the Missouris and Ottoes who speak

[1] To Washington.

very nearly the same language.   They all begged us to give
them whiskey.

The next morning the Indians mounted their horses and
received from us a canister of whiskey at parting.   We
then set sail and after passing two islands on the north came
to one on that side under some bluffs.   Here we had the
misfortune to lose one of our sergeants Charles Floyd.[1]
He was yesterday seized with a bilious colic, and all our
care and attention could not save him.   A little before
his death he said to Captain Clark "I am going to leave
you"; and he died with a composure which justified the
high opinion we had formed of his firmness and good conduct.   He was buried on the top of a bluff with the honors
due to a brave soldier, and the place of his interment
marked by a cedar post on which we put his name and the
date of his death.   We named this place after him and
also a small river about a mile to the north where we
encamped.

We shortly after passed the mouth of the great Sioux
River — this river comes in from the north and is about
one hundred and ten yards wide.   M. Durion our Sioux
interpreter says that it is navigable upwards of two hundred
miles to the falls and even beyond them.   That below the
falls a creek falls in from the Eastward after passing
through cliffs of red rock.   Of this the Indians make their
pipes: and the necessity of procuring them has introduced
a sort of law of nations, by which the banks of the creek
are sacred, so that even tribes at war meet at these quarries
without hostility.   Thus we find even among savages certain things held sacred which mitigate the rigours of their
merciless warfare.

A few days following we had a violent storm of wind
and rain in the evening and had to repair our pirogues the
next day.   At four o'clock Sergeant Pryor and his men
came back with five chiefs of the Sioux and about seventy

---

[1] The organization was military.

warriors and boys. Sergeant Pryor reported that on reaching their village twelve miles from our camp he was met by a party with a buffalo-robe on which they desired to carry their visitors: an honour which they declined informing the Indians that they were not the commanders of the party. As a mark of respect they were then presented with a fat dog, already cooked of which they partook heartily and found it well-flavored. The camps of the Sioux are of a conical form covered with buffalo-robes painted with various figures and colours, with an aperture in the top for the smoke to pass through. The lodges contain from ten to fifteen persons and the interior arrangement is compact and handsome, each lodge having a place for cooking detached from it. The next day we prepared a speech and some presents and then sent for the chiefs and warriors whom we received under a large oak-tree near to which the flag of the United States was flying. Captain Lewis delivered the speech and we gave to the grand chief a flag, a medal, and a certificate, to which we added a chief's coat; that is a richly-laced uniform of the United States Artillery Corps, and a cocked hat and red feather. A second chief and three inferior ones were given medals and a present of tobacco and articles of clothing. We then smoked the pipe of peace, and the chiefs retired to a bower formed of bushes by their young men, where they divided the presents among each other and ate and smoked and held a council on their answer to us to-morrow. The young people exercised their bows and arrows in shooting at marks for beads as prizes; and in the evening the whole party danced until a late hour. In the course of their amusement we threw among them some knives, tobacco, bells, tape and binding with which they were much pleased. Their musical instruments were the drum, and a sort of little bag made of buffalo-hide dressed white with small shot or pebbles in it and a bunch of hair tied to it for a handle. This produces a sort of rattling music with which the party was annoyed by four musicians during the council this morning.

*   *   *   *   *

These Indians are the Yanktons a tribe of the great nation of the Sioux. They are stout and well proportioned and have a certain air of dignity and boldness. They are very fond of decorations and use paint freely and porcupine quills and feathers. Some of them wear necklaces of brass chains three inches long and close strung. They have only a few fowling-pieces among them. What struck us most was an institution peculiar to them and to the Kite Indians — from whom it is copied we were told. This is an association of the bravest and most active young men who are bound to each other by attachment and secured by a vow never to retreat before danger or give way to their enemies. In war they go forward openly and without any effort at shelter. This determination became heroic — or ridiculous — a short time since when these young Yanktons were crossing the Missouri on the ice. A hole lay immediately in their course but the leader went straight ahead and was drowned. Others would have followed but were forcibly stopped by the rest of them. These young men sit and encamp and dance apart from the rest; their seats in council are superior to those even of the chiefs and their persons more respected. But their boldness diminishes their numbers; so that the band is now reduced to four warriors who were among our visitors.

*   *   *   *   *

Early in the morning of September 16th having reached a convenient spot on the south side of the river, we encamped just above a small creek which we called Corvus having killed an animal of that genus near it. Our camp is in a beautiful plain with timber thinly scattered for three-quarters of a mile, consisting chiefly of elm, cottonwood, some ash of an indifferent quality, and a considerable quantity of a small species of white oak. This tree seldom rises higher than thirty feet and branches very much,— the bark is rough, thick and of a light colour; the leaves small, deeply indented, and of a pale green; the cup which contains the acorn is fringed on the edges; the acorn itself which grows in great profusion is of an excellent flavor and has none of the roughness which most other acorns possess: they are now falling and have probably attracted the number of deer which we have seen at this place. The ground having been recently burned by the Indians is covered with young green grass and in the neighbourhood are great quantities of fine plums. We killed a few deer for the sake of their skins which we wanted to cover the pirogues, the meat being too poor for food. About a quarter of a mile behind our camp, at an elevation of twenty feet a plain extends parallel with the river for three miles. Here we saw a grove of plum trees loaded with fruit, now ripe and differing in nothing from those of the Atlantic States except that the tree is smaller and more thickly set. The ground of the plain is occupied by the burrows of multitudes of barking squirrels, who entice hither the wolves of a small kind, hawks and polecats. This plain is intersected nearly in its whole extent by deep ravines and steep irregular rising grounds of from one to two hundred feet. On ascending one of these we saw a second high level plain stretching to the south as far as the eye could reach. To the westward a high range of hills about twenty miles distant. All around the country had been recently burned and a young green grass about four inches high covered the ground which was enlivened by herds of antelopes and buffalo; the last of which were in such multitudes that we cannot exaggerate in saying that at a single glance we saw three thousand of them before us. Of all the animals we had seen the antelope seems to possess the most wonderful fleetness. Shy and timorous they generally repose only on the ridges which command a view of all the approaches of an enemy; — the acuteness of their sight distinguishes the most distant danger: the delicate sensibility of their smell defeats concealment; and when alarmed their rapid career seems more like the flight of birds than the movements of a quadruped. After many unsuccessful attempts Captain Lewis at last by winding around the ridges approached a party of seven which were on an eminence towards which the wind was unfortunately blowing. The only male of the party frequently encircled the summit of the hill as if to announce any danger to the females which formed a group at the top. Although they did not see Captain Lewis, the smell alarmed them and they fled when he was still at the distance of two hundred yards: he immediately ran to the spot where they had been; a ravine concealed him from them; but the next moment they appeared on a second ridge at a distance of three miles. He doubted whether they could be the same; but the number and the extreme rapidity with which they continued their course convinced him.

The following day we reached an island in the middle of the river nearly a mile in length and crossed with red cedar: at its extremity a small creek comes in from the north: we there met with some sand-bars and the wind being very high and ahead, we encamped having made only seven miles. In addition to the common deer which were in great abundance we saw goats, elk, buffalo, and the black-tailed deer; the large wolves too are very numerous, and have long hair with coarse fur of a light color. A small species of wolf about the size of a gray fox was also killed and proved to be the animal we had hitherto mistaken for a fox. There were also many porcupines, rabbits and barking squirrels in the neighbourhood.

In the morning we observed a man riding on horseback

down towards the boat and we were much pleased to find that it was George Shannon, one of our party for whose safety we had been very uneasy. Our two horses having strayed from us on the 26th August he was sent to search for them. After he had found them he started to rejoin us, but seeing some other tracks which must have been those of Indians, and which he mistook for our own, he concluded that we were ahead, and had been for sixteen days following the bank of the river above us. During the first four days he exhausted his bullets, being obliged to subsist for twelve days on a few grapes, and a rabbit which he had killed by making use of a hard piece of stick for a ball. One of his horses gave out and was left behind; the other he kept as a last resource for food. Despairing of overtaking us, he was returning down the river in the hope of meeting some boat with Indians, and was on the point of killing his horse when he discovered us. September 25. The morning was fine and the wind continued from the southeast. We raised a flagstaff and an awning under which we assembled at twelve o'clock with all our party [1] parading under arms. The chiefs and warriors from the camp two miles up the river met us, to the number of fifty or sixty and after smoking we delivered them a speech, and gave the chiefs presents. We then invited them on board, and showed them the boat, the air-gun and such curiosities as we thought might amuse them. In this we succeeded too well for after giving them a quarter of a glass of whiskey, which they seemed to like very much, and sucked the bottle it was with difficulty we got rid of them. Captain Clark at last started for the shore with them in a pirogue with five of our own men; but it seems they had formed a design to stop us. No sooner had the party landed than three of the Indians seized the boat's cable, and one of the soldiers of the chief put his arms around the mast — in token of possession. The second

[1] Forty-one men, full musters.

chief then said that we should not go on; that they had not received enough presents. Captain Clark told him that we were not squaws but warriors — that we could not be stopped from going on; that we were sent by our Great Father who could in a moment exterminate them. The chief replied he too had warriors and started to attack Captain Clark who immediately drew his sword, and signaled the men in the main boat to prepare for action.

The Indians surrounding him drew arrows and were just bending their bows when the swivel gun [1] was instantly trained on them — and twelve of our best men who had at once rowed over jumped ashore to help Captain Clark.

Those movements took them aback — the great chief ordered the young men away from our pirogue and they withdrew for council. Captain Clark went forward and offered his hand to the first and second chiefs but was refused. He retired and boarded the pirogue but had not got more than ten paces when both the chiefs and two of the warriors waded in after the boat and were taken on board.

September 26. Our conduct yesterday seemed to have inspired the Indians with fear of us, and as we wanted to be well with them we complied with their wish that their squaws and children also should see us and our boat — which would be a great curiosity to them.

We finally anchored on the south side of the river where a crowd of them were waiting for us. Captain Lewis went on shore and remained several hours: and finding their disposition friendly this time, we resolved to remain during the night to a dance which they were preparing for us. Captains Lewis and Clark who went on shore one after the other were met on landing by ten well-dressed young men who took them up in a robe highly decorated, and carried them to a large council-house, where they were placed on a

[1] A small cannon.

dressed buffalo-skin by the side of the grand chief. The hall or council-room was in the shape of three-quarters of a circle, covered at the top and sides with skins well-dressed and sewed together. Under this shelter sat about seventy men forming a circle round the chief, before whom were placed a Spanish flag and the one we had given them yesterday. This left a vacant circle of about six feet diameter, in which the pipe of peace was raised on two forked sticks, about six or eight inches from the ground, and under it the down of the swan was scattered; a large fire in which they were cooking provisions burned near, and in the centre about four hundred pounds of excellent buffalo-meat as a present for us. As soon as we were seated an old man got up and after approving what we had done in our own defense, begged us to take pity on their unfortunate situation. The great chief rose after and made an harangue to the same effect; then with great solemnity he took some of the most delicate parts of the dog which was cooked for the festival and held it to the flag by way of sacrifice. This done he held up the pipe of peace, and first pointing it to the heavens, then to the four quarters of the globe and then to the earth, he made a short speech, lighted it and presented it to us. As we smoked in turn he harangued his people, and then the repast was served. It consisted of the dog which they had just been cooking, this being a great dish among the Sioux and used on all festivals; to which were added pemitigon, a dish made of buffalo meat dried or jerked; pounded and mixed raw with grease and a kind of ground potato dressed like the preparation of Indian corn called hominy to which it is little inferior. Of all their luxuries, which were placed before us in platters with horn-spoons, we took the latter, but we could as yet partake but sparingly of the dog.

We ate and smoked for an hour when it became dark; everything was then cleared away for the dance, a large fire being made in the centre of the house, giving at once light and warmth to the ball-room. The orchestra was composed of about ten men, who played on a sort of tambourine formed of skin stretched across a hoop, and made a jingling noise with a long stick to which the hoofs of deer and goats were hung. The third instrument was a small skin bag with pebbles in it; these with five or six young men for the vocal part made up the band. The women then came forward highly decorated; some with poles in their hands on which were hung the scalps of their enemies; others with guns, spears or different trophies taken in war by their husbands or brothers. They arranged themselves in two columns and danced toward each other till they met in the center, when the rattles were shaken, and they all shouted and returned to do it over again. They have no step, but shuffle along the ground. The music is no more than a confusion of noises, pointed by hard or gentle blows on the buffalo skin. The song is perfectly extemporaneous. In the pauses a man comes forward and recites in a low guttural some story or incident — martial or ludicrous — or as was the case this evening voluptuous and indecent. Sometimes they alternate, the orchestra first and then the women raise their voices in chorus making a music more agreeable, that is, less intolerable than the musicians. The men dance always separate from the women and about the same except they jump up and down instead of shuffling; in their war dances the recitations are always of a military cast.

In person these Tetons are rather ugly and ill-made — their legs and arms are too small, their cheek bones are high and their eyes projecting. The females are the handsomer. Both sexes appear cheerful and sprightly; but in our intercourse we discovered they were cunning and vicious. The men shave their heads except a small tuft on top which they only sacrifice on the death of a near relation. In full dress they fasten to this a hawk's feather or calumet feather worked with porcupine quills. They paint the face and body with a mixture of grease and coal. The chief garment is a buffalo robe dressed white and adorned with loose porcupine quills to make a jingling noise when they move — and painted with uncouth symbols. The leg from the hip to the ankle is covered by leggins of dressed antelope with two inch side-seams ornamented by tufts of hair from scalps won in war. Their winter moccasins are dressed buffalo-skin soled with thick elk-skin. On great occasions or in full dress the young men drag after them the entire skin of a polecat fixed to the heel of a moccasin. Another such skin serves as a tobacco-pouch tucked into the girdle. They smoke red willow bark either alone or mixed with tobacco when they have any. The pipe is of red clay, with an ash stem of three or four feet, highly ornamented with feathers, hair, and porcupine quills. The hair of the women grows long and is parted from the forehead across the head, at the back of which it is either collected into a kind of bag or hangs down over the shoulders.

They wear the same kind of moccasins and leggins as the men but the latter do not reach below the knee where they are met by a long loose shift of skins which reaches nearly to the ankles. This is fastened over the shoulders by a string, and has no sleeves, but a few pieces of the skin hang a short distance around the arms. Sometimes a girdle fastens this skin round the waist and over is thrown a robe like that worn by the men. They seem fond of dress. They have among them officers to keep the peace — like civilized peoples — whose distinguishing mark is a collection of two or three raven skins fastened to the girdle behind the back in such a way that the tails stick out horizontally from the body. On the head too is a raven skin split into two parts and tied so as to let the beak project from the forehead.

JIM BECKWOURTH'S NARRATIVE

1824

From "Autobiography of James P. Beckwourth."

AFTER we had rested we departed for Snake River, Idaho, making the Black Foot Buttes on our way, in order to pass through the buffalo region. The second day of our march, one of our men, while fishing, detected a party of Black Feet in the act of stealing our horses in the open day. But for the man, they would have succeeded in making off with a great number. The alarm was given, and we mounted and gave immediate chase. The Indians were forty-four in number, and on foot; therefore they became an easy prey. We ran them into a thicket of dry bush, which we surrounded, and then fired in several places. It was quite dry, and, there being a good breeze at the time, it burned like chaff. This driving the Indians out, as fast as they made their appearance we shot them with our rifles. Every one of them was killed; those who escaped our bullets were consumed in the fire; and as they were all more or less roasted, we took no scalps. None of our party were hurt, except one, who was wounded by one of our men.

On the third day we found buffalo, and killed great numbers of them by a "surround." At this place we lost six horses, three of them belonging to myself, two to a Swiss, and one to Baptiste. Not relishing the idea of losing them (for they were splendid animals), and seeing no signs of Indians, I and the Swiss started along the back track in pursuit, with the understanding that we would rejoin our company at the Buttes. We followed them to the last place of rendezvous; their tracks were fresh and plain, but we could gain no sight of our horses. We then gave up the chase, and encamped in a thicket. In the morning we started to return, and had not proceeded far, when, hearing a noise in our rear, I looked round, and saw between two and three hundred Indians within a few hundred yards of us. They soon discovered us, and, from their not making immediate pursuit, I inferred that they mistook us for two of their own party. However, they soon gave chase. They being also on foot, I said to my companion, "Now we have as good a chance of escaping as they have of overtaking us."

The Swiss (named Alexander) said, "It is of no use for me to try to get away: I can not run; save yourself, and never mind me."

"No," I replied, "I will not leave you; run as fast as you can until you reach the creek; there you can secrete yourself, for they will pursue me."

He followed my advice, and saved himself. I crossed the stream, and when I again appeared in sight of the Indians I was on the summit of a small hill two miles in advance. Giving a general yell, they came in pursuit of me. On I ran, not daring to indulge the hope that they would give up the chase, for some of the Indians are great runners, and would rather die than incur the ridicule of their brethren. On, on we tore; I to save my scalp, and my pursuers to win it. At length I reached the Buttes, where I had expected to find the camp, but, to my inconceivable horror and dismay, my comrades were not there. They had found no water on their route, and had proceeded to the river, forty-five miles distant.

My feelings at this disappointment transcended expression. A thousand ideas peopled my feverish brain at once. Home, friends, and my loved one presented themselves with one lightning-flash. The Indians were close at my heels; their bullets were whizzing past me; their yells sounded painfully in my ears; and I could almost feel the knife making a circuit round my skull. On I bounded, however, following the road which our whole company had made. I was scorching with thirst, having tasted neither sup nor bit since we commenced the race. Still on I went with the speed of an antelope. I kept safely in advance of the range of their bullets, when suddenly the glorious sight of the camp-smoke caught my eye. My companions perceived me at a mile from the camp, as well as my pursuers; and, mounting their horses to meet me, soon turned the tables on my pursuers. It was now the Indians' turn to be chased. They must have suffered as badly with thirst as I did, and our men cut them off from the river. Night had begun to close in, under the protection of which the Indians escaped; our men returned with only five scalps. According to the closest calculation, I ran that day ninety-five miles.[1]

My heels thus deprived the rascally Indians of their anticipated pleasure of dancing over my scalp. My limbs were so much swollen the next morning, that for two or three days ensuing it was with great difficulty I got about. My whole system was also in great pain. In a few days, however, I was as well as ever, and ready to repay the Indians for their trouble.

The third day after my escape, my companion Aleck found his way into camp. He entered the lodge with dejection on his features.

"Oh!" he exclaimed, "I thank God for my escape, but the Indians have killed poor Jim. I saw his bones a few miles back. I will give any thing I have if a party will go with me and bury him. The wolves have almost picked his bones, but it must be he. Poor, poor Jim! gone at last!"

"Ha!" said some one present, "is Jim killed, then? Poor

---

[1] Concerning this great race for life, it may appear impossible to some for a human being to accomplish such a feat. Those who survive of Sublet's company, and who know the distances from point to point of my celebrated race, will please to correct me publicly if I am in error in the distance. I have known instances of Indian runners accomplishing more than one hundred and ten miles in one day.

fellow! Well, Aleck, let us go back and give him a Christian burial."

He had seen a body nearly devoured on the way, most likely that of the wounded Indian who had chased me in his retreat from our camp.

I came limping into the crowd at this moment, and addressed him before he had perceived me: "Halloo, Aleck, are you safe?"

He looked at me for a moment in astonishment, and then embraced me so tight that I thought he would suffocate me. He burst into a flood of tears, which for a time prevented his articulation. He looked at me again and again, as if in doubt of my identity.

At length he said, "Oh, Jim, you are safe! And how did you escape? I made sure that you were killed, and that the body I saw on the road was yours. Pshaw! I stopped and shed tears on a confounded dead Indian's carcass!"

Aleck stated that the enemy had passed within ten feet without perceiving him; that his gun was cocked and well primed, so that if he had been discovered there would have been at least one red skin less to chase me. He had seen no Indians on his way to camp.

I was satisfied that some (if not all) of my pursuers knew me, for they were Black Feet, or they would not have taken such extraordinary pains to run me down. If they had succeeded in their endeavor, they would, in subsequent years, have saved their tribe many scalps.

From this encampment we moved on to Lewis's Fork, on the Columbia River, where we made a final halt to prepare for the fall trapping season. Some small parties, getting tired of inaction, would occasionally sally out to the small mountain streams, all of which contained plenty of beaver, and would frequently come in with several skins.

I prepared my traps one day, thinking to go out alone, and see what my luck might be. I mounted my horse, and, on approaching a small stream, dismounted to take a careful survey, to see if there were any signs of beaver. Carefully ascending the bank of the stream, I peered over, and saw, not a beaver, but an Indian. He had his robe spread on the grass, and was engaged in freeing himself from vermin, with which all Indians abound. He had not seen nor heard me; his face was toward me, but inclined, and he was intently pursuing his occupation.

" Here," thought I, " are a gun, a bow, a quiver full of arrows, a good robe and a scalp."

I fired my rifle; the Indian fell over without uttering a sound. I not only took his scalp, but his head. I tied two locks of his long hair together, hung his head on the horn of my saddle, and, taking the spoils of the enemy, hurried back to camp.

The next morning our camp was invested by two thousand five hundred warriors of the Black Foot tribe. We had now something on our hands which demanded attention. We were encamped in the bend of a river — in the " horseshoe." Our lodges were pitched at the entrance, or narrowest part of the shoe, while our animals were driven back into the bend. The lodges, four deep, extended nearly across the land, forming a kind of barricade in front; not a very safe one for the inmates, since, being covered with buffalo hides, they were penetrable to bullet and arrow.

The Indians made a furious charge. We immediately placed the women and children in the rear, sending them down the bend, where they were safe unless we were defeated. We suffered the Indians for a long time to act on the offensive, being content with defending ourselves and the camp. I advised Captain Sublet to let them weary themselves with charging, by which time we would mount and charge them with greater prospect of victory; whereas, should we tire ourselves while they were fresh, we should be overwhelmed by their numbers, and, if not defeated, inevitably lose a great many men.

All the mountaineers approved of my advice, and our plans

were taken accordingly. They drove us from our first position twice, so that our lodges were between the contending ranks, but they never broke our lines. When they approached us very near we resorted to our arrows, which all our half-breeds used as skillfully as the Indians. Finally, perceiving they began to tire, I went and ordered the women to saddle the horses in haste. A horse was soon ready for each man, four hundred in number. Taking one hundred and thirty men, I passed out through the timber, keeping near the river until we could all emerge and form a line to charge them, unobserved, in the rear. While executing this diversion, the main body was to charge them in front. Defiling through the timber we came suddenly upon ten Indians who were resting from the fight, and were sitting on the ground unconcernedly smoking their pipes. We killed nine of them, the tenth one making good his retreat.

Our manœuvre succeeded admirably. The Indians were unconscious of our approach in their rear until they began to fall from their horses. Then charging on their main body simultaneously with Captain Sublet's charge in front, their whole force was thrown into irretrievable confusion, and they fled without farther resistance. We did not pursue them, feeling very well satisfied to have got rid of them as we had. They left one hundred and sixty-seven dead on the field. Our loss was also very severe; sixteen killed, mostly half-breeds, and fifty or sixty wounded. In this action I received a wound in my left side, although I did not perceive it until the battle was over.

As usual, there was a scalp-dance after the victory, in which I really feared that the fair sex would dance themselves to death. They had a crying spell afterward for the dead. After all, it was a victory rather dearly purchased.

A few days after our battle, one of our old trappers, named Le Blueux, who had spent twenty years in the mountains, came to me, and telling me he knew of a small stream full of beaver which ran into Lewis's Fork, about thirty miles from camp, wished me to accompany him there. We being free trappers at that time, the chance of obtaining a pack or two of beaver was rather a powerful incentive. Gain being my object, I readily acceded to his proposal. We put out from camp during the night, and traveled up Lewis's Fork, leisurely discussing our prospects and confidently enumerating our unhatched chickens, when suddenly a large party of Indians came in sight in our rear.

The banks of the river we were traveling along were precipitous and rocky, and skirted with a thick bush. We entered the bush without a moment's hesitation, for the Indians advanced on us as soon as they had caught sight of us. Le Blueux had a small bell attached to his horse's neck, which he took off, and, creeping to a large bush, fastened it with the end of his lariat, and returned holding the other end in his hand. This stratagem caused the Indians to expend a great amount of powder and shot in their effort to kill the bell; for, of course, they supposed the bell indicated the position of ourselves. When they approached near enough to be seen through the bushes, we fired one gun at a time, always keeping the other loaded. When we fired the bell would ring, as if the horse was started by the close proximity of the gun, but the smoke would not rise in the right place. They continued to shoot at random into the bushes without injuring us or our faithful animals, who were close by us, but entirely concealed from the sight of the Indians. My companion filled his pipe and commenced smoking with as much sang froid as if he had been in camp.

" This is the last smoke I expect to have between here and camp," said he.

" What are we to do? " I inquired, not feeling our position very secure in a brush fort manned with a company of two, and beleaguered by scores of Black Foot warriors.

In an instant, before I had time to think, crack went

his rifle, and down came an Indian, who, more bold than the rest, had approached too near to our garrison.

" Now," said Le Blueux, " bind your leggins and moccasins around your head."

I did so, while he obeyed the same order.

" Now follow me."

Wondering what bold project he was about to execute, I quietly obeyed him. He went noiselessly to the edge of the bluff, looked narrowly up and down the river, and then commenced to slide down the almost perpendicular bank, I closely following him. We safely reached the river, into which we dropped ourselves. We swam close under the bank for more than a mile, until they discovered us.

" Now," said my comrade, " strike across the stream in double quick time."

We soon reached the opposite bank, and found ourselves a good mile and a half ahead of the Indians. They commenced plunging into the river in pursuit, but they were too late. We ran across the open ground until we reached a mountain, where we could safely look back and laugh at our pursuers. We had lost our horses and guns, while they had sacrificed six or eight of their warriors, besides missing the two scalps they made so certain of getting hold of.

I had thought myself a pretty good match for the Indians, but I at once resigned all claims to merit. Le Blueux, in addition to all the acquired wiles of the Red Man, possessed his own superior art and cunning. He could be surrounded with no difficulties for which his inexhaustible brain could not devise some secure mode of escape.

We arrived safe at camp before the first guard was relieved. The following morning we received a severe reprimand from Captain Sublet for exposing ourselves on so hazardous an adventure.

As soon as the wounded were sufficiently recovered to be able to travel, we moved down the river to the junction

of Salt River with Guy's Fork, about a mile from Snake
River.   The next day the captain resolved to pass up to
Guy's Fork to a convenient camping-ground, where we were
to spend the interval until it was time to separate into small
parties, and commence trapping in good earnest ·for the
season.

One day, while moving leisurely along, two men and
myself proposed to the captain to proceed ahead of the main
party to ascertain the best road, to reconnoitre the various
streams—in short, to make it a trip of discovery.   We were
to encamp one night, and rejoin the main body the next
morning.   The captain consented, but gave us strict caution
to take good care of ourselves.

Nothing of importance occurred that day; but the next
morning, about sunrise, we were all thunderstruck at being
roused from our sleep by the discharge of guns close at hand.
Two of us rose in an instant, and gave the war-hoop as a
challenge for them to come on.   Poor Cotton, the third of
our party, was killed at the first fire.   When they saw us
arise, rifle in hand, they drew back; whereas, had they rushed
on with their battle-axes, they could have killed us in an instant.   One of our horses was also killed, which, with the
body of our dead comrade, we used for a breastwork, throwing up, at the same time, all the dirt we could to protect ourselves as far as we were able.   The Indians, five hundred in
number, showered their balls on us, but, being careful to
keep at a safe distance, they did us no damage for some
time.   At length my companion received a shot through the
heel, while carelessly throwing up his feet in crawling to get
a sight at the Indians without exposing his body.   I received
some slight scratches, but no injury that occasioned me any
real inconvenience.

Providence at last came to our relief.   Our camp was
moving along slowly, shooting buffalo occasionally, when
some of the women, hearing our guns, ran to the captain,
exclaiming, " There is a fight.   Hark! hear the guns!"

He, concluding that there was more distant fighting than is common in killing buffalo, dispatched sixty men in all possible haste in the direction of the reports. We saw them as they appeared in sight on the brow of a hill not far distant, and sent up a shout of triumph. The Indians also caught sight of them, and immediately retreated, leaving seventeen warriors dead in front of our little fort, whom we relieved of their scalps.

We returned to camp after burying our companion, whose body was literally riddled with bullets. The next day we made a very successful *surround* of buffalo, killing great numbers of them. In the evening, several of our friends, the Snakes, came to us and told us their village was only five miles farther up, wishing us to move up near them to open a trade. After curing our meat, we moved on and encamped near the friendly Snakes. We learned that there were one hundred and eighty-five lodges of Pun-naks encamped only two miles distant, a discarded band of the Snakes, very bad Indians, and very great thieves. Captain Sublet informed the Snakes that if the Pun-naks should steal any of his horses or anything belonging to his camp, he would *rub them all out,* and he wished the friendly Snakes to tell them so.

Two of our men and one of the Snakes having strolled down to the Pun-nak lodges one evening, they were set upon, and the Snake was killed, and the two of our camp came home wounded. The next morning volunteers were called to punish the Pun-naks for their outrage. Two hundred and fifteen immediately presented themselves at the call, and our captain appointed Bridger leader of the troop.

We started to inflict vengeance, but when we arrived at the site of the village, behold! there was no village there. They had packed up and left immediately after the perpetration of the outrage, they fearing, no doubt, that ample vengeance would be taken upon them.

We followed their trail forty-five miles, and came up

with them on Green River. Seeing our approach, they all made across to a small island in the river.

" What shall we do now, Jim?" inquired our leader.

"I will cross to the other side with one half the men," I suggested, " and get abreast of the island. Their retreat will be thus cut off, and we can exterminate them in their trap."

" Go," said he; " I will take them if they attempt to make this shore."

I was soon in position, and the enfilading commenced, and was continued until there was not one left of either sex or any age. We carried back four hundred and eighty-eight scalps, and, as we then supposed, annihilated the Pun-nak band. On our return, however, we found six or eight of their squaws, who had been left behind in the flight, whom we carried back and gave to the Snakes.

On informing the Snakes of what had taken place, they expressed great delight. "Right!" they said. " Pun-naks very bad Indians"; and they joined in the scalp-dance.

We afterward learned that the Pun-naks, when they fled from our vengeance, had previously sent their old men, and a great proportion of their women and children, to the mountains, at which we were greatly pleased, as it spared the effusion of much unnecessary blood. They had a great " medicine chief " slain with the others on the island; his *medicine* was not good this time, at least.

We proceeded thence to a small creek, called Black Foot Creek, in the heart of the Black Foot country.

It was always our custom, before turning out our horses in the morning, to send out spies to reconnoitre around, and see if any Indians were lurking about to steal them. When preparing to move one morning from the last-named creek, we sent out two men; but they had not proceeded twenty yards from our *corral* before a dozen shots were fired at them by a party of Black Feet, bringing them from their horses severely wounded. In a moment the whole camp was in motion. The savages made a bold and desperate attempt to rush upon the wounded men and get their scalps, but we were on the ground in time to prevent them, and drove them back, killing four of their number.

The next day we were overtaken by the Snakes, who, hearing of our skirmish, expressed great regret that they were not present to have followed them and given them battle again. We seldom followed the Indians after having defeated them, unless they had stolen our horses. It was our policy always to act on the defensive, even to tribes that were known enemies.

When the Snakes were ready, we all moved on together for the head of Green River. The Indians numbered six or seven thousand, including women and children; our number was nearly eight hundred altogether, forming quite a formidable little army, or, more properly, a moving city. The number of horses belonging to the whole camp was immense.

We had no farther difficulty in reaching Green River, where we remained six days. During this short stay our numberless horses exhausted the grass in our vicinity, and it was imperative to change position.

It was now early in September, and it was time to break up our general encampment, and spread in all directions, as the hunting and trapping season was upon us. Before we formed our dispersing parties, a number of the Crows came to our camp, and were rejoiced to see us again. The Snakes and Crows were extremely amicable.

The Crows were questioning the Snakes about some scalps hanging on our lodge-poles. They gave them the particulars of our encounter with the Black Feet, how valiantly we had fought them, and how we had defeated them. The Crows were highly gratified to see so many scalps taken from their old and inveterate foes. They wished to see the braves who had fought so nobly. I was pointed out as the one who had taken the greatest number of scalps;

they told them they had seen me fight, and that I was a very great brave. Upon this I became the object of the Crows' admiration; they were very anxious to talk to me and to cultivate my acquaintance; but I could speak very little of their language.

One of our men (named Greenwood), whose wife was a Crow, could speak their language fluently; he and his wife were generally resorted to by the Crows to afford full details of our recent victory. Greenwood, becoming tired of so much questioning, invented a fiction, which greatly amused me for its ingenuity. He informed them that White-handled Knife (as the Snakes called me) was a Crow.

They all started in astonishment at this information, and asked how that could be.

Said Greenwood in reply, " You know that so many winters ago the Cheyennes defeated the Crows, killing many hundreds of their warriors, and carrying off a great many of their women and children."

" Yes, we know it," they all exclaimed.

" Well, he was a little boy at that time, and the whites bought him of the Cheyennes, with whom he has staid ever since. He has become a great brave among them, and all your enemies fear him."

On hearing this astonishing revelation, they said that I must be given to them. Placing implicit faith in every word that they had heard, they hastened to their village to disseminate the joyful news that they had found one of their own people who had been taken by the Shi-ans when a *bar-car-ta* (child), who had been sold to the whites, and who had now become a great white chief, with his lodge-pole full of the scalps of the Black Feet, who had fallen beneath his gun and battle-axe. This excited a great commotion throughout their whole village. All the old women who remembered the defeat, when the Crows lost two thousand warriors and a host of women and children, with the ensuing captivity, were wondering if the great brave was not their own child; thereupon ensued the greatest anxiety to see me and claim me as a son.

I did not say a word impugning the authenticity of Greenwood's romance. I was greatly edified at the inordinate gullibility of the red man, and when they had gone to spread their tale of wonderment, we had a hearty laugh at their expense.

Our party now broke up; detachments were formed and leaders chosen. We issued from the camp, and started in all directions, receiving instructions to return within a certain day. There were a great many fur trappers with us, who hunted for their own profit, and disposed of their peltry to the mountain traders. The trappers were accompanied by a certain number of hired men, selected according to their individual preferences, the strength of their party being regulated by the danger of the country they were going to. If a party was going to the Black Foot country, it needed to be numerous and well armed. If going among the Crows or Snakes, where no danger was apprehended, there would go few or many, just as was agreed upon among themselves. But each party was in strict obedience to the will of its captain or leader: his word was supreme law.

My party started for the Crow country, at which I was well content; for, being a supposed Crow myself, I expected to fare well among them. It seemed a relief, also, to be in a place where we could rest from our unsleeping vigilance, and to feel, when we rose in the morning, there was some probability of our living till night.

I now parted with very many of my friends for the last time. Most of the members of that large company now sleep in death, their waking ears no longer to be filled with the death-telling yell of the savage. The manly hearts that shrunk from no danger have ceased to beat; their bones whiten in the gloomy fastnesses of the Rocky Mountains, or moulder on the ever-flowering prairies of the far West. A cloven skull is all that remains of my once gallant friends to tell the bloody death that they died, and invoke vengeance on the merciless hand that struck them down in their ruddy youth.

Here I parted from the boy Baptiste, who had been my faithful companion so long. I never saw him again.

The party that I started with consisted of thirty-one men, most of them skillful trappers (Captain Bridger[1] was in our party), and commanded by Robert Campbell. We started for Powder River, a fork of the Yellow Stone, and, arriving there without accident, were soon busied in our occupation.

A circumstance occurred in our encampment on this stream, trivial in itself (for trivial events sometimes determine the course of a man's life), but which led to unexpected results. I had set my six traps over night, and on going to them the following morning I found four beavers, but one of my traps was missing. I sought it in every direction, but without success, and on my return to camp mentioned the mystery. Captain Bridger (as skillful a hunter as ever lived in the mountains) offered to renew the search with me, expressing confidence that the trap could be found. We searched diligently along the river and the bank for a considerable distance, but the trap was among the missing. The float-pole also was gone—a pole ten or twelve feet long and four inches thick. We at length gave it up as lost.

The next morning the whole party moved farther up the river. To shorten our route, Bridger and myself crossed the stream at the spot where I had set my missing trap. It was a buffalo-crossing, and there was a good trail worn in the banks, so that we could easily cross with our horses. After passing and traveling on some two miles, I discovered what I supposed to be a badger, and we both made a rush for him. On closer inspection, however, it proved to be

[1] This is Captain Jim Bridger, a celebrated Western character who figures in " A Frontier Duel."

my beaver, with trap, chain, and float-pole. It was apparent that some buffalo, in crossing the river, had become entangled in the chain, and, as we conceived, had carried the trap on his shoulder, with the beaver pendent on one side and the pole on the other. We inferred that he had in some way got his head under the chain, between the trap and the pole, and, in his endeavors to extricate himself, had pushed his head through. The hump on his back would prevent it passing over his body, and away he would speed with his burden, probably urged forward by the four sharp teeth of the beaver, which would doubtless object to his sudden equestrian (or rather bovine) journey. We killed the beaver and took his skin, feeling much satisfaction at the solution of the mystery. When we arrived at camp we asked our companions to guess how and where we had found the trap. They all gave various guesses, but, failing to hit the truth, gave up the attempt.

"Well, gentlemen," said I, "it was stolen."

"Stolen!" exclaimed a dozen voice at once.

"Yes, it was stolen by a buffalo."

"Oh, come now," said one of the party, "what is the use of coming here and telling such a lie?"

I saw in a moment that he was angry and in earnest, and I replied, "If you deny that a buffalo stole my trap, *you* tell the lie."

He rose and struck me a blow with his fist. It was my turn now, and the first pass I made brought my antagonist to the ground. On rising, he sprang for his gun; I assumed mine as quickly. The bystanders rushed between us, and, seizing our weapons, compelled us to discontinue our strife, which would have infallibly resulted in the death of one. My opponent mounted his horse and left the camp. I never saw him afterward. I could have taken his expression in jest, for we were very free in our sallies upon one another; but in this particular instance I saw his intention was to insult me, and I allowed my passion to overcome my reflection. My companions counseled me to leave camp for a few days until the ill feeling should have subsided.

The same evening Captain Bridger and myself started out with our traps, intending to be gone three or four days. We followed up a small stream until it forked, when Bridger proposed that I should take one fork and he the other, and the one who had set his traps first should cross the hill which separated the two streams and rejoin the other. Thus we parted, expecting to meet again in a few hours. I continued my course up the stream in pursuit of beaver villages until I found myself among an innumerable drove of horses, and I could plainly see they were not wild ones.

The horses were guarded by several of their Indian owners, or horse-guards, as they term them, who had discovered me long before I saw them. I could hear their signals to each other, and in a few moments I was surrounded by them, and escape was impossible. I resigned myself to my fate: if they were enemies, I knew they could kill me but once, and to attempt to defend myself would entail inevitable death. I took the chances between death and mercy; I surrendered my gun, traps, and what else I had, and was marched to camp under a strong escort of *horse-guards.* I felt very sure that my guards were Crows, therefore I did not feel greatly alarmed at my situation. On arriving at their village, I was ushered into the chief's lodge, where there were several old men and women, whom I conceived to be members of the family. My capture was known throughout the village in five minutes, and hundreds gathered around the lodge to get a sight of the prisoner. In the crowd were some who had talked to Greenwood a few weeks before. They at once exclaimed, " That is the lost Crow, the great brave who has killed so many of our enemies. He is our brother." [1]

This threw the whole village into commotion; old and

---

[1] Beckwourth had lived in the wilds for several years and might easily have been mistaken for an Indian. — EDITOR.

young were impatient to obtain a sight of the " great brave." Orders were immediately given to summon all the old women taken by the Shi-ans at the time of their captivity so many winters past, who had suffered the loss of a son at that time. The lodge was cleared for the *examining committee,* and the old women, breathless with excitement, their eyes wild and protruding, and their nostrils dilated, arrived in squads, until the lodge was filled to overflowing. I believe never was mortal gazed at with such intense and sustained interest as I was on that occasion. Arms and legs were critically scrutinized. My face next passed the ordeal; then my neck, back, breast, and all parts of my body, even down to my feet, which did not escape the examinations of these anxious matrons, in their endeavors to discover some mark or peculiarity whereby to recognize their brave son.

At length one old woman, after having scanned my visage with the utmost intentness, came forward and said, " If this is my son, he has a mole over one of his eyes."

My eyelids were immediately pulled down to the utmost stretch of their elasticity, when, sure enough, she discovered a mole just over my left eye!

Then, and oh then! such shouts of joy as were uttered by that honest-hearted woman were seldom before heard, while all in the crowd took part in her rejoicing. It was uncultivated joy, but not the less heartfelt and intense. It was a joy which a mother can only experience when she recovers a son whom she had supposed dead in his earliest days. She has mourned him silently through weary nights and busy days for the long space of twenty years; suddenly he presents himself before her in robust manhood, and graced with the highest name an Indian can appreciate. It is but nature, either in the savage breast or civilized, that hails such a return with overwhelming joy, and feels the mother's undying affection awakened beyond all control.

All the other claimants resigning their pretensions, I was fairly carried along by the excited crowd to the lodge of the " Big Bowl," who was my father. The news of my having proved to be the son of Mrs. Big Bowl flew through the village with the speed of lightning, and, on my arrival at the paternal lodge, I found it filled with all degrees of my newly-discovered relatives, who welcomed me nearly to death. They seized me in their arms and hugged me, and my face positively burned with the enraptured kisses of my numerous fair sisters, with a long host of cousins, aunts, and other more remote kindred. All these welcoming ladies as firmly believed in my identity with the lost one as they believed in the existence of the Great Spirit.

My father knew me to be his son; told all the Crows that the dead was alive again, and the lost one was found. He knew it was fact; Greenwood had said so, and the words of Greenwood were true; his tongue was not crooked — he would not lie. He also had told him that his son was a great brave among the white men; that his arm was strong; that the Black Feet quailed before his rifle and battle-axe; that his lodge was full of their scalps which his knife had taken; that they must rally around me to support and protect me; and that his long-lost son would be a strong breast-work to their nation, and he would teach them how to defeat their enemies.

They all promised that they would do as his words had indicated.

My unmarried sisters were four in number, very pretty, intelligent young women. They, as soon as the departure of the crowd would admit, took off my old leggins, and moccasins, and other garments, and supplied their place with new ones, most beautifully ornamented according to their very last fashion. My sisters were very ingenious in such work, and they wellnigh quarreled among themselves for the privilege of dressing me. When my toilet was finished to their satisfaction, I could compare in elegance with the most popular warrior of the tribe when in full costume. They also prepared me a bed, not so high as Haman's gallows certainly, but just as high as the lodge would admit. This was also a token of their esteem and sisterly affection.

While conversing to the extent of my ability with my father in the evening, and affording him full information respecting the white people, their great cities, their numbers, their power, their opulence, he suddenly demanded of me if I wanted a wife; thinking, no doubt, that, if he got me married, I should lose all discontent, and forego any wish of returning to the whites.

I assented, of course.

" Very well," said he, " you shall have a pretty wife and a good one."

Away he strode to the lodge of one of the greatest braves, and asked one of his daughters of him to bestow upon his son, who the chief must have heard was also a great brave. The consent of the parent was readily given. The name of my prospective father-in-law was Black-lodge. He had three very pretty daughters, whose names were Still-water, Black-fish, and Three-roads.

Even the untutored daughters of the wild woods need a little time to prepare for such an important event, but long and tedious courtships are unknown among them.

The ensuing day the three daughters were brought to my father's lodge by their father, and I was requested to take my choice. " Still-water " was the eldest, and I liked her name; if it was emblematic of her disposition, she was the woman I should prefer. " Still-water," accordingly, was my choice. They were all superbly attired in garments which must have cost them months of labor, which garments the young women ever keep in readiness against such an interesting occasion as the present.

The acceptance of my wife was the completion of the ceremony, and I was again a married man, as sacredly in their eyes as if the Holy Christian Church had fastened the irrevocable knot upon us.

Among the Indians, the daughter receives no patrimony

on her wedding-day, and her mother and father never pass a word with the son-in-law after—a custom religiously observed among them, though for what reason I never learned. The other relatives are under no such restraint.

My brothers made me a present of twenty as fine horses as any in the nation—all trained war-horses. I was also presented with all the arms and instruments requisite for an Indian campaign.

My wife's deportment coincided with her name; she would have reflected honor upon many a civilized household. She was affectionate, obedient, gentle, cheerful, and, apparently, quite happy. No domestic thunder-storms, no curtain-lectures ever disturbed the serenity of our connubial lodge. I speedily formed acquaintance with all my immediate neighbors, and the Morning Star (which was the name conferred upon me on my recognition as the lost son) was soon a companion to all the young warriors in the village. No power on earth could have shaken their faith in my positive identity with the lost son. Nature seemed to prompt the old woman to recognize me as her missing child, and all my new relatives placed implicit faith in the genuineness of her discovery. Greenwood had spoken it, "and his tongue was not crooked." What could I do under the circumstances? Even if I should deny my Crow origin, they would not believe me. How could I dash with an unwelcome and incredible explanation all the joy that had been manifested on my return — the cordial welcome, the rapturous embraces of those who hailed me as a son and a brother, the exuberant joy of the whole nation for the return of a long-lost Crow, who, stolen when a child, had returned in the strength of maturity, graced with the name of a great brave, and the generous strife I had occasioned in their endeavors to accord me the warmest welcome? I could not find it in my heart to undeceive these unsuspecting people and tear myself away from their untutored caresses.

Thus I commenced my Indian life with the Crows. I

said to myself, " I can trap in their streams unmolested, and derive more profit under their protection than if among my own men, exposed incessantly to assassination and alarm." I therefore resolved to abide with them, to guard my secret, to do my best in their company, and in assisting them to subdue their enemies.[1]

[1] Beckwourth left the Crows several years afterwards and lived for many years in California, where he was a celebrated character. — EDITOR.

THE PATHFINDER
IN THE HIGH ROCKIES

JOHN C. FRÉMONT

1842

From Frémont's Journal of the First Expedition.

August 10.—The air at sunrise is clear and pure, and the morning extremely cold, but beautiful. A lofty snow peak of the mountain is glittering in the first rays of the sun, which has not yet reached us. The long mountain wall to the east, rising two thousand feet abruptly from the plain, behind which we see the peaks, is still dark, and cuts clear against the glowing sky. A fog, just risen from the river, lies along the base of the mountain. A little before sunrise, the thermometer was at 35°, and at sunrise 33°. Water froze last night, and fires are very comfortable. The scenery becomes hourly more interesting and grand, and the view here is truly magnificent; but, indeed, it needs something to repay the long prairie journey of a thousand miles. The sun has just shot above the wall, and makes a magical change. The whole valley is glowing and bright, and all the mountain peaks are gleaming like silver. Though these snow mountains are not the Alps, they have their own character of grandeur and magnificence, and will doubtless find pens and pencils to do them justice. In the scene before us, we feel how much wood improves a view. The pines on the mountain seemed to give it much additional beauty. I was agreeably disappointed in the character of the streams on this side the ridge. Instead of the creeks, which description had led me to expect, I find bold, broad streams, with

three or four feet of water, and a rapid current. The fork
on which we are encamped is upwards of a hundred feet
wide, timbered with groves or thickets of the low willow.
We were now approaching the loftiest part of the Wind
River chain; and I left the valley a few miles from our encampment, intending to penetrate the mountains, as far as
possible, with the whole party. We were soon involved in
very broken ground, among long ridges covered with fragments of granite. Winding our way up a long ravine, we
came unexpectedly in view of a most beautiful lake, set like a
gem in the mountains. The sheet of water lay transversely
across the direction we had been pursuing; and, descending
the steep, rocky ridge, where it was necessary to lead our
horses, we followed its banks to the southern extremity.
Here a view of the utmost magnificence and grandeur burst
upon our eyes. With nothing between us and their feet to
lessen the effect of the whole height, a grand bed of snow-
capped mountains rose before us, pile upon pile, glowing
in the bright light of an August day. Immediately below
them lay the lake, between two ridges, covered with dark
pines, which swept down from the main chain to the spot
where we stood. Here, where the lake glittered in the open
sunlight, its banks of yellow sand and the light foliage of
aspen groves contrasted well with the gloomy pines.
" Never before," said Mr. Preuss, " in this country or in
Europe, have I seen such magnificent, grand rocks." I was
so much pleased with the beauty of the place that I determined to make the main camp here, where our animals
would find good pasturage, and explore the mountains with
a small party of men. Proceeding a little further, we came
suddenly upon the outlet of the lake, where it found its way
through a narrow passage between low hills. Dark pines,
which overhung the stream, and masses of rock, where the
water foamed along, gave it much romantic beauty. Where
we crossed, which was immediately at the outlet, it is two
hundred and fifty feet wide, and so deep that with difficulty

we were able to ford it. Its bed was an accumulation of rocks, boulders, and broad slabs, and large angular fragments, among which the animals fell repeatedly.

The current was very swift, and the water cold and of a crystal purity. In crossing this stream, I met with a great misfortune in having my barometer broken. It was the only one. A great part of the interest of the journey for me was in the exploration of these mountains, of which so much had been said that was doubtful and contradictory; and now their snowy peaks rose majestically before me, and the only means of giving them authentically to science, the object of my anxious solicitude by night and day, was destroyed. We had brought this barometer in safety a thousand miles, and broke it almost among the snow of the mountains. The loss was felt by the whole camp. All had seen my anxiety, and aided me in preserving it. The height of these mountains, considered by the hunters and traders the highest in the whole range, had been a theme of constant discussion among them; and all had looked forward with pleasure to the moment when the instrument, which they believed to be true as the sun, should stand upon the summits and decide their disputes. Their grief was only inferior to my own.

This lake is about three miles long and of very irregular width and apparently great depth, and is the head water of the third New Fork, a tributary to Green River, the Colorado of the West. On the map and in the narrative I have called it Mountain Lake. I encamped on the north side, about three hundred and fifty yards from the outlet. This was the most western point at which I obtained astronomical observations, by which this place, called Bernier's encampment, is made in 110° 08′ 03″ west longitude from Greenwich, and latitude 43° 49′ 49″. The mountain peaks, as laid down, were fixed by bearings from this and other astronomical points. We had no other compass than the small ones used in sketching the country; but from an azimuth, in which one of them was used, the variation of the compass is 18° east. The correction made in our field work by the astronomical observations indicates that this is a very correct observation.

As soon as the camp was formed, I set about endeavoring to repair my barometer. As I have already said, this was a standard cistern barometer, of Troughton's construction. The glass cistern had been broken about midway; but, as the instrument had been kept in a proper position, no air had found its way into the tube, the end of which had always remained covered. I had with me a number of vials of tolerably thick glass, some of which were of the same diameter as the cistern, and I spent the day in slowly working on these, endeavoring to cut them of the requisite length; but, as my instrument was a very rough file, I invariably broke them. A groove was cut in one of the trees, where the barometer was placed during the night, to be out of the way of any possible danger; and in the morning I commenced again. Among the powder horns in the camp, I found one which was very transparent, so that its contents could be almost as plainly seen as through glass. This I boiled and stretched on a piece of wood to the requisite diameter, and scraped it very thin, in order to increase to the utmost its transparency. I then secured it firmly in its place on the instrument with strong glue made from a buffalo, and filled it with mercury properly heated. A piece of skin, which had covered one of the vials, furnished a good pocket, which was well secured with strong thread and glue; and then the brass cover was screwed to its place. The instrument was left some time to dry; and, when I reversed it, a few hours after, I had the satisfaction to find it in perfect order, its indications being about the same as on the other side of the lake before it had been broken. Our success in this little incident diffused pleasure throughout the camp; and we immediately set about our preparations for ascending the mountains.

As will be seen, on reference to a map, on this short mountain chain are the head waters of four great rivers of the continent, — namely, the Colorado, Columbia, Missouri, and Platte Rivers. It had been my design, after having ascended the mountains, to continue our route on the western side of the range, and, crossing through a pass at the north-western end of the chain, about thirty miles from our present camp, return along the eastern slope across the heads of the Yellowstone River, and join on the line to our station of August 7, immediately at the foot of the ridge. In this way, I should be enabled to include the whole chain and its numerous waters in my survey; but various considerations induced me, very reluctantly, to abandon this plan.

I was desirous to keep strictly within the scope of my instructions; and it would have required ten or fifteen additional days for the accomplishment of this object. Our animals had become very much worn out with the length of the journey; game was very scarce; and, though it does not appear in the course of the narrative (as I have avoided dwelling upon trifling incidents not connected with the objects of the expedition), the spirits of the men had been much exhausted by the hardships and privations to which they had been subjected. Our provisions had well-nigh all disappeared. Bread had been long out of the question; and of all our stock we had remaining two or three pounds of coffee and a small quantity of macaroni, which had been husbanded with great care for the mountain expedition we were about to undertake. Our daily meal consisted of dry buffalo meat cooked in tallow; and, as we had not dried this with Indian skill, part of it was spoiled, and what remained of good was as hard as wood, having much the taste and appearance of so many pieces of bark. Even of this, our stock was rapidly diminishing in a camp which was capable of consuming two buffaloes in every twenty-four hours. These animals had entirely disappeared, and it was not probable that we should fall in with them again until we returned to the Sweet Water.

Our arrangements for the ascent were rapidly completed. We were in a hostile country, which rendered the greatest vigilance and circumspection necessary. The pass at the north end of the mountain was generally infested by Blackfeet; and immediately opposite was one of their forts, on the edge of a little thicket, two or three hundred feet from our encampment. We were posted in a grove of beech, on the margin of the lake, and a few hundred feet long, with a narrow *prairillon* on the inner side, bordered by the rocky ridge. In the upper end of this grove we cleared a circular space about forty feet in diameter, and with the felled timber and interwoven branches surrounded it with a breastwork five feet in height. A gap was left for a gate on the inner side, by which the animals were to be driven in and secured, while the men slept around the little work. It was half hidden by the foliage, and, garrisoned by twelve resolute men, would have set at defiance any band of savages which might chance to discover them in the interval of our absence. Fifteen of the best mules, with fourteen men, were selected for the mountain party. Our provisions consisted of dried meat for two days, with our little stock of coffee and some macaroni. In addition to the barometer and a thermometer I took with me a sextant and spy-glass, and we had, of course, our compasses. In charge of the camp I left Brenier, one of my most trustworthy men, who possessed the most determined courage.

August 12. — Early in the morning we left the camp, fifteen in number, well armed, of course, and mounted on our best mules. A pack animal carried our provisions, with a coffee-pot and kettle and three or four tin cups. Every man had a blanket strapped over his saddle, to serve for his bed, and the instruments were carried by turns on their backs. We entered directly on rough and rocky ground, and, just after crossing the ridge, had the good fortune to shoot an antelope. We heard the roar, and had a glimpse of a waterfall as we rode along; and, crossing in our way two fine streams, tributary to the Colorado, in about two hours' ride we reached the top of the first row or range of the mountains. Here, again, a view of the most romantic beauty met our eyes. It seemed as if, from the vast expanse of uninteresting prairie we had passed over, Nature had collected all her beauties together in one chosen place. We were overlooking a deep valley, which was entirely occupied by three lakes, and from the brink the surrounding ridges rose precipitously five hundred and a thousand feet, covered with the dark green of the balsam pine, relieved on the border of the lake with the light foliage of the aspen. They all communicated with each other; and the green of the waters, common to mountain lakes of great depth, showed that it would be impossible to cross them. The surprise manifested by our guides when these impassable obstacles suddenly barred our progress proved that they were among the hidden treasures of the place, unknown even to the wandering trappers of the region. Descending the hill, we proceeded to make our way along the margin to the southern extremity. A narrow strip of angular fragments of rock sometimes afforded a rough pathway for our mules; but generally we rode along the shelving side, occasionally scrambling up, at a considerable risk of tumbling back into the lake.

The slope was frequently 60°. The pines grew densely together, and the ground was covered with the branches and trunks of trees. The air was fragrant with the odor of the pines; and I realized this delightful morning the pleasure of breathing that mountain air which makes a constant theme of the hunter's praise, and which now made us feel as if we had all been drinking some exhilarating gas. The depths of this unexplored forest were a place to delight the heart of a botanist. There was a rich undergrowth of plants and numerous gay-colored flowers in brilliant bloom. We reached the outlet at length, where some freshly barked willows that lay in the water showed that beaver had been recently at work. There were some small brown squirrels jumping about in the pines and a couple of large mallard ducks swimming about in the stream.

The hills on this southern end were low, and the lake looked like a mimic sea as the waves broke on the sandy beach in the force of a strong breeze. There was a pretty open spot, with fine grass for our mules; and we made our noon halt on the beach, under the shade of some large hemlocks. We resumed our journey after a halt of about an hour, making our way up the ridge on the western side of the lake. In search of smoother ground, we rode a little inland, and, passing through groves of aspen, soon found ourselves again among the pines. Emerging from these, we struck the summit of the ridge above the upper end of the lake.

We had reached a very elevated point; and in the valley below and among the hills were a number of lakes at different levels, some two or three hundred feet above others, with which they communicated by foaming torrents. Even to our great height, the roar of the cataracts came up; and we could see them leaping down in lines of snowy foam. From this scene of busy waters, we turned abruptly into the stillness of a forest, where we rode among the open bolls of the pines over a lawn of verdant grass, having strikingly the air of cultivated grounds. This led us, after a time, among masses of rock, which had no vegetable earth but in hollows and crevices, though still the pine forest continued. Toward evening we reached a defile, or rather a hole in the mountains, entirely shut in by dark pine-covered rocks.

A small stream, with a scarcely perceptible current, flowed through a level bottom of perhaps eighty yards' width, where the grass was saturated with water. Into this the mules were turned, and were neither hobbled nor picketed during the night, as the fine pasturage took away all temptation to stray; and we made our bivouac in the pines. The surrounding masses were all of granite. While supper was being prepared, I set out on an excursion in the neighborhood, accompanied by one of my men. We wandered about among the crags and ravines until dark, richly repaid for our walk by a fine collection of plants, many of them in full bloom. Ascending a peak to find the place of our camp, we saw that the little defile in which we lay communicated with the long green valley of some stream, which, here locked up in the mountains, far away to the south, found its way in a dense forest to the plains.

Looking along its upward course, it seemed to conduct by a smooth gradual slope directly toward the peak, which, from long consultation as we approached the mountain, we had decided to be the highest of the range. Pleased with the discovery of so fine a road for the next day, we hastened down to the camp, where we arrived just in time for supper. Our table service was rather scant; and we held the meat in our hands, and clean rocks made good plates on which we spread our macaroni. Among all the strange places on which we had occasion to encamp during our long journey, none have left so vivid an impression on my mind as the camp of this evening. The disorder of the masses which surrounded us, the little hole through which we saw the stars overhead, the dark pines where we slept, and the rocks lit up with the glow of our fires made a night picture of very wild beauty.

August 13. — The morning was bright and pleasant, just cool enough to make exercise agreeable; and we soon entered the defile I had seen the preceding day. It was smoothly carpeted with a soft grass and scattered over with groups of flowers, of which yellow was the predominant color. Sometimes we were forced by an occasional difficult pass to pick our way on a narrow ledge along the side of the defile, and the mules were frequently on their knees; but these obstructions were rare, and we journeyed on in the sweet morning air, delighted at our good fortune in having found such a beautiful entrance to the mountains. This road continued for about three miles, when we suddenly reached its termination in one of the grand views which at every turn meet the traveller in this magnificent region. Here the defile up which we had travelled opened out into a small lawn, where, in a little lake, the stream had its source.

There were some fine *asters* in bloom, but all the flowering plants appeared to seek the shelter of the rocks and to be of lower growth than below, as if they loved the warmth of the soil, and kept out of the way of the winds. Immediately at our feet a precipitous descent led to a confusion of defiles, and before us rose the mountains. It is not by the splendor of far-off views, which have lent such a glory to the Alps, that these impress the mind, but by a gigantic disorder of enormous masses and a savage sublimity of naked rock in wonderful contrast with innumerable green spots of a rich floral beauty shut up in their stern recesses. Their wildness seems well suited to the character of the people who inhabit the country.

I determined to leave our animals here and make the rest of our way on foot. The peak appeared so near that there was no doubt of our returning before night; and a few men were left in charge of the mules, with our provisions and blankets. We took with us nothing but our arms and instruments, and, as the day had become warm, the greater part left our coats. Having made an early dinner, we started again. We were soon involved in the most ragged precipices, nearing the central chain very slowly, and rising but little. The first ridge hid a succession of others; and when, with great fatigue and difficulty, we had climbed up five hundred feet, it was but to make an equal descent on the other side. All these intervening places were filled with small deep lakes, which met the eye in every direction, descending from one level to another, sometimes under bridges formed by huge fragments of granite, beneath which was heard the roar of the water. These constantly obstructed our path, forcing us to make long *détours,* frequently obliged to retrace our steps, and frequently falling among the rocks. Maxwell was precipitated toward the face of a precipice, and saved himself from going over by throwing himself flat on the ground. We clambered on, always expecting with every ridge that we crossed to reach the foot of the peaks, and always disappointed, until about four o'clock, when, pretty well worn out, we reached the shore of a little lake in which there was a rocky island. We remained here a short time to rest, and continued on around the lake, which had in some places a beach of white sand, and in others was bound with rocks, over which the way was difficult and dangerous, as the water from innumerable springs made them very slippery.

By the time we had reached the further side of the lake, we found ourselves all exceedingly fatigued, and, much to the satisfaction of the whole party, we encamped. The spot we had chosen was a broad, flat rock, in some measure protected from the winds by the surrounding crags, and the trunks of fallen pines afforded us bright fires. Near by was a foaming torrent which tumbled into the little lake about one hundred and fifty feet below us, and which, by way of distinction, we have called Island Lake. We had reached the upper limit of the piney region; as above this point no tree was to be seen, and patches of snow lay everywhere around us on the cold sides of the rocks. The flora of the region we had traversed since leaving our mules was extremely rich, and among the characteristic plants the scarlet flowers of the *Dodecatheon dentatum* everywhere met the eye in great abundance. A small green ravine, on the edge of which we were encamped, was filled with a profusion of alpine plants in brilliant bloom. From barometrical observations made during our three days' sojourn at this place, its elevation above the Gulf of Mexico is 10,000

feet. During the day we had seen no sign of animal life;
but among the rocks here we heard what was supposed to be
the bleat of a young goat, which we searched for with
hungry activity, and found to proceed from a small animal
of a gray color, with short ears and no tail, — probably the
Siberian squirrel. We saw a considerable number of them,
and, with the exception of a small bird like a sparrow, it is
the only inhabitant of this elevated part of the mountains.
On our return we saw below this lake large flocks of the
mountain goat. We had nothing to eat to-night.
Lajeunesse with several others took their guns and sallied
out in search of a goat, but returned unsuccessful. At sunset the barometer stood at 20.522, the attached thermometer 50°. Here we had the misfortune to break our
thermometer, having now only that attached to the barometer. I was taken ill shortly after we had encamped, and
continued so until late in the night, with violent headache
and vomiting. This was probably caused by the excessive
fatigue I had undergone and want of food, and perhaps
also in some measure by the rarity of the air. The night
was cold, as a violent gale from the north had sprung up at
sunset, which entirely blew away the heat of the fires. The
cold and our granite beds had not been favorable to sleep,
and we were glad to see the face of the sun in the morning.
Not being delayed by any preparation for breakfast, we set
out immediately.

On every side as we advanced was heard the roar of
waters and of a torrent, which we followed up a short distance until it expanded into a lake about one mile in length.
On the northern side of the lake was a bank of ice, or rather
of snow covered with a crust of ice. Carson[1] had been
our guide into the mountains, and agreeably to his advice
we left this little valley and took to the ridges again, which
we found extremely broken and where we were again involved among precipices. Here were ice fields; among which

[1] Kit Carson, the celebrated scout.

we were all dispersed, seeking each the best path to ascend the peak. Mr. Preuss attempted to walk along the upper edge of one of these fields, which sloped away at an angle of about twenty degrees; but his feet slipped from under him, and he went plunging down the plane. A few hundred feet below, at the bottom, were some fragments of sharp rock, on which he landed, and, though he turned a couple of somersets, fortunately received no injury beyond a few bruises. Two of the men, Clément Lambert and Descoteaux, had been taken ill, and lay down on the rocks a short distance below; and at this point I was attacked with headache and giddiness, accompanied by vomiting, as on the day before. Finding myself unable to proceed, I sent the barometer over to Mr. Preuss, who was in a gap two or three hundred yards distant, desiring him to reach the peak, if possible, and take an observation there. He found himself unable to proceed further in that direction, and took an observation where the barometer stood at 19.401, attached thermometer 50° in the gap. Carson, who had gone over to him, succeeded in reaching one of the snowy summits of the main ridge, whence he saw the peak towards which all our efforts had been directed towering eight or ten hundred feet into the air above him. In the mean time, finding myself grow rather worse than better, and doubtful how far my strength would carry me, I sent Basil Lajeunesse with four men back to the place where the mules had been left.

We were now better acquainted with the topography of the country; and I directed him to bring back with him, if it were in any way possible, four or five mules, with provisions and blankets. With me were Maxwell and Ayer; and, after we had remained nearly an hour on the rock, it became so unpleasantly cold, though the day was bright, that we set out on our return to the camp, at which we all arrived safely, straggling in one after the other. I continued ill during the afternoon, but became better towards sundown, when my recovery was completed by the appearance

of Basil and four men, all mounted. The men who had gone
with him had been too much fatigued to return, and were
relieved by those in charge of the horses; but in his powers
of endurance Basil resembled more a mountain goat than a
man. They brought blankets and provisions, and we enjoyed well our dried meat and a cup of good coffee. We
rolled ourselves up in our blankets, and, with our feet turned
to a blazing fire, slept soundly until morning.

August 15. — It had been supposed that we had finished
with the mountains; and the evening before it had been
arranged that Carson should set out at daylight, and return
to breakfast at the Camp of the Mules, taking with him all
but four or five men, who were to stay with me and bring
back the mules and instruments. Accordingly, at the break
of day they set out. With Mr. Preuss and myself remained
Basil Lajeunesse, Clément Lambert, Janisse, and Descoteaux. When we had secured strength for the day by a
hearty breakfast, we covered what remained, which was
enough for one meal, with rocks, in order that it might be
safe from any marauding bird, and, saddling our mules,
turned our faces once more towards the peaks. This time
we determined to proceed quietly and cautiously, deliberately
resolved to accomplish our object, if it were within the
compass of human means. We were of opinion that a long
defile which lay to the left of yesterday's route would lead
us to the foot of the main peak. Our mules had been refreshed by the fine grass in the little ravine at the island
camp, and we intended to ride up the defile as far as possible,
in order to husband our strength for the main ascent.
Though this was a fine passage, still it was a defile of the
most rugged mountains known, and we had many a rough
and steep slippery place to cross before reaching the end.
In this place the sun rarely shone. Snow lay along the
border of the small stream which flowed through it, and
occasional icy passages made the footing of the mules very
insecure; and the rocks and ground were moist with the

trickling waters in this spring of mighty rivers. We soon had the satisfaction to find ourselves riding along the huge wall which forms the central summits of the chain. There at last it rose by our sides, a nearly perpendicular wall of granite, terminating 2,000 to 3,000 feet above our heads in a serrated line of broken, jagged cones. We rode on until we came almost immediately below the main peak, which I denominated the Snow Peak, as it exhibited more snow to the eye than any of the neighboring summits. Here were three small lakes of a green color, each of perhaps a thousand yards in diameter, and apparently very deep. These lay in a kind of chasm; and, according to the barometer, we had attained but a few hundred feet above the Island Lake. The barometer here stood at 20.450, attached thermometer 70°.

We managed to get our mules up to a little bench about a hundred feet above the lakes, where there was a patch of good grass, and turned them loose to graze. During our rough ride to this place, they had exhibited a wonderful surefootedness. Parts of the defile were filled with angular, sharp fragments of rock, — three or four and eight or ten feet cube, — and among these they had worked their way, leaping from one narrow point to another, rarely making a false step, and giving us no occasion to dismount. Having divested ourselves of every unnecessary encumbrance, we commenced the ascent. This time, like experienced travellers, we did not press ourselves, but climbed leisurely, sitting down as soon as we found breath beginning to fail. At intervals we reached places where a number of springs gushed from the rocks, and about 1,800 feet above the lakes came to the snow line. From this point our progress was uninterrupted climbing. Hitherto I had worn a pair of thick moccasins, with soles of *parflêche;* but here I put on a light thin pair, which I had brought for the purpose, as now the use of our toes became necessary to a further advance. I availed my-self of a sort of comb of the mountain, which stood against the wall like a buttress, and which the wind and the solar radiation, joined to the steepness of the smooth rock, had kept almost entirely free from snow. Up this I made my way rapidly. Our cautious method of advancing in the out-set had spared my strength; and, with the exception of a slight disposition to headache, I felt no remains of yester-day's illness. In a few minutes we reached a point where the buttress was overhanging, and there was no other way of surmounting the difficulty than by passing around one side of it, which was the face of a vertical precipice of several hundred feet.

Putting hands and feet in the crevices between the blocks, I succeeded in getting over it, and, when I reached the top, found my companions in a small valley below. Descending to them, we continued climbing, and in a short time reached the crest. I sprang upon the summit, and another step would have precipitated me into an immense snow field five hundred feet below. To the edge of this field was a sheer icy precipice; and then, with a gradual fall, the field sloped off for about a mile, until it struck the foot of another lower ridge. I stood on a narrow crest, about three feet in width, with an inclination of about 20° N. 51° E. As soon as I had gratified the first feelings of curiosity, I descended, and each man ascended in his turn; for I would only allow one at a time to mount the unstable and precarious slab, which it seemed a breath would hurl into the abyss below. We mounted the barometer in the snow of the summit, and, fixing a ramrod in a crevice, unfurled the national flag to wave in the breeze where never flag waved before. During our morning's ascent we had met no sign of animal life except the small, sparrow-like bird already mentioned. A stillness the most profound and a terrible solitude forced themselves constantly on the mind as the great features of the place. Here on the summit where the stillness was absolute, unbroken by any sound, and the solitude complete, we thought ourselves beyond the region of animated life;

but, while we were sitting on the rock, a solitary bee (*bromus, the humble bee*) came winging his flight from the eastern valley, and lit on the knee of one of the men.

It was a strange place — the icy rock and the highest peak of the Rocky Mountains — for a lover of warm sunshine and flowers; and we pleased ourselves with the idea that he was the first of his species to cross the mountain barrier, a solitary pioneer to foretell the advance of civilization. I believe that a moment's thought would have made us let him continue his way unharmed; but we carried out the law of this country, where all animated nature seems at war, and, seizing him immediately, put him in at least a fit place, — in the leaves of a large book, among the flowers we had collected on our way. The barometer stood at 18.293, the attached thermometer at 44°, giving for the elevation of this summit 13,570 feet above the Gulf of Mexico, which may be called the highest flight of the bee. It is certainly the highest known flight of that insect. From the description given by Mackenzie of the mountains where he crossed them with that of a French officer still farther to the north and Colonel Long's measurements to the south, joined to the opinion of the oldest traders of the country, it is presumed that this is the highest peak of the Rocky Mountains. The day was sunny and bright, but a slight shining mist hung over the lower plains, which interfered with our view of the surrounding country. On one side we overlooked innumerable lakes and streams, the spring of the Colorado of the Gulf of California; and on the other was the Wind River Valley, where were the heads of the Yellowstone branch of the Missouri. Far to the north we just could discover the snowy heads of the *Trois Tetons,* where were the sources of the Missouri and Columbia Rivers; and at the southern extremity of the ridge the peaks were plainly visible, among which were some of the springs of the Nebraska or Platte River. Around us the whole scene had one main striking feature, which was that of terrible convulsion. Parallel to its length, the ridge was split into chasms and fissures, between which rose the thin, lofty walls, terminated with slender minarets and columns, which could be clearly discerned from the camp on Island Lake. According to the barometer, the little crest of the wall on which we stood was three thousand five hundred and seventy feet above that place and two thousand seven hundred and eighty above the little lakes at the bottom, immediately at our feet. Our camp at the Two Hills (an astronomical station) bore south 3° east, which with a bearing afterward obtained from a fixed position enabled us to locate the peak. The bearing of the *Trois Tetons* was north 50° west, and the direction of the central ridge of the Wind River Mountains south 39° east. The summit rock was gneiss, succeeded by sienitic gneiss. Sienite and feldspar succeeded in our descent to the snow line, where we found a feldspathic granite. I had remarked that the noise produced by the explosion of our pistols had the usual degree of loudness, but was not in the least prolonged, expiring almost instantaneously. Having now made what observations our means afforded, we proceeded to descend. We had accomplished an object of laudable ambition, and beyond the strict order of our instructions. We had climbed the loftiest peak of the Rocky Mountains, and looked down upon the snow a thousand feet below, and, standing where never human foot had stood before, felt the exultation of first explorers. It was about two o'clock when we left the summit; and, when we reached the bottom, the sun had already sunk behind the wall, and the day was drawing to a close. It would have been pleasant to have lingered here and on the summit longer; but we hurried away as rapidly as the ground would permit, for it was an object to regain our party as soon as possible, not knowing what accident the next hour might bring forth.

We reached our deposit of provisions at nightfall. Here was not the inn which awaits the tired traveller on his return from Mont Blanc, or the orange groves of South America, with their refreshing juices and soft, fragrant air; but we found our little *cache* of dried meat and coffee undisturbed. Though the moon was bright, the road was full of precipices, and the fatigue of the day had been great. We therefore abandoned the idea of rejoining our friends, and lay down on the rock, and in spite of the cold slept soundly.

THE WILDERNESS HUNTER

J. B. RUXTON

1845

From "Adventures in Mexico and the Rocky Mountains." John Murray, London, 1847.

THE grizzly bear is the fiercest of the feræ naturæ of the mountains. His great strength and wonderful tenacity of life render an encounter with him anything but desirable, and therefore it is a rule with the Indians and white hunters never to attack him unless backed by a strong party. Although, like every other wild animal, he usually flees from man, yet at certain seasons, when maddened by love or hunger, he not unfrequently charges at first sight of a foe; when, unless killed dead, a hug at close quarters is anything but a pleasant embrace, his strong hooked claws stripping the flesh from the bones as easily as a cook peels an onion. Many are the tales of bloody encounters with these animals which the trappers delight to recount to the " greenhorn," to enforce their caution as to the fool-hardiness of ever attacking the grizzly bear.

Some years ago a trapping party was on their way to the mountains, led, I believe, by old Sublette, a well-known captain of the West. Amongst the band was one John Glass, a trapper who had been all his life in the mountains, and had seen, probably, more exciting adventures, and had had more wonderful and hairbreadth escapes, than any of the rough and hardy fellows who make the West their home, and whose lives are spent in a succession of perils and privations. On one of the streams running from the " Black Hills," a range of mountains northward of the Platte, Glass and a companion were one day setting their traps, when, on passing through a cherry-thicket which skirted the stream, the former, who was in advance, descried a large grizzly bear quietly turning up the turf with his nose, searching for yampa-roots or pig-nuts, which there abounded. Glass immediately called his companion, and both, proceeding cautiously, crept to the skirt of the thicket, and, taking steady aim at the animal, whose broadside was fairly exposed at the distance of twenty yards, discharged their rifles at the same instant, both balls taking effect, but not inflicting a mortal wound. The bear, giving a groan of pain, jumped with all four legs from the ground, and, seeing the wreaths of smoke hanging at the edge of the brush, charged at once in that direction, snorting with pain and fury.

" Hurraw, Bill! " roared out Glass, as he saw the animal rushing towards them, " we'll be made ' meat ' of as sure as shootin'! " and, leaving the tree behind which he had concealed himself, he bolted through the thicket, followed closely by his companion. The brush was so thick, that they could scarcely make their way through, whereas the weight and strength of the bear carried him through all obstructions, and he was soon close upon them.

About a hundred yards from the thicket was a steep bluff, and between these points was a level piece of prairie; Glass saw that his only chance was to reach this bluff, and, shouting to his companion to make for it, they both broke from the cover and flew like lightning across the open space. When more than half way across, the bear being about fifty yards behind them, Glass, who was leading, tripped over a stone, and fell to the ground, and just as he rose to his feet, the beast, rising on his hind feet, confronted him. As he closed, Glass, never losing his presence of mind, cried to his companion to load up quickly, and discharged his pistol full into the body of the animal, at the same moment that the bear, with blood streaming from its nose and mouth, knocked the pistol from his hand with one blow of its paw, and, fixing his claws deep into his flesh, rolled with him to the ground.

The hunter, notwithstanding his hopeless situation, struggled manfully, drawing his knife and plunging it several times into the body of the beast, which, furious with pain, tore with tooth and claw the body of the wretched victim, actually baring the ribs of the flesh and exposing the very bones. Weak with loss of blood, and with eyes blinded with the blood which streamed from his lacerated scalp, the knife at length fell from his hand, and Glass sank down insensible, and to all appearance dead.

His companion, who, up to this moment, had watched the conflict, which, however, lasted but a few seconds, thinking that his turn would come next, and not having had presence of mind even to load his rifle, fled with might and main back to camp, where he narrated the miserable fate of poor Glass. The captain of the band of trappers, however, despatched the man with a companion back to the spot where he lay, with instructions to remain by him if still alive, or to bury him if, as all supposed he was, defunct, promising them at the same time a sum of money for so doing.

On reaching the spot, which was red with blood, they found Glass still breathing, and the bear, dead and stiff, actually lying upon his body. Poor Glass presented a horrifying spectacle: the flesh was torn in strips from his chest and limbs, and large flaps strewed the ground; his scalp hung bleeding over his face, which was also lacerated in a shocking manner.

The bear, besides the three bullets which had pierced its body, bore the marks of the fierce nature of Glass's final struggle, no less than twenty gaping wounds in the breast and belly testifying to the gallant defence of the mountaineer.

Imagining that, if not already dead, the poor fellow could not possibly survive more than a few moments, the men collected his arms, stripped him even of his hunting-shirt and mocassins, and, merely pulling the dead bear off the body, mounted their horses, and slowly followed the remainder of the party, saying, when they reached it, that Glass was dead, as probably they thought, and that they had buried him.

In a few days the gloom which pervaded the trappers' camp, occasioned by the loss of a favourite companion, disappeared, and Glass's misfortune, although frequently mentioned over the camp-fire, at length was almost entirely forgotten in the excitement of the hunt and Indian perils which surrounded them.

Months elapsed, the hunt was over, and the party of trappers were on their way to the trading-fort with their packs of beaver. It was nearly sundown, and the round adobe bastions of the mud-built fort were just in sight, when a horseman was seen slowly approaching them along the banks of the river. When near enough to discern his figure, they saw a lank cadaverous form with a face so scarred and disfigured that scarcely a feature was discernible. Approaching the leading horsemen, one of whom happened to be the companion of the defunct Glass in his memorable bear scrape, the stranger, in a hollow voice, reining in his horse before them, exclaimed, " Hurraw, Bill, my boy! you thought I was ' gone under ' that time, did you? but hand me over my horse and gun, my lad; I ain't dead yet by a dam sight! "

What was the astonishment of the whole party, and the genuine horror of Bill and his worthy companion in the burial story, to hear the well-known, though now much altered, voice of John Glass, who had been killed by a grizzly bear months before, and comfortably interred, as the two men had reported, and all had believed!

There he was, however, and no mistake about it; and all crowded round to hear from his lips, how, after the lapse of he knew not how long, he had gradually recovered, and being without arms, or even a butcher-knife, he had fed upon the almost putrid carcase of the bear for several days, until he

had regained sufficient strength to crawl, when, tearing off
as much of the bear's-meat as he could carry in his enfeebled
state, he crept down the river; and suffering excessive torture from his wounds, and hunger, and cold, he made the
best of his way to the fort, which was some eighty or ninety
miles from the place of his encounter with the bear, and,
living the greater part of the way upon roots and berries,
he after many, many days, arrived in a pitiable state, from
which he had now recovered, and was, to use his own expression, " as slick as a peeled onion."

A trapper on Arkansa, named Valentine Herring, but
better known as " Old Rube," told me that once, when visiting his traps one morning on a stream beyond the mountains,
he found one missing, at the same time that he discovered
fresh bear " sign " about the banks. Proceeding down the
river in search of the lost trap, he heard the noise of some
large body breaking through the thicket of plum-bushes
which belted the stream. Ensconcing himself behind a rock,
he presently observed a huge grizzly bear emerge from the
bush and limp on three legs to a flat rock, which he mounted,
and then, quietly seating himself, he raised one of his fore
paws, on which Rube, to his amazement, discovered his trap
tight and fast.

The bear, lifting his iron-gloved foot close to his face,
gravely examined it, turning his paw round and round, and
quaintly bending his head from side to side, looking at the
trap from the corners of his eyes, and with an air of mystery
and puzzled curiosity, for he evidently could not make out
what the novel and painful appendage could be; and every
now and then smelt it and tapped it lightly on the rock. This,
however, only paining the animal the more, he would lick
the trap, as if deprecating its anger, and wishing to con-
ciliate it.

After watching these curious antics for some time, as the
bear seemed inclined to resume his travels, Rube, to regain
his trap, was necessitated to bring the bear's cogitations

to a close, and, levelling his rifle, shot him dead, cutting off his paw and returning with it to camp, where the trappers were highly amused at the idea of trapping a b'ar.

Near the same spot where Glass encountered his " scrape," some score of Sioux squaws were one day engaged in gathering cherries in a thicket near their village, and had already nearly filled their baskets, when a bear suddenly appeared in the midst, and, with a savage growl, charged amongst them. Away ran the terrified squaws, yelling and shrieking, out of the shrubbery, nor stopped until safely ensconced within their lodges. Bruin, however, preferring fruit to meat, albeit of tender squaws, after routing the petticoats, quietly betook himself to the baskets, which he quickly emptied, and then quietly retired.

Bears are exceedingly fond of plums and cherries, and a thicket of this fruit in the vicinity of the mountains is, at the season when they are ripe, a sure " find " for Mr. Bruin. When they can get fruit they prefer such food to meat, but are, nevertheless, carnivorous animals.

The game, *par excellence,* of the Rocky Mountains, and that which takes precedence in a comestible point of view, is the carnero cimmaron of the Mexicans, the Bighorn or Mountain sheep of the Canadian hunters. This animal, which partakes both of the nature of the deer and goat, resembles the latter more particularly in its habits, and its characteristic liking to lofty, inaccessible points of the mountains, whence it seldom descends to the upland valleys excepting in very severe weather. In size the mountain-sheep is between the domestic animal and the common red deer of America, but more strongly made than the latter. Its colour is a brownish dun (the hair being tipped with a darker tinge as the animal's age increases), with a whitish streak on the hind quarters, the tail being shorter than a deer's, and tipped with black. The horns of the male are enormous, curved backwards, and often three feet in length with a circumference of twenty inches near the head. The hunters assert that, in descending the precipitous sides of the mountains, the sheep frequently leap from a height of twenty or thirty feet, invariably alighting on their horns, and thereby saving their bones from certain dislocation.

They are even more acute in the organs of sight and smell than the deer; and as they love to resort to the highest and most inaccessible spots, whence a view can readily be had of approaching danger, and particularly as one of the band is always stationed on the most commanding pinnacle of rock as sentinel, whilst the others are feeding, it is no easy matter to get within rifle-shot of the cautious animals. When alarmed they ascend still higher up the mountain: halting now and then on some overhanging crag, and looking down at the object which may have frightened them, they again commence their ascent, leaping from point to point, and throwing down an avalanche of rocks and stones as they bound up the steep sides of the mountain. They are generally very abundant in all parts of the main chain of the Rocky Mountains, but particularly so in the vicinity of the " Parks " and the Bayou Salado, as well as in the range between the upper waters of the Del Norte and Arkansa, called the " Wet Mountain " by the trappers. On the Sierra Madre, or Cordillera of New Mexico and Chihuahua, they are also numerous.

The first mountain-sheep I killed, I got within shot of in rather a curious manner. I had undertaken several unsuccessful hunts for the purpose of procuring a pair of horns of this animal, as well as some skins, which are of excellent quality when dressed, but had almost given up any hope of approaching them, when one day, having killed and butchered a black-tail deer in the mountains, I sat down with my back to a small rock and fell asleep. On awaking, feeling inclined for a smoke, I drew from my pouch a pipe, and flint and steel, and began leisurely to cut a charge of tobacco. Whilst thus engaged I became sensible of a peculiar odour which was wafted right into my face by the breeze, and which, **on** snuffing it once or twice, I immediately recognised as that which emanates from sheep and goats. Still I never thought that one of the former animals could be in the neighbourhood, for my mule was picketed on the little plateau where I sat, and was leisurely cropping the buffalo-grass which thickly covered it.

Looking up carelessly from my work, as a whiff stronger than before reached my nose, what was my astonishment at seeing five mountain-sheep within ten paces, and regarding me with a curious and astonished gaze! Without drawing a breath, I put out my hand and grasped the rifle, which was lying within reach; but the motion, slight as it was, sufficed to alarm them, and with a loud bleat the old ram bounded up the mountain, followed by the band, and at so rapid a pace that all my attempts to " draw a bead " upon them were ineffectual. When, however, they reached a little plateau about one hundred and fifty yards from where I stood, they suddenly stopped, and, approaching the edge, looked down at me, shaking their heads, and bleating their displeasure at the intrusion. No sooner did I see them stop than my rifle was at my shoulder, and covering the broadside of the one nearest to me. An instant after and I pulled the trigger, and at the report the sheep jumped convulsively from the rock, and made one attempt to follow its flying companions; but its strength failed, and, circling round once or twice at the edge of the plateau, it fell over on its side, and, rolling down the steep rock, tumbled dead very near me. My prize proved a very fine young male, but had not a large pair of horns. It was, however, " seal " fat, and afforded me a choice supply of meat, which was certainly the best I had eaten in the mountains, being fat and juicy, and in flavour somewhat partaking both of the domestic sheep and buffalo.

Several attempts have been made to secure the young of these animals and transport them to the States; and, for this purpose, an old mountaineer, one Billy Williams, took with him a troop of milch-goats, by which to bring up the young sheep; but although he managed to take several fine lambs, I believe that he did not succeed in reaching the frontier with one living specimen out of some half-score. The hunters frequently rear them in the mountains; and they become greatly attached to their masters, enlivening the camp with their merry gambols.

The elk, in point of size, ranks next to the buffalo. It is found in all parts of the mountains, and descends not unfrequently far down into the plains in the vicinity of the larger streams. A full-grown elk is as large as a mule, with rather a heavy neck and body, and stout limbs, its feet leaving a track as large as that of a two-year-old steer. They are dull, sluggish animals, at least in comparison with others of the deer tribe, and are easily approached and killed. In winter they congregate in large herds, often numbering several hundreds; and at that season are fond of travelling, their track through the snow having the appearance of a broad beaten road. The elk requires less killing than any other of the deer tribe (whose tenacity of life is remarkable); a shot anywhere in the fore part of the animal brings it to the ground. On one occasion I killed two with one ball, which passed through the neck of the first, and struck the second, which was standing a few paces distant, through the heart: both fell dead. A deer, on the contrary, often runs a considerable distance, strike it where you will. The meat of the elk is strong flavoured, and more like " poor bull " than venison: it is only eatable when the animal is fat and in good condition; at other times it is strong tasted and stringy.

The antelope, the smallest of the deer tribe, affords the hunter a sweet and nutritious meat, when that of nearly every other description of game, from the poorness and scarcity of the grass during the winter, is barely eatable. They are seldom seen now in very large bands on the grand prairies, having been driven from their old pastures by the Indians and white hunters. The former, by means of " surrounds," an enclosed space formed in one of the passes used by these animals, very often drive into the toils an entire band of antelope of several hundreds, when not one escapes slaughter.

I have seen them on the western sides of the mountains, and in the mountain valleys, in herds of several thousands. They are exceedingly timid animals, but at the same time wonderfully curious; and their curiosity very often proves their death, for the hunter, taking advantage of this weakness, plants his wiping-stick in the ground, with a cap or red handkerchief on the point, and, concealing himself in the long grass, waits, rifle in hand, the approach of the inquisitive antelope, who, seeing an unusual object in the plain, trots up to it, and, coming within range of the deadly tube, pays dearly for his temerity. An antelope, when alone, is one of the stupidest of beasts, and becomes so confused and frightened at sight of a travelling party, that it frequently runs right into the midst of the danger it seeks to avoid.

I had heard most wonderful accounts from the trappers of an animal, the existence of which was beyond all doubt, which, although exceedingly rare, was occasionally met with in the mountains, but, from its supposed dangerous ferocity, and the fact of its being a cross between the devil and a bear, was never molested by the Indians or white hunters, and a wide berth given whenever the animal made its dreaded appearance. Most wonderful stories were told of its audacity and fearlessness; how it sometimes jumps from an overhanging rock on a deer or buffalo, and, fastening on its neck, soon brings it to the ground; how it has been known to leap upon a hunter when passing near its place of concealment, and devour him in a twinkling — often charging furiously into a camp, and playing all sorts of pranks on the goods and chattels of the mountaineers. The general belief was that the animal owes its paternity to the old gentleman himself; but the most reasonable declare it to be a cross between the bear and wolf.

Hunting one day with an old Canadian trapper, he told me that, in a part of the mountains which we were about to visit on the morrow, he once had a battle with a " carcagieu," which lasted upwards of two hours, during which he fired a pouchful of balls into the animal's body, which spat them out as fast as they were shot in. To the truth of this probable [improbable] story he called all the saints to bear witness.

Two days after, as we were toiling up a steep ridge after a band of mountain-sheep, my companion, who was in advance, suddenly threw himself flat behind a rock, and exclaimed in a smothered tone, signalling me with his hand to keep down and conceal myself, " Sacré enfant de Gârce, mais here's von dam carcagieu! "

I immediately cocked my rifle, and, advancing to the rock, and peeping over it, saw an animal, about the size of a large badger, engaged in scraping up the earth about a dozen paces from where we were concealed. Its colour was dark, almost black; its body long, and apparently tailless; and I at once recognised the mysterious beast to be a " glutton." After I had sufficiently examined the animal, I raised my rifle to shoot, when a louder than common "Enfant de Gârce " from my companion alarmed the animal, and it immediately ran off, when I stood up and fired both barrels after it, but without effect; the attempt exciting a derisive laugh from the Canadian, who exclaimed, " Pe gar, may be you got fifty balls; vel, shoot 'em all at de dam carcagieu, and he not care a dam! "

The skins of these animals are considered " great medicine " by the Indians, and will fetch almost any price. They are very rarely met with on the plains, preferring the upland valleys and broken ground of the mountains, which afford them a better field for their method of securing game, which is by lying in wait behind a rock, or on the steep bank of a ravine, concealed by a tree or shrub, until a deer or antelope passes underneath, when they spring upon the animal's back, and, holding on with their strong and sharp claws, which they bury in the flesh, soon bring it bleeding to the ground. The Indians say they are purely carnivorous; but I imagine that, like the bear, they not unfrequently eat fruit and roots, when animal food is not to be had.

I have said that the mountain wolves, and, still more so, the coyote of the plains, are less frightened at the sight of man than any other beast. One night, when encamped on an affluent of the Platte, a heavy snow-storm falling at the time, I lay down in my blanket, after first heaping on the fire a vast pile of wood, to burn till morning. In the middle of the night I was awakened by the excessive cold, and, turning towards the fire, which was burning bright and cheerfully, what was my astonishment to see a large grey wolf sitting quietly before it, his eyes closed, and his head nodding in sheer drowsiness! Although I had frequently seen wolves evince their disregard to fires, by coming within a few feet of them to seize upon any scraps of meat which might be left exposed, I had never seen or heard of one approaching so close as to warm his body, and for that purpose alone. However, I looked at him for some moments without disturbing the beast, and closed my eyes and went to sleep, leaving him to the quiet enjoyment of the blaze.

This is not very wonderful when I mention that it is a very common thing for these animals to gnaw the straps of a saddle on which your head is reposing for a pillow.

When I turned my horse's head from Pike's Peak I quite regretted the abandonment of my mountain life, solitary as it was, and more than once thought of again taking the trail to the Bayou Salado, where I had enjoyed such good sport.

Apart from the feeling of loneliness which any one in my situation must naturally have experienced, surrounded by stupendous works of nature, which in all their solitary grandeur frowned upon me, and sinking into utter insignifi-

cance the miserable mortal who crept beneath their shadow;
still there was something inexpressibly exhilarating in the
sensation of positive freedom from all worldly care, and a
consequent expansion of the sinews, as it were, of mind and
body, which made me feel elastic as a ball of Indian rubber,
and in a state of such perfect *insouciance* that no more dread
of scalping Indians entered my mind than if I had been
sitting in Broadway, in one of the windows of Astor House.
A citizen of the world, I never found any difficulty in in-
vesting my resting-place, wherever it might be, with all
the attributes of a home; and hailed, with delight equal to
that which the artificial comforts of a civilized home would
have caused, the, to me, domestic appearance of my hobbled
animals, as they grazed around the camp, when I returned
after a hard day's hunt. By the way, I may here remark
that my *sporting* feeling underwent a great change when I
was necessitated to follow and kill game for the support
of life, and as a means of subsistence; and the slaughter
of deer and buffalo no longer became *sport* when the object
was to fill the larder, and the excitement of the hunt was
occasioned by the alternative of a plentiful feast or a
banyan; and, although ranking under the head of the most
red-hot of sportsmen, I can safely acquit myself of ever
wantonly destroying a deer or buffalo unless I was in need
of meat; and such consideration for the feræ naturæ is
common to all the mountaineers who look to game alone for
their support. Although liable to an accusation of barbarism, I must confess that the very happiest moments of
my life have been spent in the wilderness of the far West;
and I never recall but with pleasure the remembrance of my
solitary camp in the Bayou Salado, with no friend near me
more faithful than my rifle, and no companions more
sociable than my good horse and mules, or the attendant
coyote which nightly serenaded us. With a plentiful supply
of dry pine-logs on the fire, and its cheerful blaze streaming
far up into the sky, illuminating the valley far and near, and

exhibiting the animals, with well-filled bellies, standing contentedly at rest over their picket-pins, I would sit cross-legged enjoying the genial warmth, and, pipe in mouth, watch the blue smoke as it curled upwards, building castles in its vapoury wreaths, and, in the fantastic shapes it assumed, peopling the solitude with figures of those far away. Scarcely, however, did I ever wish to change such hours of freedom for all the luxuries of civilized life, and, unnatural and extraordinary as it may appear, yet such is the fascination of the life of the mountain hunter, that I believe not one instance could be adduced of even the most polished and civilized of men, who had once tasted the sweets of its attendant liberty and freedom from every worldly care, not regretting the moment when he exchanged it for the monotonous life of the settlements, nor sighing, and sighing again, once more to partake of its pleasures and allurements.

Nothing can be more social and cheering than the welcome blaze of the camp fire on a cold winter's night, and nothing more amusing or entertaining, if not instructive, than the rough conversation of the single-minded mountaineers, whose simple daily talk is all of exciting adventure, since their whole existence is spent in scenes of peril and privation; and consequently the narration of their every-day life is a tale of thrilling accidents and hair-breadth 'scapes, which, though simple matter-of-fact to them, appear a startling romance to those who are not acquainted with the nature of the lives led by these men, who, with the sky for a roof and their rifles to supply them with food and clothing, call no man lord or master, and are free as the game they follow.

A hunter's camp in the Rocky Mountains is quite a picture. He does not always take the trouble to build any shelter unless it is in the snow-season, when a couple of deerskins stretched over a willow frame shelter him from the storm. At other seasons he is content with a mere breakwind. Near at hand are two upright poles, with another supported on the top of these, on which is displayed, out of reach of hungry wolf or coyote, meat of every variety the mountains afford. Buffalo dépouillés, hams of deer and mountain-sheep, beaver-tails, &c., stock the larder. Under the shelter of the skins hang his powder-horn and bullet-pouch; while his rifle, carefully defended from the damp, is always within reach of his arm. Round the blazing fire the hunters congregate at night, and whilst cleaning their rifles, making or mending mocassins, or running bullets, spin long yarns of their hunting exploits, &c.

Some hunters, who have married Indian squaws, carry about with them the Indian lodge of buffalo-skins, which are stretched in a conical form round a frame of poles. Near the camp is always seen the " graining-block," a log of wood with the bark stripped and perfectly smooth, which is planted obliquely in the ground, and on which the hair is removed from the skins to prepare them for being dressed. There are also " stretching-frames," on which the skins are placed to undergo the process of dubbing, which is the removal of the flesh and fatty particles adhering to the skin, by means of the *dubber,* an instrument made of the stock of an elk's horn. The last process is the " smoking," which is effected by digging a round hole in the ground and lighting in it an armful of rotten wood or punk. Three sticks are then planted round the hole, and their tops brought together and tied. The skin is then placed on this frame, and all the holes by which the smoke might escape carefully stopped: in ten or twelve hours the skin is thoroughly smoked and ready for immediate use.

The camp is invariably made in a picturesque locality, for, like the Indian, the white hunter has ever an eye to the beautiful. The broken ground of the mountains, with their numerous tumbling and babbling rivulets, and groves and thickets of shrubs and timber, always afford shelter from the boisterous winds of winter, and abundance of fuel and water. Facing the rising sun the hunter invariably erects his shanty, with a wall of precipitous rock in rear to defend it from the gusts which often sweep down the gorges of the mountains. Round the camp his animals, well hobbled at night, feed within sight, for nothing does a hunter dread more than a visit from the horse-stealing Indians; and to be "afoot" is the acme of his misery.

AT FORT LARAMIE

FRANCIS PARKMAN

1846

LOOKING back, after the expiration of a year, upon Fort Laramie and its inmates, they seem less like a reality than like some fanciful picture of the olden time; so different was the scene from any which this tamer side of the world can present. Tall Indians, enveloped in their white buffalo-robes, were striding across the area or reclining at full length on the low roofs of the buildings which enclosed it. Numerous squaws, gayly bedizened, sat grouped in front of the rooms they occupied; their mongrel offspring, restless and vociferous, rambled in every direction through the fort; and the trappers, traders and *engagés* of the establishment were busy at their labor or their amusements.

We were met at the gate, but by no means cordially welcomed. Indeed we seemed objects of some distrust and suspicion, until Henry Chatillon explained that we were not traders, and we, in confirmation, handed to the *bourgeois* a letter of introduction from his principals. He took it, turned it upside down, and tried hard to read it; but his literary attainments not being adequate to the task, he applied for relief to the clerk, a sleek, smiling Frenchman, named Monthalon. The letter read, Bordeaux (the *bourgeois*) seemed gradually to awaken to a sense of what was expected of him. Though not deficient in hospitable intentions, he was wholly unaccustomed to act as master of ceremonies. Discarding all formalities of reception, he did not honor us with a single word, but walked swiftly across the area, while we followed in some admiration to a railing and a flight of steps opposite the entrance. He signed to us that we had better fasten our horses to the railing; then he walked up the steps, tramped along a rude balcony, and, kicking open a door, displayed a large room, rather more elaborately furnished than a barn. For furniture it had a rough bedstead, but no bed, two chairs, a chest of drawers, a tin pail to hold water, and a board to cut tobacco upon. A brass crucifix hung on the wall, and close at hand a recent scalp, with hair full a yard long, was suspended from a nail. I shall again have occasion to mention this dismal trophy, its history being connected with that of our subsequent proceedings.

This apartment, the best in Fort Laramie, was that usually occupied by the legitimate *bourgeois,* Papin, in whose absence the command devolved upon Bordeaux. The latter, a stout, bluff little fellow, much inflated by a sense of his new authority, began to roar for buffalo-robes. These being brought and spread upon the floor formed our beds, — much better ones than we had of late been accustomed to. Our arrangements made, we stepped out to the balcony to take a more leisurely survey of the long looked-for haven at which we had arrived at last. Beneath us was the square area surrounded by little rooms, or rather cells, which opened upon it. These were devoted to various purposes, but served chiefly for the accommodation of the men employed at the fort, or of the equally numerous squaws whom they were allowed to maintain in it. Opposite to us rose the blockhouse above the gateway; it was adorned with the figure of a horse at full speed, daubed upon the boards with red paint, and exhibiting a degree of skill which might rival that displayed by the Indians in executing similar designs upon their robes and lodges. A busy scene was enacting in the area.

The wagons of Vaskiss, an old trader, were about to set out for a remote post in the mountains, and the Canadians were going through their preparations with all possible bustle, while here and there an Indian stood looking on with imperturbable gravity.

Fort Laramie is one of the posts established by the " American Fur Company," which well-nigh monopolizes the Indian trade of this region. Here its officials rule with an absolute sway; the arm of the United States has little force; for when we were there, the extreme outposts of her troops were about seven hundred miles to the eastward. The little fort is built of bricks dried in the sun, and externally is of an oblong form, with bastions of clay, in the form of ordinary blockhouses, at two of the corners. The walls are about fifteen feet high, and surmounted by a slender palisade. The roofs of the apartments within, which are built close against the walls, serve the purpose of a banquette. Within, the fort is divided by a partition: on one side is the square area, surrounded by the store-rooms, offices, and apartments of the inmates; on the other is the *corral,* a narrow place, encompassed by the high clay walls, where at night, or in presence of dangerous Indians, the horses and mules of the fort are crowded for safe keeping. The main entrance has two gates, with an arched passage intervening. A little square window, high above the ground, opens laterally from an adjoining chamber into this passage; so that when the inner gate is closed and barred, a person without may still hold communication with those within, through this narrow aperture. This obviates the necessity of admitting suspicious Indians, for purposes of trading, into the body of the fort; for when danger is apprehended, the inner gate is shut fast, and all traffic is carried on by means of the window. This precaution, though necessary at some of the Company's posts, is seldom resorted to at Fort Laramie; where, though men are frequently killed in the neighborhood, no apprehensions are felt of any general designs of hostility from the Indians.

We did not long enjoy our new quarters undisturbed. The door was silently pushed open, and two eyeballs and a visage as black as night looked in upon us; then a red arm and shoulder intruded themselves, and a tall Indian, gliding in, shook us by the hand, grunted his salutation, and sat down on the floor. Others followed, with faces of the natural hue, and letting fall their heavy robes from their shoulders, took their seats, quite at ease, in a semi-circle before us. The pipe was now to be lighted and passed from one to another; and this was the only entertainment that at present they expected from us. These visitors were fathers, brothers, or other relatives of the squaws in the fort, where they were permitted to remain, loitering about in perfect idleness. All those who smoked with us were men of standing and repute. Two or three others dropped in also; young fellows who neither by their years nor their exploits were entitled to rank with the old men and warriors, and who, abashed in the presence of their superiors, stood aloof, never withdrawing their eyes from us. Their cheeks were adorned with vermilion, their ears with pendants of shell, and their necks with beads. Never yet having signalized themselves as hunters, or performed the honorable exploit of killing a man, they were held in slight esteem, and were diffident and bashful in proportion. Certain formidable inconveniences attended this influx of visitors. They were bent on inspecting everything in the room; our equipments and our dress alike underwent their scrutiny, for though the contrary has been asserted, few beings have more curiosity than Indians in regard to subjects within their ordinary range of thought. As to other matters, indeed, they seem utterly indifferent. They will not trouble themselves to inquire into what they cannot comprehend, but are quite contented to place their hands over their mouths in token of wonder, and exclaim that it is " great medicine." With this comprehensive solution, an Indian never is at a loss. He never launches into speculation and conjecture; his reason moves in its beaten track. His soul is dormant; and no exertions of the missionaries, Jesuit or Puritan, of the old world or of the new, have as yet availed to arouse it.

As we were looking, at sunset, from the wall, upon the desolate plains that surround the fort, we observed a cluster of strange objects like scaffolds, rising in the distance against the red western sky. They bore aloft some singular-looking burdens; and at their foot glimmered something white, like bones. This was the place of sepulture of some Dakota chiefs, whose remains their people are fond of placing in the vicinity of the fort, in the hope that they may thus be protected from violation at the hands of their enemies. Yet it has happened more than once, and quite recently, that war parties of the Crow Indians, ranging through the country, have thrown the bodies from the scaffolds, and broken them to pieces, amid the yells of the Dakota, who remained pent up in the fort, too few to defend the honored relics from insult. The white objects upon the ground were buffalo skulls, arranged in the mystic circle commonly seen at Indian places of sepulture upon the prairie.

We soon discovered, in the twilight, a band of fifty or sixty horses approaching the fort. These were the animals belonging to the establishment; who, having been sent out to feed, under the care of armed guards, in the meadows below, were now being driven into the *corral* for the night. A gate opened into this inclosure; by the side of it stood one of the guards, an old Canadian, with gray bushy eyebrows, and a dragoon pistol stuck into his belt; while his comrade, mounted on horseback, his rifle laid across the saddle in front, and his long hair blowing before his swarthy face, rode at the rear of the disorderly troop, urging them up the ascent. In a moment the narrow *corral* was thronged with the half-wild horses, kicking, biting, and crowding restlessly together.

The discordant jingling of a bell, rung by a Canadian in the area, summoned us to supper. The repast was served on a rough table in one of the lower apartments of the fort, and consisted of cakes of bread and dried buffalo meat, an excellent thing for strengthening the teeth. At this meal were seated the *bourgeois* and superior dignitaries of the establishment, among whom Henry Chatillon was worthily included. No sooner was it finished than the table was spread a second time (the luxury of bread being now, however, omitted), for the benefit of certain hunters and trappers of an inferior standing; while the ordinary Canadian *engagés* were regaled on dried meat in one of their lodging rooms. By way of illustrating the domestic economy of Fort Laramie, it may not be amiss to introduce in this place a story current among the men when we were there.

There was an old man named Pierre, whose duty it was to bring the meat from the store-room for the men. Old Pierre, in the kindness of his heart, used to select the fattest and the best pieces for his companions. This did not long escape the keen-eyed *bourgeois,* who was greatly disturbed at such improvidence, and cast about for some means to stop it. At last he hit on a plan that exactly suited him. At the side of the meat-room, and separated from it by a clay partition, was another apartment, used for the storage of furs. It had no communication with the fort, except through a square hole in the partition; and of course it was perfectly dark. One evening the *bourgeois,* watching for a moment when no one observed him, dodged into the meat-room, clambered through the hole, and ensconced himself among the furs and buffalo-robes. Soon after, old Pierre came in with his lantern, and muttering to himself, began to pull over the bales of meat and select the best pieces, as usual. But suddenly a hollow and sepulchral voice proceeded from the inner room: "Pierre, Pierre! Let that fat meat alone. Take nothing but lean." Pierre dropped his lantern, and bolted out into the fort, screaming, in an agony of terror, that the devil was in the store-room; but tripping on the threshold, he pitched over upon the gravel, and lay senseless, stunned by the fall. The Canadians ran out to the rescue. Some lifted the unlucky Pierre; and others, making an extempore crucifix of two sticks, were proceeding to attack the devil in his stronghold, when the *bourgeois,* with a crestfallen countenance, appeared at the door. To add to his mortification, he was obliged to explain the whole stratagem to Pierre, in order to bring him to his senses.

We were sitting, on the following morning, in the passage-way between the gates, conversing with the traders Vaskiss and May. These two men, together with our sleek friend, the clerk Monthalon, were, I believe, the only persons then in the fort who could read and write. May was telling a curious story about the traveller Catlin, when an ugly, diminutive Indian, wretchedly mounted, came up at a gallop, and rode by us into the fort. On being questioned, he said that Smoke's village was close at hand. Accordingly only a few minutes elapsed before the hills beyond the river were covered with a disorderly swarm of savages, on horseback and on foot. May finished his story; and by that time the whole array had descended to Laramie Creek, and begun to cross it in a mass. I walked down to the bank. The stream is wide, and was then between three and four feet deep, with a swift current. For several rods the water was alive with dogs, horses, and Indians. The long poles used in pitching the lodges are carried by the horses, fastened by the heavier end, two or three on each side, to a rude sort of pack-saddle, while the other end drags on the ground. About a foot behind the horse, a kind of large basket or pannier is suspended between the poles, and firmly lashed in its place. On the back of the horse are piled various articles of luggage; the basket also is well filled with domestic utensils, or, quite as often, with a litter of puppies, a brood of small children, or a superannuated old man. Numbers of these curious vehicles, *traineaux,* or, as the

Canadians called them, *travois,* were now splashing together through the stream. Among them swam countless dogs, often burdened with miniature *traineaux;* and dashing forward on horseback through the throng came the warriors, the slender figure of some lynx-eyed boy clinging fast behind them. The women sat perched on the pack-saddles, adding not a little to the load of the already over-burdened horses. The confusion was prodigious. The dogs yelled and howled in chorus; the puppies in the *travois* set up a dismal whine as the water invaded their comfortable retreat; the little black-eyed children, from one year of age upward, clung fast with both hands to the edge of their basket, and looked over in alarm at the water rushing so near them, sputtering and making wry mouths as it splashed against their faces. Some of the dogs, encumbered by their load, were carried down by the current, yelping piteously; and the old squaws would rush into the water, seize their favorites by the neck, and drag them out. As each horse gained the bank, he scrambled up as he could. Stray horses and colts came among the rest, often breaking away at full speed through the crowd, followed by the old hags, screaming after their fashion on all occasions of excitement. Buxom young squaws, blooming in all the charms of vermilion, stood here and there on the bank, holding aloft their master's lance, as a signal to collect the scattered portions of his household. In a few moments the crowd melted away; each family with its horses and equipage, filing off to the plain at the rear of the fort; and here, in the space of half an hour, arose sixty or seventy of their tapering lodges. Their horses were feeding by hundreds over the surrounding prairie, and their dogs were roaming everywhere. The fort was full of warriors, and the children were whooping and yelling incessantly under the walls.

These new-comers were scarcely arrived, when Bordeaux ran across the fort, shouting to his squaw to bring him his spy-glass. The obedient Marie, the very model of a squaw, produced the instrument, and Bordeaux hurried with it to the wall. Pointing it eastward, he exclaimed, with an oath, that the families were coming. But a few moments elapsed before the heavy caravan of the emigrant wagons could be seen, steadily advancing from the hills. They gained the river, and, without turning or pausing, plunged in, passed through, and slowly ascending the opposing bank, kept directly on their way by the fort and the Indian village, until, gaining a spot a quarter of a mile distant, they wheeled into a circle. For some time our tranquillity was undisturbed. The emigrants were preparing their encampment; but no sooner was this accomplished than Fort Laramie was taken by storm. A crowd of broad-brimmed hats, thin visages, and staring eyes, appeared suddenly at the gate. Tall, awkward men, in brown homespun, women, with cadaverous faces and long lank figures, came thronging in together, and, as if inspired by the very demon of curiosity, ransacked every nook and corner of the fort. Dismayed at this invasion we withdrew in all speed to our chamber, vainly hoping that it might prove a sanctuary. The emigrants prosecuted their investigations with untiring vigor. They penetrated the rooms, or rather dens, inhabited by the astonished squaws. Resolved to search every mystery to the bottom, they explored the apartments of the men, and even that of Marie and the *bourgeois*. At last a numerous deputation appeared at our door, but found no encouragement to remain.

Having at length satisfied their curiosity, they next proceeded to business. Their men occupied themselves in procuring supplies for their onward journey,— either buying them, or giving in exchange superfluous articles of their own.

The emigrants felt a violent prejudice against the French Indians, as they called the trappers and traders. They thought, and with some reason, that these men bore them no good-will. Many of them were firmly persuaded that the French were instigating the Indians to attack and cut them off. On visiting the encampment we were at once struck with the extraordinary perplexity and indecision that prevailed among them. They seemed like men totally out of their element, — bewildered and amazed, like a troop of schoolboys lost in the woods. It was impossible to be long among them without being conscious of the bold spirit with which most of them were animated. But the *forest* is the home of the backwoodsman. On the remote prairie he is totally at a loss. He differs as much from the genuine " mountain-man " as a Canadian voyageur, paddling his canoe on the rapids of the Ottawa, differs from an American sailor among the storms of Cape Horn. Still my companion and I were somewhat at a loss to account for this perturbed state of mind. It could not be cowardice; these men were of the same stock with the volunteers of Monterey and Buena Vista. Yet, for the most part, they were the rudest and most ignorant of the frontier population; they knew absolutely nothing of the country and its inhabitants; they had already experienced much misfortune, and apprehended more; they had seen nothing of mankind, and had never put their own resources to the test.

A full share of suspicion fell upon us. Being strangers, we were looked upon as enemies. Having occasion for a supply of lead and a few other necessary articles, we used to go over to the emigrant camps to obtain them. After some hesitation, some dubious glances, and fumbling of the hands in the pockets, the terms would be agreed upon, the price tendered, and the emigrant would go off to bring the article in question. After waiting until our patience gave out, we would go in search of him, and find him seated on the tongue of his wagon.

" Well, stranger," he would observe, as he saw us approach, " I reckon I won't trade."

Some friend of his had followed him from the scene of the bargain, and whispered in his ear that clearly we meant to cheat him, and he had better have nothing to do with us.

This timorous mood of the emigrants was doubly unfortunate, as it exposed them to real danger. Assume, in the presence of Indians, a bold bearing, self-confident yet vigilant, and you will find them tolerably safe neighbors. But your safety depends on the respect and fear you are able to inspire. If you betray timidity or indecision, you convert them from that moment into insidious and dangerous enemies. The Dakota saw clearly enough the perturbation of the emigrants, and instantly availed themselves of it. They became extremely insolent and exacting in their demands. It has become an established custom with them to go to the camp of every party, as it arrives in succession at the fort, and demand a feast. Smoke's village had come with this express design, having made several days' journey with no other object than that of enjoying a cup of coffee and two or three biscuit. So the " feast " was demanded, and the emigrants dared not refuse it.

One evening about sunset the village was deserted. We met old men, warriors, squaws, and children in gay attire, trooping off to the encampment with faces of anticipation; and, arriving here, they seated themselves in a semicircle. Smoke occupied the centre, with his warriors on either hand; the young men and boys came next, and the squaws and children formed the horns of the crescent. The biscuit and coffee were promptly despatched, the emigrants staring open-mouthed at their savage guests. With each emigrant party that arrived at Fort Laramie this scene was renewed; and every day the Indians grew more rapacious and presumptuous. One evening they broke in pieces, out of mere wantonness, the cups from which they had been feasted; and this so exasperated the emigrants that many of them seized their rifles and could scarcely be restrained from firing on the insolent mob of Indians. Before we left the country this dangerous spirit on the part of the Dakota had mounted to a yet higher pitch. They began openly to threaten the emigrants with destruction, and actually fired upon one or two parties of them. A military force and military law are urgently called for in that perilous region; and unless troops are speedily stationed at Fort Laramie, or elsewhere in the neighborhood, both emigrants and other travellers will be exposed to most imminent risks.

The Ogillallah, the Brulé, and the other western bands of the Dakota or Sioux, are thorough savages, unchanged by any contact with civilization. Not one of them can speak a European tongue, or has ever visited an American settlement. Until within a year or two, when the emigrants began to pass through their country on the way to Oregon, they had seen no whites, except a few employed about the Fur Company's posts. They thought them a wise people, inferior only to themselves, living in leather lodges, like their own, and subsisting on buffalo. But when the swarm of *Meneaska,* with their oxen and wagons, began to invade them, their astonishment was unbounded. They could scarcely believe that the earth contained such a multitude of white men. Their wonder is now giving way to indignation; and the result, unless vigilantly guarded against, may be lamentable in the extreme.

But to glance at the interior of a lodge. Shaw and I used often to visit them. Indeed we spent most of our evenings in the Indian village, Shaw's assumption of the medical character giving us a fair pretext. As a sample of the rest I will describe one of these visits. The sun had just set, and the horses were driven into the *corral.* The Prairie Cock, a noted beau, came in at the gate with a bevy of young girls, with whom he began a dance in the area, leading them round and round in a circle, while he jerked up from his chest a succession of monotonous sounds, to which they kept time in a rueful chant. Outside the gate boys and young men were idly frolicking; and close by, looking grimly upon them, stood a warrior in his robe, with his face painted jet-black, in token that he had lately taken a Pawnee scalp. Passing these, the tall dark lodges rose between us and the red western sky. We repaired at once to the lodge of Old Smoke himself. It was by no means better than the others; indeed, it was rather shabby; for in this democratic community the chief never assumes superior state. Smoke sat cross-legged on a buffalo-robe, and his grunt of salutation as we entered was unusually cordial, out of respect, no doubt, to Shaw's medical character. Seated around the lodge were several squaws, and an abundance of children. The complaint of Shaw's patients was, for the most part, a severe inflammation of the eyes, occasioned by exposure to the sun, a species of disorder which he treated with some success. He had brought with him a homœopathic medicine-chest, and was, I presume, the first who introduced that harmless system of treatment among the Ogillallah. No sooner had a robe been spread at the head of the lodge for our accommodation, and we had seated ourselves upon it, than a patient made her appearance, — the chief's daughter herself, who, to do her justice, was the best-looking girl in the village. Being on excellent terms with the physician, she placed herself readily under his hands, and submitted with a good grace to his applications, laughing in his face during the whole process, for a squaw hardly knows how to smile. This case despatched, another of a different kind succeeded. A hideous, emaciated old woman sat in the darkest corner of the lodge, rocking to and fro with pain, and hiding her eyes from the light by pressing the palms of both hands against her face. At Smoke's command she came forward, very unwillingly, and exhibited a pair of eyes that had nearly disappeared from excess of inflammation. No sooner had the doctor fastened his grip upon her, than she set up a dismal moaning, and writhed so in his grasp that he lost all patience; but being resolved to carry his point, he succeeded at last in applying his favorite remedies.

" It is strange," he said when the operation was finished, " that I forgot to bring any Spanish flies with me; we must have something here to answer for a counter-irritant."

So, in the absence of better, he seized upon a red-hot brand from the fire, and clapped it against the temple of the old squaw, who set up an unearthly howl, at which the rest of the family broke into a laugh.

During these medical operations Smoke's eldest squaw entered the lodge, with a mallet in her hand, the stone head of which, precisely like those sometimes ploughed up in the fields of New England, was made fast to the handle by a covering of raw hide. I had observed some time before a litter of well-grown black puppies, comfortably nestled among some buffalo-robes at one side; but this new-comer speedily disturbed their enjoyment; for seizing one of them by the hind paw, she dragged him out and carrying him to the entrance of the lodge, hammered him on the head till she killed him. Aware to what this preparation tended, I looked through a hole in the back of the lodge to see the next steps of the process. The squaw, holding the puppy by the legs, was swinging him to and fro through the blaze of a fire, until the hair was singed off. This done, she unsheathed her knife and cut him into small pieces, which she dropped into a kettle to boil. In a few moments a large wooden dish was set before us filled with this delicate preparation. A dog-feast is the greatest compliment a Dakota can offer to his guest; and, knowing that to refuse eating would be an affront, we attacked the little dog, and devoured him before the eyes of his unconscious parent. Smoke in the mean time was preparing his great pipe. It was lighted when we had finished our repast, and we passed it from one to another till the bowl was empty. This done, we took our leave without further ceremony, knocked at the gate of the fort, and after making ourselves known, were admitted.

GOLD! GOLD!

SUTTER'S FORT

CHARLES PETTIGREW

1848-1849

From *The Caledonian*. Reprinted by permission of the publishers, Caledonian Publishing Company, New York.

In the year 1839, while California was still a part of the Mexican Republic, there appeared before the Governor at Monterey, a man named Johann August Sutter, asking for a grant of land on which he proposed to found a colony. Though born in Baden, Germany, his parents were Swiss, and when a young man he served as captain in the Swiss army, and later was in business, but failed. He then came to America, and crossing to the Pacific Coast on the Oregon trail, he rambled about the Northwest, went to Honolulu, and finally landed at Yerba Buena (San Francisco), going from there to Monterey. Governor Alvarado, in answer to his request for a grant of land, told him that he must first become a citizen of Mexico, then select the land for which he wished a grant, and come back to him in a year, when perhaps his naturalization papers would be issued, and a grant of the land given him.

Sutter acted as directed, and was not only made a Mexican citizen and given a grant of the land he had selected but was also made an official of the government, an alcalde (mayor with judicial powers), with jurisdiction over a territory running eighty-five miles northward along the Sacramento river from near the place where the American river joins it, and eastward from the Sacramento a distance varying from ten to twelve miles, Sutter's grant being eleven square leagues (48,000 acres) within that territory. Having previously selected his location, he at once began to build a fort with adobe brick (bricks of sun dried clay), with walls three feet thick and eighteen feet high, enclosing a space five hundred feet long, by a hundred feet wide. The walls were pierced at suitable places with loopholes for muskets, and at the southeast and northwest corners of the enclosure were towers or bastions in which small cannon were mounted, so that they commanded the four sides of the enclosure. In this fort Sutter's house, together with quarters for his people, and all necessary storehouses and workshops were located. The fort stood on high ground, on the south bank of the American river, about a quarter of a mile from the water's edge, and about a mile from the Sacramento river. His original company of colonists consisted of five white men, ten Indians, two of whom were squaws, and a large bulldog. That Captain Sutter chose his location wisely was strongly confirmed in 1854, when the site of his fort was chosen as the capital of the newly organized State of California; and now the great city of Sacramento, with its population of 75,000, has risen on the place of his selection. He named the place New Helvetta, to remind him of his native Switzerland; but somehow that name did not stick, and it was popularly known as Sutter's Fort, the site of which has long since been absorbed by the great city. But the grateful citizens of Sacramento have preserved and restored the ruins of the old fort in one of their parks, so that its memory may be forever cherished.

During the five years that intervened between the time he became a citizen of the Mexican Republic and the ceding of the whole territory of Alta California by Mexico to the United States, Sutter was lord of all he surveyed. He had studied Dr. McLaughlin's (the agent of the Hudson Bay Company) method of handling the Indians, and he followed it strictly. He treated them kindly, without fear, paying them exactly as agreed for their services, and punishing them when they stole or disturbed the peace and order of the camp; and if they showed any disposition to act against him in force, he easily frightened them by the use of his three cannon, which always terrified them.

Sutter's Fort soon became the rendezvous for all the trappers, hunters and wandering people of all sorts in the surrounding territory, besides the emigrants that all the time came from the East over the Oregon trail, the fort being its terminal.

When the territory came under the Stars and Stripes, Sutter swore allegiance to the flag and anglicized his name, becoming John Augustus Sutter. By 1847 his colony had developed wonderfully. He had a thousand acres of land growing wheat; he owned 8,000 head of cattle, 2,000 horses and mules, 2,000 sheep and 1,000 hogs.

Commodore Stockton had confirmed him as alcalde, or justice of the peace, and General Kearney later made him Indian Agent. He had now come to the point where it became necessary to have a flour mill for the colony, and that a flour mill might be built, a saw-mill was necessary, to prepare timbers, planks and boards. The machinery for these mills had been recently brought to the fort in 1844 by the ship *Lexington*.

Among the immigrants that came to the fort in 1844 was a man from New Jersey named James Wilson Marshall, a millwright by trade. He worked for Sutter for a time, but being taken with an attack of land-hunger, he undertook to work land of his own. Tiring of that, he came back to Sutter in 1847, when the necessity for the mills became so urgent. They formed a partnership in the saw-mill, and Marshall, with two white men and an Indian guide, left the fort on May 16, 1847, to search for a site and build the saw-mill. He found a place on the south fork of the American river, about forty-five miles from the fort, adjacent to timber, that he thought suitable. This place now bears the name of Coloma. Work on the mill and dam was at once begun, and in January of the following year the mill and dam had been constructed, and they were at work on the tail-race that was to lead the water, after it had done its work on the wheel, back to the river.

Marshall found conditions such that considerable time and labor could be saved by simply loosening up the earth with a pick and by turning on the water washing it out into the river.

On the afternoon of January 24, while directing this operation and walking along on the bank of the tail-race, his eye was attracted by some yellow specks that glittered in the sunlight. At first he took little notice of them, till seeing still more of them, the thought flashed through his mind — " Can these be gold? " He picked up a piece larger than the rest and examined it. He had never seen gold in its native state, but understood in a general way that it was heavier than lead and that it was a soft, not a brittle metal. He weighed it in his hands, bit it with his teeth, then laid it on a rock and pounded it with a smaller stone, and found that he could mash it a little. Being of a morose disposition, he became very thoughtful, and as he sat at supper with his mates he scarcely spoke a word; but at last he quietly remarked: " Boys, I think I have found a gold mine." One of the men spoke up and said, " I reckon not — no such luck for us."

He could not dismiss it from his mind, and was up betimes in the morning, again looking over the tail-race, and found more of the yellow particles. The thought that it might be gold thrilled him. He and his men picked up about four ounces of the yellow stuff, and Mrs. Wimmer, the camp cook, boiled them, which only made them brighter. This more and more convinced Marshall that they were gold. He begged his men to go on with the work and say nothing about it. On the morning of January 28 he mounted his horse and started for the fort, where he arrived early in the afternoon. He was covered with mud, for he had ridden hard, and it was raining so that he was wet to the skin, and he was very much excited. Walking into Sutter's office, he at once asked for a private interview. Whispering that the doors must be locked, this rather alarmed Sutter. Marshall then announced that he was sure he had found gold, and taking a little bag from his pocket he dumped his few ounces of nuggets on the table. Incredulous at first, Sutter soon became convinced that this was gold, especially after he had tested them with acid, and bringing from his drug store a small pair of scales, he put some silver coins in one of the saucers, and balancing them with gold in the other, he lowered them into a basin of water. When the yellow metal dropped lower than the silver coins, he knew for sure that they were gold.

So excited was Marshall that though Sutter urged him to stay at the fort till the next morning, cold and wet as he was, he returned to the mill the same night, hardly taking time to eat a bit of supper. The next morning he was back on the road to meet Sutter, who had agreed to come then. They spent two days together looking the ground over and trying to decide what was the best thing to do.

Gold they found everywhere they looked for it, along the river. Marshall's chief anxiety was to secure for themselves all the rights to the gold in the ground to which they might be entitled. Sutter's viewpoint was somewhat different. He had developed a very valuable agricultural property, and at this time owned 12,000 head of cattle, 2,000 horses and mules, 10,000 to 15,000 sheep, and 1,000 hogs; he had grown during the past year 20,000 bushels of wheat, and had several thousand hides in process of tanning or waiting to be tanned. Then there were the two unfinished mills. He at once saw that if his men once broke away from him and went after the gold his mills would never be finished, and they were now more than ever absolutely necessary. So he decided to try and keep the whole matter secret, at least until the mills were finished, and he pledged his men to stay on the job and say nothing about the gold for the next six weeks. He thought that he could easily keep them isolated for that time. He also took the precaution of obtaining from the Indians living in the district the exclusive use of their lands for all or any purpose, for himself and Marshall, for the next three years, the tract consisting of twelve miles square.

The excitement within the camp increased daily. One of the men, Bilger by name, had been assigned the duty of occasionally going along the river and its tributaries, to shoot deer and ducks, to give variety to the bill of fare. He always brought back with him specimens of gold that he easily found wherever he searched for it in the streams. Sutter himself became more and more uneasy as the weeks passed. His title to the land grant given him by the Mexican Government had not been confirmed by the United States authorities, that had so recently come into control of the new territory. There had not been time for such detail. At last he decided to send one of his trusted assistants, one Charles Bennett, to Monterey, to see the Acting Governor, Mason, and ask him to make a special grant, or at least give him and his partner exclusive milling and mining rights and privileges on the land they were developing. Mason had no power or authority to make such a grant. Bennett, though strictly enjoined to say nothing about the gold find, let the secret slip.

About the same time, supplies were needed at the saw-mill, and a teamster whom Sutter thought he could trust was sent with them. He, of course, heard from the workmen at the mill about the finding of gold, and being very incredulous, was given a few small nuggets to convince him. Returning to the fort, and still doubtful of the value of the yellow stuff he had gotten from the men at the saw-mill, the idea occurred to him that a good way to test the matter was to try to trade it for whiskey, so he offered his few pieces of yellow metal at the store that had been recently opened at New Helvetta by Smith & Brannan. Smith, to whom he offered the gold, though distrustful of its being gold, made the trade. The whiskey loosened the teamster's tongue, and the secret was out. This was about a week before the six weeks of agreed secrecy had expired.

Unaware that they stood at the threshold of a great era, at the birthplace, one might say, of a mighty empire, Sutter and Marshall were reluctant to change the future of peaceful plodding pursuits that they had marked out for themselves, for they knew not what, nor did they dream that they would be the first to suffer disaster from this discovery.

The news that had been let loose by the trusted assistant and the drunken teamster spread like fire when touched to a pile of straw, to San Francisco, Monterey, Los Angeles and San Diego, almost to every settlement in California and up into Oregon, going almost like a flash. The men at the saw-mill and at the fort at once traded the particles of yellow metal they had found for picks, shovels, pans, blankets, boots, bacon, beef and flour, on the basis of eight dollars an ounce; this the traders were willing to risk as the value.

People poured in by the hundred from everywhere. The wheat in Sutter's fields was never harvested; his mills were never completed; no man now wanted to do his work. His sheep, cattle and hogs were stolen and devoured by hungry men who squatted on his lands, dug over and wasted them, till little by little his vast properties melted away. He spent his money in litigation that was fruitless, trying to reclaim the title to his lands, and was saved from dire poverty by a pension from the State. He died in Washington, D. C., in 1880.

Marshall fared no better. The squatters took possession of the land, dividing it into mining claims; he wandered about the district, a broken, homeless man, till finally in 1865 he obtained a grant to a piece of land due him for services in the Mexican War, on which he lived, growing grapes, till death called him. A simple monument now marks the spot where Marshall first found the gold, and Sutter's Fort has been reproduced in one of Sacramento's parks to keep their memories green.

The news of the gold find spread the world over, to wherever news could be carried, and California, like a great lodestone, attracted the attention of all peoples, and became a Mecca for many. A great human tide flowed to it in three great streams; one of these being by sailing vessels around Cape Horn, that might take from six to nine months or longer, depending on the weather. Another stream went by the Isthmus of Panama; the very best time that could be made across was five days, which was made chiefly by mule-back, though often on foot, baggage being carried on mules, or on the shoulders of peons. The road was nothing more than a trail, a very poor one, at that. Arriving at Panama, the trip was continued up the coast by sailing vessel, or by the one steamer that had recently been put on by the Pacific Mail Steamship Company.

The third stream went overland across the plains and mountains by the Oregon or the Santa Fe trail, by wagons or pack trains. Either of these routes brought untold hardships, toil and suffering to the gold-seeker; tales of these experiences of many are truly heart-rending, and we may relate some of these later.

The ships that left ports on the Atlantic coast late in December, 1848, for the trip around the Horn bound for San Francisco, began to arrive early in July, and by the end of that month fifty-four of them had anchored in the bay. Each succeeding month brought more and more, and besides there came from ports all over the world, ships that altogether, by the end of 1849, made up a total of 540, all of them laden to full capacity with a human cargo of all sorts and conditions, bankers, merchants, manufacturers, ship owners, mechanics, farmers, laborers, professional men, students, artists, and even women who had caught the vision of great riches, braved the dangers of ocean, mountain and desert to reach the land of gold.

Arriving at San Francisco, everybody, including the officers and crews of the ships, headed for the diggings. This went on during the next five years, until there were more deserted ships rotting at their anchor cables in San Francisco Bay than ever before or since in the history of the world. The city itself became almost deserted; at the time of the discovery it had a population of 800 that speedily shrunk to 150.

Food and miners' supplies of all kinds became very scarce; flour sold at $400 a barrel, and sugar at $4 a pound, and a very poor grade of coffee at the same price. In many cases flour brought $2 a pound and whiskey $20 a quart. Rowboats that ordinarily sold for $50 or less, by the end of May, 1849, had jumped to $500, for people could go to Sutter's Fort by rowboat. A shovel that formerly sold for a dollar now cost ten; picks, crowbars, pans and knives all advanced in the same ratio. In like manner, clothing of all kinds, especially that of the coarser quality, advanced in price, and was hard to get.

The first news of the discovery reached Monterey (then the capital of the territory) on May 20, Colonel of Dragoons R. B. Mason being governor of the new territory, and the Rev. Walter Cotton, alcalde of the City of Monterey. At first the news was considered very doubtful, till on June 5th, what seemed more reliable information was received, and the day following Cotton despatched a messenger to the American River, to ascertain, as he wrote, "whether the reported gold was a tangible reality on the earth or a fanciful treasure at the base of some rainbow."

On the 12th of June a straggler wandered into the town with a nugget weighing an ounce, and a few days later a man who had worked for Cotton as a body servant, after being absent for a short time, returned with $2,000 worth of native gold. A rough-looking man who did not appear to have enough about him to buy a loaf of bread, came to Monterey with a sack on his shoulder, from which he shook $15,000 worth of gold dust. Four citizens of Monterey who had employed some Indians on the Feather River, collected $76,844 worth of gold in seven weeks and three days; a man who had worked sixty-four days on the Yuba River brought back $5,356 in gold; another resident of Monterey, who worked fifty-seven days on the North Fork of the American River, brought back $4,534; a party of fourteen who worked fifty-four days on the Mokelumne River, had $3,467; a woman who had worked with pan and shovel in dry diggings forty-six days cleaned up $2,125. All these incidents did not seem to satisfy either the Governor or the Alcalde, and in order that absolute proof of the truth of the whole matter might be had, it was decided in September that the Alcalde should visit the mines in person, a party of responsible citizens accompanying him. Let us take the trip with them and note what they saw.

As they neared the mines, they met returning gold hunters, of whom Cotton wrote: " A more forlorn looking group never knocked at the gate of a pauper asylum. Most of them were on foot, with rags tied on their blistered feet." They asked for bread and meat; Cotton's party gave them some, supposing that they were giving in charity, and were surprised when one of the party passed out a pound or two of nuggets in payment. Cotton afterwards learned that the ragged travelers had with them over a hundred thousand dollars in virgin gold. On arrival at the mines, the eager Alcalde borrowed a pick, and in five minutes found enough gold to make a seal ring. He found seventy people at work in a small ravine, each of them getting an ounce a day. A sailor whom he had known when he was chaplain on the *Savannah* had found a nugget that weighed three ounces.

He found another man picking at a spot on the canyon side who presently uncovered a pocket from which he took nearly two pounds of nuggets, all shaped like water-melon seeds, and near to this spot, on the following day, he uncovered a pound and a half.

A Welshman whom the Alcalde had a short time before fined for being drunk, and disturbing the peace, met him with a hearty greeting, assuring him that he held no grudge against him, and turning to resume his work, uncovered a nugget that weighed an ounce or more; picking it up, he handed it to Mr. Cotton, saying: " Senor Alcalde, accept that, and when you reach home, have a bracelet made of it for your good lady." A German picked up a piece weighing three ounces, from the ground in front of Cotton's tent, and later in the same day Cotton himself took half an ounce from a crevice in a rock. A little girl playing in a ravine near her mother's tent, picked up a curious-looking stone that proved to be nearly pure gold; it weighed over six pounds. A much larger lump, twenty-three pounds in weight, was later found nearby.

Two men invited Cotton to come and see their claim. He found them working in a hole up to their waists in water; they were getting from fifteen to twenty dollars out of every pan they washed, and the day that he was with them they took $1,000 for their day's work. He found at a place about three miles from his camp a woman working alone. He had known her in San Jose; she was washing gravel in a wooden bowl, and had averaged an ounce a day for three weeks.

Just before leaving the mines at the end of his stay of six weeks, he found seated on a stone under a tree, in rather a dejected condition, an old man, who bewailed the fact that he had worked for many days and gotten little or nothing, and that he would move to another place. Cotton said to him, " Why not turn over the stone you are sitting on?" He replied, " It ain't worth while, but I will do it if you say so." He turned it over, and clearing away a little dirt, found a lot of nuggets that weighed nearly a half a pound.

On the way home, his party overtook another old man with his grandson; they had been in the mines and collected twenty pounds of nuggets, of which they had been robbed, and were poorer than when they began.

Governor Mason also visited the mines, and made a report of his trip to the Adjutant-General of the United States. The report was dated August 17, 1848. With his report he sent two hundred and twenty-eight ounces of nuggets as specimens of the product of the mines. He had visited mines on all the rivers in the gold-bearing territory; his report relates many interesting incidents, among them the following: He was shown a trench about a hundred yards long, four feet wide and three feet deep, from which there had been taken in one week $17,000; a small ravine near to it had yielded $12,000; men were picking gold out of the crevices of the rocks with butcher knives, in pieces weighing from one to six ounces. At Weber's store in Helvetta, a man had given an ounce and a half of gold worth $24 for a box of seidlitz powders; another man had paid one dollar for a drop of laudanum.

He estimated the whole output of the mines at that time from thirty to fifty thousand dollars a day, and stated that he thought that the mines in the Sacramento and San Joaquin Valleys would easily repay the cost of the late war with Mexico, together with all that the Government had paid for lands ceded. All this gold was being taken from land which now belonged to the Government, and he thought something should be paid for the privilege of mining, but he saw no way to collect it, having but few soldiers, not enough to cover the large territory that was being worked over. He had considerable trouble holding enlisted men to the performance of their duties, so concluded not to make any rules that he could not enforce. The gold-

bearing region known at that time was about two hundred
miles long, averaging about thirty miles wide.

This report he despatched by special messenger by way
of Panama; it reached Washington in time for President
Polk to mention the discovery in his message to Congress
in December, thus transmitting it to the people. It attracted wide attention, creating great interest everywhere,
so that every newspaper in the country, nay, in the world,
was daily scanned for news from the California gold
diggings.

Enough has been said, and the many instances related
will give readers a fair idea of the magnitude and importance
of Marshall's discovery. It will be of interest to add further
that from the time of the discovery in 1848 to January 1st,
1903, California had produced $1,379,275,408 in gold.
There were two periods of intense excitement, the first ending in 1854. From 1850 to 1853, the greatest yield from
washings was probably not less than $65,000,000 a year.
The average production per year for the years 1851 to 1854,
inclusive, was $75,570,087, reaching $81,294,270 in 1852;
this was the banner year, and from 1850 to 1862 the average production was $55,882,861, never falling below
$50,000,000.

The ardent hope that ever lured the plodding miner and
the prospector as well, was that they would come upon some
rich deposits of dust, or a big nugget, that would make them
rich at once. Let me quote from Eldridge's history:
" Some nuggets of surprising size were found in the early
years, the largest recorded being one of one hundred and
forty-one pounds four ounces of almost pure gold, found
in 1854. One of perhaps equal value was found by some
Chinamen, who cut it to pieces with cold chisels, and sold
it bit by bit with their gold dust, fearing that it would be
taken away from them if shown to anyone in the shape in
which they found it. A single lump weighing one hundred
and six pounds was found in Baltimore ravine, near Auburn,

and another of one hundred and three pounds, and still another of ninety-six pounds near Downieville. A seventy-two pound chunk was found near Columbia, one worth $10,000 at Ophir, in Sutter County; one of fifty pounds on the Yuba; one of forty-four pounds near Dogtown, Butte County; one of fifty-one pounds near French ravine, in Sierra County, and one of eighty pounds from the American River.

"Pieces weighing from ten to forty pounds have been found in many places, and sometimes in the most casual manner. A farmer strolling through his pasture on or near the lower Mokelumne River, one Sunday morning, kicked at what appeared to be a stone lying in his path, but which proved to be so heavy that he examined it more carefully. It proved to be a lump of almost pure gold worth several thousand dollars. Many lucky miners made their fortunes within a few months after arriving at the mines in 1849 and 1850. Many were more easily satisfied, and returned east after they had found enough to buy a farm near the old homestead, or to pay off a mortgage, or start in some business for which they had long striven. Many lost their health and even their lives. The number of those who died in their tents or cabins, or under the open sky, during the fierce struggle of the first years after the discovery, will never be known.

"Of the thousands that were attracted to the West by the gold discovery, few, if any, ever thought that gold digging would be a permanent occupation for them, and so it proved. It was only a stepping stone to the acquiring of a farm and a home. It took but a few years to find and pick up all the yellow metal that Nature had so profusely scattered on or near the surface of California's lovely valleys and foothills. That done, large numbers of the gold-seekers remained to help develop and cultivate her soil that was to produce still greater riches than the combined efforts of the vast crowd who came to search her soil for the yellow metal."

Those who made the trip across the plains usually began the long journey at Independence or Westport, Missouri, for at that time the Missouri River was considered the western boundary of all civilization, and as these gold-hunters launched out on the almost trackless prairies that lay west of that mighty stream, many considered themselves as entering a country of peculiar freedom, and it was often said that "law and morality never crossed the Missouri River."

Many parties came to this starting place by steamer via the Mississippi and Missouri rivers. There trains or companies, sometimes consisting of several hundred people, organized for the trip; this they did for mutual protection from the Indians. The usual outfit was a stout wagon with a cover of white canvas or sheeting that was oiled or painted, stretched over hickory or oak, the same prairie schooner that had brought thousands to the Middle West.

I have read many books that tell the stories of many parties who crossed, all of them filled with thrilling incidents of hardships and heroisms that are almost unbelievable. The book entitled *Death Valley in '49,* by William Lewis Manley, is perhaps the most striking, being a story of personal experiences.

At the age of twenty, W. L. Manley left his father's home on the frontiers of civilization, near Jackson, Michigan, that was then, in 1840, still a territory. He was starting in life for himself with seven dollars in his pocket. He and a companion together bought enough pine boards with which to build a boat, on which they paddled down Grand River to the place where the city of Grand Rapids now is. There they found a schooner, loaded with lumber, about to sail across the lake to Wisconsin, and for a dollar each they were permitted to cross on her. They were put ashore at Southport. At that time Wisconsin was practically a wild waste, but they tramped clear across it to Mineral Point, arriving there with blistered feet, Manley having thirty-five cents in his pocket. They found it hard to obtain employment, but finally did so, receiving the sum of thirteen dollars a month; a little later he went to work digging lead ore in the summer, and in the winter hunted fur-bearing animals.

In the spring of 1849 he caught the gold fever, and arranged to go to California with a man named Bennett, who with his wife and two children was about to go there. Through a misunderstanding as to the time of starting, the Bennetts started two weeks before Manley knew that they had gone. They had taken his outfit with them, thinking that he would overtake them. This he tried to do, but did not find them for many months after, when he accidentally met them at Salt Lake City. At Council Bluffs, he found himself with nothing but the clothes he wore, an extra shirt, a light gun, a small light tent, a frying-pan, a tin cup, his mules, but no money. He had come to the conclusion to return to Michigan, when he met a man named Charles Dallas, from Iowa, who was preparing to join a train of wagons bound for California. Dallas offered to feed Manley if he would drive one of his teams clear through; this he very reluctantly agreed to do.

The train was made up of a number of ox teams; the one Manley drove consisted of two oxen and two cows. After much hardship and many hair breadth escapes, they reached a point near the Mormon settlement at Salt Lake City, where they found a band of emigrants, camped among them being Manley's friends, the Bennetts, from whom he received his complete outfit just as he had left it with them months before in Wisconsin. He at once decided to join the Bennetts, and as Mr. Dallas had decided to stay at Salt Lake City until spring, he had no compunction in doing so. This other train consisted of one hundred and seven wagons, with about 500 horses and cattle. The company had a semblance of military organization, being made up of seven divisions, each having its own captain, whom they elected; one Captain Hunt was engaged to act as guide and commander (he called himself Dictator), acting under rules that had been framed by the whole body. These rules, it was understood, could be amended by a majority of the whole; each member was to pay Captain Hunt ten dollars for acting as their pilot. Hunt was a Mormon, and pretended to know the best routes to California. It was planned that they should move with military precision, division number one taking the lead the first day, division number two the second day, and so on in regular routine.

The route chosen was a new one for a wagon train, though there was a trail over which the Mormons traveled to their settlement or colony at San Bernardino, located about sixty miles east of Los Angeles.

A few days after starting, they met with another party of emigrants, spoken of in the histories as the Smith party, its leader's name being Smith. Captain Smith had a map procured at Salt Lake City, from an engineer named Williams, that showed a route still different from the one Hunt was taking; this map pretended to show every place on the route where grass and water could be found. Hunt had no map, and many of his party who had lost confidence in him, were inclined to go with the Smith party. There was much discussion on the subject, and finally, when they reached the place where the two trails diverged, many of the Hunt party joined Smith's, among them the Bennetts, and, of course, Manley. About three days after the breaking up of the Hunt party, the Smith train discovered that they had made a mistake. They came to a place beyond which it seemed the wagons could not go. Many in the train then turned back to go by the Hunt trail, so that the Smith party was reduced to twenty-seven wagons, among them the Bennetts.

Parties that had been sent out to find a pass shortly

returned, reporting that they had found one, so on the twenty-seven wagons went. Soon they found a broad, well-defined trail that became known as the Jay-Hawker's trail; at this point it ran over rolling hills covered with juniper trees, and through grassy valleys, with plenty of water, and all went very well. It was now November.

They plodded on, ever westward, but day after day getting farther away from game that was now the only source of food for themselves, and from water and grass so necessary for their animals as well as themselves. The party to which the Bennetts clung had been reduced to seven wagons, for dissensions due to difference of opinion had sprung up, so that a large number had broken away. Each day their supply of food diminished, so that at last they had to kill one of their steers to keep them supplied with food.

Manley spent all his time on scouting expeditions, searching for water and game, climbing to high points on the hills to spy out the land and decide what route should be taken, using a field glass owned by one of the party. Out on one of these expeditions, far ahead of the party, he came upon a dead ox that had fallen by the way. With his knife he cut into one of its hams and found that, on account of the dryness and purity of the atmosphere, the meat was fresh and sweet, though probably dead for many days. He was glad to eat it raw as he walked along.

All around, as far as the eye could reach, was dry desolation, not a spear of grass, not a drop nor sign of water anywhere. Night came on; he crept under a projecting rock to try to sleep, being afraid to make a fire, for he had seen signs of Indians, whom he feared. When he awoke it was Christmas day. They were now in what a little later came to be known as Death Valley, because so many of those who entered it never came out.

One day their eyes were gladdened by the sight of water. It was far ahead of them, but it gleamed in the sunlight and cheered them on.   But alas! it proved to be salt water. Soon they reached a condition where it was decided that all the provisions of civilized life should be pooled, and served only to the women and children and that, as occasion required, an ox should be killed, the meat dried and served to the men; every scrap of the ox, the hide and horns excepted, was used for food, every drop of blood was as precious to them as the grains of gold they were in search of.   Four of the teamsters now decided to take their share of the provisions, together with their blankets and guns, leave the party and push on to try to save themselves.

The party crawled along, the oxen hardly able to stand, having had no food or water for many days, and as far as Manley could see, there was no prospect of any being found.   A solemn council was held, at which it was agreed that they could only live till the last of their cattle had been eaten up.   It was then agreed that they should turn back to the place where they had last found a spring of water and grass, and that there the party should camp, while two of the youngest men, taking some of the food, should push on till they found a settlement where they could get help and food, and return as fast as possible; they hoped that in ten days they might be able to return with the needed relief.

The next morning the oxen were hitched up and started back to the spring.   Shortly after they had started, one of them became so feeble that he lay down and never rose again, and when they were within two miles of the spring, another one could travel no further, and also lay down. Arriving at the spring, they carried water back to him, so that he recovered and came on to the spring.

Manley and a man named Rodgers, from Tennessee, were selected, and agreed to undertake the hazardous journey.   Preparations were at once made for their departure; the weakest of the oxen was slaughtered, and the meat dried; the women made rawhide moccasins and knapsacks, and packed as much of the dried meat as could be comfortably carried. Manley and Rodgers started off with the expressed hopes and blessings of each member of the party.

Manley writes: " I wore no coat or vest, but took half a light blanket, while Rodgers wore a thin summer coat, and took no blanket; we each had a small tin cup and a small camp kettle that held a quart. Bennett had me take his seven-shooter rifle, and Rodgers had a good double-barreled shotgun; we each had a sheath-knife, and our hats were small-brimmed affairs, fitting close to the head, and not very conspicuous to the enemy, as we might rise up from behind a hill, or a hiding-place, into view. We tried on our packs and fitted the straps a little, so that they would carry easy, and started off."

The party they left in camp consisted of thirteen adults and six children; there was very little civilized food, the oxen that might be killed when necessary being their chief reliance.

Manley and Rodgers took a course due west as nearly as the mountains would permit. Days passed, but they found no water. A big snow-capped mountain in the distance lured them on, and not till they came within its influence did they find relief. In order not to miss a possible chance of finding water, they separated, agreeing on a general course each would take, and that if either found water he should fire his gun as a signal. In a little while Rodgers fired his gun, and going to him, Manley saw that he had found a little ice as thick as window glass; eagerly they put some of it into their mouths and gathered all they could. It just filled their quart kettle; this they melted, and thus saved their lives. They had become so thirsty and their mouths and tongues became so dry that they could not chew their dried beef; the saliva would not flow. On they went again; in a few days they found a well developed trail leading toward the west. This they followed and came up with a party written of in the histories as the Jay-Hawkers. They were camped at some water holes where they had killed an ox and were drying the meat.

From them they received some fresh meat, and were also much refreshed by the water; they filled their canteens and pressed on, every moment being precious. When they parted, tears flowed freely from all eyes. Many of the larger company, being men past middle life, had about concluded that their chances of surviving the hardships through which they were passing were rather slim. They gave Manley and Rodgers the names and addresses of the friends they had left in the old home, asking them to tell their friends where and how they had found them, provided that they themselves were fortunate enough to reach a post office.

Soon after leaving the camp of the Jay-Hawkers, Manley and Rodgers realized that they had crossed the divide and that every step they took was down the Pacific slope; soon they began to see signs of life; a crow came in sight and perched within gunshot, and very promptly he was shot and bagged in Rodgers' knapsack. A little later a hawk hove in sight, and it was very promptly taken care of in the same way; then a little further along they spied a quail; it also they shot.

Trees began to appear, and stumbling into a narrow ravine and following it for many miles, it led them to a much larger one, and O joy! there was a babbling brook of clear, sparkling water that literally sang them welcome as it wimpled over the stones in its course. They drank liberally of its life-giving stream, then dressed and cooked their three birds, and began to feel that life still held something for them. Soon a broad, grassy meadow opened before them. I will quote Manley's words describing this incident.

" Before us was a spur from the hills that reached nearly across the valley and shut out further sight in that direction, and when we came to it we climbed up over it to shorten the distance. When the summit was reached, a most pleasing sight filled our sick hearts with a most indescribable joy.

" I shall never have the ability to adequately describe the beauty of the scene as it appeared to us, and so long as I live that landscape will be impressed on my mind. There before us was a beautiful meadow of a thousand acres, green as a thick carpet of grass could make it, and shaded with oaks, wide-branching and symmetrical, equal to those of an old English park. While all over the low mountains that bordered it on the south, and over the broad acres of luxuriant grass was a herd of cattle numbering many hundreds, if not thousands. All seemed happiness and contentment, and such a scene of abundance and rich plenty and comfort, bursting thus upon our eyes, which for months had seen only the desolation and sadness of the desert, was like getting a glimpse of Paradise, and tears of joy ran down our faces. The day was bright with sunshine as well as with hope, and it was the first day of January, 1850."

Not a human being was in sight, and they were very hungry; down in a deep gully cut out by the rains, a yearling steer was feeding; Manley, gun in hand, crawled near to him and fired two shots, and as quickly as possible they were enjoying some of his meat that they roasted at once. They ate till they were satisfied, the first time in many long, dreary weeks. They then dried the balance of the meat, one of them sleeping while the other worked, relieving each other every few hours. The miserable dried meat that had been so long in their knapsacks they threw away, and refilled them with this good, fresh meat store.

They also made for themselves moccasins from the hide of the steer, and then continued their journey, though not very sure that they might not be pounced on at any moment for shooting the yearling steer. Soon they came to a strange-looking house of the adobe Mexican type, that proved to be the home of a farmer. There they found the woman of the house, but she could not speak or understand a word of English.

They had come out from the Sierra Madre Mountains into the San Fernando Valley at a point not far from the mission of that name. They went there and were entertained for the night, sleeping on the floor, but indoors. Here they met an American, with whom they talked over their troubles, and concluded, under his advice, that they would save time by returning to the settler's house at which they had stopped on the previous day, and get the provisions they wanted. They might go on to Los Angeles, some thirty miles away, and fare no better, that place being very badly demoralized on account of the rush to the gold mines.

Their new found friend agreed to go with them and act as interpreter. There they procured three horses, a little mule, a sack of beans, a sack of unbolted flour, and one of wheat, which they would have to grind themselves; also some dried meat. This food their friends showed them how to pack on the backs of the horses, and as quickly as possible they started on the return journey, to try and save the other members of the party.

About the fourth day out the horses got so worn out and feeble for the want of food and water that they could hardly crawl along; their heads flung low, almost touching the ground. They then concluded to bury the sack of wheat, hoping to find it on their return; this they did, and loaded the other sacks on the mule, which seemed to be in better condition.

The next day the ground became so rough and the grade so steep that the horses were unable to get over it, and had to be abandoned. Then, too, they found the bodies of two men who had traveled with them in the Jay-Hawkers' party. They had died by the side of the trail and had to be left there. This, of course, was all very disconcerting to our brave fellows, and only the thought that many other lives depended on their efforts urged them on.

At last, on the twenty-sixth day after leaving their friends camped at the spring, they were again in its vicinity. Their first sight or sign of their fellow travelers was to find the dead body of one of them — Captain Culverwell — lying on the trail. He lay on his back, his arms extended, his little canteen, made of two powder flasks, lying by his side. Manley writes: " This looked, indeed, as if some of our saddest forebodings were coming true. How many more bodies should we find? — or should we find the camp deserted, and never find a trace of the former occupants?

" We marched toward camp like two Indians, silent and alert, looking out for dead bodies and live Indians, for really we expected to find the camp devastated by those rascals, rather than to find that it still contained our friends. About noon we came in sight of the wagons, still a long way off, but in the clear air we could make them out.

" No signs of life were anywhere about, and the thought of our hard struggles between life and death, to go out and return with the fruitless results that now seemed apparent, was almost more than human heart could bear. When should we know their fate? Where should we find their remains, and how learn their sad history, if we ourselves should live to get back again to settlements and life? If ever two men were troubled, Rodgers and I surely passed through the furnace. One hundred yards to the wagons, and still no sign of life; we fear that perhaps there are Indians in ambush, and with nervous, irregular breathing, we counsel what to do. Finally Rodgers suggested that he had two charges in his shotgun, and I seven in the Colts rifle, and that I fire one of mine and await results before we ventured any nearer. I fired, and in a moment a man came from under one of the wagons and stood up. Then he threw up his arms and shouted, ' The boys have come! ' Then other bare heads appeared, and Mr. Bennett and wife and Mr. Arcane came running toward us. They caught us in their arms and embraced us with all their strength. Mrs. Bennett fell on her knees and clung to me like a maniac in the great emotion that came to her, and not a word was spoken."

They estimated that they had traveled five hundred miles since they had left the camp, and found on their return that the party had been reduced till only Mr. and Mrs. Bennett and their four children and Mr. and Mrs. Arcane and their boy remained; the others had pressed forward from time to time to try to escape from the desert. Immediately they began to prepare for the long journey. There were five oxen still left. It was at once decided that everything should be left behind, only things absolutely necessary for the sustaining of life to be taken along — a kettle, a tin cup for each, a few knives, forks and spoons, and all the blankets and the clothes they wore. It was planned that the two women should each ride on an ox; though they had never known or heard of such a thing being done, they thought it practicable. The cloth in the wagon covers and in bed ticks was made into harness, the blankets being used for saddles, and one of the oxen, old Crump, the gentlest of them, was rigged out with saddle bags made from two of the men's hickory shirts, in which the two youngest children were to be carried; the older ones were to ride like the women. Manley and Rodgers made new moccasins for themselves, and in a very few days they were ready to start.

It was very soon found that riding an ox was impracticable, and the women and older children had to walk. In a few days they were out of the valley, to which they had given the gruesome name, " Death Valley." Their food consisted of soup made from the beans and flour boiled with some of the dried beef, some of which they also ate. When five days out, their stock of beans became entirely exhausted, but at the place where they were to camp for the night was the sack of whole wheat that Manley and Rodgers had buried. This they had hidden so well that they had considerable trouble locating it. When found, although it had been buried in the dry desert sand, it had absorbed enough moisture from it that it had swollen so that the bag was nearly at the bursting point. But it was sweet and quite fit for food. At this camp they had to kill an ox.

They had had no water all day. Manley and Rodgers had gone on ahead and started a fire, and made what preparations they could to ease the hardship of the situation, selecting the best spots on which to sleep, spreading the blankets, and having the soup ready to serve, so that when the weary, bedraggled women and children arrived, they could at once lie down and be served with their share.

The women declared that but for the children they would cheerfully lie down and die, rather than endure another such day. The distance from the last camp to this spring was longer and the trail much rougher than on any of the previous days. Near to this camp, too, they had to pass the place where the bodies of Mr. Fish and Mr. Isham lay, and which Manley and Rodgers had covered with sand.

At this camp they had to make moccasins for themselves and also for the oxen, whose feet had become so lacerated and tender from tramping over knife-edged stones, it was feared that they might give out altogether. These moccasins they made from the hide of the ox they had just slaughtered.

It was four days' travel to the next water hole, and all the water they could have during that time was what they could carry in their canteens. This they did not dare use during the day, but must save for their soup; none but the children could have any water, and they only at long intervals, and after they had cried hard for it.

The third night they had to make their soup with salt water which they found in a water hole; the next day they had no water at all for themselves or the oxen, only a little for the children, till they arrived at water holes at the base of a snow mountain. The oxen had to subsist on greasewood, a shrub resembling a currant bush.

They were nine days from camp, their beans, flour and wheat all used up. They must now subsist on the beef obtained by killing their oxen. An ox yielded very little meat, and it was of the very poorest quality, giving very little nutrition; always they had to kill the poorest-conditioned one, so as to make sure the others could travel on, for they were now reduced to skin and bone.

The moccasins of the entire party were again completely worn out, so that, as one of the women expressed it, their feet ached like the tooth-ache; not only were their feet blistered and sore, but their dresses were worn off nearly to their knees by being draggled through the chaparral of the desert. But they could not stop long enough to kill an ox or make moccasins, but must plod on that the lives of the whole party might be saved. Their camp would be at a spring, and they must reach it that day, but they were caught by darkness four hours short of it, and did not reach it till four hours after daylight the next day; and to make matters worse, a rain-storm, the second they had encountered since leaving Wisconsin, came up that turned to snow, and at sunrise there were two inches of snow on the ground. Their condition was truly miserable. They rested long enough at the next spring to kill an ox and make moccasins. The amount of meat procured from the ox when dried was easily carried in the mule's pack, it was so very small.

The next morning, after their meal of soup made from the meat of the ox, they felt somewhat refreshed, and in better spirits. It was a two days' journey to the next water hole. They were now in what later came to be called the Mojave Desert, a waterless, barren plain, on which nothing grew with which they could make a fire, nothing to which they could even tie their animals, and

when they camped that night, they simply tied them together. They could not make a fire; they had to content
themselves with a little dried meat, and a little sip of water,
for they were still another day from water, that they reached
late the following afternoon, and also found a little grass
for the cattle.

The next day, a few hours after starting, they lost the
trail; the ground was of such a nature it could not retain
marks of a trail. It was plenteously covered with the bones
of animals, however, showing that many had passed that
way, all of which so depressed the women that they had to
go into camp until the next morning. That night they came
to the water hole they had planned to reach the night before;
all that the cattle could have for food was a few sage bushes
at which they nibbled. The next day they were in a hilly
country, and the day following they came to the little babbling
brook that had so delighted Manley and Rodgers the first
time they saw it.

Here Manley writes in his journal, " New life seemed to
come to the dear women. ' O what a beautiful stream! '
they cried, and they dip in a tin cup and drink, and drink
again, then watch the rollicking brook as if it was the most
entertaining thing in the whole wide earth."

It was now the seventh day of March, 1850, twenty-two
days since they left their wagons, and four months since
they entered Death Valley, and about a year since they left
Wisconsin. It had been for them a year of wandering,
struggle and terrible hardship. They took a long rest, the
cattle eating their fill, and then slowly traveled to the home
of the settler where Manley and Rodgers had obtained their
supplies. The woman recognized them, and when the men
came home they were handsomely treated.

None of our travelers had a cent of money. Mr. Arcane
sold his two steers, all the property he had in the world, to
the Mexicans, and with the money obtained started for
San Pedro, the post of Los Angeles; there he hoped to

obtain a passage on a sailing vessel to San Francisco. The Bennetts, Manley and Rodgers leisurely went on to Los Angeles, some thirty miles away, and from there found their way to the mines.

A FRONTIER DUEL

EMERSON HOUGH

1848

From "The Covered Wagon." Reprinted by permission of the publishers, D. Appleton and Company, New York.[1]

ONCE more the train, now permanently divided into two, faced the desert, all the men and many women now afoot, the kine low-headed, stepping gingerly in their new rawhide shoes. Gray, grim work, toiling over the dust and sand. But at the head wagon, taking over an empire foot by foot, flew the great flag. Half fanatics? That may be. Fanatics, so called, also had prayed and sung and taught their children, all the way across to the Great Salt Lake. They, too, carried books. And within one hour after their halt near the Salt Lake they began to plow, began to build, began to work, began to grow, and made a country.

The men at the trading post saw the Missouri wagons pull out ahead. Two hours later the Wingate train followed, as the lot had determined. Woodhull remained with his friends in the Wingate group, regarded now with an increasing indifference, but biding his time.

Bridger held back his old friend Jackson even after the last train pulled out. It was midafternoon when the start was made.

"Don't go just yet, Bill," said he. "Ride on an' overtake 'em. Nothin' but rattlers an' jack rabbits now fer a while. The Shoshones won't hurt 'em none. I'm pow-

<hr>

[1] Copyright, 1922, by Emerson Hough. Copyright, 1922, by the Curtis Publishing Co.

erful lonesome, somehow.   Let's you an' me have one more
drink."

"That sounds reas'nable," said Jackson.   "Shore that
sounds reas'nable to me."

They drank of a keg which the master of the post had
hidden in his lodge, back of his blankets; drank again of
high wines diluted but uncolored — the "likker" of the
fur trade.

They drank from tin cups, until Bridger began to chant,
a deepening sense of his old melancholy on him.

"Good-by!" he said again and again, waving his hand
in general vagueness to the mountains.

"We was friends, wasn't we, Bill?" he demanded again
and again; and Jackson, drunk as he, nodded in like maudlin
gravity.   He himself began to chant.   The two were savages again.

"Well, we got to part, Bill.   This is Jim Bridger's last
rendyvous.   I've rid around an' said good-by to the mount-
ings.   Why don't we do it the way the big partisans allus
done when the rendyvous was over?   'Twas old Mike Fink
an' his friend Carpenter begun hit fifty year ago.   Keel-
boat men on the river, they was.   There's as good shots
left to-day as then, and as good friends.   You an' me has
seed hit; we seed hit at the very last meetin' o' the Rocky
Mountain Company men, before the families come.   An'
nary a man spilled the whisky on his partner's head."

"That's the truth," assented Jackson, "though some
I wouldn't trust now."

"Would ye trust me, Bill, like I do you, fer sake o'
the old times, when friends was friends?"

"Shore I would, no matter how come, Jim.   My hand's
stiddy as a rock, even though my shootin' shoulder's a leetle
stiff from that Crow arrer."

Each man held out his firing arm, steady as a bar.

"I kin still see the nail heads on the door yan.   Kin ye,
Bill?"

"Plain! It's a waste o' likker, Jim, fer we'd both drill the cups."

"Are ye a-skeered?"

"I told ye not."

"Chardon!" roared Bridger to his clerk. "You, Chardon, come here!"

The clerk obeyed, though he and others had been discreet about remaining visible as this bout of old-timers at their cups went on. Liquor and gunpowder usually went together.

"Chardon, ye git two fresh tin cups an' bring 'em here. Bring a piece o' charcoal to spot the cups. We're goin' to shoot 'em off each other's heads, in the old way. You know what I mean."

Chardon, trembling, brought the two tin cups, and Bridger with a burnt ember sought to mark plainly on each a black bull's-eye. Silence fell on the few observers, for all the emigrants had now gone and the open space before the rude trading building was vacant, although a few faces peered around corners. At the door of the tallest tepee two native women sat, a young and an old, their blankets drawn across their eyes, accepting fate, and not daring to make a protest.

"How!" exclaimed Bridger as he filled both cups and put them on the ground. "Have ye wiped yer barrel?"

"Shore I have. Let's wipe again."

Each drew his ramrod from the pipes and attached the cleaning worm with its twist of tow, kept handy in belt pouch in muzzle-loading days.

"Clean as a whistle!" said Jackson, holding out the end of the rod.

"So's mine, pardner. Old Jim Bridger never disgraced hisself with a rifle."

"Ner me," commented Jackson. "Hold a hair full, Jim, an' cut high the top o' the tin. That'll be safer fer my skelp, an' hit'll let less whisky out'n the hole. We got to drink what's left.   S'pose'n' we have a snort now?"

"Atter we both shoot we kin drink," rejoined his friend, with a remaining trace of judgment. "Go take stand whar we marked the scratch. Chardon, damn ye, carry the cup down an' set hit on his head, an' ef you spill a drop I'll drill ye, d'ye hear?"

The *engagé's* face went pale.

"But Monsieur Jim ——" he began.

"Don't ' Monsieur Jim ' me or I'll drill a hole in ye anyways! Do-ee-do what I tell ye, boy! Then if ye crave fer to see some ol'-time shootin' come on out, the hull o' ye, an' take a lesson, damn ye!"

"Do-ee ye shoot first, Bill," demanded Bridger. "The light's soft, an' we'll swap atter the fust fire, to git hit squar for the hindsight, an' no shine on the side o' the front sight."

"No, we'll toss fer fust," said Jackson, and drew out a Spanish dollar. "Tails fer me last!" he called as it fell. "An' I win! You go fust, Jim."

"Shore I will ef the toss-up says so," rejoined his friend. "Step off the fifty yard. What sort o' iron ye carryin', Bill?"

"Why do ye ask? Ye know ol' Mike Sheets in Virginia never bored a better. I've never changed."

"Ner I from my old Hawken. Two good guns, an' two good men, Bill, o' the ol' times — the ol' times! We kain't say fairer'n this, can we, at our time o' life, fer favor o' the old times, Bill? We got to do somethin', so's to kind o' git rested up."

"No man kin say fairer," said his friend.

They shook hands solemnly and went onward with their devil-may-care test, devised in a historic keel-boat man's brain, as inflamed then by alcohol as their own were now.

Followed by the terrified clerk, Bill Jackson, tall, thin and grizzled, stoical as an Indian, and too drunk to care much for consequences, so only he proved his skill and his courage, walked steadily down to the chosen spot and stood, his arms folded, after leaning his own rifle against the door of the trading room. He faced Bridger without a tremor, his head bare, and cursed Chardon for a coward when his hand trembled as he balanced the cup on Jackson's head.

"Damn ye," he exclaimed, "there'll be plenty lost without any o' your spillin'!"

"Air ye all ready, Bill?" called Bridger from his station, his rifle cocked and the delicate triggers set, so perfect in their mechanism that the lightest touch against the trigger edge would loose the hammer.

"All ready!" answered Jackson.

The two, jealous still of the ancient art of the rifle, which nowhere in the world obtained nicer development than among men such as these, faced each other in what always was considered the supreme test of nerve and skill; for naturally a man's hand might tremble, sighting three inches above his friend's eyes, when it would not move a hair sighting center between the eyes of an enemy.

Bridger spat out his tobacco chew and steadily raised his rifle. The man opposite him stood steady as a pillar, and did not close his eyes. The silence that fell on those who saw became so intense that it seemed veritably to radiate, reaching out over the valley to the mountains as in a hush of leagues.

For an instant, which to the few observers seemed an hour, these two figures, from which motion seemed to have passed forever, stood frozen. Then there came a spurt of whitish-blue smoke and the thin dry crack of the border rifle.

The hand and eye of Jim Bridger, in spite of advancing years, remained true to their long training. At the rifle crack the tin cup on the head of the statuelike figure opposite him was flung behind as though by the blow of an invisible hand. The spin of the bullet, acting on the liquid contents, ripped apart the seams of the cup and flung the fluid wide. Then and not till then did Jackson move.

He picked up the empty cup, bored center directly through the black spot, and turning walked with it in his hand toward Bridger, who was wiping out his rifle once more.

"I call hit mighty careless shootin'," said he, irritated. "Now look what ye done to the likker! If ye'd held a leetle higher, above the level o' the likker, like I told ye, she wouldn't have busted open thataway. It's nacherl, thar warn't room in the cup fer both the likker an' the ball. That's wastin' likker, Jim, an' my mother told me when I was a boy, 'Willful waste makes woeful want!'"

"I call hit a plumb-center shot," grumbled Bridger. "Do-ee look now! Maybe ye think ye kin do better shootin' yerself than old Jim Bridger!"

"Shore I kin, an' I'll show ye! I'll bet my rifle aginst yourn — ef I wanted so sorry a piece as yourn — I kin shoot that close to the mark an' not spill no likker a-tall! An' ye can fill her two-thirds full an' put yer thumb in fer the balance ef ye like."

"I'll just bet ye a new mule agin yer pony ye kain't do nothin' o' the sort!" retorted Bridger.

"All right, I'll show ye. O' course, ye got to hold still."

"Who said I wouldn't hold still?"

"Nobody. Now you watch me."

He stooped at the little water ditch which had been led in among the buildings from the stream and kneaded up a little ball of mud. This he forced into the handle of the tin cup, entirely filling it, then washed off the body of the cup.

"I'll shoot the fillin' out'n the handle an' not out'n the cup!" said he. "Mud's cheap, an' all the diff'runce in holdin' is, ef I nicked the side o' yer haid it'd hurt ye 'bout the same as ef what I nicked the center of hit. Ain't that so? We'd orto practice inderstry an' 'conomy, Jim. Like my mother said, ' Penny saved is er penny yearned.' ' Little drops o' water, little grains o' sand,' says she, ' a-makes the mighty o-o-ocean an' the plea-ea-sant land.' "

" I never seed it tried," said Bridger, with interest, " but I don't see why hit hain't practical. Whang away, an' ef ye spill the whisky shootin' to one side, or cut ha'r shootin' too low, your *caballo* is mine — an' he ain't much! "

With no more argument, he in turn took up his place, the two changing positions so that the light would favor the rifleman. Again the fear-smitten Chardon adjusted the filled cup, this time on his master's bared head.

" Do-ee turn her sideways now, boy," cautioned Bridger. " Set the han'le sideways squar', so she looks wide. Give him a fa'r shot now, fer I'm interested in this yere thing, either way she goes. Either I lose ha'r er a mule."

But folding his arms he faced the rifle without batting an eye, as steady as had been the other in his turn.

Jackson extended his long left arm, slowly and steadily raising the silver bead up from the chest, the throat, the chin, the forehead of his friend, then lowered it, rubbing his sore shoulder.

" Tell him to turn that han'le squar' to me, Jim! " he called. " The damn fool has got her all squegeed around to one side."

Bridger reached up a hand and straightened the cup himself.

" How's that? " he asked.

" All right! Now hold stiddy a minute."

Again the Indian women covered their faces, sitting motionless. And at last came again the puff of smoke, the faint crack of the rifle, never loud in the high, rarefied air.

The straight figure of the scout never wavered. The cup still rested on his head. The rifleman calmly blew the smoke from his barrel, his eye on Bridger as the latter now raised a careful hand to his head. Chardon hastened to aid, with many ejaculations.

The cup still was full, but the mud was gone from inside the handle as though poked out with a finger!

"That's what I call shootin', Jim," said Jackson, "an' reas'nable shootin' too. Now spill half o' her where she'll do some good, an' give me the rest. I got to be goin' now. I don't want yer mule. I fust come away from Missoury to git shet o' mules."

Chardon, cupbearer, stood regarding the two wild souls whom he never in his own more timid nature was to understand. The two mountain men shook hands. The alcohol had no more than steadied them in their rifle work, but the old exultation of their wild life came to them now once more. Bridger clapped hand to mouth and uttered his old war cry before he drained his share of the fiery fluid.

"To the ol' days, friend!" said he once more; "the days that's gone, when men was men, an' a friend could trust a friend!"

"To the ol' days!" said Jackson in turn. "An' I'll bet two better shots don't stand to-day on the soil o' Oregon! But I got to be goin', Jim. I'm goin' on to the Columby. I may not see ye soon. It's far."

He swung into his saddle, the rifle in its loop at the horn. But Bridger came to him, a hand on his knee.

"I hate to see ye go, Bill."

"Shore!" said Jackson. "I hate to go. Take keer yerself, Jim."

The two Indian women had uncovered their faces and gone inside the lodge. But old Jim Bridger sat down, back against a cottonwood, and watched the lopping figure of his friend jog slowly out into the desert. He himself was singing now, chanting monotonously an old Indian refrain that lingered in his soul from the days of the last rendezvous.

At length he arose and, animated by a sudden thought, sought out his tepee once more. Dang Yore Eyes greeted him with shy smiles of pride.

"Heap shoot, Jeem!" said she. "No kill-um. Why?"

She was decked now in her finest, ready to use all her blandishments on her lord and master. Her cheeks were painted red, her wrists were heavy with copper. On a thong at her neck hung a piece of yellow stone which she had bored through with an awl, or rather with three or four awls, after much labor, that very day.

Bridger picked up the ornament between thumb and finger. He said no word, but his fingers spoke.

" Other pieces.   Where? "

" White man. Gone — out there."   She answered in the same fashion.

" How, cola! " she spoke aloud. " Him say, ' How, cola,' me."   She smiled with much pride over her conquest, and showed two silver dollars.   " Swap! "

In silence Bridger went into the tepee and pulled the door flaps.

EL DORADO

BAYARD TAYLOR

From "Eldorado." Reprinted by permission of the authorized publishers, G. P. Putnam's Sons, New York.

I

ACROSS THE ISTHMUS

I LEFT the Falcon at day-break in the ship's boat. We rounded the high bluff on which the castle stands and found beyond it a shallow little bay, on the eastern side of which, on low ground, stand the cane huts of Chagres. Piling up our luggage on the shore, each one set about searching for the canoes which had been engaged the night previous, but, without a single exception, the natives were not to be found, or when found, had broken their bargains. The canoes were beached on the mud, and their owners engaged in re-thatching their covers with split leaves of the palm. The doors of the huts were filled with men and women, each in a single cotton garment, composedly smoking their cigars, while numbers of children, in Nature's own clothing, tumbled about in the sun. Having started without break-fast, I went to the " Crescent City " Hotel, a hut with a floor to it, but could get nothing. Some of my friends had fared better at one of the native huts, and I sat down to the remains of their meal, which was spread on a hen-coop beside the door. The pigs of the vicinity and several lean dogs surrounded me to offer their services, but maintained a respectful silence, which is more than could be said of pigs at home. Some pieces of pork fat, with fresh bread and a draught of sweet spring water from a cocoa shell, made me a delicious repast.

A returning Californian had just reached the place, with a box containing $22,000 in gold-dust, and a four-pound lump in one hand. The impatience and excitement of the passengers, already at a high pitch, was greatly increased by his appearance. Men ran up and down the beach, shouting, gesticulating, and getting feverishly impatient at the deliberate habits of the natives; as if their arrival in California would thereby be at all hastened. The boatmen, knowing very well that two more steamers were due the next day, remained provokingly cool and unconcerned. They had not seen six months of emigration without learning something of the American habit of going at full speed. Captain C—— and Mr. M——, of Baltimore, and myself, were obliged to pay $15 each, for a canoe to Cruces. We chose a broad, trimly-cut craft, which the boatmen were covering with fresh thatch. We stayed with them until all was ready, and they had pushed it through the mud and shoal water to the bank before Ramos's house. Our luggage was stowed away, we took our seats and raised our umbrellas, but the men had gone off for provisions and were not to be found. The sun blazed down on the swampy shores, and visions of yellow fever came into the minds of the more timid travelers. The native boys brought to us bottles of fresh water, biscuits and fruit, presenting them with the words: " bit! " " picayune! " " Your bread is not good," I said to one of the shirtless traders. " Si, *Señor!* " was his decided answer, while he tossed back his childish head with a look of offended dignity which charmed me. Our own men appeared towards noon, with a bag of rice and dried pork, and an armful of sugar-cane. A few strokes of their broad paddles took us from the excitement and noise of the landing-place to the seclusion and beauty of the river scenery.

Our chief boatman, named Ambrosio Mendez, was of the

mixed Indian and Spanish race. The second, Juan Crispin Bega, belonged to the lowest class, almost entirely of negro blood. He was a strong, jovial fellow, and took such good care of some of our small articles as to relieve us from all further trouble about them. This propensity is common to all of his caste on the Isthmus. In addition to these, a third man was given to us, with the assurance that he would work his passage; but just as we were leaving, we learned that he was a runaway soldier, who had been taken up for theft and was released on paying some sub-alcalde three bottles of liquor, promising to quit the place at once. We were scarcely out of sight of the town before he demanded five dollars a day for his labor. We refused, and he stopped working. Upon our threatening to set him ashore in the jungle, he took up the paddle, but used it so awkwardly and perversely that our other men lost all patience. We were obliged, however, to wait until we could reach Gatun, ten miles distant, before settling matters. Juan struck up " Oh Susanna! " which he sang to a most ludicrous imitation of the words, and I lay back under the palm leaves, looking out of the stern of the canoe on the forests of the Chagres River.

There is nothing in the world comparable to these forests. The river, broad, and with a swift current of the sweetest water I ever drank, winds between walls of foliage that rise from its very surface. From the rank jungle of canes and gigantic lilies, and the thickets of strange shrubs that line the water, rise the trunks of the mango, the ceiba, the cocoa, the sycamore and the superb palm. Plantains take root in the banks, hiding the soil with their leaves, shaken and split into immense plumes by the wind and rain. The zapote, with a fruit the size of a man's head, the gourd tree, and other vegetable wonders, attract the eye on all sides. Blossoms of crimson, purple and yellow, of a form and magnitude unknown in the North, are mingled with the leaves, and flocks of paroquets and brilliant butterflies circle through the air like blossoms blown away. Every turn of the stream only disclosed another and more magnificent vista of leaf, bough and blossom. All outline of the landscape is lost under this deluge of vegetation. No trace of the soil is to be seen; lowland and highland are the same; a mountain is but a higher swell of the mass of verdure. As on the ocean, you have a sense rather than a perception of beauty. The sharp, clear lines of our scenery at home are here wanting. What shape the land would be if cleared, you cannot tell.

In the afternoon we reached Gatun, a small village of bamboo huts, thatched with palm-leaves, on the right bank of the river. We ejected our worthless passenger on landing, notwithstanding his passive resistance, and engaged a new boatman in his place, at $8. I shall never forget the forlorn look of the man as he sat on the bank beside his bag of rice, as the rain began to fall. Ambrosio took us to one of the huts and engaged hammocks for the night. Two wooden drums, beaten by boys, in another part of the village, gave signs of a coming fandango, and, as it was Sunday night, all the natives were out in their best dresses. They are a very cleanly people, bathing daily, and changing their dresses as often as they are soiled. The children have their heads shaved from the crown to the neck, and as they go about naked, with abdomens unnaturally distended, from an exclusive vegetable diet, are odd figures enough. They have bright black eyes, and are quick and intelligent in their speech and motions.

The inside of our hut was but a single room, in which all the household operations were carried on. A notched pole, serving as a ladder, led to a sleeping loft, under the pyramidal roof of thatch. Here a number of the emigrants who arrived late were stowed away on a rattling floor of cane, covered with hides. After a supper of pork and coffee, I made my day's notes by the light of a miserable starveling candle, stuck in an empty bottle, but had not written far before my paper was covered with fleas. The owner of the hut swung my hammock meanwhile, and I turned in, to secure it for the night. To lie there was one thing, to sleep another. A dozen natives crowded round the table, drinking their aguardiente and disputing vehemently; the cooking fire was on one side of me, and every one that passed to and fro was sure to give me a thump, while my weight swung the hammock so low, that all the dogs on the premises were constantly rubbing their backs under me.

Our men were to have started at midnight, but it was two hours later before we could rouse and muster them together. We went silently and rapidly up the river till sunrise, when we reached a cluster of huts called Dos Hermanos (Two Brothers). There had been only a slight shower since we started; but the clouds began to gather heavily, and by the time we had gained the ranche of Palo Matida a sudden cold wind came over the forests, and the air was at once darkened. We sprang ashore and barely reached the hut, a few paces off, when the rain broke over us, as if the sky had caved in. The rain drove into one side of the cabin and out the other, but we wrapped ourselves in India-rubber cloth and kept out the wet and chilling air. During the whole day the river rose rapidly and we were obliged to hug the bank closely, running under the boughs of trees and drawing ourselves up the rapids by those that hung low.

I crept out of the snug nest where we were all stowed as closely as three unfledged sparrows, and took my seat between Juan and Ambrosio, protected from the rain by an India-rubber poncho. The clothing of our men was likewise waterproof, but without seam or fold. It gave no hindrance to the free play of their muscles, as they deftly and rapidly plied the broad paddles. Juan kept time to the Ethiopian melodies he had picked up from the emigrants, looking round from time to time with a grin of satisfaction at his skill. I preferred, however, hearing the native songs, which the boatmen sing with a melancholy drawl on the final syllable of every line, giving the music a peculiar but not unpleasant effect, when heard at a little distance. Singing begets thirst, and perhaps Juan sang the more that he might have a more frequent claim on the brandy. The bottle was then produced and each swallowed a mouthful, after which he dipped his cocoa shell in the river and took a long draught. This is a universal custom among the boatmen, and the traveler is obliged to supply them. As a class, they are faithful, hard-working and grateful for kindness. They have faults, the worst of which are tardiness, and a propensity to filch small articles; but good treatment wins upon them in almost every case. Juan said to me in the beginning " *soy tu amigo yo*," (*Americanice:* I am thy friend, *well* I am,) but when he asked me, in turn, for every article of clothing I wore, I began to think his friendship not the most disinterested. Ambrosio told me that they would serve no one well who treated them badly. " If the Americans are good, we are good; if they abuse us, we are bad. We are black, but *muchos caballeros*" (very much of gentlemen), said he. Many blustering fellows, with their belts stuck full of pistols and bowie-knives, which they draw on all occasions, but take good care not to use, have brought reproach on the country by their silly conduct. It is no bravery to put a revolver to the head of an unarmed and ignorant native, and the boatmen have sense enough to be no longer terrified by it.

We stopped the second night at Peña Blanca (the White Rock), where I slept in the loft of a hut, on the floor, in the midst of the family and six other travelers. We started at sunrise, hoping to reach Gorgona the same night, but ran upon a sunken log and were detained some time. Ambrosio finally released us by jumping into the river and swimming ashore with a rope in his teeth. We passed the ranches of Agua Salud, Varro Colorado and Palanquilla, and shortly after were overtaken by a storm on the river. We could hear the rush and roar of the rain, as it came towards us like the trampling of myriad feet on the leaves. Shooting under a broad sycamore we made fast to the boughs, covered ourselves with India-rubber, and lay under our cool, rustling thatch of palm, until the storm had passed over.

The character of the scenery changed somewhat as we advanced. The air was purer, and the banks more bold and steep. The country showed more signs of cultivation, and in many places the forest had been lopped away to make room for fields of maize, plantain and rice. But the vegetation was still that of the tropics and many were the long and lonely reaches of the river, where we glided between piled masses of bloom and greenery.

We stopped four hours short of Gorgona, at the hacienda of San Pablo, the residence of Padre Dutaris, curé of all the interior. Ambrosio took us to his house by a path across a rolling, open savanna, dotted by palms and acacias of immense size. Herds of cattle and horses were grazing on the short, thick-leaved grass, and appeared to be in excellent condition. The padre owns a large tract of land, with a thousand head of stock, and his ranche commands a beautiful view up and down the river. Ambrosio was acquainted with his wife, and by recommending us as *buenos caballeros*, procured us a splendid supper of fowls, eggs, rice boiled in cocoa milk, and chocolate, with baked plantains for bread. The padre was absent at the time, but his son Felipe, a boy of twelve years old, assisted in doing the honors with wonderful grace and self-possession. His tawny skin was as soft as velvet, and his black eyes sparkled like jewels. He sat in the hammock with me, leaning over my shoulder as I noted down the day's doings, and when I had done, wrote his name in my book, in an elegant hand. I slept soundly in the midst of an uproar, and only awoke at four o'clock next morning, to hurry our men in leaving for Gorgona.

The current was very strong and in some places it was almost impossible to make headway. Our boatmen worked hard, and by dint of strong poling managed to jump through most difficult places. Their naked, sinewy forms, bathed in sweat, shone like polished bronze. Ambrosio was soon exhausted, and lay down; but Miguel, our *corps de reserve,* put his agile spirit into the work and flung himself upon the pole with such vigor that all the muscles of his body quivered as the boat shot ahead and relaxed them. About half-way to Gorgona we rounded the foot of Monte Carabali, a bold peak clothed with forests and crowned with a single splendid palm. This hill is the only one in the province from which both oceans may be seen at once.

As we neared Gorgona, our men began repeating the ominous words: *"Cruces — mucha colera."* We had, in fact, already heard of the prevalence of cholera there, but doubted, none the less, their wish to shorten the journey. On climbing the bank to the village, I called immediately at the store of Mr. Miller, the only American resident, who informed me that several passengers by the Falcon had already left for Panama, the route being reported passable. In the door of the alcalde's house, near at hand, I met Mr. Powers, who had left New York a short time previous to my departure, and was about starting for Panama on foot, mules being very scarce. While we were deliberating whether to go on to Cruces, Ambrosio beckoned me into an adjoining hut. The owner, a very venerable and dignified native, received me swinging in his hammock. He had six horses which he would furnish us the next morning, at $10 the head for riding animals, and $6 for each 100 lbs. of freight. The bargain was instantly concluded.

As we were leaving Gorgona, our party was joined by a long Mississippian, whose face struck me at the first glance as being peculiarly cadaverous. He attached himself to us without the least ceremony, leaving his own party behind. We had not ridden far before he told us he had felt symptoms of cholera during the night, and was growing worse. We insisted on his returning to Gorgona at once, but he refused, saying he was "bound to go through." At the first ranche on the road we found another traveler, lying on the ground in a state of entire prostration. He was attended by a friend, who seemed on the point of taking the epidemic, from his very fears. The sight of this case no doubt operated on the Mississippian, for he soon became so racked with pain as to keep his seat with great difficulty. We were alarmed; it was impossible to stop in the swampy forest, and equally impossible to leave him, now that all his dependence was on us. The only thing resembling medicine in our possession, was a bottle of claret. It was an unusual remedy for cholera, but he insisted on drinking it.

After urging forward our weary beasts till late in the afternoon, we were told that Panama was four hours further. We pitied the poor horses, but ourselves more, and determined to push ahead. After a repetition of all our worst experience, we finally struck the remains of the paved road constructed by the buccaneers when they held Panama. I now looked eagerly forward for the Pacific, but every ridge showed another in advance, and it grew dark with a rain coming up. Our horses avoided the hard pavement and took by-paths through thickets higher than our heads. The cholera-stricken emigrant, nothing helped by the claret he drank, implored us, amid his groans, to hasten forward. We were far in advance of our Indian guide and lost the way more than once in the darkness. At last he overtook us, washed his feet in a mudhole, and put on a pair of pantaloons. This was a welcome sign to us, and in fact, we soon after smelt the salt air of the Pacific, and could distinguish huts on either side of the road. These gave place to stone houses and massive ruined edifices, overgrown with vegetation. We passed a plaza and magnificent church, rode down an open space fronting the bay, under a heavy gate-way, across another plaza and through two or three narrow streets, hailed by Americans all the way with: "Are you the Falcon's passengers?" "From Gorgona?" "From

Cruces?" till our guide brought us up at the Hotel Americano.

Thus terminated my five days' journey across the Isthmus — decidedly more novel, grotesque and adventurous than any trip of similar length in the world. It was rough enough, but had nothing that I could exactly call hardship, so much was the fatigue balanced by the enjoyment of unsurpassed scenery and a continual sensation of novelty. In spite of the many dolorous accounts which have been sent from the Isthmus, there is nothing, at the worst season, to deter any one from the journey.

II

HO! FOR SAN FRANCISCO

There were about seven hundred emigrants waiting for passage, when I reached Panama. All the tickets the steamer could possibly receive had been issued and so great was the anxiety to get on, that double price, $600, was frequently paid for a ticket to San Francisco. A few days before we came, there was a most violent excitement on the subject, and as the only way to terminate the dispute, it was finally agreed to dispose by lot of all the tickets for sale. The emigrants were all numbered, and those with tickets for sailing vessels or other steamers excluded. The remainder then drew, there being fifty-two tickets to near three hundred passengers. The disappointed candidates, for the most part, took passage in sailing vessels, with a prospect of seventy days' voyage before them. A few months previous, when three thousand persons were waiting on the Isthmus, several small companies started in the log canoes of the natives, thinking to reach San Francisco in them! After a voyage of forty days, during which they went no further than the Island of Quibo, at the mouth of the Gulf, nearly all of them returned; the rest have not since been heard of.

The passengers were engaged in embarking all the afternoon of the second day after my arrival. The steamer came up to within a mile and a half of the town, and numbers of canoes plied between her and the sea-gateway. Native porters crowded about the hotels, clamoring for luggage, which they carried down to the shore under so fervent a heat that I was obliged to hoist my umbrella. One of the boatmen lifted me over the swells for the sake of a *medio,* and I was soon gliding out along the edge of the breakers, startling the pelicans that flew in long lines over the water. I was well satisfied to leave Panama at the time; the cholera, which had already carried off one-fourth of the native population, was making havoc among the Americans, and several of the Falcon's passengers lay at the point of death.

A voyage from Panama to San Francisco in the year 1849 can hardly be compared to sea-life in any other part of the world or at any previous period. Our vessel was crowded fore and aft: exercise was rendered quite impossible and sleep was each night a new experiment, for the success of which we were truly grateful. We were roused at daylight by the movements on deck, if not earlier, by the breaking of a hammock-rope and the thump and yell of the unlucky sleeper. Coffee was served in the cabin; but, as many of the passengers imagined that, because they had paid a high price for their tickets, they were conscientiously obligated to drink three cups, the late-comers got a very scanty allowance. The breakfast hour was nine, and the table was obliged to be fully set twice. At the first tingle of the bell, all hands started as if a shot had exploded among them; conversation was broken off in the middle of a word; the deck was instantly cleared, and the passengers, tumbling pell-mell down the cabin-stairs, found every seat taken by others who had probably been sitting in them for half an hour. The bell, however, had an equally convulsive effect upon these. There was a confused grabbing motion for a few seconds, and lo! the plates were cleared. While about half the passengers had all their breakfast piled at once upon their plates, the other half were regaled by a "plentiful lack." The second table was but a repetition of these scenes, which dinner — our only additional meal — renewed in the afternoon. Among our company of two hundred and fifty, there were, of course, many gentlemen of marked refinement and intelligence from various parts of the Union. I believe the controlling portion of the California emigration is intelligent, orderly and peaceable; yet I never witnessed so many disgusting exhibitions of the lowest passions of humanity, as during the voyage. At sea or among the mountains, men completely lose the little arts of dissimulation they practise in society. They show in their true light, and very often, alas! in a light little calculated to encourage the enthusiastic believer in the speedy perfection of our race.

* * * * * * *

"There is California!" was the cry next morning at sunrise. "Where?" "Off the starboard bow." I rose on my bunk in one of the deck state-rooms, and looking out of the window, watched the purple mountains of the Peninsula, as they rose in the fresh, inspiring air. We were opposite its southern extremity, and I scanned the brown and sterile coast with a glass, searching for anything like vegetation. The whole country appeared to be a mass of nearly naked rock, nourishing only a few cacti and some stunted shrubs. At the extreme end of the Peninsula the valley of San José opens inland between two ranges of lofty granite mountains. Its beautiful green level, several miles in width, stretched back as far as the eye could reach. The town lies near the sea; it is noted for the siege sustained by Lieut. Haywood and a small body of American troops during the war. Lying deep amid the most frightfully barren and rugged mountains I ever saw, the valley of San José which is watered by a small river, might be made a paradise. In spite of the forbidding appearance of the coast, a more peculiar and interesting picture than it gave can hardly be found on the Pacific. Cape San Lucas, which we passed toward evening, is a bold bluff of native granite, broken into isolated rocks at its points, which present the appearance of three distinct and perfectly-formed pyramids. The white, glistening rock is pierced at its base by hollow caverns and arches, some of which are fifteen or twenty feet high, giving glimpses of the ocean beyond. . . . In a few minutes after our gun was fired, we could see horsemen coming down from San Diego at full gallop, one of whom carried behind him a lady in graceful riding costume. In the first boat were Colonel Weller, U. S. Boundary Commissioner, and Major Hill, of the Army. Then followed a number of men, lank and brown " as is the ribbed sea-sand " — men with long hair and beards, and faces from which the rigid expression of suffering was scarcely relaxed. They were the first of the overland emigrants by the Gila route, who had reached San Diego a few days before. Their clothes were in tatters, their boots, in many cases, replaced by moccasins, and, except their rifles and some small packages rolled in deerskin, they had nothing left of the abundant stores with which they left home.

We hove anchor in half an hour, and again rounded Point Loma, our number increased by more than fifty passengers.

The emigrants we took on board at San Diego were objects of general interest. The stories of their adventures by the way sounded more marvellous than anything I had heard or read since my boyish acquaintance with Robinson Crusoe, Captain Cook and John Ledyard. Taking them as the average experience of the thirty thousand emigrants who last year crossed the Plains, this California Crusade will more than equal the great military expeditions of the

Middle Ages in magnitude, peril and adventure. The amount of suffering which must have been endured in the savage mountain passes and herbless deserts of the interior, cannot be told in words. Some had come by way of Santa Fé and along the savage hills of the Gila; some, starting from Red River, had crossed the Great Stake Desert and taken the road from Paso del Norte to Tucson in Arizona; some had passed through Mexico and after spending one hundred and four days at sea, run into San Diego and given up their vessel; some had landed, weary with a seven months' passage around Cape Horn, and some, finally, had reached the place on foot, after walking the whole length of the Californian Peninsula.

We were within sight of the Coast Range of California all day, after passing Cape Conception. Their sides are spotted with timber, which in the narrow valleys sloping down to the sea appeared to be of large growth. From their unvarying yellow hue, we took them to be mountains of sand, but they were in reality covered with natural harvests of wild oats, as I afterwards learned, on traveling into the interior. A keen, bracing wind at night kept down the fog, and although the thermometer fell to 52°, causing a general shiver on board, I walked the deck a long time, noting the extraordinary brilliancy of the stars in the pure air. The mood of our passengers changed very visibly as we approached the close of the voyage; their exhilarant anticipations left them, and were succeeded by a reaction of feeling that almost amounted to despondency. The return to laborious life after a short exemption from its cares, as in the case of travel, is always attended with some such feeling, but among the California emigrants it was intensified by the uncertainty of their venture in a region where all the ordinary rules of trade and enterprise would be at fault.

When I went on deck in the clear dawn we were rounding Point Pinos into the harbor of Monterey. As we drew near, the white, scattered dwellings of the town, situated on a gentle slope, behind which extended on all sides the celebrated Pine Forest, became visible in the grey light.   A handsome fort, on an eminence near the sea, returned our salute.   The town is larger than I expected to find it, and from the water has the air of a large New-England village, barring the *adobe* houses.   As we were preparing to leave, the sun rose over the mountains, covering the air with gold brighter than ever was scratched up on the Sacramento.   The picturesque houses of Monterey, the pine woods behind and the hills above them, glowed like an illuminated painting, till a fog-curtain which met us at the mouth of the harbor dropped down upon the water and hid them all from sight.

————

At last the voyage is drawing to a close.   Fifty-one days have elapsed since leaving New York, in which time we have, in a manner, coasted both sides of the North-American Continent, from the parallel of 40° N. to its termination, within a few degrees of the Equator, over seas once ploughed by the keels of Columbus and Balboa, of Grijalva and Sebastian Viscaino.   All is excitement on board; the Captain has just taken his noon observation.   We are running along the shore, within six or eight miles' distance; the hills are bare and sandy, but loom up finely through the deep blue haze.   The coast trends somewhat more to the westward and a notch or gap is at last visible in its lofty outline.

An hour later; we are in front of the entrance to San Francisco Bay.   As the view opens through the splendid strait, three or four miles in width, the island rock of Alcatraz appears, gleaming white in the distance.

At last we are through the Golden Gate — fit name for such a magnificent portal to the commerce of the Pacific! Yerba Buena Island is in front; southward and westward opens the renowned harbor, crowded with the shipping of the world, mast behind mast and vessel behind vessel, the flags of all nations fluttering in the breeze! Around the curving shore of the Bay and upon the sides of three hills which rise steeply from the water, the middle one receding so as to form a bold amphitheatre, the town is planted and seems scarcely yet to have taken root, for tents, canvas, plank, mud and adobe houses are mingled together with the least apparent attempt at order and durability. But I am not yet on shore. The gun of the Panama has just announced our arrival to the people on land. We glide on with the tide, past the U. S. ship Ohio and opposite the main landing, outside of the forest of masts. A dozen boats are creeping out to us over the water; the signal is given — the anchor drops — our voyage is over.

III

SAN FRANCISCO

After a prolonged search on the first day of my arrival I obtained a room with two beds at $25 per week, meals being in addition $20 per week. I asked the landlord whether he could send a porter for our trunks. " There is none belonging to the house," said he; " every man is his own porter here." I returned to the Parker House,[1] shouldered a heavy trunk, took a valise in my hand and carried them to my quarters, in the teeth of the wind. Our room was in a sort of garret over the only story of the hotel; two cots, evidently of California manufacture, and covered only with a pair of blankets, two chairs, a rough table and a small looking-glass, constituted the furniture. There was not space enough between the bed and the bare rafters overhead, to sit upright, and I gave myself a severe blow in rising the next morning without the proper heed.

[1] Named for the celebrated Parker House in Boston.

Through a small roof-window of dim glass, I could see the opposite shore of the bay, then partly hidden by the evening fogs. The wind whistled around the eaves and rattled the tiles with a cold, gusty sound, that would have imparted a dreary character to the place, had I been in a mood to listen.

Many of the passengers began speculation at the moment of landing. The most ingenious and successful operation was made by a gentleman of New York, who took out fifteen hundred copies of The Tribune and other papers, which he disposed of in two hours, at one dollar a-piece! Hearing of this I bethought me of about a dozen papers which I had used to fill up crevices in packing my valise. There was a newspaper merchant at the corner of the City Hotel, and to him I proposed the sale of them, asking him to name a price. " I shall want to make a good profit on the retail price," said he, "and can't give more than ten dollars for the lot." I was satisfied with the wholesale price, which was a gain of just four thousand per cent!

I set out for a walk before dark and climbed a hill back of the town, passing a number of tents pitched in the hollows. The scattered houses spread out below me and the crowded shipping in the harbor, backed by a lofty line of mountains, made an imposing picture. The restless, feverish tide of life in that little spot, and the thought that what I then saw and was yet to see will hereafter fill one of the most marvellous pages of all history, rendered it singularly impressive.

I was forced to believe many things, which in my communications to The Tribune I was almost afraid to write, with any hope of their obtaining credence. It may be interesting to give here a few instances of the enormous and unnatural value put upon property at the time of my arrival. The Parker House rented for $110,000 yearly, at least $60,000 of which was paid by gamblers, who held nearly all the second story. Adjoining it on the right was a canvas-tent fifteen by twenty-five feet, called " El dorado," and occupied likewise by gamblers, which brought $40,000. On

the opposite corner of the plaza, a building called the
"Miner's Bank," used by Wright & Co., brokers, about
half the size of a fire-engine house in New York, was held
at a rent of $75,000. A mercantile house paid $40,000 rent
for a one-story building of twenty feet front; the United
States Hotel, $36,000; the Post-Office, $7,000, and so on
to the end of the chapter. A friend of mine, who wished
to find a place for a law-office, was shown a cellar in the
earth, about twelve feet square and six deep, which he could
have at $250 a month. One of the common soldiers at
the battle of San Pasquale was reputed to be among the
millionaires of the place, with an income of $50,000 *monthly*.
A citizen of San Francisco died insolvent to the amount
of $41,000 the previous Autumn. His administrators were
delayed in settling his affairs, and his real estate advanced
so rapidly in value meantime, that after his debts were paid
his heirs had a yearly income of $40,000. These facts were
indubitably attested; every one believed them, yet hearing
them talked of daily, as matters of course, one at first could
not help feeling as if he had been eating of "the insane
root."

The prices paid for labor were in proportion to everything else. The carman of Mellus, Howard & Co. had a
salary of $6,000 a year, and many others made from $15
to $20 daily. Servants were paid from $100 to $200 a
month, but the wages of the rougher kinds of labor had
fallen to about $80. Yet, notwithstanding the number of
gold-seekers who were returning enfeebled and disheartened
from the mines, it was difficult to obtain as many workmen
as the forced growth of the city demanded. A gentleman
who arrived in April told me he then found but thirty or
forty houses; the population was then so scant that not more
than twenty-five persons would be seen in the streets at any
one time. Now, there were probably five hundred houses,
tents and sheds, with a population, fixed and floating, of
six thousand. People who had been absent six weeks came

back and could scarcely recognize the place. Streets were regularly laid out, and already there were three piers, at which small vessels could discharge. It was calculated that the town increased daily by from fifteen to thirty houses; its skirts were rapidly approaching the summits of the three hills on which it is located.

A curious result of the extraordinary abundance of gold and the facility with which fortunes were acquired, struck me at the first glance. All business was transacted on so extensive a scale that the ordinary habits of solicitation and compliance on the one hand and stubborn cheapening on the other, seemed to be entirely forgotten. You enter a shop to buy something; the owner eyes you with perfect indifference, waiting for you to state your want; if you object to the price, you are at liberty to leave, for you need not expect to get it cheaper; he evidently cares little whether you buy it or not. One who has been some time in the country will lay down the money, without wasting words. This disregard for all the petty arts of money-making was really a refreshing feature of society. Another equally agreeable trait was the punctuality with which debts were paid and the general confidence which men were obliged to place, perforce, in each other's honesty. Perhaps this latter fact was owing, in part, to the impossibility of protecting wealth, and consequent dependence on an honorable regard for the rights of others.

About the hour of twilight the wind fell; the sound of a gong called us to tea, which was served in the largest room of the hotel. The fare was abundant and of much better quality than we expected — better, in fact, than I was able to find there two months later. The fresh milk, butter and excellent beef of the country were real luxuries after our sea-fare. Thus braced against the fog and raw temperature, we sallied out for a night-view of San Francisco, then even more peculiar than its daylight look. Business was over about the usual hour, and then the harvest-time of the gamblers commenced. Every "hell" in the place, and I did not pretend to number them, was crowded, and immense sums were staked at the monte and faro tables. A boy of fifteen, in one place, won about $500, which he coolly pocketed and carried off. One of the gang we brought in the Panama won $1,500 in the course of the evening, and another lost $2,400. A fortunate miner made himself conspicuous by betting large piles of ounces on a single throw. His last stake of 100 oz. was lost, and I saw him the following morning dashing through the streets, trying to break his own neck or that of the magnificent *garañon* he bestrode.

Walking through the town the next day, I was quite amazed to find a dozen persons busily employed in the street before the United States Hotel, digging up the earth with knives and crumbling it in their hands. They were actual gold-hunters, who obtained in this way about $5 a day. After blowing the fine dirt carefully in their hands, a few specks of gold were left, which they placed in a piece of white paper. A number of children were engaged in the same business, picking out the fine grains by applying to them the head of a pin, moistened in their mouths. I was told of a small boy having taken home $14 as the result of one day's labor. On climbing the hill to the Post Office I observed in places, where the wind had swept away the sand, several glittering dots of the real metal, but, like the Irishman who kicked the dollar out of his way, concluded to wait till I should reach the heap. The presence of gold in the streets was probably occasioned by the leakings from the miners' bags and the sweepings of stores; though it may also be, to a slight extent, native in the earth, particles having been found in the clay thrown up from a deep well.

The arrival of a steamer with a mail ran the usual excitement and activity of the town up to its highest possible notch. The little Post Office, half-way up the hill, was almost hidden from sight by the crowds that clustered around it. Mr. Moore, the new Postmaster, who was my fellow-traveler from New York, barred every door and window from the moment of his entrance, and with his sons and a few clerks, worked steadily for two days and two nights, till the distribution of twenty thousand letters was completed.

*   *   *   *   *   *   *

As early as half-past six the bells begin to sound to breakfast, and for an hour thenceforth, their incessant clang and the braying of immense gongs drown all the hammers that are busy on a hundred roofs. The hotels, restaurants and refectories of all kinds are already as numerous as gaming-tables, and equally various in kind. The tables d'hôte of the first class (which charge $2 and upwards the meal) are abundantly supplied. There are others, with more simple and solid fare, frequented by the large class who have their fortunes yet to make. At the United States and California restaurants, on the plaza, you may get an excellent beef-steak, scantily garnished with potatoes, and a cup of good coffee or chocolate for $1. Fresh beef, bread, potatoes, and all provisions which will bear importation, are plenty; but milk, fruit and vegetables are classed as luxuries, and fresh butter is rarely heard of.

By nine o'clock the town is in the full flow of business. The streets running down to the water, and Montgomery street which fronts the Bay, are crowded with people, all in hurried motion. The variety of characters and costumes is remarkable. Our own countrymen seem to lose their local peculiarities in such a crowd, and it is by chance epithets rather than by manner, that the New-Yorker is distinguished from the Kentuckian, the Carolinian from the Down-Easter, the Virginian from the Texan. The German and Frenchman are more easily recognized. Peruvians and Chilians go by in their brown ponchos, and the sober Chinese, cool and impassive in the midst of excitement, look out of the oblique corners of their long eyes at the bustle, but are never tempted to venture from their own line of business. The eastern side of the plaza, in front of the Parker House and a canvas hell called the Eldorado, are the general rendezvous of business and amusement — combining 'change, park, club-room and promenade all in one. There, everybody not constantly employed in one spot, may be seen at some time of the day. The character of the groups scattered along the plaza is oftentimes very interesting. In one place are three or four speculators bargaining for lots, buying and selling " fifty varas square" in towns, some of which are canvas and some only paper; in another, a company of miners, brown as leather, and rugged in features as in dress; in a third, perhaps, three or four naval officers speculating on the next cruise, or a knot of genteel gamblers, talking over the last night's operations.

The day advances. The mist which after sunrise hung low and heavy for an hour or two, has risen above the hills, and there will be two hours of pleasant sunshine before the wind sets in from the sea. The crowd in the streets is now wholly alive. Men dart hither and thither, as if possessed with a never-resting spirit. You speak to an acquaintance — a merchant, perhaps. He utters a few hurried words of greeting, while his eyes send keen glances on all sides of you; suddenly he catches sight of somebody in the crowd; he is off, and in the next five minutes has bought up half a cargo, sold a town lot at treble the sum he gave, and taken a share in some new and imposing speculation. The very air is pregnant with the magnetism of bold, spirited, unwearied action, and he who but ventures into the outer circle of the whirlpool, is spinning, ere he has time for thought, in its dizzy vortex.

About twelve o'clock, a wind begins to blow from the north-west, sweeping with most violence through a gap between the hills, opening towards the Golden Gate. The bells and gongs begin to sound for dinner, and these two causes tend to lessen the crowd in the streets for an hour or two. Two o'clock is the usual dinner-time for business men, but some of the old and successful merchants have adopted the fashionable hour of five. Where shall we dine to-day? the restaurants display their signs invitingly on all sides; we have choice of the United States, Tortoni's, the Alhambra, and many other equally classic resorts, but Delmonico's, like its distinguished original in New York, has the highest prices and the greatest variety of dishes. We go down Kearney street to a two-story wooden house on the corner of Jackson. The lower story is a market. We enter a little door at the end of the building, ascend a dark, narrow flight of steps and find ourselves in a long, low room, with ceiling and walls of white muslin and a floor covered with oil-cloth.

There are about twenty tables disposed in two rows, all of them so well filled that we have some difficulty in finding places. Taking up the written bill of fare, we find such items as the following:

SOUPS.		ENTREES.	
Mock Turtle	$0.75	Filet of Beef, mushroom sauce	$1.75
St. Julien	1.00	Veal Cutlets, breaded	1.00
FISH.		Mutton Chop	1.00
Boiled Salmon Trout, Anchovy sauce	1.75	Lobster Salad	2.00
BOILED.		Sirloin of Venison	1.50
Leg Mutton, caper sauce	1.00	Baked Macaroni	0.75
Corned Beef, Cabbage	1.00	Beef Tongue, sauce piquante	1.00
Ham and Tongues	0.75		

So that, with but a moderate appetite, the dinner will cost us $5, if we are at all epicurean in our tastes. There are cries of " steward! " from all parts of the room — the word " waiter " is not considered sufficiently respectful, seeing that the waiter may have been a lawyer or merchant's clerk a few months before. The dishes look very small as they are placed on the table, but they are skilfully cooked and very palatable to men that have ridden in from the diggings. The appetite one acquires in California is something remarkable. For two months after my arrival, my sensations were like those of a famished wolf.

The afternoon is less noisy and active than the forenoon. Merchants keep within-doors, and the gambling-rooms are crowded with persons who step in to escape the wind and dust. The sky takes a cold gray cast, and the hills over the bay are barely visible in the dense, dusty air. Towards sunset, the plaza is nearly deserted; the wind is merciless in its force, and a heavy overcoat is not found unpleasantly warm. As it grows dark, there is a lull, though occasional gusts blow down the hill and carry the dust of the city out among the shipping.

The appearance of San Francisco at night, from the water, is unlike anything I ever beheld. The houses are mostly of canvas, which is made transparent by the lamps within, and transforms them, in the darkness, to dwellings of solid light. Seated on the slopes of its three hills, the tents pitched among the chaparral to the very summits, it gleams like an amphitheatre of fire. Here and there shine out brilliant points, from the decoy-lamps of the gaming-houses; and through the indistinct murmur of the streets comes by fits the sound of music from their hot and crowded precincts.

The only objects left for us to visit are the gaming-tables, whose day has just fairly dawned. We need not wander far in search of one. Denison's Exchange, the Parker House and Eldorado stand side by side; across the way are the Verandah and Aguila de Oro; higher up the plaza the St. Charles and Bella Union; while dozens of second-rate establishments are scattered through the less frequented streets. The greatest crowd is about the Eldorado; we find it difficult to effect an entrance. There are about eight tables in the room, all of which are thronged; copper-hued Kanakas, Mexicans rolled in their sarapes and Peruvians thrust through their ponchos, stand shoulder to shoulder with the brown and bearded American miners. The stakes are generally small, though when the bettor gets into " a streak of luck," as it is called, they are allowed to double until all is lost or the bank breaks. Along the end of the room is a spacious bar, supplied with all kinds of bad liquors, and in a sort of gallery, suspended under the ceiling, a female violinist tasks her talent and strength of muscle to minister to the excitement of play.

The Verandah, opposite, is smaller, but boasts an equal attraction in a musician who has a set of Pandean pipes fastened at his chin, a drum on his back, which he beats with sticks at his elbows, and cymbals in his hands. The piles of coin on the monte tables clink merrily to his playing, and the throng of spectators, jammed together in a sweltering mass, walk up to the bar between the tunes and drink out of sympathy with his dry and breathless throat. At the Aguila de Oro there is a full band of Ethiopian serenaders, and at the other hells, violins, guitars or wheezy accordeons, as the case may be. The atmosphere of these places is rank with tobacco-smoke, and filled with a feverish, stifling heat, which communicates an unhealthy glow to the faces of the players.

There are rare chances here for seeing human nature in one of its most dark and existing phases. They are playing monte, the favorite game in California, since the chances are considered more equal and the opportunity of false play very slight. The dealer throws out his cards with a cool, nonchalant air; indeed, the gradual increase of the hollow square of dollars at his left hand is not calculated to disturb his equanimity. The two Mexicans in front, muffled in their dirty sarapes, put down their half-dollars and dollars and see them lost, without changing a muscle. Gambling is a born habit with them, and they would lose thousands with the same indifference. Very different is the demeanor of the Americans who are playing; their good or ill luck is betrayed at once by involuntary exclamations and changes of countenance, unless the stake should be very large and absorbing, when their anxiety, though silent, may be read with no less certainty. They have no power to resist the fascination of the game. Now counting their winnings by thousands, now dependent on the kindness of a friend for a few dollars to commence anew, they pass hour after hour in those hot, unwholesome dens. There is no appearance of arms, but let one of the players, impatient with his losses and maddened by the poisonous fluids he has drunk, threaten one of the profession, and there will be no scarcity of knives and revolvers.

There are other places, where gaming is carried on privately and to a more ruinous extent — rooms in the rear of the Parker House, in the City Hotel and other places, frequented only by the initiated. Here the stakes are almost unlimited, the players being men of wealth and apparent respectability. Frequently, in the absorbing interest of some desperate game the night goes by unheeded and morning breaks upon haggard faces and reckless hearts. Here are lost, in a few turns of a card or rolls of a ball, the product of fortunate ventures by sea or months of racking labor on land.

IV

AT THE DIGGINGS

MOKELUMNE

In the evening of the day of our arrival we sat down to a supper prepared by Baptiste and his partner, Mr. Fisher, which completed my astonishment at the resources of that wonderful land. There, in the rough depth of the hills, where three weeks before there was scarcely a tent, and where we expected to live on jerked beef and bread, we saw on the table green corn, green peas and beans, fresh oysters, roast turkey, fine Goshen butter and excellent coffee. I will not pretend to say what they cost, but I began to think that the fable of Aladdin was nothing very remarkable, after all.

I slept soundly that night on the dining-table, and went down early to the river, where I found the party of ten bailing out the water which had leaked into the river-bed during the night. They were standing in the sun, and had two hours' hard work before they could begin to wash for gold. The prospect looked uninviting, but when I went there again towards noon, one of them was scraping up the sand from the bed with his knife, and throwing it into a basin, the bottom of which glittered with gold. Every knifeful brought out a quantity of grains and scales, some of which were as large as the finger-nail. At last a two-ounce lump fell plump into the pan, and the diggers, now in the best possible humor, went on with their work with great alacrity. Their forenoon's digging amounted to nearly six pounds. It is only by such operations as these, through associated labor, that great profits are to be made in those districts which have been visited by the first eager horde of gold hunters. The deposits most easily reached are soon exhausted by the crowd, and the labor required to carry on further work successfully deters single individuals from attempting it. Those who, retaining their health, return home disappointed, say they have been humbugged about the gold, when in fact, they have humbugged themselves about the *work*. If any one expects to dig treasures out of the earth, in California, without severe labor, he is wofully mistaken. Of all classes of men, those who pave streets and quarry limestone are best adapted for gold diggers.

Dr. Gillette, to whom we were indebted for many kind attentions, related to me the manner of his finding the rich gulch which attracted so many to the Mokelumne Diggings. About two months previous to our arrival, Dr. Gillette came down from the Upper Bar with a companion, to "prospect" for gold among the ravines in the neighborhood. There were no persons there at the time, except some

Indians belonging to the tribe of José Jesus. One day at noon, while resting in the shade of a tree, Dr. G. took a pick and began carelessly turning up the ground. Almost on the surface, he struck and threw out a lump of gold of about two pounds weight. Inspired by this unexpected result, they both went to work, laboring all that day and the next, and even using part of the night to quarry out the heavy pieces of rock. At the end of the second day they went to the village on the Upper Bar and weighed their profits, which amounted to fourteen pounds! They started again the third morning under pretence of hunting, but were suspected and followed by the other diggers, who came upon them just as they commenced work. The news rapidly spread, and there was soon a large number of men on the spot, some of whom obtained several pounds per day, at the start. The gulch had been well dug up for the large lumps, but there was still great wealth in the earth and sand, and several operators only waited for the wet season to work it in a systematic manner.

The next day Col. Lyons, Dr. Gillette and myself set out on a visit to the scene of these rich discoveries. Climbing up the rocky bottom of the gulch, as by a staircase, for four miles, we found nearly every part of it dug up and turned over by the picks of the miners. Deep holes, sunk between the solid strata or into the precipitous sides of the mountains, showed where veins of the metal had been struck and followed as long as they yielded lumps large enough to pay for the labor. The loose earth, which they had excavated, was full of fine gold, and only needed washing out. A number of Sonorians were engaged in dry washing this refuse sand — a work which requires no little skill, and would soon kill any other men than these lank and skinny Arabs of the West. Their mode of work is as follows: — Gathering the loose dry sand in bowls, they raise it to their heads and slowly pour it upon a blanket spread at their feet. Repeating this several times, and throwing out the worthless pieces of rock, they reduce the dust to about half its bulk; then, balancing the bowl on one hand, by a quick, dexterous motion of the other they cause it to revolve, at the same time throwing its contents into the air and catching them as they fall. In this manner everything is finally winnowed away except the heavier grains of sand mixed with gold, which is carefully separated by the breath. It is a laborious occupation, and one which, fortunately, the American diggers have not attempted. This breathing the fine dust from day to day, under a more than torrid sun, would soon impair the strongest lungs.

We found many persons at work in the higher part of the gulch, searching for veins and pockets of gold, in the holes which had already produced their first harvest. Some of these gleaners, following the lodes abandoned by others as exhausted, into the sides of the mountain, were well repaid for their perseverance. Others, again, had been working for days without finding anything. Those who understood the business obtained from one to four ounces daily. Their only tools were the crowbar, pick and knife, and many of them, following the veins under strata of rock which lay deep below the surface, were obliged to work while lying flat on their backs, in cramped and narrow holes, sometimes kept moist by springs. They were shielded, however, from the burning heats, and preserved their health better than those who worked on the bars of the river.

There are thousands of similar gulches among the mountains, nearly all of which undoubtedly contain gold. Those who are familiar with geology, or by carefully noting the character of the soil and strata where gold is already found, have learned its indications, rarely fail in the selection of new spots for digging. There is no such thing as accident in Nature, and in proportion as men understand her, the more sure a clue they have to her buried treasures. There is more gold in California than ever was said or imagined: ages will not exhaust the supply.

I went up in the ravines one morning, for about two miles, looking for game. It was too late in the day for deer, and I saw but one antelope, which fled like the wind over the top of the mountain. I started a fine hare, similar in appearance to the European, but of larger size. A man riding down the trail, from the Double Spring, told us he had counted seven deer early in the morning, beside numbers of antelopes and partridges. The grizzly bear and large mountain wolf are frequently seen in the more thickly timbered ravines. The principal growth of the mountains is oak and the California pine, which rises like a spire to the height of two hundred feet. The *piñons*, or cones, are much larger and of finer flavor, than those of the Italian stonepine. As far as I could see from the ridges which I climbed, the mountains were as well timbered as the soil and climate will allow. A little more rain would support as fine forests as the world can produce. The earth was baked to a cinder, and from 11 A. M. to 4 P. M. the mercury ranged between 98° and 110°.

The largest piece found in the rich gulch weighed eleven pounds. Mr. James, who had been on the river since April, showed me a lump weighing sixty-two ounces — pure, unadulterated gold.

From all I saw and heard, while at the Mokelumne Diggings, I judged there was as much order and security as could be attained without a civil organization. The inhabitants had elected one of their own number Alcalde, before whom all culprits were tried by a jury selected for the purpose. Several thefts had occurred, and the offending parties been severely punished after a fair trial. Some had been whipped and cropped, or maimed in some other way, and one or two of them hung. Two or three who had stolen largely had been shot down by the injured party, the general feeling among the miners justifying such a course when no other seemed available. We met near Livermore's Ranche, on the way to Stockton, a man whose head had been shaved and his ears cut off, after receiving one hundred lashes, for stealing ninety-eight pounds of gold. It may conflict with popular ideas of morality, but, nevertheless, this extreme course appeared to have produced good results. In fact, in a country without not only bolts and bars, but any effective system of law and government, this Spartan severity of discipline seemed the only security against the most frightful disorder. The result was that, except some petty acts of larceny, thefts were rare. Horses and mules were sometimes taken, but the risk was so great that such plunder could not be carried on to any extent. The camp or tent was held inviolate, and like the patriarchal times of old, its cover protected all it enclosed. Among all well-disposed persons there was a tacit disposition to make the canvas or pavilion of rough oak-boughs as sacred as once were the portals of a church.

The history of law and society in California, from the period of the golden discoveries, would furnish many instructive lessons to the philosopher and the statesman. The first consequence of the unprecedented rush of emigration from all parts of the world into a country almost unknown, and but half reclaimed from its original barbarism was to render all law virtually null, and bring the established authorities to depend entirely on the humor of the population for the observance of their orders. The countries which were nearest the golden coast — Mexico, Peru, Chili, China and the Sandwich Islands — sent forth their thousands of ignorant adventurers, who speedily outnumbered the American population. Another fact, which none the less threatened serious consequences, was the readiness with which the worthless and depraved class of our own country came to the Pacific Coast. From the beginning, a state of things little short of anarchy might have been reasonably awaited.

Instead of this, a disposition to maintain order and secure the rights of all, was shown throughout the mining districts. In the absence of all law or available protection, the

people met and adopted rules for their mutual security —
rules adapted to their situation, where they had neither
guards nor prisons, and where the slightest license given
to crime or trespass of any kind must inevitably have led to
terrible disorders. Small thefts were punished by banish-
ment from the placers, while for those of large amount or
for more serious crimes, there was the single alternative
of hanging. These regulations, with slight change, had
been continued up to the time of my visit to the country.
In proportion as the emigration from our own States increased, and the digging community assumed a more orderly
and intelligent aspect, their severity had been relaxed, though
punishment was still strictly administered for all offences.
There had been, as nearly as I could learn, not more than
twelve or fifteen executions in all, about half of which
were inflicted for the crime of murder. This awful re-
sponsibility had not been assumed lightly, but after a fair
trial and a full and clear conviction, to which was added,
I believe in every instance, the confession of the criminal.

In all the large digging districts, which had been worked
for some time, there were established regulations, which
were faithfully observed. Alcaldes were elected, who decided on all disputes of right or complaints of trespass, and
who had power to summon juries for criminal trials. When
a new placer or gulch was discovered, the first thing done
was to elect officers and extend the area of order. The result was, that in a district five hundred miles long, and inhabited by 100,000 people, who had neither government,
regular laws, rules, military or civil protection, nor even
locks or bolts, and a great part of whom possessed wealth
enough to tempt the vicious and depraved, there was as
much security to life and property as in any part of the
Union, and as small a proportion of crime. The capacity
of a people for self-government was never so triumphantly
illustrated. Never, perhaps, was there a community formed
of more unpropitious elements; yet from all this seeming

chaos grew a harmony beyond what the most sanguine apostle of Progress could have expected.

The rights of the diggers were no less definitely marked and strictly observed. Among the hundreds I saw on the Mokelumne and among the gulches, I did not see a single dispute nor hear a word of complaint. A company of men might mark out a race of any length and turn the current of the river to get at the bed, possessing the exclusive right to that part of it, so long as their undertaking lasted. A man might dig a hole in the dry ravines, and so long as he left a shovel, pick or crowbar to show that he still intended working it, he was safe from trespass. His tools might remain there for months without being disturbed. I have seen many such places, miles away from any camp or tent, which the digger had left in perfect confidence that he should find all right on his return. There were of course exceptions to these rules — the diggings would be a Utopia if it were not so — but they were not frequent.

The treatment of the Sonorians by the American diggers was one of the exciting subjects of the summer. These people came into the country in armed bands, to the number of ten thousand in all, and took possession of the best points on the Tuolumne, Stanislaus and Mokelumne Rivers. At the Sonorian camp on the Stanislaus there were, during the summer, several thousands of them, and the amount of ground they dug up and turned over is almost incredible. For a long time they were suffered to work peaceably, but the opposition finally became so strong that they were ordered to leave. They made no resistance, but quietly backed out and took refuge in other diggings. In one or two places, I was told, the Americans, finding there was no chance of having a fight, coolly invited them back again! At the time of my visit, however, they were leaving the country in large numbers, and there were probably not more than five thousand in all scattered along the various rivers. Several parties of them, in revenge for the treatment they experienced, committed outrages on their way home, stripping small parties of the emigrants by the Gila route of all they possessed. It is not likely that the country will be troubled with them in future.

Abundance of gold does not always beget, as moralists tell us, a grasping and avaricious spirit. The principles of hospitality were as faithfully observed in the rude tents of the diggers as they could be by the thrifty farmers of the North and West. The cosmopolitan cast of society in California, resulting from the commingling of so many races and the primitive mode of life, gave a character of good-fellowship to all its members; and in no part of the world have I ever seen help more freely given to the needy, or more ready coöperation in any humane proposition. Personally, I can safely say that I never met with such unvarying kindness from comparative strangers.

FRÉMONT'S GREAT RIDE

FREDERICK S. DELLENBAUGH

1849

From "Frémont and '49." Reprinted by permission of the publishers, G. P. Putnam's Sons, New York.[1]

FOR a period of about fifty days, from January 16, 1847, Colonel Frémont was recognised everywhere in California as Governor, under Stockton's appointment. Kearny went up to Monterey, and in March Frémont thought he had discovered signs of another outbreak which he believed should be immediately reported to the General. H. H. Bancroft declares: "These alarms were invented later as an excuse for disobeying Kearny's orders." But it seems somewhat unreasonable to suppose that Frémont would make such a tremendous effort as he did in the long ride to be described, merely to inaugurate, or cover up, insubordination. At the same time one may ask, "Why was it necessary for him to carry the news in person?" He writes, "I made a most extraordinary ride to give information to prevent an insurrection. The only thing, it would seem, that I came for in that interview, was to insult General Kearny, and to offer my resignation; and he [pretends he] does not even know what I went for. Certainly the public service, to say nothing of myself as an officer, required a different kind of reception from the one I received."

The immediate trouble seems partly to have arisen from General Kearny's insisting that Colonel Mason should remain through the interview, on the ground that he was the

---

[1] Copyright, 1914, by G. P. Putnam's Sons.

officer appointed to succeed to command in California after the approaching departure of General Kearny. The situation was antagonistic. Kearny finally gave Frémont a limited time in which to declare himself as to obeying the General's orders, and after an hour's consideration he returned agreeing to obey. He was then directed to report at Monterey at the earliest possible moment. Of the impending insurrection at Los Angeles nothing more is heard.

The great ride which culminated at Monterey in this unsatisfactory interview was one of the most remarkable on record for speed and distance. Few men would have the endurance necessary to accomplish such a feat, but Frémont was a man of iron. At dawn, March 22, 1847, he rode out of Los Angeles accompanied by his devoted friend Don Jesus Pico, like all Californians of that day a superb horseman full of endurance, and by the equally devoted coloured man Jacob Dodson, now, by his long experience, the equal of a Californian in riding and lasso-throwing. Besides their three mounts they drove before them six other horses in good condition, all unshod, and from time to time (about every twenty miles), Dodson or Pico would rope fresh horses from the free band to relieve the tired mounts. Changing saddles was but the work of a few seconds, and off they sped again. By night of this first day they had made 120 miles, over mountains and valleys, part of the way by the Rincon, the precarious path along the coast, possible only at low tide, and they slept beyond Santa Barbara at the ranch of Señor Robberis. The second day the distance covered was 135 miles, over the mountains where the Battalion had been so furiously beaten down by the terrible storm described by Bryant, and they counted the skeletons of fifty horses that had succumbed on that day of exposure and suffering.

Sunset found them at Captain Dana's place taking supper; and the home of Pico, San Luis Obispo, was reached by nine in the night. Here a warm welcome met Frémont for his clemency to Pico in the matter of the parole, and it was eleven o'clock the next morning before they were again in the saddle, with eight fresh horses and a Spanish boy for herder, and riding for Monterey. Seventy miles to their credit brought them to a halt for the night in the valley of the Salinas, where they were barred from sleep by a number of grizzly bears prowling near and frightening the horses. Frémont was for shooting them but Pico said no, and he shouted at them something in Spanish when they forthwith retired! But a large fire was then built, breakfast was prepared, and at break of day the last stretch of the road to Monterey was taken at a fine pace, the ninety miles being covered by three in the afternoon (March 25th) making a grand total in *four days of 420 miles.* Frémont, that evening, had the interview, with General Kearny, above referred to, which H. H. Bancroft regards as the " turning point " in the Kearny-Frémont affair. The next day, at four in the afternoon, the party started on the return to Los Angeles and they made 40 miles. The following day 120 miles more were put between them and Monterey, and with 130 miles then on each of the two succeeding days, the Colonel and his companions rode into Los Angeles on the ninth day after his start from there; a total journey of 840 miles over rough country in 76 actual riding hours by the use of 17 horses. To test one of them Frémont rode him without change for 130 miles in 24 hours. The famous ride from Ghent to Aix, immortalised by Browning, was barely more than the least one of these eight days of Frémont. Browning missed an opportunity. Riding with a herd of loose horses running ahead from which the lasso any moment can bring one a fresh mount is highly exhilarating. I tried it once, with 25 horses, for some 300 miles across Utah, but I was not bent on saving Aix or even Los Angeles.

THE LUCK OF ROARING CAMP

BRET HARTE

From "The Luck of Roaring Camp and Other Sketches." Reprinted by permission of the publishers, Houghton, Mifflin Company, Boston.[1]

THERE was commotion in Roaring Camp. It could not have been a fight, for in 1850 that was not novel enough to have called together the entire settlement. The ditches and claims were not only deserted, but "Tuttle's grocery" had contributed its gamblers, who, it will be remembered, calmly continued their game the day that French Pete and Kanaka Joe shot each other to death over the bar in the front room. The whole camp was collected before a rude cabin on the outer edge of the clearing. Conversation was carried on in a low tone, but the name of a woman was frequently repeated. It was a name familiar enough in the camp, — "Cherokee Sal."

Perhaps the less said of her the better. She was a coarse, and, it is to be feared, a very sinful woman. But at that time she was the only woman in Roaring Camp, and was just then lying in sore extremity, when she most needed the ministration of her own sex. Dissolute, abandoned and irreclaimable, she was yet suffering a martyrdom hard enough to bear even when veiled by sympathizing womanhood, but now terrible in her loneliness. The primal curse had come to her in that original isolation which must have made the punishment of the first transgression so dreadful. It was, perhaps, part of the expiation of her sin, that, at a moment when she most lacked her sex's intuitive tenderness

[1] Copyright, 1899, by Bret Harte.

and care, she met only the half-contemptuous faces of her masculine associates. Yet a few of the spectators were, I think, touched by her sufferings. Sandy Tipton thought it was "rough on Sal," and, in the contemplation of her condition, for a moment rose superior to the fact that he had an ace and two bowers in his sleeve.

It will be seen, also, that the situation was novel. Deaths were by no means uncommon in Roaring Camp, but a birth was a new thing. People had been dismissed from the camp effectively, finally, and with no possibility of return; but this was the first time that anybody had been introduced *ab initio*. Hence the excitement.

"You go in there, Stumpy," said a prominent citizen known as "Kentuck," addressing one of the loungers. "Go in there, and see what you kin do. You've had experience in them things."

Perhaps there was a fitness in the selection. Stumpy, in other climes, had been the putative head of two families; in fact, it was owing to some legal informality in these proceedings that Roaring Camp — a city of refuge — was indebted to his company. The crowd approved the choice, and Stumpy was wise enough to bow to the majority. The door closed on the extempore surgeon and midwife, and Roaring Camp sat down outside, smoked its pipe, and awaited the issue.

The assemblage numbered about a hundred men. One or two of these were actual fugitives from justice, some were criminal, and all were reckless. Physically, they exhibited no indication of their past lives and character. The greatest scamp had a Raphael face, with a profusion of blond hair; Oakhurst, a gambler, had the melancholy air and intellectual abstraction of a Hamlet; the coolest and most courageous man was scarcely over five feet in height, with a soft voice and an embarrassed, timid manner. The term "roughs" applied to them was a distinction rather than a definition. Perhaps in the minor details of fingers, toes, ears, etc., the camp may have been deficient, but these slight omissions did not detract from their aggregate force. The strongest man had but three fingers on his right hand; the best shot had but one eye.

Such was the physical aspect of the men that were dispersed around the cabin. The camp lay in a triangular valley, between two hills and a river. The only outlet was a steep trail over the summit of a hill that faced the cabin, now illuminated by the rising moon. The suffering woman might have seen it from the rude bunk whereon she lay, — seen it winding like a silver thread until it was lost in the stars above.

A fire of withered pine-boughs added sociability to the gathering. By degrees the natural levity of Roaring Camp returned. Bets were freely offered and taken regarding the result. Three to five that " Sal would get through with it "; even, that the child would survive; side bets as to the sex and complexion of the coming stranger. In the midst of an excited discussion, an exclamation came from those nearest the door, and the camp stopped to listen. Above the swaying and moaning of the pines, the swift rush of the river, and the crackling of the fire, rose a sharp, querulous cry, — a cry unlike anything heard before in the camp. The pines stopped moaning, the river ceased to rush, and the fire to cackle. It seem as if Nature had stopped to listen too.

The camp rose to its feet as one man! It was proposed to explode a barrel of gunpowder, but, in consideration of the situation of the mother, better counsels prevailed, and only a few revolvers were discharged; for, whether owing to the rude surgery of the camp, or some other reason, Cherokee Sal was sinking fast. Within an hour she had climbed, as it were, that rugged road that led to the stars, and so passed out of Roaring Camp, its sin and shame forever. I do not think that the announcement disturbed them much, except in speculation as to the fate of the child. " Can he live now? " was asked of Stumpy. The answer was doubtful. The only other being of Cherokee Sal's sex and maternal condition in the settlement was an ass. There was some conjecture as to fitness, but the experiment was tried. It was less problematical than the ancient treatment of Romulus and Remus, and apparently as successful.

When these details were completed, which exhausted another hour, the door was opened, and the anxious crowd of men who had already formed themselves into a queue, entered in single file. Beside the low bunk or shelf, on which the figure of the mother was starkly outlined below the blankets stood a pine table. On this a candle-box was placed, and within it, swathed in staring red flannel, lay the last arrival at Roaring Camp. Beside the candle-box was placed a hat. Its use was soon indicated. " Gentlemen," said Stumpy, with a singular mixture of authority and *ex officio* complacency, — " Gentlemen will please pass in at the front door, round the table, and out at the back door. Them as wishes to contribute anything toward the orphan will find a hat handy." The first man entered with his hat on; he uncovered, however, as he looked about him, and so, unconsciously, set an example to the next. In such communities good and bad actions are catching. As the procession filed in, comments were audible, — criticisms addressed, perhaps, rather to Stumpy, in the character of showman, — " Is that him? " " mighty small specimen "; " hasn't mor'n got the color "; " ain't bigger nor a derringer." The contributions were as characteristic: A silver tobacco-box; a doubloon; a navy revolver, silver mounted; a gold specimen; a very beautifully embroidered lady's handkerchief (from Oakhurst the gambler); a diamond breastpin; a diamond ring (suggested by the pin, with the remark from the giver that he " saw that pin and went two diamonds better "); a slung shot; a Bible (contributor not detected); a golden spur; a silver teaspoon (the initials, I regret to say, were not the giver's); a pair of surgeon's shears; a lancet; a Bank of England note for £5; and about $200 in loose gold and silver coin. During these proceedings Stumpy maintained a silence as impassive as the dead on his left, a gravity as inscrutable as that of the newly born on his right. Only one incident occurred to break the monotony of the curious procession. As Kentuck bent over the candle-box half curiously, the child turned, and, in a spasm of pain, caught at his groping finger, and held it fast for a moment. Kentuck looked foolish and embarrassed. Something like a blush tried to assert itself in his weather-beaten cheek. "The d—d little cuss!" he said, as he extricated his finger, with, perhaps, more tenderness and care than he might have been deemed capable of showing. He held that finger a little apart from its fellows as he went out, and examined it curiously. The examination provoked the same original remark in regard to the child. In fact, he seemed to enjoy repeating it. "He rastled with my finger," he remarked to Tipton, holding up the member, "the d—d little cuss!"

It was four o'clock before the camp sought repose. A light burnt in the cabin where the watchers sat, for Stumpy did not go to bed that night. Nor did Kentuck. He drank quite freely, and related with great gusto his experience, invariably ending with his characteristic condemnation of the new-comer. It seemed to relieve him of any unjust implication of sentiment, and Kentuck had the weaknesses of the nobler sex. When everybody else had gone to bed, he walked down to the river, and whistled reflectingly. Then he walked up the gulch, past the cabin, still whistling with demonstrative unconcern. At a large redwood tree he paused and retraced his steps, and again passed the cabin. Half-way down to the river's bank he again paused, and then returned and knocked at the door. It was opened by Stumpy. "How goes it?" said Kentuck, looking past Stumpy toward the candle-box. "All serene," replied Stumpy. "Anything up?" "Nothing." There was a pause — an embarrassing one — Stumpy still holding the door. Then Kentuck had recourse to his finger, which he held up to Stumpy. "Rastled with it, — the d—d little cuss," he said, and retired.

The next day Cherokee Sal had such rude sepulture as Roaring Camp afforded. After her body had been committed to the hillside, there was a formal meeting of the camp to discuss what should be done with her infant. A resolution to adopt it was unanimous and enthusiastic. But an animated discussion in regard to the manner and feasibility of providing for its wants at once sprung up. It was remarkable that the argument partook of none of those fierce personalities with which discussions were usually conducted at Roaring Camp. Tipton proposed that they should send the child to Red Dog, — a distance of forty miles, — where female attention could be procured. But the unlucky suggestion met with fierce and unanimous opposition. It was evident that no plan which entailed parting from their new acquisition would for a moment be entertained. "Besides," said Tom Ryder, "them fellows at Red Dog would swap it, and ring in somebody else on us." A disbelief in the honesty of other camps prevailed at Roaring Camp as in other places.

The introduction of a female nurse in the camp also met with objection. It was argued that no decent woman could be prevailed to accept Roaring Camp as her home, and the speaker urged that "they didn't want any more of the other kind." This unkind allusion to the defunct mother, harsh as it may seem, was the first spasm of propriety, — the first symptom of the camp's regeneration. Stumpy advanced nothing. Perhaps he felt a certain delicacy in interfering with the selection of a possible successor in office. But when questioned, he averred stoutly that he and "Jinny" — the mammal before alluded to — could manage to rear the child. There was something original, independent, and heroic about the plan that pleased the camp. Stumpy was retained. Certain articles were sent for to Sacramento. " Mind," said the treasurer, as he pressed a bag of gold-dust into the expressman's hand, " the best that can be got, — lace, you know, and filigree-work and frills, — d—m the cost ! "

Strange to say, the child thrived. Perhaps the invigorating climate of the mountain camp was compensation for material deficiencies. Nature took the foundling to her broader breast. In that rare atmosphere of the Sierra foothills, — that air pungent with balsamic odor, that ethereal cordial at once bracing and exhilarating, — he may have found food and nourishment, or a subtle chemistry that transmuted asses' milk to lime and phosphorus. Stumpy inclined to the belief that it was the latter and good nursing. " Me and that ass," he would say, " has been father and mother to him. Don't you," he would add, apostrophizing the helpless bundle before him, " never go back on us."

By the time he was a month old, the necessity of giving him a name became apparent. He had generally been known as " the Kid," " Stumpy's boy," " the Cayote " (an allusion to his vocal powers), and even by Kentuck's endearing diminutive of " the d—d little cuss." But these were felt to be vague and unsatisfactory, and were at last dismissed under another influence. Gamblers and adventurers are generally superstitious, and Oakhurst one day declared that the baby had brought " the luck " to Roaring Camp. It was certain that of late they had been successful. " Luck " was the name agreed upon, with the prefix of Tommy for greater convenience. No allusion was made to the mother, and the father was unknown. " It's better," said the philosophical Oakhurst, " to take a fresh deal all round. Call him Luck, and start him fair." A day was accordingly set apart for the christening. What was meant by this ceremony the reader may imagine, who has already gathered some idea of the reckless irreverence of Roaring Camp. The master of ceremonies was one " Boston," a noted wag, and the occasion seemed to promise the greatest facetiousness. This ingenious satirist had spent two days in preparing a burlesque of the church service, with pointed local allusions. The choir was properly trained, and Sandy Tipton was to stand godfather. But after the procession had marched to the grove with music and banners, and the child had been deposited before a mock altar, Stumpy stepped before the expectant crowd. " It ain't my style to spoil fun, boys," said the little man, stoutly, eyeing the faces around him, " but it strikes me that this thing ain't exactly on the squar. It's playing it pretty low down on this yer baby to ring in fun on him that he ain't going to understand. And ef there's going to be any godfathers round, I'd like to see who's got any better rights than me." A silence followed Stumpy's speech. To the credit of all humorists be it said, that the first man to acknowledge its justice was the satirist, thus stopped of his fun. " But," said Stumpy, quickly, following up his advantage, " we're here for a christening, and we'll have it. I proclaim you Thomas Luck, according to the laws of the United States and the State of California, so help me God." It was the first time that the name of the Deity had been uttered otherwise than profanely in the camp. The form of christening was perhaps even more ludicrous than the satirist had conceived; but, strangely enough, nobody saw it and nobody laughed. " Tommy " was christened as seriously as he would have been under a Christian roof, and cried and was comforted in as orthodox fashion.

And so the work of regeneration began in Roaring Camp. Almost imperceptibly a change came over the settlement. The cabin assigned to " Tommy Luck " — or " The Luck," as he was more frequently called — first showed signs of improvement. It was kept scrupulously clean and white-washed. Then it was boarded, clothed, and papered. The rosewood cradle — packed eighty miles by mule — had, in Stumpy's way of putting it, " sorter killed the rest of the furniture." So the rehabilitation of the cabin became a necessity. The men who were in the habit of lounging in at Stumpy's to see "how The Luck got on" seemed to appreciate the change, and, in self-defence, the rival establishment of "Tuttle's grocery" bestirred itself, and imported a carpet and mirrors. The reflections of the latter on the appearance of Roaring Camp tended to produce stricter habits of personal cleanliness. Again, Stumpy imposed a kind of quarantine upon those who aspired to the honor and privilege of holding "The Luck." It was a cruel mortification to Kentuck — who, in the carelessness of a large nature and the habits of frontier life, had begun to regard all garments as a second cuticle, which, like a snake's, only sloughed off through decay — to be debarred this privilege from certain prudential reasons. Yet such was the subtle influence of innovation that he thereafter appeared regularly every afternoon in a clean shirt, and face still shining from his ablutions. Nor were moral and social sanitary laws neglected. "Tommy," who was supposed to spend his whole existence in a persistent attempt to repose, must not be disturbed by noise. The shouting and yelling which had gained the camp its infelicitous title were not permitted within hearing distance of Stumpy's. The men conversed in whispers, or smoked with Indian gravity. Profanity was tacitly given up in these sacred precincts, and throughout the camp a popular form of expletive, known as "D — n the luck!" and "Curse the luck!" was abandoned, as having a new personal bearing. Vocal music was not interdicted, being supposed to have a soothing, tranquillizing quality, and one song, sung by "Man-o' War Jack," an English sailor, from her Majesty's Australian colonies, was quite popular as a lullaby. It was a lugubrious recital of the exploits of "the Arethusa, Seventy-four," in a muffled minor, ending with a prolonged dying fall at the burden of each verse, "On b-o-o-o-ard of the Arethusa." It was a fine sight to see Jack holding The Luck, rocking from side to side as if with the motion of a ship, and crooning forth this naval ditty. Either through the peculiar rocking of Jack or the length of his song, — it contained ninety stanzas, and was continued with conscientious deliberation to the bitter end, — the lullaby generally had the desired effect. At such times the men would lie at full length under the trees, in the soft summer twilight, smoking their pipes and drinking in the melodious utterances. An indistinct idea that this was pastoral happiness pervaded the camp. "This 'ere kind o' think," said the Cockney Simmons, meditatively reclining on his elbow, "is 'evingly." It reminded him of Greenwich.

On the long summer days The Luck was usually carried to the gulch, from whence the golden store of Roaring Camp was taken. There, on a blanket spread over pine-boughs, he would lie while the men were working in the ditches below. Latterly, there was a rude attempt to decorate this bower with flowers and sweet-smelling shrubs, and generally some one would bring him a cluster of wild honeysuckles, azaleas, or the painted blossoms of Las Mariposas. The men had suddenly awakened to the fact that there were beauty and significance in these trifles, which they had so long trodden carelessly beneath their feet. A flake of glittering mica, a fragment of variegated quartz, a bright pebble from the bed of the creek, became beautiful to eyes thus cleared and strengthened, and were invariably put aside for "The Luck." It was wonderful how many treasures the woods and hillsides yielded that "would do for Tommy." Surrounded by playthings such as never child out of fairy-land had before, it is to be hoped that Tommy was content. He appeared to be securely happy, albeit there was an infantine gravity about him, a contemplative light in his round gray eyes, that sometimes worried Stumpy. He was always tractable and quiet, and it is recorded that once, having crept beyond his "corral," —

a hedge of tessellated pine-boughs, which surrounded his bed, — he dropped over the bank on his head in the soft earth, and remained with his mottled legs in the air in that position for at least five minutes with unflinching gravity. He was extricated without a murmur. I hesitate to record the many other instances of his sagacity, which rest, unfortunately, upon the statements of prejudiced friends. Some of them were not without a tinge of superstition. "I crep' up the bank just now," said Kentuck one day, in a breathless state of excitement, "and dern my skin if he wasn't a talking to a jaybird as was a sittin' on his lap. There they was, just as free and sociable as anything you please, a jawin' at each other just like two cherry-bums." Howbeit, whether creeping over the pine-boughs or lying lazily on his back blinking at the leaves above him, to him the birds sang, the squirrels chattered, and the flowers bloomed. Nature was his nurse and playfellow. For him she would let slip between the leaves golden shafts of sunlight that fell just within his grasp; she would send wandering breezes to visit him with the balm of bay and resinous gums; to him the tall red-woods nodded familiarly and sleepily, the bumble-bees buzzed, and the rooks cawed a slumbrous accompaniment.

Such was the golden summer of Roaring Camp. They were "flush times," — and the Luck was with them. The claims had yielded enormously. The camp was jealous of its privileges and looked suspiciously on strangers. No encouragement was given to immigration, and, to make their seclusion more perfect, the land on either side of the mountain wall that surrounded the camp they duly pre-empted. This, and a reputation for singular proficiency with the revolver, kept the reserve of Roaring Camp inviolate. The expressman — their only connecting link with the surrounding world — sometimes told wonderful stories of the camp. He would say, "They 've a street up there in 'Roaring,' that would lay over any street in Red Dog. They 've got

vines and flowers round their houses, and they wash themselves twice a day. But they're mighty rough on strangers,
and they worship an Ingin baby."

With the prosperity of the camp came a desire for further
improvement. It was proposed to build a hotel in the following spring, and to invite one or two decent families
to reside there for the sake of " The Luck," — who might
perhaps profit by female companionship. The sacrifice that
this concession to the sex cost these men, who were fiercely
sceptical in regard to its general virtue and usefulness, can
only be accounted for by their affection for Tommy. A
few still held out. But the resolve could not be carried
into effect for three months, and the minority meekly yielded
in the hope that something might turn up to prevent it.
And it did.

The winter of 1851 will long be remembered in the
foot-hills. The snow lay deep on the Sierras, and every
mountain creek became a river, and every river a lake.
Each gorge and gulch was transformed into a tumultuous
watercourse that descended the hillsides, tearing down giant
trees and scattering its drift and débris along the plain.
Red Dog had been twice under water, and Roaring Camp
had been forewarned. " Water put the gold into them
gulches," said Stumpy. " It's been here once and will be
here again! " And that night the North Fork suddenly
leaped over its banks, and swept up the triangular valley
of Roaring Camp.

In the confusion of rushing water, crushing trees, and
crackling timber, and the darkness which seemed to flow
with the water and blot out the fair valley, but little could
be done to collect the scattered camp. When the morning
broke, the cabin of Stumpy nearest the river-bank was gone.
Higher up the gulch they found the body of its unlucky
owner; but the pride, the hope, the joy, the Luck, of Roaring Camp had disappeared. They were returning with
sad hearts, when a shout from the bank recalled them.

It was a relief-boat from down the river. They had picked up, they said, a man and an infant, nearly exhausted, about two miles below. Did anybody know them, and did they belong here?

It needed but a glance to show them Kentuck lying there, cruelly crushed and bruised, but still holding the Luck of Roaring Camp in his arms. As they bent over the strangely assorted pair, they saw that the child was cold and pulseless. "He is dead," said one. Kentuck opened his eyes. "Dead?" he repeated feebly. "Yes, my man, and you are dying too." A smile lit the eyes of the expiring Kentuck. "Dying," he repeated, "he's a taking me with him, — tell the boys I've got the Luck with me now"; and the strong man, clinging to the frail babe as a drowning man is said to cling to a straw, drifted away into the shadowy river that flows forever to the unknown sea.

THE CITY OF THE SAINTS

SIR RICHARD BURTON

I

ON the road we saw for the first time a train of Mormon wagons, twenty-four in number, slowly wending their way toward the Promised Land. The "Captain" — those who fill the dignified office of guides are so designated, and once a captain always a captain is the Far Western rule — was young Brigham Young, a nephew of the Prophet; a *blondin,* with yellow hair and beard, an intelligent countenance, a six-shooter by his right, and a bowie-knife by his left side. It was impossible to mistake, even through the veil of freckles and sun-burn with which a two months' journey had invested them, the nationality of the emigrants; "British-English" was written in capital letters upon the white eyelashes and tow-colored curls of the children, and upon the sandy brown hair and staring eyes, heavy bodies, and ample extremities of the adults. One young person concealed her facial attractions under a manner of mask. I thought that perhaps she might be a sultana, reserved for the establishment of some very magnificent Mormon bashaw; but the driver, when appealed to, responded with contempt, "Guess old Briggy won't stampede many o' that 'ere lot!" Though thus homely in appearance, few showed any symptoms of sickness or starvation; in fact, their condition first impressed us most favorably with the excellence of the Perpetual Emigration Funds' traveling arrangements.

The Mormons who can afford such luxury generally purchase for the transit of the plains an emigrant's wagon, which in the West seldom costs more than $185. They take a full week before well *en route,* and endeavor to leave the Mississippi in early May, when " long forage " is plentiful upon the prairies. Those prospecting parties who are bound for California set out in March or April, feeding their animals with grain till the new grass appears; after November the road over the Sierra Nevada being almost impassable to way-worn oxen. The ground in the low parts of the Mississippi Valley becomes heavy and muddy after the first spring rains, and by starting in good time the worst parts of the country will be passed before the travel becomes very laborious. Moreover, grass soon disappears from the higher and less productive tracts; between Scott's Bluffs and Great Salt Lake City we were seldom out of sight of starved cattle, and on one spot I counted fifteen skeletons. Travelers, however, should not push forward early, unless their animals are in good condition and are well supplied with grain; the last year's grass is not quite useless, but cattle can not thrive upon it as they will upon the grammas, festucas, and buffalo clover (*Trifolium reflexum*) of Utah and New Mexico. The journey between St. Jo and the Mormon capital usually occupies from two to three months. The Latter-Day Saints march with a quasi-military organization. Other emigrants form companies of fifty to seventy armed men — a single wagon would be in imminent danger from rascals like the Pawnees, who, though fonder of bullying than of fighting, are ever ready to cut off a straggler — elect their " Cap.," who holds the office only during good conduct, sign and seal themselves to certain obligations, and bind themselves to stated penalties in case of disobedience or defection. The " Prairie Traveler " strongly recommends this systematic organization, without which, indeed, no expedition, whether emigrant, commercial, or exploratory, ought ever or in any part of the world to begin its labors; justly observing that, without it, discords and dissensions sooner or later arise which invariably result in breaking up the company.

In this train I looked to no purpose for the hand-carts with which the poorer Saints add to the toils of earthly travel a semi-devotional work of supererogation expected to win a proportionate reward in heaven.

Near the Pine-Tree Stream we met a horse-thief driving four bullocks: he was known to Macarthy, and did not look over comfortable. We had now fallen into the regular track of Mormon emigration, and saw the wayfarers in their worst plight, near the end of the journey. We passed several families, and parties of women and children trudging wearily along: most of the children were in rags or half nude, and all showed gratitude when we threw them provisions. The greater part of the men were armed, but their weapons were far more dangerous to themselves and their fellows than to the enemy. There is not on earth a race of men more ignorant of arms as a rule than the lower grades of English; becoming an emigrant, the mechanic hears that it may be necessary to beat off Indians, so he buys the first old fire-arm he sees, and probably does damage with it. Only last night a father crossed Green River to beg for a piece of cloth; it was intended to shroud the body of his child, which during the evening had been accidentally shot, and the station people seemed to think nothing of the accident, as if it were of daily recurrence. I was told of three, more or less severe, that happened in the course of a month. The Western Americans, who are mostly accustomed to the use of weapons, look upon these awkwardnesses with a profound contempt. We were now in a region of graves, and their presence in this wild was not a little suggestive.

Presently we entered a valley in which green grass, low and dense willows, and small but shady trees, an unusually vigorous vegetation, refreshed, as though with living water, our eyes, parched and dazed by the burning glare. Stock strayed over the pasture, and a few Indian tents rose at the farther side; the view was probably *pas grand chose,* but we thought it splendidly beautiful. At midday we reached Ham's Fork, the northwestern influent of Green River, and there we found a station. The pleasant little stream is called by the Indians Turugempa, the " Blackfoot Water."

Again we advanced. The air was like the breath of a furnace; the sun was a blaze of fire — accounting, by-the-by, for the fact that the human nose in these parts seems invariably to become cherry-red — all the nullahs were dried up, and the dust-pillars and mirage were the only moving objects on the plain. Three times we forded Black's Fork, and then debouched once more upon a long flat. The ground was scattered over with pebbles of granite, obsidian, flint, and white, yellow, and smoky quartz, all water-rolled. After twelve miles we passed Church Butte, one of many curious formations lying to the left hand or south of the road. This isolated mass of still clay has been cut and ground by wind and rain into folds and hollow channels which from a distance perfectly simulate the pillars, groins, and massive buttresses of a ruinous Gothic cathedral. The foundation is level, except where masses have been swept down by the rain, and not a blade of grass grows upon any part. An architect of genius might profitably study this work of Nature: upon that subject, however, I shall presently have more to say. The Butte is highly interesting in a geological point of view; it shows the elevation of the adjoining plains in past ages, before partial deluges and the rains of centuries had effected the great work of degradation.

Again we sighted the pretty valley of Black's Fork, whose

cool clear stream flowed merrily over its pebbly bed. The road was now populous with Mormon emigrants; some had good teams, others hand-carts, which looked like a cross between a wheel-barrow and a tax-cart. There was nothing repugnant in the demeanor of the party; they had been civilized by traveling, and the younger women, who walked together and apart from the men, were not too surly to exchange a greeting. The excessive barrenness of the land presently diminished; gentian and other odoriferous herbs appeared, and the greasewood, which somewhat reminded me of the Sindhian camel-thorn, was of a lighter green than elsewhere, and presented a favorable contrast with the dull glaucous hues of the eternal prairie sage. We passed a dwarf copse so strewed with the bones of cattle as to excite our astonishment: Macarthy told us that it was the place where the 2d Dragoons encamped in 1857, and lost a number of their horses by cold and starvation. The wolves and coyotes seemed to have retained a predilection for the spot; we saw troops of them in their favorite " location " — the crest of some little rise, whence they could keep a sharp look-out upon any likely addition to their scanty larder.

An American artist might extract from such scenery as Church Butte and Echo Kanyon a system of architecture as original and national as Egypt ever borrowed from her sandstone ledges, or the North of Europe from the solemn depths of her fir forests. But Art does not at present exist in America; as among their forefathers farther east, of artists they have plenty, of Art nothing.

After a few minutes' delay to stand and gaze, we resumed the footpath way, while the mail-wagon, with wheels rough-locked, descended what appeared to be an impracticable slope. The summit of the Pass was well-nigh cleared of timber; the woodman's song informed us that the evil work was still going on, and that we are nearly approaching a large settlement. Thus stripped of their protecting fringes, the mountains are exposed to the heat of summer, that sends forth countless swarms of devastating crickets, grasshoppers, and blue-worms; and to the wintry cold, that piles up, four to six feet high — the mountain-men speak of thirty and forty — the snows drifted by the unbroken force of the winds. The Pass from November to February can be traversed by nothing heavier than " sleighs," and during the snow-storms even these are stopped. Falling into the gorge of Big Kanyon Creek, after a total of twelve hard miles from Bauchmin's Fork, we reached at 11:30 the station that bears the name of the water near which it is built. We were received by the wife of the proprietor, who was absent at the time of our arrival; and half stifled by the thick dust and the sun, which had raised the glass to 103°, we enjoyed copious draughts — *tant soit peu* qualified — of the cool but rather hard water that trickled down the hill into a trough by the house side. Presently the station-master, springing from his light " sulky," entered, and was formally introduced to us by Mr. Macarthy as Mr. Ephe Hanks. I had often heard of this individual as one of the old triumvirate of Mormon desperadoes, the other two being Orrin Porter Rockwell and Bill Hickman — as the leader of the dreaded Danite band, and, in short, as a model ruffian. The ear often teaches the eye to form its pictures: I had eliminated a kind of mental sketch of those assassin faces which one sees on the Apennines and Pyrenees, and was struck by what met the eye of sense. The " vile villain," as he has been called by anti-Mormon writers, who verily do not try to *ménager* their epithets, was a middle-sized, light-haired, good-looking man, with regular features, a pleasant and humorous countenance, and the manly manner of his early sailor life, touched with the rough cordiality of the mountaineer. " Frank as a bear-hunter " is a proverb in these lands. He had, like the rest of the triumvirate, and like most men (Anglo-Americans) of desperate courage and fiery, excitable temper, a clear, pale blue eye, verging upon gray, and looking as if it wanted nothing better than to light up, together with a cool and quiet glance that seemed to shun neither friend nor foe.

The terrible Ephe began with a facetious allusion to all our new dangers under the roof of a Danite, to which, in similar strain, I made answer that Danite or Damnite was pretty much the same to me. After dining, we proceeded to make trial of the air-cane, to which he took, as I could see by the way he handled it, and by the nod with which he acknowledged the observation, "almighty convenient sometimes not to make a noise, Mister," a great fancy. He asked me whether I had a mind to "have a slap" at his namesake,[1] an offer which was gratefully accepted, under the promise that "cuffy" should previously be marked down so as to save a long ride and a troublesome trudge over the mountains. His battery of "killb'ars" was heavy and in good order, so that on this score there would have been no trouble, and the only tool he bade me bring was a Colt's revolver, dragoon size. He told me that he was likely to be in England next year, when he had set the "ole woman" to her work. I suppose my look was somewhat puzzled, for Mrs. Dana graciously explained that every Western wife, even when still, as Mrs. Ephe was, in her teens, commands that venerable title, venerable, though somehow not generally coveted.

From Big Kanyon Creek Station to the city, the driver "reckoned," was a distance of seventeen miles. We waited till the bright and glaring day had somewhat burned itself out; at noon heavy clouds came up from the south and southwest, casting a grateful shade and shedding a few drops of rain. After taking friendly leave of the "Danite" chief — whose cordiality of manner had prepossessed me strongly in his favor — we entered the mail-wagon, and

---

[1] "Ole Ephraim" is the mountain-man's *sobriquet* for the grizzly bear.

prepared ourselves for the finale over the westernmost ridge of the stern Wasach.

After advancing about 1.50 mile over the bench ground, the city by slow degrees broke upon our sight. It showed, one may readily believe, to special advantage after the succession of Indian lodges, Canadian ranchos, and log-hut mail-stations of the prairies and the mountains. The site has been admirably chosen for drainage and irrigation — so well, indeed, that a " Deus ex machinâ " must be brought to account for it.[1] About two miles north, and overlooking the settlements from a height of 400 feet, a detached cone, called Ensign Peak or Ensign Mount, rises at the end of a chain which, projected westward from the main range of the heights, overhangs and shelters the north-eastern corner of the valley. Upon this " big toe of the Wasach range," as it is called by a local writer, the spirit of the martyred prophet, Mr. Joseph Smith, appeared to his successor, Mr. Brigham Young, and pointed out to him the position of the New Temple, which, after Zion had " got up into the high mountain," was to console the Saints for the loss of Nauvoo the Beautiful. The city — it is about two miles broad — runs parallel with the right bank of the Jordan, which forms its western limit. It is twelve to fifteen miles distant from the western range, ten from the debouchure of the river, and eight to nine from the nearest point of the lake — a respectful distance, which is not the least of the position's merits. It occupies the rolling brow of a slight decline at the western base of the Wasach — in

[1] I have frequently heard this legend from Gentiles, never from Mormons; yet even the Saints own that as early as 1842 visions of the mountains and kanyons, the valley and the lake, were revealed to Mr. Joseph Smith, jun., who declared it privily to the disciples whom he loved. Thus Messrs. O. Pratt and E. Snow, apostles, were enabled to recognize the Promised Land, as, the first of the pioneers, they issued from the ravines of the Wasach. Of course the Gentiles declare that the exodists hit upon the valley by the purest chance. The spot is becoming classical: here Judge and Apostle Phelps preached his " Sermon on the Mount," which, anti-Mormons say, was a curious contrast to the first discourse so named.

fact, the lower, but not the lowest level of the eastern valley-bench; it has thus a compound slope from north to south, on the line of its water supplies, and from east to west, thus enabling it to drain off into the river.

The city revealed itself, as we approached, from behind its screen, the inclined terraces of the upper table-land, and at last it lay stretched before us as upon a map. The fields were large and numerous, but the Saints have too many and various occupations to keep them, Moravian-like, neat and trim; weeds overspread the ground; often the wild sun-flower-tops outnumbered the heads of maize. The fruit had suffered from an unusually nipping frost in May; the peach-trees were barren; the vines bore no produce; only a few good apples were in Mr. Brigham Young's garden, and the watermelons were poor, yellow, and tasteless, like the African. On the other hand, potatoes, onions, cab-bages, and cucumbers were good and plentiful, the tomato was ripening everywhere, fat full-eared wheat rose in stacks, and crops of excellent hay were scattered about near the houses. The people came to their doors to see the mail-coach, as if it were the "Derby dilly" of old, go by. I could not but be struck by the modified English appearance of the colony, and by the prodigious numbers of the white-headed children.

Presently we debouched upon the main thoroughfare, the centre of population and business, where the houses of the principal Mormon dignitaries and the stores of the Gentile merchants combine to form the city's only street which can be properly so called. It is, indeed, both street and market, for, curious to say, New Zion has not yet built for herself a bazar or market-place. Nearly opposite the Post-office, in a block on the eastern side, with a long veranda, supported by trimmed and painted posts, was a two-storied, pent-roofed building, whose sign-board, swinging to a tall, gibbet-like flag-staff, dressed for the occasion, announced it to be the Salt Lake House, the principal if not the only establishment of the kind in New Zion. In the Far West, one learns not to expect much of the hostelry;[1] I had not seen aught so grand for many a day. Its depth is greater than its frontage, and behind it, secured by a *porte cochère,* is a large yard for corralling cattle. A rough-looking crowd of drivers, drivers' friends, and idlers, almost every man openly armed with revolver and bowie-knife, gathered round the doorway to greet Jim, and " prospect" the "new lot "; and the host came out to assist us in transporting our scattered effects. We looked vainly for a bar on the ground floor; a bureau for registering names was there, but (temperance, in public at least, being the order of the day) the usual tempting array of bottles and decanters was not forthcoming; up stairs we found a Gentile ballroom, a tolerably furnished sitting-room, and bedchambers, apparently made out of a single apartment by partitions too thin to be strictly agreeable. The household had its deficiencies; blacking, for instance, had run out, and servants could not be engaged till the expected arrival of the hand-cart train. However, the proprietor, Mr. Townsend, a Mormon, from the State of Maine — when expelled from Nauvoo, he had parted with land, house, and furniture for $50 — who had married an Englishwoman, was in the highest degree civil and obliging, and he attended personally to our wants, offered his wife's services to Mrs. Dana, and put us all in the best of humors, despite the closeness of the atmosphere, the sadness ever attending one's first entrance into a new place, the swarms of " emigration flies " — so called because they appear in September with the emigrants, and, after living for a month, die off with the first snow — and a certain populousness of bedstead, concerning which the less said the better. Such, gentle reader, are the results of my

---

[1] I subjoin one of the promising sort of advertisements:

" Tom Mitchell!!! dispenses comfort to the weary (!), feeds the hungry (!!), and cheers the gloomy (!!!), at his old, well-known stand, thirteen miles east of Fort Des Moines. *Don't pass by me.*"

first glance at Zion on the tops of the mountains, in the
Holy City of the Far West.

Our journey had occupied nineteen days, from the 7th to
the 25th of August, both included; and in that time we had
accomplished not less than 1136 statute miles.

Walking in a northward direction up Main, otherwise
called Whisky Street, we could not but observe the "magnificent distances" of the settlement, which, containing
9000–12,000 souls, covers an area of three miles.   This
broadway is 132 feet wide, including the side-walks, which
are each twenty, and, like the rest of the principal avenues,
is planted with locust and other trees.   There are twenty
or twenty-one wards or cantons, numbered from the S.E.
"boustrophedon" to the N.W. corner.   They have a common fence and a bishop apiece.   They are called after the
creeks, trees, people, or positions, as Mill-Creek Ward,
Little Cotton-wood, Denmark, and South Ward.   Every
ward contains about nine blocks, each of which is forty
rods square.   The area of ten acres is divided into four to
eight lots, of two and a half to one and a quarter acres
each, 264 feet by 132.   A city ordinance places the houses
twenty feet behind the front line of the lot, leaving an inter-
mediate place for shrubbery or trees.   This rule, however,
is not observed in Main Street.

The streets are named from their direction to the Temple
Block.   Thus Main Street is East Temple Street No. 1;
that behind it is State Road, or East Temple Street 2, and
so forth, the ward being also generally specified.   Temple
Block is also the point to which latitude and longitude are
referred.   It lies in N. lat. 40° 45′ 44″, W. long. (G.)
112° 6′ 8″, and 4300 feet above sea level.

Main Street is rapidly becoming crowded.   The western
block, opposite the hotel, contains about twenty houses of
irregular shape and size.   The buildings are intended to
supply the principal wants of a far-Western settlement,
as bakery, butchery, and blacksmithery, hardware and

crockery, paint and whip warehouse, a " fashionable tailor "
— and " fashionable " in one point, that his works are more
expensive than Poole's [1] — shoe-stores, tannery and cur-
riery; the Pantechnicon, on a more pretentious style than
its neighbors, kept by Mr. Gilbert Clements, Irishman and
orator; dry-goods, groceries, liquors, and furniture shops,
Walker's agency, and a kind of restaurant for ice-cream, a
luxury which costs 25 cents a glass; saddlers, dealers in
" food, flour, and provisions," hats, shoes, clothing, sash
laths, shingles, timber, copper, tin, crockery-ware, carpenters' tools, and mouse-traps. . . . . . . The Tabernacle is
126 feet long from N. to S., and 64 wide from E. to W.; its
interior, ceilinged with an elliptical arch — the width being
its span — can accommodate 2000-3000 souls. It urgently
requires enlarging. Over the entrances at the gable ends,
which open to the N. and S., is a wood-work representing
the sun, with his usual coiffure of yellow beams, like a
Somali's wig, or the symbol of the Persian empire. The roof
is of shingles: it shelters under its projecting eaves a whole
colony of swallows, and there are four chimneys — a number insufficient for warmth at one season, or for ventilation
at the other. The speaker or preacher stands on the west
side of the building, which is reserved for the three highest
dignities, viz., the First Presidency, the " Twelve " (Apostles), and the President of the State of Zion: distinguished strangers are also admitted. Of late, as in the old
Quaker meeting-houses at Philadelphia, the brethren in the
Tabernacle have been separated from the " sistern," who
sit on the side opposite the preacher's left; and, according
to Gentiles, it is proposed to separate the Christians from
the Faithful, that the " goats " may no longer mingle with
the sheep.

Immediately north of the Tabernacle is the Bowery — in
early spring a canopy of green leafy branches, which are
left to wither with the year, supported on wooden posts.

[1] Poole — the celebrated London tailor.

In the extreme northwest angle of the block is the Endowment, here pronounced *On-dewment House,* separated from the Tabernacle by a high wooden paling. The building, of which I made a pen and ink sketch from the west, is of adobe, with a pent roof and four windows, one blocked up: the central and higher portion is flanked by two wings, smaller erections of the same shape. The Endowment House is the place of great medicine, and all appertaining to it is carefully concealed from Gentile eyes and ears: the result is that human sacrifices are said to be performed within its walls. Mrs. Smith and Mr. Hyde have described the mysterious rites performed within these humble walls, but, for reasons given before, there is reason to doubt the truth of their descriptions; such orgies as they describe could not coexist with the respectability which is the law of the land. M. Remy has detailed the programme with all the exactitude of an eye-witness, which he was not. The public declare that the ceremonies consist of some show, which in the Middle Ages would be called a comedy or mystery — possibly Paradise Lost and Paradise Regained — and connect it with the working of a mason's lodge. The respectable Judge Phelps, because supposed to take the place of the Father of Sin when tempting Adam and Eve, is popularly known as " the Devil." The two small wings are said to contain fonts for the two sexes, where baptism by total immersion is performed. According to Gentiles, the ceremony occupies eleven or twelve hours. The neophyte, after bathing, is anointed with oil, and dressed in clean white cotton garments, cap and shirt, of which the latter is rarely removed — Dr. Richards saved his life at the Carthage massacre by wearing it — and a small square masonic apron, with worked or painted fig-leaves: he receives a new name and a distinguishing grip, and is bound to secrecy by dreadful oaths. Moreover, it is said that, as in all such societies, there are several successive degrees, all of which are not laid open to initiation till the Temple shall be finished. But — as every mason knows — the "red-hot poker" and other ideas concerning masonic institutions have prevailed when juster disclosures have been rejected. Similarly in the Mormonic mystery, it is highly probable that, in consequence of the conscientious reserve of the people upon a subject which it would be indelicate to broach, the veriest fancies have taken the deepest root.

After dining with the governor, we sat under the stoop enjoying, as we might in India, the cool of the evening. Several visitors dropped in, among them Mr. and Mrs. Stenhouse. He — Elder T. B. H. Stenhouse — is a Scotchman by birth, and has passed through the usual stages of neophyte (larva), missionary (pupa), and elder or fully-developed Saint (imago). Madame was from Jersey, spoke excellent French, talked English without nasalization or cantalenation, and showed a highly cultivated mind. She had traveled with her husband on a propagandist tour to Switzerland and Italy, where, as president of the missions for three years, he was a "diligent and faithful laborer in the great work of the last dispensation."

He became a Saint in 1846, at the age of 21; lived the usual life of poverty and privation, founded the Southampton Conference, converted a lawyer among other great achievements, and propagated the Faith successfully in Scotland as in England. The conversation turned — somehow, in Great Salt Lake City it generally does — upon polygamy, or rather plurality, which here is the polite word, and for the first time I heard that phase of the family tie sensibly, nay, learnedly advocated on religious grounds by fair lips. Mr. Stenhouse kindly offered to accompany me on the morrow, as the first hand-cart train was expected to enter, and to point out what might be interesting. I saw Elder and High-Priest Stenhouse almost every day during my stay at Great Salt Lake City, and found in his society both pleasure and profit. We of course avoided those mysterious points, into which, as an outsider, I had no right to enter; the elder was communicative enough upon all others, and freely gave me leave to use his information. The reader, however, will kindly bear in mind that, being a strict Mormon, Mr. Stenhouse could enlighten me only upon one side of the subject; his statements were therefore carefully referred to the " other part " ; moreover, as he could never see any but the perfections of his system, the blame of having pointed out what I deem its imperfections is not to be charged upon him. His power of faith struck me much. I had once asked him what became of the Mormon Tables of the Law, the Golden Plates which, according to the Gentiles, were removed by an angel after they had done their work. He replied that he knew not; that his belief was independent of all such accidents; that Mormonism is and must be true to the exclusion of all other systems. I saw before me an instance how the brain or mind of man can, by mere force of habit and application, imbue itself with any idea.

Long after dark I walked home alone. There were no lamps in any but Main Street, yet the city is as safe as at St. James's Square, London. There are perhaps not more than twenty-five or thirty constables or policemen in the whole place, under their captain, a Scotchman, Mr. Sharp, " by name as well as nature so " ; and the guard on public works is merely nominal. Its excellent order must be referred to the perfect system of private police, resulting from the constitution of Mormon society, which in this point resembles the caste system of Hindooism. There is no secret from the head of the Church and State; every thing, from the highest to the lowest detail of private and public life, must be brought to the ear and submitted to the judgment of the father-confessor-in-chief. Gentiles often declare that the Prophet is acquainted with their every word half an hour after it is spoken; and from certain indices, into which I hardly need enter, my opinion is that, allowing something for exaggeration, they are not very far wrong.

In London and Paris the foreigner is subjected, though perhaps he may not know it, to the same surveillance, and till lately his letters were liable to be opened at the Post-office. We can not, then, wonder that at Great Salt Lake City, a stranger, before proving himself at least to be harmless, should begin by being an object of suspicion.

Mr. Stenhouse circulated freely among the crowd, and introduced me to many whose names I do not remember; in almost every case the introduction was followed by some invitation. He now exchanged a word with this " brother," then a few sentences with that " sister," carefully suppressing the Mr. and Madam of the Eastern States. The fraternal address gives a patriarchal and somewhat Oriental flavor to Mormon converse; like other things, however, it is apt to run into extremes. If a boy in the streets be asked, " What's your name? " he will reply — if he condescends to do so — " I'm brother such-and-such's son." In order to distinguish children of different mothers, it is usual to prefix the maternal to the paternal parent's name, suppressing the given or Christian name of monogamic lands. Thus, for instance, my sons by Miss Brown, Miss Jones, and Miss Robinson, would call themselves Brother Brown Burton, Brother Jones Burton, and so on. The Saints — even the highest dignitaries — waive the Reverend; and the ridiculous Esquire, that " title much in use among vulgar people," which in Old and New England applies to every body, gentle or simple, has not yet extended to Great Salt Lake City. The Mormon pontiff and the eminences around him are simply Brother or Mister — they have the substance, and they disdain the shadow of power. *En revanche,* among the crowd there are as many colonels and majors — about ten being the proportion to one captain — as in the days when Mrs. Trollope set the Mississippi on fire. Sister is applied to women of all ages, thus avoiding the difficulty of addressing a dowager, as in the Eastern States, Madam, in contradistinction to Mrs., her daughter-in-law, or, what is worse, of calling her after the English way, old Mrs. A., or, *Scotticè,* Mrs. A. senior.

The dress of the fair sex has, I observed, already become peculiar. The article called in Cornwall a " gowk," in other parts of England a " cottage bonnet," and in the United States a " sun-bonnet," is here universally used, with the difference, however that the Mormons provide it with a long thick veil behind, which acts like a cape or shawl. A loose jacket and a petticoat, mostly of calico or of some inexpensive stuff, compose the *tout visible.* The wealthier affect silks, especially black. The merchants are careful to keep on hand a large stock of fancy goods, and millinery.

*   *   *   *   *   *   *

About noon, after a preliminary visit to Mr. Gilbert — and a visit in these lands always entails a certain amount of " smiling " — I met Governor Cumming in Main Street, and we proceeded together to our visit to the Prophet. After a slight scrutiny we passed the guard — which is dressed in plain clothes, and to the eye unarmed — and walking down the veranda, entered the Prophet's private office. Several people who were sitting there rose at Mr. Cumming's entrance. At a few words of introduction, Mr. Brigham Young advanced, shook hands with complete simplicity of manner, asked me to be seated on a sofa at one side of the room, and presented me to those present.

Under ordinary circumstances it would be unfair in a visitor to draw the portrait of one visited. But this is no common case. I have violated no rites of hospitality. Mr. Brigham Young is a " seer, revelator, and prophet, having all the gifts of God which he bestows upon the Head of the Church ": his memoirs, lithographs, photographs, and portraits have been published again and again; I add but one more likeness; and, finally, I have nothing to say except in his favor.

The Prophet was born at Whittingham, Vermont, on the 1st of June, 1801; he was consequently, in 1860, fifty-nine years of age; he looks about forty-five. *La célébrité vieillit* — I had expected to see a venerable-looking old man. Scarcely a gray thread appears in his hair, which is parted on the side, light colored, rather thick, and reaches below the ears with a half curl. He formerly wore it long, after the Western style; now it is cut level with the ear-lobes. The forehead is somewhat narrow, the eyebrows are thin, the eyes between gray and blue, with a calm, composed, and somewhat reserved expression: a slight droop in the left lid made me think that he had suffered from paralysis; I afterward heard that the ptosis is the result of a neuralgia which has long tormented him. For this reason he usually covers his head, except in his own house or in the Tabernacle. Mrs. Ward, who is followed by the " Revue des Deux-Mondes," therefore errs again in asserting that " his Mormon majesty never removes his hat in public." The nose, which is fine and somewhat sharp-pointed, is bent a little to the left. The lips are close like the New Englander's, and the teeth, especially those of the under jaw, are imperfect. The cheeks are rather fleshy, and the line between the alæ of the nose and the mouth is broken; the chin is somewhat peaked, and the face clean shaven, except under the jaws, where the beard is allowed to grow. The hands are well made, and not disfigured by rings. The figure is somewhat large, broad-shouldered, and stooping a little when standing.

The Prophet's dress was neat and plain as a Quaker's, all gray homespun except the cravat and waistcoat. His coat was of antique cut, and, like the pantaloons, baggy, and the buttons were black. A neck-tie of dark silk, with a large bow, was loosely passed round a starchless collar, which turned down of its own accord. The waistcoat was of black satin — once an article of almost national dress — single-breasted, and buttoned nearly to the neck, and a plain gold chain was passed into the pocket. The boots were Wellingtons, apparently of American make.

Altogether the Prophet's appearance was that of a gentleman farmer in New England — in fact, such as he is: his father was an agriculturist and revolutionary soldier, who settled " down East." He is a well-preserved man; a fact which some attribute to his habit of sleeping as the Citizen Proudhon so strongly advises, in solitude. His manner is at once affable and impressive, simple and courteous: his want of pretension contrasts favorably with certain pseudo-prophets that I have seen, each and every one of whom holds himself to be a " Logos," without other claim save a semi-maniacal self-esteem. He shows no signs of dogmatism, bigotry, or fanaticism, and never once entered — with me at least — upon the subject of religion. He impresses a stranger with a certain sense of power; his followers are, of course, wholly fascinated by his superior strength of brain. It is commonly said there is only one chief in Great Salt Lake City, and that is " Brigham." His temper is even and placid; his manner is cold — in fact, like his face, somewhat bloodless; but he is neither morose nor methodistic, and, where occasion requires, he can use all the weapons of ridicule to direful effect, and " speak a bit of his mind " in a style which no one forgets. He often reproves his erring followers in purposely violent language, making the terrors of a scolding the punishment in lieu of hanging for a stolen horse or cow. His powers of observation are intuitively strong, and his friends declare him to be gifted with an excellent memory and a perfect judgment of character. If he dislikes a stranger at the first interview, he never sees him again. Of his temperance and sobriety there is but one opinion. His life is ascetic: his favorite food is baked potatoes with a little buttermilk, and his drink water; he disapproves, as do all strict Mormons, of spirituous liquors, and never touches any thing stronger than a glass of thin Lager-bier; moreover, he abstains from tobacco. Mr. Hyde has accused him of habitual intemperance: he is, as his appearance shows, rather disposed to abstinence than to the reverse. Of his education I can not speak: " men, not books — deeds, not words," has ever been his motto; he probably has, as Mr. Randolph said of Mr. Johnston, " a mind uncorrupted by books." In the only discourse which I heard him deliver, he pronounced impĕtus, impētus. Yet he converses with ease and correctness, has neither snuffle nor pompousness, and speaks as an authority upon certain subjects, such as agriculture and stock-breeding. He assumes no airs of extra sanctimoniousness, and has the plain, simple manners of honesty. His followers deem him an angel of light, his foes a goblin damned: he is, I presume, neither one nor the other. I can not pronounce about his scrupulousness: all the world over, the sincerest religious belief and the practice of devotion are sometimes compatible not only with the most disorderly life, but with the most terrible crimes; for mankind mostly believes that

" Il est avec le ciel des accommodements."

He has been called hypocrite, swindler, forger, murderer. No one looks it less. The best authorities — from those who accuse Mr. Joseph Smith of the most heartless deception, to those who believe that he began as an impostor and ended as a prophet — find in Mr. Brigham Young " an earnest, obstinate egotistic enthusiasm, fanned by persecution and inflamed by bloodshed." He is the St. Paul of the new Dispensation: true and sincere, he gave point, and energy, and consistency to the somewhat disjointed turbulent, and unforeseeing fanaticism of Mr. Joseph Smith; and if he has not been able to create, he has shown himself great in controlling circumstances. Finally, there is a total absence of pretension in his manner, and he has been so long used to power that he cares nothing for its display.

The arts by which he rules the heterogeneous mass of conflicting elements are indomitable will, profound secrecy, and uncommon astuteness.

Such is His Excellency President Brigham Young, "painter and glazier" — his earliest craft — prophet, revelator, translator, and seer; the man who is revered as king or kaiser, pope or pontiff never was; who, like the Old Man of the Mountain, by holding up his hand could cause the death of any one within his reach; who, governing as well as reigning, long stood up to fight with the sword of the Lord, and with his few hundred guerrillas, against the then mighty power of the United States; who has outwitted all diplomacy opposed to him; and, finally, who made a treaty of peace with the President of the Great Republic as though he had wielded the combined power of France, Russia, and England.

Remembering the frequent query, "What shall be done with the Mormons?" I often asked the Saints, Who will or can succeed Mr. Brigham Young? No one knows, and no one cares. They reply, with a singular disdain for the usual course of history, with a perfect faith that their Cromwell will know no Richard as his successor, that, as when the crisis came the Lord raised up in him, then unknown and little valued, a fitting successor to Mr. Joseph Smith — of whom, by-the-by, they now speak with a respectful reverential *sotto voce,* as Christians name the Founder of their faith — so, when the time for deciding the succession shall arrive, the chosen Saints will not be left without a suitable leader.

The conversation, which lasted about an hour, ended by the Prophet asking me the line of my last African exploration, and whether it was the same country traversed by Dr. Livingstone. I replied that it was about ten degrees north of the Zambezi. Mr. A. Carrington rose to point out the place upon a map which hung against the wall, and placed his finger too near the equator, when Mr. Brigham Young said, " A little lower down." There are many educated men in England who could not have corrected the mistake as well: witness the "London Review," in which the gentleman who " does the geography " — not having the fear of a certain society in Whitehall Place before his eyes — confounds, in all the pomp of criticism upon the said exploration, lakes which are not less than 200 miles apart.

When conversation began to flag, we rose up, shook hands, as is the custom here, all round, and took leave. The first impression left upon my mind by this short *séance,* and it was subsequently confirmed, was, that the Prophet is no common man, and that he has none of the weakness and vanity which characterize the common uncommon man. A desultory conversation can not be expected to draw out a master spirit, but a truly distinguished character exercises most often an instinctive — some would call it a mesmeric — effect upon those who come in contact with it; and as we hate or despise at first sight, and love or like at first sight, so Nature teaches us at first sight what to respect. It is observable that, although every Gentile writer has represented Mr. Joseph Smith as a heartless impostor, few have ventured to apply the term to Mr. Brigham Young. I also remarked an instance of the veneration shown by his followers, whose affection for him is equaled only by the confidence with which they intrust to him their dearest interests in this world and in the next. After my visit many congratulated me, as would the followers of the Tien Wong, or heavenly King, upon having at last seen what they consider "a per se" the most remarkable man in the world.

I was unwilling to add to the number of those who had annoyed the Prophet by domestic allusions, and therefore have no direct knowledge of the extent to which he carries polygamy; some Gentiles allow him seventeen, others thirty-six, out of a household of seventy members; others an indefinite number of wives scattered through the different settlements. Of these, doubtless, many are but wives by name, such, for instance, as the widows of the late Prophet; and others are married more for the purpose of building up for themselves spiritual kingdoms than for the normal purpose of matrimony. I should judge the Prophet's progeny to be numerous from the following circumstance: On one occasion, when standing with him on the belvidere, my eye fell upon a new erection: it could be compared externally to nothing but an English gentleman's hunting stables, with their little clock-tower, and I asked him what it was intended for. "A private school for my children," he replied, "directed by Brother E. B. Kelsey." The harem is said to have cost $30,000.

On the extreme west of this block, backed by a pound for estrays, which is no longer used, lies the Tithing House and Deserét Store, a long, narrow, upper-storied building, with cellars, store-rooms, receiving-rooms, pay-rooms, and writing offices. At this time of the year it chiefly contains linseed, and rags for paper-making; after the harvest it is well stuffed with grains and cereals, which are taken instead of money payment. There is nothing more unpopular among the American Gentiles, or, indeed, more unintelligible to them, than these Mosaic tithes, which the English converts pay, from habit, without a murmur. They serve for scandalous insinuations, viz., that the chiefs are leeches that draw the people's golden blood; that the imposts are compulsory, and that they are embezzled and peculated by the principal dignitaries. I have reason to believe that the contrary is the case. The tithes which are paid into the "Treasury of the Lord" upon the property of a Saint on profession, and afterward upon his annual income, or his time, or by substitute, are wholly voluntary. It sometimes happens that a man casts his all into the bosom of the Church; in this case the all is not refused, but — may I ask — by what Church body, Islamitic, Christian, or pagan, would it be? If the Prophet takes any thing from the Tithing House, he pays for it like other men. The writers receive stipends like other writers, and no more; of course, if any one — clerk or lawyer — wishes to do the business of the Church gratis, he is graciously allowed to.

*   *   *   *   *   *   *

I was eager to attend the services at the Tabernacle on my first Sunday in Zion and found it, as I expected, overcrowded. All wore their hats till the address began, and then all uncovered. By my side was the face of a bleareyed English servant-girl; *en revanche* in front was a charming American mother and child: she had, what I have remarked in Mormon meetings at Saville House and other places in Europe, an unusual development of the organ which phrenologists call veneration. I did not see any Bloomers " displaying a serviceable pair of brogues," or " pictures of Grant Thorburn in petticoats." There were a few specimens of the " Yankee woman," formerly wondrous grim, with a shrewd, thrifty gray eye, at once cold and eager, angular in body and mind, tall, bony, and squareshouldered, now softened and humanized by transplantation and transposition to her proper place. The number of old people astonished me; half a dozen were sitting on the same bench; these broken-down men and decrepit crones had come to lay their bones in the Holy City; their presence speaks equally well for their faith and for the kind-heartedness of those who had brought the encumbrance. I remarked some Gentiles in the Bowery; many, however, do not care to risk what they may hear there touching themselves.

At 10 A.M. the meeting opened with a spiritual song. Then Mr. Wallace — a civilized-looking man lately returned from foreign travel — being called upon by the presiding elder for the day, opened the meeting with prayer, of which the two short-hand writers in the tribune proceeded to take notes. The matter, as is generally the case with returned missionaries delivering their budget, was good; the manner was somewhat Hibernian; the " valleys of the mountains " — a stock phrase, appeared and reappeared like the speechifying Patlander's eternal " emerald green hills and beautiful pretty valleys." He ended by imploring a blessing upon the (Mormon) President, and all those in authority; Gentiles of course were included. The conclusion was an amen, in which all hands joined: it reminded me of the historical practice of " humming " in the seventeenth century, which caused the universities to be called *" Hum et Hissimi auditores."*

Next arose Bishop Abraham O. Smoot, second mayor of Zion, and successor to the late Jedediah M. Grant, who began with " Brethering," and proceeded at first in a low and methody tone of voice, " hardly audible in the gallery," to praise the Saints, and to pitch into the apostates. His delivery was by no means fluent, even when he warmed. He made undue use of the regular Wesleyan organ — the nose; but he appeared to speak excellent sense in execrable English. He recalled past persecutions without over-asperity, and promised future prosperity without over-prophecy. As he was in the midst of an allusion to the President, entered Mr. Brigham Young, and all turned their faces, even the old lady — who, dear soul! from Hanover Square to far San Francisco, placidly reposes through the discourse.

The Prophet was dressed, as usual, in gray homespun and homewoven: he wore, like most of the elders, a tall, steeple-crowned straw hat, with a broad black ribbon, and he had the rare refinement of black kid gloves. He entered the tribune covered and sat down, apparently greeting those near him. A man in a fit was carried out pumpward. Bishop Smoot concluded with informing us that we should live for God. Another hymn was sung. Then a great silence, which told us that something was about to happen: *that* old man held his cough; *that* old lady awoke with a start; *that* child ceased to squall. Mr. Brigham Young removed his hat, advanced to the end of the tribune, expectorated stooping over the spittoon, which was concealed from sight by the boarding, restored the balance of fluid by a glass of water from a well-filled decanter on the stand, and, leaning slightly forward upon both hands propped on the green baize of the tribune, addressed his followers.

The discourse began slowly; word crept titubantly after word, and the opening phrases were hardly audible; but as the orator warmed, his voice rose high and sonorous, and a fluency so remarkable succeeded falter and hesitation, that — although the phenomenon is not rare in strong speakers — the latter seemed almost to have been a work of art. The manner was pleasing and animated, and the matter fluent, impromptu, and well turned, spoken rather than preached: if it had a fault it was rather rambling and unconnected. Of course, colloquialisms of all kinds were introduced, such as " he become," " for you and I," and so forth. The gestures were easy and rounded, not without a certain grace, though evidently untaught; one, however, must be excepted, namely, that of raising and shaking the forefinger; this is often done in the Eastern States, but the rest of the world over it is considered threatening and bullying. The address was long. God is a mechanic. Mormonism is a great fact. Religion had made him (the speaker) the happiest of men. He was ready to dance like a Shaker. At this sentence the Prophet, who is a good mimic, and has much of the old New English quaint humor, raised his right arm, and gave, to the amusement of the congregation, a droll imitation of Anne Lee's followers. The Gentiles had sent an army to lay waste Zion, and what had they done? Why hung one of their own tribe! and that, too, on the Lord's day![1] The Saints have a glorious destiny

[1] Alluding to one Thos. H. Ferguson, a Gentile; he killed, on Sept. 17th, 1859, in a drunken moment, A. Carpenter, who kept a boot and shoe store. Judge Sinclair, according to the Mormons, was exceedingly anxious that somebody should be *sus. per coll.*, and, although intoxication is usually admitted as a plea in the Western States, he ignored it,

before them, and their morality is remarkable as the beauty of the Promised Land: the soft breeze blowing over the Bowery, and the glorious sunshine outside, made the allusion highly appropriate. The Lamanites, or Indians, are a religious people. All races know a God and may be saved. After a somewhat lengthy string of sentences concerning the great tribulation coming on earth — it has been coming for the last 1800 years — he concluded with good wishes to visitors and Gentiles generally, with a solemn blessing upon the President of the United States, the territorial governor, and all such as be in authority over us, and, with an amen which was loudly re-echoed by all around, he restored his hat and resumed his seat.

Having heard much of the practical good sense which characterizes the Prophet's discourse, I was somewhat disappointed: probably the occasion had not been propitious. During the discourse, a Saint, in whose family some accident had occurred, was called out, but the accident failed to affect the riveted attention of the audience.

Then arose Mr. Heber C. Kimball, the second President. He is the model of a Methodist, a tall and powerful man, a " gentleman in black," with small, dark, piercing eyes, and clean-shaven blue face. He affects the Boanerges style, and does not at times disdain the part of Thersites: from a certain dislike to the Nonconformist rant and whine, he prefers an every-day manner of speech, which savors rather of familiarity than of reverence. The people look more amused when he speaks than when others harangue them, and they laugh readily, as almost all crowds will, at the thinnest phantom of a joke. Mr. Kimball's movements contrasted strongly with those of his predecessors; they consisted now

and hanged the man on Sunday. Mr. Ferguson was executed in a place behind the city; he appeared costumed in a Robin Hood style, and complained bitterly to the Mormon troops, who were drawn out, that his request to be shot had not been granted.

of a stone-throwing gesture delivered on tiptoe, then of a descending movement, as

> "When pulpit, drum ecclesiastic,
> Was beat with fist and not with stick."

He began with generalisms about humility, faithfulness, obeying counsel, and not beggaring one's neighbor. Addressing the hand-cart emigrants, newly arrived from the " sectarian world," he warned them to be on the look-out, or that every soul of them would be taken in and shaved (a laugh). Agreeing with the Prophet — Mr. Kimball is said to be his echo — in a promiscuous way concerning the morality of the Saints, he felt it notwithstanding his duty to say that among them were " some of the greatest rascals in the world " (a louder laugh, and N.B., the Mormons are never spared by their own preachers). After a long suit of advice, *à propos de rien,* to missionaries, he blessed, amen'd, and sat down.

After Mr. Kimball's address, a list of names for whom letters were lying unclaimed was called from the platform. Mr. Eldridge, a missionary lately returned from foreign travel, adjourned the meeting till 2 P.M., delivered the prayer of dismissal, during which all stood up, and ended with the benediction and amen. The Sacrament was not administered on this occasion. It is often given, and reduced to the very elements of a ceremony; even water is used instead of wine, because the latter is of Gentile manufacture. Two elders walk up and down the rows, one carrying a pitcher, the other a plate of broken bread, and each Saint partakes of both.

ON THE COMSTOCK

J. ROSS BROWNE

"A Peep at Washoe," and "Washoe Revisited." Reprinted by permission of *Harper's New Monthly Magazine,* Vol. XXII, No. 123 and Vol. XXXI, No. 181. Harper and Brothers, New York.

I

1860

I WAS desirous of seeing as much of the mining region as possible, and with this view took the stage for Virginia City. The most remarkable peculiarity on the road was the driver, whose likeness I struck in a happy moment of inspiration. At Silver City, eight miles from Carson, I dismounted, and proceeded the rest of the way on foot. The road here becomes rough and hilly, and but little is to be seen of the city except a few tents and board shanties. Half a mile beyond is a remarkable gap cut by Nature through the mountain, as if for the express purpose of giving the road an opportunity to visit Virginia City.

As I passed through the Devil's Gate it struck no indecorous sense. I was simply about to ask where he lived, when, looking up the road, I saw amidst the smoke and din of shivered rocks, where grimy imps were at work blasting for ore, a string of adventurers laden with picks, shovels, and crowbars; kegs of powder, frying-pans, pitchforks, and other instruments of torture — all wearily toiling in the same direction; decrepit old men, with avarice imprinted upon their furrowed brows; Jews and Gentiles, foot-weary and haggard; the young and the old, the strong and the weak, all alike burning with an unhallowed lust for lucre; and then I shuddered as the truth flashed upon me that they were going straight to — Virginia City.

Every foot of the cañon was claimed, and gangs of miners were at work all along the road, digging and delving into the earth like so many infatuated gophers. Many of these unfortunate creatures lived in holes dug into the side of the hill, and here and there a blanket thrown over a few stakes served as a domicile to shield them from the weather.

At Gold Hill, two miles beyond the Gate, the excitement was quite pitiable to behold. Those who were not at work, burrowing holes into the mountain, were gathered in gangs around the whisky saloons, pouring liquid fire down their throats and swearing all the time in a manner so utterly reckless as to satisfy me they had long since bid farewell to hope.

This district is said to be exceedingly rich in gold, and I fancy it may well be so, for it is certainly rich in nothing else. A more barren-looking and forbidding spot could scarcely be found elsewhere on the face of the earth. The whole aspect of the country indicates that it must have been burned up in hot fires many years ago and reduced to a mass of cinders; or scraped up from all the desolate spots in the known world, and thrown over the Sierra Nevada Mountains in a confused mass to be out of the way. I do not wish to be understood as speaking disrespectfully of any of the works of creation; but it is inconceivable that this region should ever have been designed as an abode for man.

A short distance beyond Gold Hill we came in sight of the great mining capital of Washoe, the far famed Virginia City. In the course of a varied existence it had been my fortune to visit the city of Jerusalem, the city of Constantinople, the city of the Sea, the City of the Dead, the Seven Cities, and others of historical celebrity in the Old World; and many famous cities in the New, including Port Townsend, Crescent City, Benicia, and the New York of the Pacific; but I had never yet beheld such a city as that which now burst upon my distended organs of vision.

On a slope of mountains speckled with snow, sage-bushes, and mounds of upturned earth, without any apparent beginning or end, congruity or regard for the eternal fitness of things, lay outspread the wondrous city of Virginia.

Frame shanties, pitched together as if by accident; tents of canvas, of blankets, of brush, of potato-sacks and old shirts, with empty whisky barrels for chimneys; smoky hovels of mud and stone; coyote holes in the mountain-side forcibly seized and held by men; pits and shafts with smoke issuing from every crevice; piles of goods and rubbish on craggy points, in the hollows, on the rocks, in the mud, in the snow, everywhere, scattered broadcast in pell-mell confusion, as if the clouds had suddenly burst overhead and rained down the dregs of all the flimsy, rickety, filthy little hovels and rubbish of merchandise that had ever undergone the process of evaporation from the earth since the days of Noah. The intervals of space, which may or may not have been streets, were dotted over with human beings of such sort, variety, and numbers that the famous ant-hills of Africa were as nothing in the comparison. To say that they were rough, muddy, unkempt and unwashed, would be but faintly expressive of their actual appearance; they were all this by reason of exposure to the weather; but they seemed to have caught the very diabolical tint and grime of the whole place. Here and there, to be sure, a San Francisco dandy of the " boiled shirt " and " stove-pipe " pattern loomed up in proud consciousness of the triumphs of art under adverse circumstances; but they were merely peacocks in the barn-yard.

A fraction of the crowd, as we entered the precincts of the town, were engaged in a lawsuit relative to a question of title. The arguments used on both sides were empty whisky-bottles, after the fashion of the *Basilinum,* or club law, which, according to Addison, prevailed in the colleges of learned men in former times. Several of the disputants had already been knocked down and convinced, and various others were freely shedding their blood in the cause of justice. Even the bull-terriers took an active part — or, at least, a very prominent part. The difficulty was about the ownership of a lot, which had been staked out by one party and " jumped " by another. Some two or three hundred disinterested observers stood by, enjoying the spectacle, several of them with their hands on their revolvers, to be ready in case of any serious issue; but these dangerous weapons are only used on great occasions — a refusal to drink, or some illegitimate trick at monte.

Upon fairly reaching what might be considered the centre of the town, it was interesting to observe the manners and customs of the place. Groups of keen speculators were huddled around the corners, in earnest consultation about the rise and fall of stocks; rough customers, with red and blue flannel shirts, were straggling in from the Flowery Diggings, the Desert, and other rich points, with specimens of croppings in their hands, or offering bargains in the " Rogers," the " Lady Bryant," the " Mammoth," the " Woolly Horse," and Heaven knows how many other valuable *leads,* at prices varying from ten to seventy-five dollars a foot. Small knots of the knowing ones were in confidential interchange of thought on the subject of every other man's business; here and there a loose man was caught by the button, and led aside behind a shanty to be " stuffed " ; every body had some grand secret, which nobody else could find out; and the game of "dodge " and " pump " was universally played. Jew clothing-men were setting out their goods and chattels in front of wretched-looking tenements; monte-dealers, gamblers, thieves, cut-throats, and murderers were mingling miscellaneously in the dense crowds gathered around the bars of the drinking saloons. Now and then a half-starved Pah-Ute or Washoe Indian came tottering along under a heavy press of fagots and whisky. On the main street, where the mass of the population were gathered, a jaunty fellow who had " made a good thing of it " dashed through the crowds on horseback, accoutred in genuine Mexican style, swinging his *reata* over his head, and yelling like a devil let loose. All this time the wind blew in terrific gusts from the four quarters of the compass, tearing away signs, capsizing tents, scattering the grit from the gravel-banks with blinding force in every body's eyes, and sweeping furiously around every crook and corner in search of some sinner to smite. Never was such a wind as this—so scathing, so searching, so given to penetrate the very core of suffering humanity; disdaining overcoats, and utterly scornful of shawls and blankets. It actually seemed to double up, twist, pull, push, and screw the unfortunate biped till his muscles cracked and his bones rattled — following him wherever he sought refuge, pursuing him down the back of the neck, up the coat-sleeves, through the legs of his panta-loons, into his boots — in short, it was the most villainous and persecuting wind that ever blew, and I boldly protest that it did nobody good.

Yet, in the midst of the general wreck and crash of mat-ter, the business of trading in claims, " bucking," and " bear-ing " went on as if the zephyrs of Virginia were as soft and balmy as those of San Francisco.

This was surely — No matter; nothing on earth could aspire to competition with such a place. It was essentially infernal in every aspect, whether viewed from the Comstock Ledge or the summit of Gold Hill. Nobody seemed to own the lots except by right of possession; yet there was trading in lots to an unlimited extent. Nobody had any money; yet every body was a millionaire in silver claims. Nobody had any credit, yet every body bought thousands of feet of glittering ore. Sales were made in the " Mammoth," the " Lady Bryant," the " Sacramento," the " Winnebunk," and the innumerable other " outside claims," at the most astounding figures — but not a dime passed hands. All was silver underground, and deeds and mortgages on top; silver, silver every where, but scarce a dollar in coin. The small change had somehow gotten out of the hands of the public into the gambling saloons.

Every speck of ground covered by canvas, boards, baked mud, brush, or other architectural material, was jammed to suffocation; there were sleeping houses, twenty feet by thirty, in which from one hundred and fifty to two hundred solid sleepers sought slumber at night, at a dollar a head; tents, eight by ten, offering accommodations to the multitude; any thing or any place, even a stall in a stable, would have been a luxury.

The chief hotel, called, if I remember, the " Indication," or the " Hotel de Haystack," or some such euphonious name, professed to accommodate three hundred live men, and it doubtless did so, for the floors were covered from the attic to the solid earth — three hundred human beings in a tinder-box not bigger than a first-class hencoop! But they were sorry-looking sleepers as they came forth each morning, swearing at the evil genius who had directed them to this miserable spot — every man a dollar and a pound of flesh poorer. I saw some, who perhaps were short of means, take surreptitious naps against the posts and walls in the bar-room, while they ostensibly professed to be mere spectators.

In truth, wherever I turned there was much to confirm the forebodings with which I had entered the Devil's Gate. The deep pits on the hill-sides; the blasted and barren appearance of the whole country; the unsightly hodge-podge of a town; the horrible confusion of tongues; the roaring, raving drunkards at the bar-rooms, swilling fiery liquids from morning till night; the flaring and flaunting gambling-saloons, filled with desperadoes of the vilest sort; the ceaseless torrent of imprecations that shocked the ear on every side; the mad speculations and feverish thirst for gain —

all combined to give me a forcible impression of the un-hallowed character of the place.

What dreadful savage is that? I asked, as a ferocious-looking monster in human shape stalked through the crowd. Is it — can it be the — No; that's only a murderer. He shot three men a few weeks ago, and will probably shoot another before night. And this aged and decrepit man, his thin locks floating around his haggard and unshaved face, and matted with filth? That's a speculator from San Francisco. See how wildly he grasps at every " indication," as if he had a lease of life for a thousand years! And this bull-dog fellow, with a mutilated face, button-holing every by-passer? That fellow? Oh, he's only a " bummer " in search of a cocktail. And this — and this — all these crazy-look-ing wretches, running hither and thither with hammers and stones in their hands, calling one another aside, hurrying to the assay-offices, pulling out papers, exchanging mysteri-ous signals — who and what are all these? Oh, these are Washoe millionaires. They are deep in " outside claims." The little fragments of rock they carry in their hands are " croppings " and " indications " from the " Wake-up-Jake," " Root-Hog-or-Die," " Wild-Cat," " Grizzly Hill," " Dry-up," " Same Horse," " Let-her-Rip," " You Bet," " Gouge-Eye," and other famous ledges and companies, in which they own some thousands of feet. Hold, good friend; I am convinced there is no rest for the wicked. All night long these dreadful noises continue; the ears are distracted with an unintelligible jargon of "croppings," " ledges," " lodes," " leads," " indications," " feet," and " strikes," and the nostrils offended with foul odors of boots, old pipes, and dirty blankets — who can doubt the locality? If the climate is more rigorous than Dante describes it — if Calypso might search in vain for Ulysses in such a motley crowd — these apparent differences are not inconsistent with the general theory of changes produced by American emigration and the sudden conglomeration of such incongruous elements.

I slept, or rather tried to sleep, at one " Zip's," where there were only twenty " bunks " in the room, and was fortunate in securing a bunk even there. But the great Macbeth himself, laboring under the stings of an evil conscience, could have made a better hand of sleeping than I did at Zip's. It proved to be a general meeting-place for my San Francisco friends, and as they were all very rich in mining claims, and bent on getting still richer, they were continually making out deeds, examining titles, trading and transferring claims, discussing the purchases and prospects of the day, and exhibiting the most extraordinary " indications " yet discovered, in which one or other of them held an interest of fifty or a hundred feet, worth, say, a thousand dollars a foot. Between the cat-naps of oblivion that visited my eyes there was a constant din of " croppings " — " feet " — " fifty thousand dollars " — " struck it rich! " — " the Comstock Ledge! " — " the Billy Choller! " — " Miller on the rise! " — " Mammoth! " — " Sacramento! " — " Lady Bryant! " — " a thousand feet more! " — " great bargain " — " forty dollars a foot! " — crash! rip! bang! — "an earthquake! " — " run for your lives! "

What the deuce is the matter?

It happened thus one night. The wind was blowing in terrific gusts. In the midst of the general clatter on the subject of croppings, bargains, and indications, down came our next neighbor's house on the top of us with a terrific crash. For a moment it was difficult to tell which house was the ruin. Amidst projecting and shivered planks, the flapping of canvas, and the howling of the wind, it really seemed as if chaos had come again. But " Zip's " was well braced, and stood the shock without much damage, a slight heel and lurch to leeward being the chief result. I could not help thinking, as I turned in again after the alarm, that there could no longer be a doubt on the subject which had already occasioned me so many unpleasant reflections. It even seemed as if I smelled something like brimstone; but upon calling to Zip to know what was the matter, he informed me that he was " only dryin' the boots on the stove."

Notwithstanding the number of physicians who had already hoisted their " shingles," there was much sickness in Virginia, owing chiefly to exposure and dissipation, but in some measure to the deleterious quality of the water. Nothing more was wanting to confirm my original impressions. The water was certainly the worst ever used by man. Filtered through the Comstock Lead, it carried with it much of the plumbago, arsenic, copperas, and other poisonous minerals alleged to exist in that vein. The citizens of Virginia had discovered what they conceived to be an infallible way of " correcting it " ; that is to say, it was their practice to mix a spoonful of water in half a tumbler of whisky, and then drink it. The whisky was supposed to neutralize the bad effects of the water. Sometimes it was considered good to mix it with gin. I was unable to see how any advantage could be gained in this way. The whisky contained strychnine, oil of tobacco, tarantula juice, and various effective poisons of the same general nature, including a dash of corrosive sublimate; and the gin was manufactured out of turpentine and whisky, with a sprinkling of Prussic acid to give it flavor. For my part, I preferred taking poison in its least complicated form, and therefore adhered to the water. With hot saleratus bread, beans fried in grease, and such drink as this, it was no wonder that scores were taken down sick from day to day.

Sickness is bad enough at the best of times; but here the condition of the sick was truly pitiable. There was scarcely a tenement in the place that could be regarded as affording shelter against the piercing wind; and crowded as every tent and hovel was to its utmost capacity, it was hard even to find a vacant spot to lie down, much less sleep or rest in comfort. Many had come with barely means sufficient to defray their expenses to the diggings, in the confident belief that they would immediately strike "something rich." Or, if they failed in that, they could work a while on wages. But the highest wages here for common labor were three dollars a day, while meals were a dollar each, and lodgings the same. It was a favor to get work for "grub." Under such circumstances, when a poor fellow fell sick, his recovery could only be regarded as a matter of luck. No record of the deaths was kept. The mass of the emigration were strangers to each other, and it concerned nobody in particular when a man "pegged out," except to put him in a hole somewhere out of the way.

I soon felt the bad effects of the water. Possibly I had committed an error in not mixing it with the other poisons; but it was quite poisonous enough alone to give me violent pains in the stomach and a very severe diarrhea. At the same time, I was seized with an acute attack of rheumatism in the shoulder and neuralgic pains in the head. The complication of miseries which I now suffered was beyond all my calculations of the hardships of mining life. As yet I had struck nothing better than " Winn's Restaurant," where I took my meals. The Comstock Ledge was all very fine; but a THOUSAND DOLLARS A FOOT! Who ever had a thousand dollars to put in a running foot of ground, when not even the great Comstock himself could tell where it was running to. On the whole, I did not consider the prospect cheering.

At this period there were no laws of any kind in the district for the preservation of order. Some regulations had been established to secure the right of discovery to claimants; but they were loose and indefinite, differing in each district according to the caprice of the miners, and subject to no enforcement except that of the revolver. In some localities the original discoverer of a vein was entitled to 400 running feet; he could put down the names of as many friends as he chose at 200 feet each. Notice had to be recorded at certain places of record, designating the date and location of discovery. All " leads " were taken up with their " dips, spurs, and angles." But who was to judge of the " dips, spurs, and angles " ? That was the difficulty. Every man ran them to suit himself. The Comstock Ledge was in a mess of confusion. The shareholders had the most enlarged views of its " dips, spurs, and angles " ; but those who struck croppings above and below were equally liberal in their notions; so that, in fine, every body's spurs were running into every body else's angles. The Cedar Hill Company were spurring the Miller Company; the Virginia Ledge was spurring the Continuation; the Dow Company were spurring the Billy Choller, and so on. It was a free fight all round, in which the dips, spurs, and angles might be represented after the pattern of a bunch of snakes.

The contention was very lively. Great hopes were entertained that when Judge Cradlebaugh arrived he would hold Court, and then there would be some hope of settling these conflicting claims. I must confess I did not share in the opinion that law would settle any dispute in which silver was concerned. The Almaden Mine case is not yet settled, and never will be as long as there are judges and juries to sit upon it, and lawyers to argue it, and silver to pay expenses. Already Virginia City was infested with gentlemen of the bar, thirsting and hungering for chances at the Comstock. If it could only be brought into Court, what a picking of bones there would be!

When the snow began to clear away there was no end to the discoveries alleged to be made every day. The Flowery Diggings, six miles below Virginia, were represented to be wonderfully rich — so rich, indeed, that the language of every speculator who held a claim there partook of the flowery character of the diggings. The whole country was staked off to the distance of twenty or thirty miles. Every hill-side was grubbed open, and even the Desert was pegged, like the sole of a boot, with stakes designating claims.

Those who could not spare time to go out "prospecting" hired others, or furnished provisions and pack-mules, and went shares. If the prospecting party struck "any thing rich," it was expected they would share it honestly; but I always fancied they would find it more profitable to hold on to that, and find some other rich lead for the resident partners.

In Virginia City a man who had been at work digging a cellar found rich indications. He immediately laid claim to a whole street covered with houses. The excitement produced by this "streak of luck" was perfectly frantic. Hundreds went to work grubbing up the ground under their own and their neighbors' tents; and it was not long before the whole city seemed in a fair way of being undermined. The famous *Winn,* as I was told, struck the richest lead of all directly under his restaurant, and was next day considered worth a million of dollars. The dips, spurs, and angles of these various discoveries covered every foot of ground within an area of six miles. It was utterly impossible that a fraction of the city could be left. Owners of lots protested in vain. The mining laws were paramount where there was no law at all. There was no security to personal property, or even to persons. He who turned in to sleep at night might find himself in a pit of silver by morning. At least it was thus when I made up my mind to escape from that delectable region; and now, four months later, I really don't know whether the great City of Virginia is still in existence, or whether the inhabitants have not found a "deeper deep, still threatening to devour."

It must not be supposed, from the general character of the population, that Virginia City was altogether destitute of men skilled in scientific pursuits. There were few, indeed, who did not profess to know something of geology; and as for assayers and assay offices, they were almost as numerous as bar-keepers and groggeries. A tent, a furnace, half a dozen crucibles, a bottle of acid, and a hammer, generally comprised the entire establishment; but it is worthy of remark that the assays were always satisfactory. Silver, or indications of silver, were sure to be found in every specimen. I am confident some of these learned gentlemen in the assay business could have detected the precious metals in an Irish potato or a round of cheese for a reasonable consideration.

It was also a remarkable peculiarity of the country that the great "Comstock Lead" was discovered to exist in almost every locality, however remote or divergent from the original direction of the vein. I know a gentleman who certainly discovered a continuation of the Comstock forty miles from the Ophir mines, and at an angle of more than sixty degrees. But how could the enterprising adventurer fail to hit upon something rich, when every clod of earth and fragment of rock contained, according to the assays, both silver and gold? There was not a coyote hole in the ground that did not develop "indications." I heard of one lucky fellow who struck upon a rich vein, and organized an extensive company on the strength of having stumped his toe. Claims were even staked out and companies organized on "indications" rooted up by the squirrels and gophers. If they were not always indications of gold or silver, they were sure to contain copper, lead, or some other valuable mineral — plumbago or iridium, for instance. One man actually professed to have discovered "ambergris"; but I think he must have been an old whaler.

The complications of ills which had befallen me soon became so serious that I resolved to get away by hook or crook, if it was possible to cheat the —— corporate authorities of their dues. I had not come there to enlist in the service of Mammon at such wages.

Bundling up my pack one dark morning, I paid " Zip " the customary dollar, and while the evil powers were roistering about the grog-shops, taking their early bitters, made good my escape from the accursed place. Weak as I was, the hope of never seeing it again gave me nerve; and when I ascended the first elevation on the way to Gold Hill, and cast a look back over the confused mass of tents and hovels, and thought of all I had suffered there in the brief space of a few days, I involuntarily exclaimed, "If ever I put foot in that hole again, may the —"

But perhaps I had better not use strong language till I once more get clear of the Devil's Gate.

II

1864

I was prepared to find great changes on the route from Carson to Virginia City. At Empire City — which was nothing but a sage-desert inhabited by Dutch Nick on the occasion of my early explorations — I was quite bewildered with the busy scenes of life and industry. Quartz-mills and sawmills had completely usurped the valley along the head of the Carson River; and now the hammering of stamps, the hissing of steam, the whirling clouds of smoke from tall chimneys, and the confused clamor of voices from a busy multitude, reminded one of a manufacturing city. Here, indeed, was progress of a substantial kind.

Further beyond, at Silver City, there were similar evidences of prosperity. From the descent into the cañon through the Devil's Gate, and up the grade to Gold Hill, it is almost a continuous line of quartz-mills, tunnels, dumps, sluices, water-wheels, frame shanties, and grog-shops.

Gold Hill itself has swelled into the proportions of a city. It is now practically a continuation of Virginia. Here the evidences of busy enterprise are peculiarly striking. The whole hill is riddled and honey-combed with shafts and tunnels. Engine-houses for hoisting are perched on points apparently inaccessible; quartz-mills of various capacities line the sides of the cañon; the main street is well flanked by brick stores, hotels, express-offices, saloons, restaurants, groggeries, and all those attractive places of resort which go to make up a flourishing mining town. Even a newspaper is printed here, which I know to be a spirited and popular institution, having been viciously assailed by the same. A runaway team of horses, charging full tilt down the street, greeted our arrival in a lively and characteristic manner, and came very near capsizing our stage. One man was run over some distance below, and partially crushed; but as somebody was killed nearly every day, such a meagre result afforded no general satisfaction.

Descending the slope of the ridge that divides Gold Hill from Virginia City a strange scene attracts the eye. He who gazes upon it for the first time is apt to doubt if it be real. Perhaps there is not another spot upon the face of the globe that presents a scene so weird and desolate in its natural aspect, yet so replete with busy life, so animate with human interest. It is as if a wondrous battle raged, in which the combatants were man and earth. Myriads of swarthy, bearded, dust-covered men are piercing into the grim old mountains, ripping them open, thrusting murderous holes through their naked bodies; piling up engines to cut out their vital arteries; stamping and crushing up with infernal machines their disemboweled fragments, and holding fiendish revels amidst the chaos of destruction; while the mighty earth, blasted, barren, and scarred by the tempests of ages, fiercely affronts the foe, smiting him with disease and death; scoffing at his puny assaults with a grim scorn; ever grand in his desolation, ever dominant in the infinity of his endurance. "Come!" he seems to mutter, " dig, delve, pierce, and bore, with your picks, your shovels, and your infernal machines; wring out of my veins a few globules of the precious blood; hoard it, spend it, gamble for it, bring perdition to your souls with it — do what you will, puny insects! Sooner or later the death-blow smites you, and Earth swallows you! From earth you came — to earth you go again!"

The city lies on a rugged slope, and is singularly diversified in its uprisings and downfallings. It is difficult to determine, by any system of observation or measurement, upon what principle it was laid out. My impression is that it was never laid out at all, but followed the dips, spurs, and angles of the immortal Comstock. Some of the streets run straight enough; others seem to dodge about at acute angles in search of an open space, as miners explore the subterranean regions in search of a lead. The cross-streets must have been forgotten in the original plan — if ever there was a plan about this eccentric city. Sometimes they happen accidentally at the most unexpected points; and sometimes they don't happen at all where you are sure to require them. A man in a hurry to get from the upper slope of the town to any opposite point below must try it under-ground or over the roofs of the houses, or take the customary circuit of half a mile. Every body seems to have built wherever he could secure a lot. The two main streets, it must be admitted, are so far regular as to follow pretty nearly the direction of the Comstock lead. On the lower slope, or plateau, the town, as viewed from any neighboring eminence, presents much the appearance of a vast number of shingle-roofs shaken down at random, like a jumbled pack of cards. All the streets are narrow, except where there are but few houses, and there they are wide enough at present. The business part of the town has been built up with astonishing rapidity. In the spring of 1860 there was nothing of it save a few frame shanties and canvas tents, and one or two rough stone cabins. It now presents some of the distinguishing features of a metropolitan city. Large and substantial brick houses, three or four stories high, with ornamental fronts, have filled up most of the gaps, and many more are still in progress of erection. The oddity of the plan, and variety of its architecture — combining most of the styles known

to the ancients, and some but little known to the moderns —
give this famous city a grotesque, if not picturesque, appearance, which is rather increased upon a close inspection.

Immense freight-wagons, with ponderous wheels and
axles, heavily laboring under prodigious loads of ore for
the mills, or groaning with piles of merchandise in boxes,
bales, bags, and crates, block the narrow streets. Powerful
teams of horses, mules, or oxen, numbering from eight to
sixteen animals to each wagon, make frantic efforts to drag
these land schooners over the ruts, and up the sudden rises,
or through the sinks of this rut-smitten, ever-rising, ever-
sinking city. A pitiable sight it is to see them! Smoking
hot, reeking with sweat, dripping with liquefied dust, they
pull, jerk, groan, fall back, and dash forward, tumble down,
kick, plunge, and bite; then buckle to it again, under the
galling lash; and so live and so struggle these poor beasts,
for their pittance of barley and hay, till they drop down
dead. How they would welcome death if they had souls!
Yet men have souls, and work hard too for their miserable
pittance of food. How many of the countless millions of
the earth yearn for death or welcome its coming? Even
the teamsters that drive these struggling labor-worn brutes
seem so fond of life that they scorn eternity. Brawny,
bearded fellows they are; their faces so ingrained with the
dust and grit of earth, and tanned to such an uncertain hue
by the scorching suns and dry winds of the road, that for
the matter of identity they might as well be Hindoos or
Belooches. With what malignant zeal they crack their
leather-thonged whips, and with what ferocious vigor they
rend the air with their imprecations! O Plutus! such swearing — a sliding scale of oaths to which swearing in all other
parts of the world is as the murmuring of a gentle brook to
the volume and rush and thunder of a cataract. The fertility of resource displayed by these reckless men; their ready
command of metaphor; their marvelous genius for strange,
startling and graphic combinations of slang and profanity;

their grotesque originality of inflexion and climax; their infatuated credulity in the understanding of dumb animals; would in the pursuit of any nobler art elevate them to a niche in the temple of fame. Surely if murder be deemed one of the Fine Arts in Virginia City, swearing ought not to be held in such common repute.

Entering the main street you pass on the upper side huge piles of earth and ore, hoisted out of the shafts or run out of the tunnels, and cast over the " dumps." The hill-sides, for a distance of more than a mile, are perfectly honeycombed. Steam-engines are puffing off their steam; smokestacks are blackening the air with their thick volumes of smoke; quartz-batteries are battering; hammers are hammering; subterranean blasts are bursting up the earth; picks and crow-bars are picking and crashing into the precious rocks; shanties are springing up, and carpenters are sawing and ripping and nailing; store-keepers are rolling their merchandise in and out along the way-side; fruit vendors are peddling their fruits; wagoners are tumbling out and piling in their freights of dry goods and ore; saloons are glittering with their gaudy bars and fancy glasses, and many-colored liquors, and thirsty men are swilling the burning poison; auctioneers, surrounded by eager and gaping crowds of speculators, are shouting off the stocks of delinquent stockholders; organ-grinders are grinding their organs and torturing consumptive monkeys; hurdy-gurdy girls are singing bacchanalian songs in bacchanalian dens; Jew clothiers are selling off prodigious assortments of worthless garments at ruinous prices; bill-stickers are sticking up bills of auctions, theatres, and new saloons; news-boys are crying the city papers with the latest telegraphic news; stages are dashing off with passengers for " Reese " ; and stages are dashing in with passengers from " Frisco " ; and the inevitable Wells, Fargo, and Co. are distributing letters, packages, and papers to the hungry multitude, amidst tempting piles of silver bricks and wonderful complications of scales, letter-boxes, clerks, account-books, and twenty-dollar pieces. All is life, excitement, avarice, lust, deviltry, and enterprise. A strange city truly, abounding in strange exhibitions and startling combinations of the human passions. Where upon earth is there such another place?

One of the most characteristic features of Virginia is the inordinate passion of the inhabitants for advertising. Not only are the columns of the newspapers filled with every possible species of advertisement, but the streets and hillsides are pasted all over with flaming bills. Says the proprietor of a small shanty, in letters that send a thrill of astonishment through your brain:

"LOOK HERE! *For fifty cents* YOU CAN GET A GOOD SQUARE MEAL at the HOWLING WILDERNESS SALOON!"

A square meal is not, as may be supposed, a meal placed upon the table in the form of a solid cubic block, but a substantial repast of pork and beans, onions, cabbage, and other articles of sustenance that will serve to fill up the corners of a miner's stomach.

The Jew clothing-stores present the most marvelous fertility of invention in this style of advertising. Bills are posted all over the doorways, in the windows, on the pavements, and on the various articles of clothing hung up for sale. He who runs may read:

"Now or Never! *Cheapest coats in the world!!* Pants given away!!! WALK IN, GENTS."

And so on without limit. New clothes and clothes doubtful are offered for sale at these prolific establishments, which are always selling off at cost or suicidal prices, yet never seem to be reduced in stock. I verily believe I saw hanging at the door of one of these shops the identical pair of stockings stolen from me several years ago at Strawberry.

Drinking establishments being rather numerous, the competition in this line of business gives rise to a very persuasive and attractive style of advertising. The bills are usually printed in florid and elaborately gilt letters, and frequently abound in pictures of an imaginative character. "Cosy Home," "Miner's Retreat," "Social Hall," "Empire," "Indication," "Fancy-Free," "Snug," "Shades," etc., are a few of the seductive names given to these places of popular resort; and the announcements are generally followed by a list of "choice liquors" and the gorgeous attractions of the billiard department, together with a hint that Dick, Jack, Dan, or Jerry "is always on hand, and while grateful for past favors will spare no pains to merit a continuance of the same. By catering to the public taste he hopes to make his house in the future, as it has been in the past, a real HOME for the Boys!" Nice homes these, and a nice family of boys that will come out of them! Where will they live when they grow to be men? A good idea it was to build a stone penitentiary.

"Oh yes! Oh yes! Oh yes!"
"AUCTION SALES EVERY DAY!"

This is another form of advertisement for a very prolific branch of trade. Day and night auctions are all the rage in Virginia as in San Francisco. Every thing that can't go any other way, and many things that can, go by auction. Stocks, horses, mules, boots, groceries, tinware, drugs and medicines, and rubbish of all kinds are put in flaming bills and auctioned off to the highest bidder for cash. "An'af! an'af! an'af! shall I have it?" is a part of the language popularly spoken on the principal streets.

A cigar store not much bigger than a dry-goods box must have its mammoth posters out over the town and hill-sides, displaying to the public eye the prodigious assortments of Regalias, Principes, Cheroots, etc., and choice brands of "Yellow-leaf," "Honey-dew," "Solace," and "Eureka," to be had within the limits of their cigar and tobacco emporium. If Archimedes were to rush from the solace of a bath and run naked through the streets of Virginia, shouting, " Eureka! Eureka! " it would merely be regarded as a dodge to dispose of an invoice of Fine-Cut.

Quack pills, sirups, tonics, and rectifiers stare you in the face from every mud-bank, rock, post, and corner, in red, black, blue, and white letters; in hieroglyphics, in cadaverous pictures of sick men, and astounding pictures of well men.

Every branch of trade, every conceivable species of amusement, is forced upon the public eye in this way. Bill-posting is one of the fine arts. Its professors are among the most notable characters in Virginia. They have a specific interest in certain corners, boards, boxes, and banks of earth and rock, which, with the brush and pot of paste, yield them a handsome revenue. To one who witnesses this bill-mania for the first time the effect is rather peculiar. He naturally imagines that the whole place is turned inside out. Every man's business fills his eye from every point of view, and he can not conceive the existence of a residence unless it be that where so much of the inside is out some portion of the outside may be in. With the exception of the silver mines this is, to a casual observer, an inverted city, and may well claim to be a city of anomalies.

I had occasion, during my stay, to avail myself of the services of a professional bill-sticker. For the sum of six dollars he agreed to make me notorious. The bills were printed in the approved form: " A Trip to Iceland," etc. Special stress was given to the word " ICELAND," and my name was printed in extravagantly conspicuous letters. In the course of a day or two I was shocked at the publicity the Professor of Bill-Posting had given me. From every rock, corner, dry-goods box, and awning post; from every screen in every drinking saloon, I was confronted and browbeaten by my own name. I felt disposed to shrink into my boots. Had any body walked up to me and said, " Sir, you are a humbug!" it would have been an absolute relief. I would have grasped him by the hand, and answered, "I know it, my dear fellow, and honor you for your frankness!" But there was one consolation: I was suffering in company. A lady, popularly known as "The Menken" (the afterwards celebrated actress, Adah Isaacs Menken) had created an immense sensation in San Francisco, and was about to favor the citizens of Virginia with a classical equestrian exhibition entitled "Mazeppa." She was represented as tied in an almost nude state to the back of a wild horse, which was running away with her at a fearful rate of speed. My friend the Professor was an artist in the line of bill-sticking, and carefully studied effects. He evidently enjoyed Mazeppa. It was a flaming and a gorgeous bill. Its colors were of the most florid character; and he posted accordingly. First came Mazeppa on the mustang horse; then came the Trip to Iceland and myself. If I remember correctly we (that is to say "The Menken" and I) were followed by "Ayer's Tonic Pills," "Brown's Bronchial Troches," and "A good Square Meal at the Howling Wilderness Saloon." Well, I suppose it was all right, though it took me rather aback at the first view. If the lady had no reason to complain, it was not for me, an old traveler, to find fault with the bill-sticker for placing me prominently before the public. Perhaps the juxtaposition was unfortunate in a pecuniary point of view; perhaps the citizens of Virginia feel no great interest in icy regions. Be that as it may, never again so long as I live will I undertake to run "Iceland" in the vicinity of a beautiful woman tied to the back of a wild horse.

*   *   *   *   *   *   *

Making due allowance for the atmosphere of exaggeration through which a visitor sees every thing in this wonderful mining metropolis, its progress has been sufficiently remarkable to palliate in some measure the extraordinary flights of fancy in which its inhabitants are prone to indulge. I was not prepared to see so great a change within the brief period of three years; for when people assure me " the world never saw any thing like it," " California is left in the shade," " San Francisco is eclipsed," " Montgomery Street is nowhere now," my incredulity is excited, and it takes some little time to judge of the true state of the case without prejudice. Speaking then strictly within bounds, the growth of this city is remarkable. When it is considered that the surrounding country affords but few facilities for the construction of houses; that lumber has to be hauled a considerable distance at great expense; that lime, bricks, iron-work, sashes, doors, etc., cost three or four times what similar articles do in San Francisco; that much indispensable material can only be had by transporting it over the mountains a distance of more than a hundred and fifty miles; and that the average of mechanical labor, living, and other expenses is correspondingly higher than in California, it is really wonderful how much has been done in so short a space of time.

Yet, allowing all this, what would be the impressions of a Fejee Islander sent upon a mission of inquiry to this strange place? His earliest glimpse of the main street would reveal the curious fact that it is paved with a conglomerate of dust, mud, splintered planks, old boots, clippings of tinware, and playing-cards. It is especially prolific in the matter of cards. Mules are said to fatten on them during seasons of scarcity when the straw gives out. The next marvelous fact that would strike the observation of this wild native is that so many people live in so many saloons, and do nothing from morning till night, and from night till morning again, but drink fiery liquids and indulge in profane language. How can all these able-bodied men afford to be idle? Who pays their expenses? And why do they carry pistols, knives, and other deadly weapons, when no harm could possibly befall them if they went unarmed and devoted themselves to some useful occupation? Has the God of the white men done them such an injury in furnishing all this silver for their use that they should treat His name with contempt and disrespect? Why do they send missionaries to the Fejee Islands and leave their own country in such a dreadful state of neglect? The Fejeeans devour their enemies occasionally as a war measure; the white man swallows his enemy all the time without regard to measure. Truly the white man is a very uncertain native! Fejeeans can't rely upon him.

When I was about to start on my trip to Washoe, friends from Virginia assured me I would find hotels there almost, if not quite, equal to the best in San Francisco. There was, but little difference, they said, except in the matter of extent. The Virginia hotels were quite as good, though not quite so large. Of course I believed all they told me. Now I really don't consider myself fastidious on the subject of hotels. Having traveled in many different countries I have enjoyed an extensive experience in the way of accommodations, from my mother-earth to the foretop of a whale-ship, from an Indian wigwam to a Parisian hotel, from an African palm-tree to an Arctic snowbank. I have slept in the same bed with two donkeys, a camel, half a dozen Arabs, several goats, and a horse. I have slept on beds alive with snakes, lizards, scorpions, centipedes, bugs, and fleas — beds in which men stricken with the plague had died horrible deaths — beds that might reasonably be suspected of small-pox, measles and Asiatic cholera. I have slept in beds of rivers and beds of sand, and on the bare bed rock. Standing, sitting, lying down, doubled up, and hanging over; twisted, punched, jammed, and elbowed by drunken men; snored at in the cars; sat upon and smothered by the nightmare; burnt by fires, rained upon, snowed upon, and bitten by frost — in all these positions, and subject to all these discomforts, I have slept with comparative satisfaction. There are pleasanter ways of sleeping, to be sure, but there are times when any way is a blessing. In respect to the matter of eating I am even less particular. Frogs, horse-leeches, snails, and grasshoppers are luxuries to what I have eaten. It has pleased Providence to favor me with appetites and tastes appropriate to a great variety of circumstances and many conditions of life. These facts serve to show that I am not fastidious on the subject of personal accommodations.

Perhaps my experience in Virginia was exceptional; perhaps misfortune was determined to try me to the utmost extremity. I endeavored to find accommodations at a hotel recommended as the best in the place, and was shown a room over the kitchen stove, in which the thermometer ranged at about 130 to 150 degrees of Fahrenheit. To be lodged and baked at the rate of $2 per night, cash in advance, was more than I could stand, so I asked for another room. There was but one more, and that was pre-empted by a lodger who might or might not come back and claim possession in the middle of the night. It had no window except one that opened into the passage, and the bed was so arranged that every other lodger in the house could take a passing observation of the sleeper and enjoy his style of sleeping. Nay, it was not beyond the resources of the photographic art to secure his negative and print his likeness for general distribution. It was bad enough to be smothered for want of light and air; but I had no idea of paying $2 a night for the poor privilege of showing people how I looked with my eyes shut, and possibly my mouth open. A man may have an attack of nightmare; his countenance may be distorted by horrible dreams; he may laugh immoderately at a very bad pun made in his sleep — in all which conditions of body and mind he doubtless presents an interesting spectacle to the critical eyes of a stranger, but he doesn't like to wake up suddenly and be caught in the act.

The next hotel to which I was recommended was eligibly located on a street composed principally of grog-shops and gambling-houses. I was favored with a front-room about eight feet square. The walls were constructed of boards fancifully decorated with paper, and afforded this facility to a lodger — that he could hear all that was going on in the adjacent rooms. The partitions might deceive the eye, but the ear received the full benefit of the various oaths, ejaculations, conversations, and perambulations in which his neighbors indulged. As for the bed, I don't know how long it had been in use, or what race of people had hitherto slept in it, but the sheets and blankets seemed to be sadly discolored by age — or lack of soap and water. It would be safe to say washing was not considered a paying investment by the managers of this establishment. Having been over twenty-four hours without sleep or rest I made an attempt to procure a small supply, but miserably failed in consequence of an interesting conversation carried on in the passage between the chamber-maids, waiters, and other ladies and gentlemen respecting the last free fight. From what I could gather this was considered the best neighborhood in the city for free fights. Within the past two weeks three or four men had been shot, stabbed, or maimed close by the door. " Oh, it's a lively place, you bet! " said one of the ladies (the chamber-maid, I think), " an oncommon lively place — reely hexcitin'. I look out of the winder every mornin' jist to see how many dead men are layin' around. I declare to gracious the bullets flies around here sometimes like hailstones! " " An' shure," said a voice in that rich brogue which can never be mistaken, " it's no wondher the boys shud be killin' an' murtherin' themselves forninst the door, whin they're all just like me, dyin' in love wid yer beauteeful self! " A smart slap and a general laugh followed this suggestion. " Git away wid ye, Dinnis; yer always up to yer mischief! As I was sayin', no later than this mornin', I see two men a poppin' away at each other wid six-shooters — a big man an' a little man. The big man he staggered an' fell right under the winder, wid his head on the curb-stone, an' his legs a stickin' right up in the air. He was all over blood, and when the boys picked him up he was dead as a brickbat. 'Tother chap he run into a saloon. You better b'leeve this is a lively neighborhood. I tell you hailstones is nothink to the way the bullets flies around." "That's so," chimes in another female voice; " I see myself, with my own eyes, Jack's corpse an' two more carried away in the last month. If I'd a had a six-shooter then you bet they'd a carried away the fellow that nipped Jack! "

Now taking into view the picturesque spectacle that a few dead men dabbled in blood must present to the eye on a fine morning, and the chances of a miscellaneous ball carrying away the top of one's cranium, or penetrating the thin board wall and ranging upward through his body as he lies in bed, I considered it best to seek a more secluded neighborhood, where the scenery was of a less stimulating character and the hail-storms not quite so heavy. By the kind aid of a friend I secured comparatively agreeable quarters in a private lodging-house kept by a widow lady. The rooms were good and the beds clean, and the price not extravagant for this locality — $12 a week without board.

So much for the famous hotels of Virginia. If there are any better, neither myself, nor some fellow-travelers who told me their experiences, succeeded in finding them. The concurrent testimony was that they are dirty, ill-kept, badly attended by rough, ill-mannered waiters — noisy to such a degree that a sober man can get but little rest, day or night, and extravagantly high in proportion to the small comfort they afford. One of the newspapers published a statement which the author probably intended for a joke, but which is doubtless founded upon fact — namely, that a certain hotel advertised for 300 chickens to serve the same number of guests. Only one chicken could be had for love or money — a very ancient rooster, which was made into soup and afterward served up in the form of a fricassee for the 300 guests. The flavor was considered extremely delicate — what there was of it; and there was plenty of it such as it was.

Still if we are to credit what the Virginia newspapers say — and it would be dangerous to intimate that they ever deal in any thing save the truth — there are other cities on the eastern slope of the Sierras which afford equally attractive accommodations. On the occasion of the recent Senatorial contest at Carson City, the prevailing rates charged for lodgings, according to the Virginia *Enterprise,* were as follows: "For a bed in a house, barn, blacksmith-shop, or hay-yard (none to be had — all having been engaged shortly before election); horse-blanket in an old sugar hogshead per night, $10; crockery-crate, with straw, $7 50; without straw, $5 75; for cellar door, $4; for roosting on a smooth pole $3 50; pole, common, rough, $3; plaza fence, $2 50; walking up and down the Warm Springs road — if cloudy, $1 50; if clear, $1 25. (In case the clouds are very thick and low $1 75 is generally asked.) Very good roosting in a pine-tree, back of Camp Nye, may still be had free, but we understand that a company is being formed to monopolize all the more accessible trees. We believe they propose to improve by putting two pins in the bottom of each tree, or keep a man to boost regular customers. They talk of charging six bits."

I could scarcely credit this, if it were not that a friend of mine, who visited Reese River last summer, related some experiences of a corroborative character. Unable to secure lodgings elsewhere, he undertook to find accommodations in a vacant sheep corral. The proprietor happening to come home about midnight found him spread out under the lee of the fence. "Look-a-here, stranger!" said he gruffly "that's all well enough, but I gen'rally collect in advance. Just fork over four bits or mizzle!" My friend indignantly mizzled. Cursing the progressive spirit of the age, he walked some distance out of town, and was about to finish the night under the lee of a big quartz boulder, when a fierce-looking speculator, with a six-shooter in his hand, suddenly appeared from a cavity in the rock, saying, " No yer don't! Take a fool's advice now, and git! When you go a prospectin' around ov nights agin, jest steer ov this boulder ef you please! " In vain my friend attempted to explain. The rising wrath of the squatter was not to be appeased by soft words, and the click of the trigger, as he raised his pistol and drew a bead, warned the trespasser that it was time to be off. He found lodgings that night on the public highway to Virginia City and San Francisco.

ALDER GULCH

NATHANIEL P. LANGFORD

1863

From "Vigilante Days and Ways." Reprinted by permission of the publishers, A. C. McClurg and Company, Chicago.[1]

IN May, 1863, a company of miners, while returning from an unsuccessful exploring expedition, discovered the remarkable placer afterwards known as Alder Gulch. They gave the name of one of their number, Fairweather, to the district. Several of the company went immediately to Bannack, communicated the intelligence, and returned with supplies to their friends. The effect of the news was electrical. Hundreds started at once to the new placer, each striving to outstrip the other, in order to secure a claim. In the hurry of departure, among many minor accidents, a man whose body, partially concealed by the willows, was mistaken for a beaver, was shot by Mr. Arnold. Discovering the fatal mistake, Arnold gave up the chase and bestowed his entire attention upon the unfortunate victim until his death, a few days afterwards. The great stampede with its numerous pack-animals, penetrated the dense alder thicket which filled the gulch, a distance of eight miles, to the site selected for building a town. An accidental fire occurring, swept away the alders for the entire distance in a single night. In less than a week from the date of the first arrival, hundreds of tents, brush wakiups, and rude log cabins, extemporized for immediate occupancy, were

[1] Copyright, 1890, by Nathaniel P. Langford. Copyright, 1912, by A. C. McClurg & Co.

scattered at random over the spot, now for the first time trodden by white men. For a distance of twelve miles from the mouth of the gulch to its source in Bald Mountain, claims were staked and occupied by the men fortunate enough first to assert an ownership. Laws were adopted, judges selected, and the new community was busy in up-heaving, sluicing, drifting, and cradling the inexhaustible bed of auriferous gravel, which has yielded under these various manipulations a greater amount of gold than any other placer on the continent.

The Southern sympathizers of the Territory gave the name of Varina to the new town which had sprung up in Alder Gulch, in honor of the wife of President Jefferson Davis. Dr. Bissell, one of the miners' judges of the gulch, was an ardent Unionist. Being called upon to draw up some papers before the new name had been generally adopted, and requested to date them at " Varina City," he declared, with a very emphatic expletive, he would not do it, and wrote the name " Virginia City," — by which name the place has ever since been known.

The road agents were among the first to follow in the track of the miners. Prominent among them were Cyrus Skinner, Jack Gallagher, Buck Stinson, and Ned Ray, — the last three as deputies of Plummer in the sheriffalty. Ripe for the commission of any deed, however atrocious, which gave the promise of plunder, jackal-like they watched the gathering crowd and its various industries, marking each and all for early and unceasing depredation.

The Hon. Washington Stapleton who had been at work in the Bannack mines from the time of their discovery, a miner named Dodge, and another man, each supposed to possess a considerable amount of gold, having determined to go to Virginia City, Dodge was privately informed by Dillingham, one of Plummer's deputies, on the eve of their intended departure, that Buck Stinson, Hayes Lyons, and Charley Forbes had laid plans for robbing them on the way, and had requested him (Dillingham) to join them in the robbery. When the time for their going came, Dodge expressed his fear of an attack, and announced his determination to remain. His friends rallied him, until, smarting under their taunts, he revealed the information given by Dillingham. Stinson, Lyons, and Forbes heard of it, and determined to kill the informer. Stapleton left his companions, and started for Virginia City alone. At Rattlesnake he encountered Hayes Lyons, who rode up and asked him if he had heard of the robbery which Dillingham alleged had been planned against him. Stapleton replied in the negative; but when telling the story since, says that he has felt more comfortable even when sleeping in church, than when he saw that scoundrel approaching him. He told him, he says, that this was the first he had heard of it, adding, " If you want my money, I have only one hundred dollars in greenbacks. You had better take that, and let me go."

Lyons replied with an oath that the story was a lie, and that he was then on his way to kill Dillingham for putting such a story in circulation, but he feared Dillingham had heard of his intention and left the country.

Stapleton accomplished his trip without molestation. Lyons and Forbes rode on to Virginia City, also, and finding Dillingham there, they, in company with Stinson, met the next day and arranged for his assassination.

A miners' court for the trial of a civil case was in session the following morning near the bank of the creek fronting the town. To the observation of a person unaccustomed to the makeshifts and customs of a mining community, the picture presented by this court of justice would have exhibited many amusing features — not the least of which was the place wherein it was held. The Temple of Justice was a wakiup of brush and twigs, gathered from the different coppices of willow and alder growing upon the banks of the creek, thrown together in conical form, and of barely sufficient capacity to accommodate the judge, clerk, parties, and jurors. Spectators were indebted to the interstices in this primitive structure for a view of the proceedings; and as no part of the person except the eyes was visible to those within, the appearance of those visual orbs bore no inapt comparison to a constellation in a brush heap.

Dr. Steele, president of the gulch, acted as judge. He united with much native good sense, great modesty of demeanor. He was not a lawyer. On his trip from the States, while crossing the plains, an unfriendly gust had swept his only hat beyond recovery, and he came into Montana with his brows bound in a parti-colored cotton handkerchief, which, for want of something more appropriate, not obtainable at the stores, he had worn until some friendly miner possessing an extra hat presented him with it. Proving too small to incase his intellectual organs, the doctor had, by a series of indented slits encircling the rim, increased its elasticity, so that, saving a succession of gaps, through which his hair bristled " like quills upon the fretful porcupine," it answered the purpose of its creation. With this upon his head he sat upon the bench, an embodiment of the dignity, law, and learning of this little mountain judiciary.

In the progress of the trial, the defendant's counsel asked for a nonsuit, on account of some informality of service.

" A what? " inquired the judge with a puzzled expression, as if he had not rightly understood the word.

" A nonsuit," was the rejoinder.

" What's a — " The question partly asked, was left incomplete. The judge blushed, but reflecting that he would probably learn the office of a nonsuit in the course of the argument, he broke through the dilemma by asking,

" Upon what ground? "

The argument followed, and the judge, soon comprehending the meaning of a nonsuit, decided that unless the defendant could show that he had suffered by reason of the informal service, the case must proceed. Some of the friends of the magistrate, seated near the door, understanding the cause of his embarrassment, enjoyed the scene hugely, and as it presented an opportunity for returning in kind some of the numerous jokes which he had played at their expense, one of them, thinking it too good to be lost, with much mock sobriety of manner and tone, arose and said,

" Most righteous decision! "

All eyes were turned upon the speaker, but before they could comprehend the joke at the bottom, another arose, and with equal solemnity, exclaimed,

" Most just judge! "

Dr. Steele, though embarrassed by his ill-timed jocularity, was so well satisfied with his sagacity in finding out what a nonsuit meant, without betraying his legal unlearnedness, that the joke was taken in good part, and formed a subject of frequent merriment in after times.

Charley Forbes was the clerk of the court, and sat beside the judge taking notes of the trial. After the decision denying the motion, the plaintiff passed around a bottle of liquor, of which the court and jury partook. Not to be outdone, the defendant circulated a box of cigars. And it was while the spectators were giving expression in various forms to their approval of the decision, that Stinson and Lyons came into the court, and proceeding to the seat occupied by Forbes, engaged with him in a whispered conversation inaudible to the bystanders. After a few moments, Forbes suddenly rose in his place, and, with an oath, exclaimed,

" Well, we'll kill the scoundrel then, at once," and accompanied Stinson and Lyons out of the wakiup. The audience, startled by the announcement, hurriedly followed. Dillingham had come over from Bannack in his capacity as deputy sheriff, to look for some stolen horses. He had come on the ground a moment before, in search of Mr. Todd, the deputy at Virginia City, for assistance.

An assemblage of a hundred or more miners and others was congregated in and about the place where the court was in progress, — some intent upon the trial, others sauntering through the crowd and along the bank of Alder Creek. The three ruffians, after a moment's conversation, approached in company the spot where Dillingham stood.

"We want to see you," said Lyons, addressing him. "Step this way a moment."

Stinson advanced a few paces, and looking over his shoulder said to his companions,

"Bring him along. Make him come."

Dillingham waited for no second invitation. Evidently supposing that they had some matter of business to communicate, he accompanied them to an open spot not more than ten paces distant. There they all stopped, and facing Dillingham, with a muttered curse Lyons said to him,

"Take back those lies," when with the quickness of thought, they drew their revolvers, — Charley Forbes at the same time exclaiming, "Don't shoot, don't shoot," — and fired upon him simultaneously. The groan which Lyons' ball drew from the poor victim as it entered his thigh, was hushed by the bullet of Forbes, as it passed through his breast, inflicting a mortal wound. He fell, and died in a few moments. Jack Gallagher, who was in the plot, rushed up, and in his capacity as a deputy sheriff, seized the pistols of the three ruffians, one of which, while unobserved, he reloaded, intending thereby to prevent the identification of the villain who fired the fatal shot.

The deed was committed so quickly that the bystanders hardly knew what had happened till they saw Dillingham stretched upon the ground in the death agony. The court broke up instantly, and the jury dispersed. Aghast at the bloody spectacle, for some moments the people surveyed it in speechless amazement. The ruffians meanwhile sauntered quietly away, chuckling at their own adroitness. They had not gone far, until several of the miners, by direction of Dr. Steele, arrested them. The reaction from terror to reason was marked by the adoption of vigorous measures for the punishment of the crime, and but for the calm self-possession of a few individuals, the murderers would have been summarily dealt with. An officer elected by the people, with a detail of miners, took them into custody, and having confined them in a log building, preparations were made for their immediate trial.

Here again, as at the trial of Moore and Reeves, the difficulty of a choice between a trial by the people, and by a jury of twelve, occasioned an obstinate and violent discussion. The reasons for the latter, though strongly urged, were finally overcome by the paramount consideration that the selection of a jury would devolve upon a deputy sheriff who was in league with the prisoners, and, as it was afterwards ascertained, an accomplice in the crime for which they were arrested.

The people assembled *en masse* upon the very spot where the murder had been committed. Dr. Steele, by virtue of his office as president of the gulch, was appointed judge, and at his request Dr. Bissell, the district judge, and Dr. Rutar, associates, to aid with their counsel in the decisions of such questions as should arise in the progress of the trial. E. R. Cutler, a blacksmith, and James Brown acted as public prosecutors, and H. P. A. Smith, a lawyer of ability, appeared on behalf of the prisoners.

A separate trial was assigned to Forbes, because the pistol which Gallagher had privately reloaded, was claimed by him, a fact of which he wished to avail himself. In fact, however, the pistol belonged to Stinson. It was midday when the trial of Lyons and Stinson commenced. At dark it was not concluded, and the prisoners were put under a strong guard for the night. They were confined in a small, half-roofed, unchinked cabin, overlooking Daylight

Creek, which ran through a hollow filled with willows. Dr. Six and Major Brookie had charge of the prisoners. Soon after dark their attention was attracted by the repeated shrill note of a night-hawk, apparently proceeding from the willows. After each note, Forbes commenced singing. This being noticed by the guard, on closer investigation they discovered that the note was simulated by some person as a signal for the prisoners. They immediately ordered Forbes to stop singing. He refused. They then proposed to chain the prisoners, they objecting, and Forbes remarking,

" I will suffer death before you shall do it."

He receded, however, under the persuasion of six shot-guns drawn upon a line with his head, and in a subdued tone, said,

" Chain me."

During the night Lyons sent for one of the citizens, who, under cover of the guns of the guard, approached and asked him what he wanted.

" I want you," said he, " to release Stinson and Forbes. I killed Dillingham. I came here for that express purpose. They are innocent. I was sent here by the best men in Bannack to kill him."

" Who sent you? " inquired the citizen.

After naming several of the best citizens of Bannack, who knew nothing of the murder until several days after it was committed, he added,

" Henry Plummer told me to shoot him." It was afterwards proven that this was true.

Hayes Lyons was greatly unnerved, and cried a great part of the night; but Buck Stinson was wholly unconcerned and slept soundly.

The trial was resumed the next morning. At noon, the arguments being concluded, the question of " guilty or not guilty," was submitted to the people, and decided almost unanimously in the affirmative.

" What shall be their punishment? " asked the president of the now eager crowd.

" Hang them," was the united response.

Men were immediately appointed to erect a scaffold, and dig the graves of the doomed criminals, who were taken into custody to await the result of the trial of Forbes. This followed immediately; and the loaded pistol, and the fact that when the onslaught was made upon Dillingham, he called out, " Don't shoot, don't shoot," were used in evidence with good effect. When the question was finally put, Forbes, who was a young man of fine personal appearance, and possessed of good powers as a speaker, made a personal appeal to the crowd, which so wrought upon their sympathies, and was so eloquent withal, that they acquitted him by a large majority. In marked contrast with the spirit which they had exhibited a few hours before while condemning Stinson and Lyons to a violent death, the people, upon the acquittal of Forbes, crowded around him with shouts and laughter, eager to shake hands with and congratulate him upon his escape. Months afterwards, when the excitement of the occasion, with the memory of it, has passed from men's minds, Charley Forbes was heard vauntingly to say that he was the slayer of Dillingham. He was known to deride the tender susceptibilities of the people, who gave him liberty to renew his desperate career, and chuckle over the exercise of powers of person and mind that could make so many believe even Truth herself to be a liar. Among the villains belonging to Plummer's band, not one, not even Plummer himself, possessed a more depraved nature than Forbes; and with it, few, if any, were gifted with as many shining accomplishments. He was a prince of cut-throats, uniting with the coolness of Augustus Tomlinson all the adaptability of Paul Clifford. On one occasion he said to a gentleman about to leave the Territory,

" You will be attacked on your way to Salt Lake City."

" You can't do it, Charley," was the reply. " Your boys are scattered, we are together, and will prove too many for you." Nevertheless, the party drove sixty miles the first day out, and thus escaped molestation.

His early life was passed in Grass Valley, California. While comparatively a youth, he was convicted of robbery. On the expiration of his sentence, he visited his old friends, and on his promise of reformation, they obtained employment for him in McLaughlin's gas works. For a while his conduct was unexceptionable, and he was rapidly regaining the esteem of all; but in an evil hour he indulged in a game of poker for money. From that moment he yielded to this temptation, until it became a besetting vice. Not long after he entered upon this career, he provoked a quarrel with one " Dutch John," who threatened to kill him.

Forbes told McLaughlin, saying in conclusion, " When Dutch John says so, he means it."

" Take my revolver out of the case," said McLaughlin, " put it in your breast-pocket, and defend yourself as occasion may require."

Forbes obeyed. Soon after, as he was passing along with a ladder on his shoulder, an acquaintance said to him,

" Dutch John is looking for you to kill you."

" So I hear," replied Forbes. " He'll find me sooner than he wants to."

A few rods farther on he saw John coming from the Magnolia saloon, where he had been looking for Forbes. Forbes sprang towards him, exclaiming with an oath,

" Here I am," and immediately fired four shots at him. John fired once in return, and throwing up his hands in affright at the rapid firing of Forbes, ejaculated,

" *O mein Gott!* Will I be murdered? "

A bystander who had witnessed the meeting, and saw that John, who had expected an easy victory, was paralyzed with fear, called to him,

" Turn your artillery loose! "

Forbes was tried for this crime, and acquitted. He was afterwards convicted of crime of some kind in Carson City, and imprisoned. On New Year's day he succeeded in removing his handcuffs, broke jail, and went to the sheriff's house, as he said upon entering, "to make a New Year's call." The officer returned him to prison. From this time, his career of crime knew no impediment.

On his first arrival in the mountains he corresponded for some of the California and Nevada papers. His letters were highly interesting. His true name was Edward Richardson.

To return to Stinson and Lyons. After the demonstration of joy at Forbes's escape had subsided, the people remembered that there was an execution on the *tapis*. Drawing up a wagon in front of the building where the criminals were confined, they ordered them to get in. They obeyed, followed by several of their friends, who took seats beside them. Lyons became almost uproarious in his appeals for mercy. The women, of whom there were many, began to cry, begging earnestly for the lives of the criminals. Smith, their lawyer, joined his petitions to those of the women, and the entire crowd began to give way under this pressure of sympathy. Meantime the wagon was drawn slowly towards the place of execution. When the excitement was at its highest pitch, a man demanded in a loud tone that the people should listen to a letter which Lyons had written to his mother. This document, which had been prepared by some person for the occasion, was now read. It was filled with expressions of love for the aged mother, regret for the crime, repentance, acknowledgments of misspent life, and strong promises of amendment, if only life could be spared a little longer. Every sentence elicited fresh grief from the women, who now became perfectly clamorous in their calls for mercy to the prisoners. After the letter was read, some one cried out, in derision,

"Give him a horse, and let him go to his mother."

Another immediately moved that they take a vote upon that proposition. Sheriff Todd, whose duty it was only to carry out the sentence of the court, consented to this, and the question was submitted to ayes and noes. Both parties claimed the victory. It was then agreed that those in favor of hanging should go up, and those opposed, down the side of a neighboring hill. Neither party being satisfied, as a final test, four men were selected, and those who wished the sentence enforced were to pass between two of them, and those who opposed, between the other two. The votes for liberty were increased to meet the occasion, by a second passage of as many as were necessary to carry the question. An Irish miner, while the voting was in progress, exclaimed in a loud voice, as a negro passed through the acquittal bureau,

"Bedad, there's a bloody nagur that's voted three times."

But this vote, dishonest as it was, settled the question; for Jack Gallagher, pistol in hand, shouted,

"Let them go. They're cleared."

This was a signal for a general uproar, and amid shouts from both parties, expressive of the opinions which each entertained, some one mounted the assassins upon a horse standing near, which belonged to a Blackfoot squaw, and cutting the lariat, started them off at a gallop down the gulch. At this moment one of the guard pointed to the gallows, and said to another,

"There stands a monument of disappointed justice."

Immediately after sentence of death had been passed upon Stinson and Lyons, Dr. Steele returned to his cabin, two miles down the gulch. The result of the trial had furnished him with food for sad reflection, — especially as the duty of passing death sentence had devolved upon him. Other considerations followed in quick succession. He has since, when speaking of it, said that he never indulged in a more melancholy reverie, than while returning home from this trial. The youth of the convicts; their evident fitness, both by culture and manners, for any sphere of active business; the effect that their execution must have upon distant parents and friends, — all these thoughts presented themselves in sad array before his mental vision; when, as he was about entering his cabin, a quick clatter of hoofs roused him and turning to see the cause, he beheld the subjects of his gloomy reflections both mounted upon the Indian pony, approaching at the animal's swiftest pace. He had hardly time to recover from his surprise, and realize that the object was not a vision, until the animal with its double rider passed him, — and Lyons, nodding familiarly, waved his hand, accompanying the gesture with the parting words,

" Good-bye, Doc."

The body of the unfortunate Dillingham lay neglected upon a gambling table in a tent near by, until this wretched travesty was completed. Then a wagon was obtained, and, followed by a small procession, it was hurriedly buried. The tears had all been shed for the murderers.

" I cried for Dillingham," said one, on being told that his wife and daughters had expended their grief upon the wrong persons.

" Oh, you did," was the reply. " Well thought of. Who will pray for him? Will you do it, judge? "

Judge Bissell responded by kneeling upon the spot and offering up an appropriate prayer, as the body of the unfortunate young man was consigned to its mother earth.

Soon after the murder of Dillingham, Charley Forbes suddenly disappeared. No one knew what became of him, but it was supposed that he had fallen a victim to the vengeance of his comrades for the course he had taken in securing for himself a separate trial. This supposition was afterwards confirmed by some of the robbers themselves, who stated that in a quarrel with Moore at the Big Hole River, Forbes was killed. Fearing that the friends of the murdered ruffian would retaliate, Moore killed Forbes's horse at the same time, and burned to ashes the bodies of horse and rider. This fact was known to Plummer only, at the time of its occurrence.

Dillingham was a straightforward, honest young man, and his office as deputy sheriff was given him under the supposition that he would readily affiliate with the roughs. Lyons, Stinson, and Forbes, who were also deputies, supposed him to be as bad as they were.

On my trip east in 1863, the Overland coach in which I had taken passage was detained a night by snow at Hook's Station in Nebraska. Ascertaining that I was from Bannack, a young man at the station asked me many questions about Hayes Lyons, telling me that he had heard that he narrowly escaped hanging the previous summer. I narrated to him the circumstances attending the murder of Dillingham and the trial.

"He is my brother," said the young man, and invited me to go with him and see his mother and sister. I learned that Hayes had been well brought up, but was the victim of evil associations. His mother wept while deploring his criminal career, which she ascribed to bad company.

CHEYENNES AND SIOUX

GENERAL GEORGE A. CUSTER

1867

From "My Life on the Plains." Reprinted by permission of the publishers, J. D. Sheldon Company, New York.[1]

OF the many important expeditions organized to operate in the Indian country, none, perhaps, of late years has excited more general and unfriendly comment, considering the slight loss of life inflicted upon the Indians, than the expedition organized and led in person by Major-General Hancock in the spring of 1867. The clique generally known as the " Indian ring " were particularly malevolent and bitter in their denunciations of General Hancock for precipitating, as they expressed it, an Indian war. This expedition was quite formidable in appearance, being made up of eight troops of cavalry, seven companies of infantry, and one battery of light artillery, numbering altogether about 1,400 men.

It may be asked, What had the Indians done to make this incursion necessary? They had been guilty of numerous thefts and murders during the preceding summer and fall, for none of which had they been called to account. They had attacked the stations of the overland mail route, killed the employees, burned the station, and captured the stock. Citizens had been murdered in their homes on the frontier of Kansas; murders had been committed on the Arkansas route. The principal perpetrators of these acts were the Cheyennes and Sioux. The agent of the former, if not a

[1] Entered, according to Act of Congress, in the year 1874, by Sheldon & Co., in the Office of the Librarian of Congress.

party to the murder on the Arkansas, knew who the guilty persons were, yet took no steps to bring the murderers to punishment. Such a course would have interfered with his trade and profits. It was not to punish for these sins of the past that the expedition was set on foot, but rather by its imposing appearance and its early presence in the Indian country to check or intimidate the Indians from a repetition of their late conduct. This was deemed particularly necessary from the fact that the various tribes from which we had greatest cause to anticipate trouble had during the winter, through their leading chiefs and warriors, threatened that as soon as the grass was up in spring a combined outbreak would take place along our entire frontier, and especially against the main routes of travel. To assemble the tribes for the desired council, word was sent early in March to the agents of those tribes whom it was desirable to meet. The agents sent runners to the villages inviting them to meet us at some point near the Arkansas river.

General Hancock, with the artillery and six companies of infantry, reached Fort Riley, Kansas, from Fort Leavenworth by rail the last week in March; here he was joined by four companies of the Seventh Cavalry and an additional company of the Thirty-seventh Infantry. It was at this point that I joined the expedition. And as a very fair sample of the laurels which military men may win in an Indian campaign by a zealous discharge of what they deem their duty, I will here state, in parenthesis, that after engaging in the expedition, some of the events of which I am about to relate, and undergoing fatigue, privations, and dangers equal to those of a campaign during the Rebellion, I found myself at the termination of the campaign again at Fort Riley *in arrest*. This is not mentioned in a fault-finding spirit. I have no fault to find. It is said that blessings sometimes come in disguise. Such proved to be true in this instance, although I must say the disguise for some little time was most perfect.

From Fort Riley we marched to Fort Harker, a distance of ninety miles, where our force was strengthened by the addition of two more troops of cavalry. Halting only long enough to replenish our supplies, we next directed our march toward Fort Larned, near the Arkansas, about seventy miles to the southeast. A march from the 3d to the 7th of April brought us to Fort Larned. The agent for the Comanches and Kiowas accompanied us. At Fort Larned we found the agent of the Cheyennes, Arapahoes, and Apaches; from the latter we learned that he had, as requested, sent runners to the chiefs of his agency inviting them to the council, and that they had agreed to assemble near Fort Larned on the 10th of the month, requesting that the expedition would remain there until that date. To this request General Hancock acceded.

On the 9th of April, while encamped awaiting the council, which was to be held the following day, a terrible snow-storm occurred, lasting all day until late in the evening. It was our good fortune to be in camp rather than on the march; had it been otherwise, we could not well have escaped without loss of life from the severe cold and blinding snow. The cavalry horses suffered seriously, and were only preserved by doubling their ration of oats, while to prevent their being frozen during the intensely cold night which followed, the guards were instructed to keep passing along the picket lines with a whip, and to keep the horses moving constantly. The snow was eight inches in depth. The council, which was to take place the next day, had to be postponed until the return of good weather. Now began the display of a kind of diplomacy for which the Indian is peculiar. The Cheyennes and a band of the Sioux were encamped on Pawnee Fork, about thirty miles above Fort Larned. They neither desired to move nearer to us nor have us approach nearer to them. On the morning of the 11th they sent us word that they had started to visit us, but discovering a large herd of buffalo near their camp, they had stopped to procure a supply of meat. This message was not received with much confidence, nor was a buffalo hunt deemed of sufficient importance to justify the Indians in breaking their engagement. General Hancock decided, however, to delay another day, when, if the Indians still failed to come in, he would move his command to the vicinity of their village and hold the conference there.

Orders were issued on the evening of the 12th for the march to be resumed on the following day. Later in the evening two chiefs of the " Dog Soldiers," a band composed of the most warlike and troublesome Indians on the Plains, chiefly made up of Cheyennes, visited our camp. They were accompanied by a dozen warriors, and expressed a desire to hold a conference with General Hancock, to which he assented. A large council fire was built in front of the General's tent, and all the officers of his command assembled there. A tent had been erected for the accommodation of the chiefs a short distance from the General's. Before they could feel equal to the occasion, and in order to obtain time to collect their thoughts, they desired that supper might be prepared for them, which was done. When finally ready they advanced from their tent to the council fire in single file, accompanied by their agent and an interpreter. Arrived at the fire, another brief delay ensued. No matter how pressing or momentous the occasion, an Indian invariably declines to engage in a council until he has filled his pipe and gone through with the important ceremony of a smoke. This attended to, the chiefs announced that they were ready " to talk." They were then introduced to the principal officers of the group, and seemed much struck with the flashy uniforms of the few artillery officers who were present in all the glory of red horsehair plumes, aigulets, etc. The chiefs seemed puzzled to determine whether these insignia designated chieftains or medicine men. General Hancock began the conference by a speech, in which he explained to the Indians his purpose in coming to see them, and what he expected of them in the future. He particularly informed them that he was not there to make war, but to promote peace. Then expressing his regret that more of the chiefs had not visited him, he announced his intention of proceeding on the morrow with his command to the vicinity of their village and there holding a council with all of the chiefs. Tall Bull, a fine, warlike-looking chieftain, replied to General Hancock, but his speech contained nothing important, being made up of allusions to the growing scarcity of the buffalo, his love for the white man, and the usual hint that a donation in the way of refreshments would be highly acceptable; he added that he would have nothing new to say at the village.

Several years prior to the events referred to, our people had captured from the Indians two children. I believe they were survivors of the Chivington massacre at Sand Creek, Colorado. These children had been kindly cared for, and were being taught to lead a civilized mode of life. Their relatives, however, made demands for them, and we by treaty stipulation agreed to deliver them up. One of them, a little girl, had been cared for kindly in a family living near Denver, Colorado; the other, a boy, had been carried East to the States, and it was with great difficulty that the Government was able to learn his whereabouts and obtain possession of him. He was finally discovered, however, and sent to General Hancock, to be by him delivered up to his tribe. He accompanied the expedition, and was quite a curiosity for the time being. He was dressed comfortably, in accordance with civilized custom; and, having been taken from his people at so early an age, was apparently satisfied with the life he led. The Indians who came to our camp expressed a great desire to see him, and when he was brought into their presence they exhibited no emotion such as white men under similar circumstances might be expected to show. They evidently were not pleased to see him clothed in the white man's dress. The little fellow, then some eight or ten years of age, seemed little disposed to go back to his people.

I saw him the following year in the village of his tribe; he then had lost all trace of civilization, had forgotten his knowledge of the English language, and was as shy and suspicious of the white men as any of his dusky comrades. From older persons of the tribe we learned that their first act after obtaining possession of him was to deprive him of his "store clothes," and in their stead substitute the blanket and leggings.

Rightly concluding that the Indians did not intend to come to our camp as they had at first agreed to, it was decided to move nearer to their village. On the morning following the conference held with the two chiefs of the " Dog Soldiers," our entire force therefore marched from Fort Larned up Pawnee Fork in the direction of the main village, encamping the first night about twenty-one miles from the fort. Several parties of Indians were seen in our advance during the day, evidently watching our movements; while a heavy smoke, seen to rise in the direction of the Indian village, indicated that something more than usual was going on. This smoke we afterwards learned arose from the burning grass. The Indians, thinking to prevent us from encamping in their vicinity, had set fire to and burned all the grass for miles in the direction from which they expected us. Before we arrived at our camping-ground we were met by several chiefs and warriors belonging to the Cheyennes and Sioux. Among the chiefs were Pawnee Killer of the Sioux, and White Horse of the Cheyennes. It was arranged that these chiefs should accept our hospitality and remain with us during the night, and in the morning all the chiefs of the two tribes then in the village were to come to General Hancock's headquarters and hold a council. On the morning of the 14th Pawnee Killer left our camp at an early hour, for the purpose, as he said, of going to the village to bring in the other chiefs to the council. Nine o'clock had been agreed upon as the hour at which the council should assemble. The hour came, but the chiefs did not. Now **an**

Indian council is not only often an important but always an interesting occasion. And, somewhat like a famous recipe for making a certain dish, the first thing necessary in holding an Indian council is to get the Indian. Half-past nine o'clock came, and still we were lacking this one important part of the council. At this juncture Bull Bear, an influential chief among the Cheyennes, came in and reported that the chiefs were on their way to our camp, but would not be able to reach it for some time. This was a mere artifice to secure delay. General Hancock informed Bull Bear that as the chiefs could not arrive for some time, he would move his forces up the stream nearer to the village, and the council could be held at our camp that night. To this proposition Bull Bear gave his assent.

At 11 A. M. we resumed the march, and had proceeded but a few miles when we witnessed one of the finest and most imposing military displays, prepared according to the Indian art of war, which it has ever been my lot to behold. It was nothing more nor less than an Indian line of battle drawn directly across our line of march; as if to say, Thus far and no further. Most of the Indians were mounted; all were bedecked in their brightest colors, their heads crowned with the brilliant war-bonnet, their lances bearing the crimson pennant, bows strung, and quivers full of barbed arrows. In addition to these weapons, which with the hunting-knife and tomahawk are considered as forming the armament of the warrior, each one was supplied with either a breech-loading rifle or revolver, sometimes with both — the latter obtained through the wise foresight and strong love of fair play which prevails in the Indian Department, which, seeing that its wards are determined to fight, is equally determined that there shall be no advantage taken, but that the two sides shall be armed alike; proving, too, in this manner the wonderful liberality of our Government, which not only is able to furnish its soldiers with the latest improved style of breech-loaders to defend it and themselves, but is equally able and willing to give the same pattern of arms to their common foe. The only difference is, that the soldier, if he loses his weapon, is charged double price for it; while to avoid making any such charge against the Indian, his weapons are given him without conditions attached. In the line of battle before us there were several hundred Indians, while further to the rear and at different distances were other organized bodies acting apparently as reserves. Still further were small detachments who seemed to perform the duty of couriers, and were held in readiness to convey messages to the village. The ground beyond was favorable for an extended view, allowing the eye to sweep the plain for several miles. As far as the eye could reach small groups or individuals could be seen in the direction of the village; these were evidently parties of observation, whose sole object was to learn the result of our meeting with the main body and hasten with the news to the village.

For a few moments appearances seemed to foreshadow anything but a peaceful issue. The infantry was in the advance, followed closely by the artillery, while my command, the cavalry, was marching on the flank. General Hancock, who was riding with his staff at the head of the column, coming suddenly in view of the wild fantastic battle array, which extended far to our right and left and not more than half a mile in our front, hastily sent orders to the infantry, artillery, and cavalry to form line of battle, evidently determined that if war was intended we should be prepared. The cavalry, being the last to form on the right, came into line on a gallop, and, without waiting to align the ranks carefully, the command was given to " draw sabre." As the bright blades flashed from their scabbards into the morning sunlight, and the infantry brought their muskets to a carry, a most beautiful and wonderfully interesting sight was spread out before and around us, presenting a contrast which, to a military eye, could but be striking. Here in battle array, facing each other, were the representatives of civilized and barbarous warfare. The one, with but few modifications, stood clothed in the same rude style of dress, bearing the same patterned shield and weapon that his ancestors had borne centuries before; the other confronted him in the dress and supplied with the implements of war which the most advanced stage of civilization had pronounced the most perfect. Was the comparative superiority of these two classes to be subjected to the mere test of war here? Such seemed the prevailing impression on both sides. All was eager anxiety and expectation. Neither side seemed to comprehend the object or intentions of the other; each was waiting for the other to deliver the first blow. A more beautiful battle-ground could not have been chosen. Not a bush or even the slightest irregularity of ground intervened between the two lines which now stood frowning and facing each other. Chiefs could be seen riding along the line as if directing and exhorting their braves to deeds of heroism.

After a few moments of painful suspense, General Hancock, accompanied by General A. J. Smith and other officers, rode forward, and through an interpreter invited the chiefs to meet us midway, for the purpose of an interview. In response to this invitation Roman Nose, bearing a white flag, accompanied by Bull Bear, White Horse, Gray Beard, and Medicine Wolf on the part of the Cheyennes, and Pawnee Killer, Bad Wound, Tall Bear that Walks under the Ground, Left Hand, Little Bear, and Little Bull on the part of the Sioux, rode forward to the middle of the open space between the two lines. Here we shook hands with all of the chiefs, most of them exhibiting unmistakable signs of gratification at this apparently peaceful termination of our encounter. General Hancock very naturally inquired the object of the hostile attitude displayed before us, saying to the chiefs that if war was their object we were ready then and there to participate. Their immediate answer was that they did not desire war, but were peacefully disposed. They were then told that we would continue our march toward the village, and encamp near it, but would establish such regulations that none of the soldiers would be permitted to approach or disturb them. An arrangement was then effected by which the chiefs were to assemble at General Hancock's headquarters as soon as our camp was pitched. The interview then terminated, and the Indians moved off in the direction of their village, we following leisurely in rear.

A march of a few miles brought us in sight of the village, which was situated in a beautiful grove on the banks of the stream up which we had been marching. The village consisted of upwards of three hundred lodges, a small fraction over half belonging to the Cheyennes, the remainder to the Sioux. Like all Indian encampments, the ground chosen was a most romantic spot, and at the same time fulfilled in every respect the requirements of a good camping-ground; wood, water, and grass were abundant. The village was placed on a wide, level plateau, while on the north and west, at a short distance off, rose high bluffs, which admirably served as a shelter against the cold winds which at that season of the year prevail from these directions. Our tents were pitched within half a mile of the village. Guards were placed between to prevent intrusion upon our part. A few of the Indian ponies found grazing near our camp were caught and returned to them, to show that our intentions were at least neighborly. We had scarcely pitched our tents when Roman Nose, Bull Bear, Gray Beard, and Medicine Wolf, all prominent chiefs of the Cheyennes, came into camp, with the information that upon our approach their women and children had all fled from the village, alarmed by the presence of so many soldiers, and imagining a second Chivington massacre to be intended. General Hancock insisted that they should all return, promising protection and good treatment to all; that if the camp was abandoned he would hold it responsible. The chiefs then stated their belief in their ability to recall the fugitives, could they be furnished with horses to overtake them. This was accordingly done, and two of them set out mounted on two of our horses. An agreement was also entered into at the same time that one of our interpreters, Ed. Gurrier, a half-breed Cheyenne who was in the employ of the Government, should remain in the village and report every two hours as to whether any Indians were leaving the village. This was about seven o'clock in the evening. At half past nine the half-breed returned to headquarters, with the intelligence that all the chiefs and warriors were saddling up to leave, under circumstances showing that they had no intention of returning, such as packing up such articles as could be carried with them, and cutting and destroying their lodges, this last being done to obtain small pieces for temporary shelter.

I had retired to my tent, which was located some few hundred yards from that of General Hancock, when a messenger from the latter awakened me with the information that General Hancock desired my presence at his tent. Imagining a movement on the part of the Indians, I made no delay in responding to the summons. General Hancock briefly stated the situation of affairs, and directed me to mount my command as quickly and as silently as possible, surround the Indian village, and prevent the departure of its inhabitants. Easily said, but not so easily done. Under ordinary circumstances, silence not being necessary, I could have returned to my camp, and by a few blasts from the trumpet placed every soldier in his saddle almost as quickly as it has taken time to write this sentence. No bugle calls must be sounded; we were to adopt some of the stealth of the Indian — how successfully remains to be seen. By this time every soldier, officers as well as men, was in his tent sound asleep. How to awaken them and impart to each the necessary order? First going to the tent of the adjutant and arousing him, I procured an experienced assistant in my labors.   Next the captains of companies were awakened and orders imparted to them.   They in turn transmitted the order to the first sergeant, who similarly aroused the men.   It has often surprised me to observe the alacrity with which disciplined soldiers, experienced in campaigning, will hasten to prepare themselves for the march in an emergency like this.   No questions are asked, no time is wasted.   A soldier's toilet, on an Indian campaign, is a simple affair, and requires little time for arranging.   His clothes are gathered up hurriedly, no matter how, so long as he retains possession of them.   The first object is to get his horse saddled and bridled, and until this is done his own toilet is a matter of secondary importance, and one button or hook must do the duty of half a dozen.   When his horse is ready for the mount the rider will be seen completing his own equipment; stray buttons will receive attention, arms be overhauled, spurs restrapped; then, if there still remain a few spare moments, the homely black pipe is filled and lighted, and the soldier's preparation is completed.

The night was all that could be desired for the success of our enterprise.   The air was mild and pleasant; the moon, although nearly full, kept almost constantly behind the clouds, as if to screen us in our hazardous undertaking. I say hazardous, because there were none of us who imagined for one moment that if the Indians discovered us in our attempt to surround them and their village, we would escape without a fight — a fight, too, in which the Indians, sheltered behind the trunks of the stately forest trees under which their lodges were pitched, would possess all the advantage.   General Hancock, anticipating that the Indians would discover our approach, and that a fight would ensue, ordered the artillery and infantry under arms, to await the result of our moonlight venture.   My command was soon in the saddle, and silently making its way toward the village.   Instructions had been given forbidding all conversation except in a whisper. Sabres were so disposed of as to prevent clanging. Taking a camp-fire which we could see in the village as our guiding point, we made a detour so as to place the village between ourselves and the infantry. Occasionally the moon would peep out from behind the clouds and enable us to catch a hasty glance at the village. Here and there under the thick foliage we could see the white, conical-shaped lodges. Were their inmates slumbering, unaware of our close proximity, or were their dusky defenders concealed, as well they might have been, along the banks of the Pawnee, quietly awaiting our approach, and prepared to greet us with their well-known war-whoop? These were questions that were probably suggested to the mind of each individual of my command. If we were discovered approaching in the stealthy, suspicious manner which characterized our movements, the hour being midnight, it would require a more confiding nature than that of the Indian to assign a friendly or peaceful motive to our conduct. The same flashes of moonlight which gave us hurried glimpses of the village enabled us to see our own column of horsemen stretching its silent length far into the dim darkness, and winding its course, like some huge anaconda about to envelop its victim.

The method by which it was determined to establish a cordon of armed troopers about the fated village, was to direct the march in a circle, with the village in the centre, the commanding officer of each rear troop halting his command at the proper point, and deploying his men similarly to a line of skirmishers — the entire circle, when thus formed, facing toward the village, and distant from it perhaps a few hundred yards. No sooner was our line completely formed than the moon, as if deeming darkness no longer essential to our success, appeared from behind her screen and lighted up the entire scene. And a beautiful scene it was. The great circle of troops, each individual of which sat on his steed silent as a statue, the beautiful and in some places dense foliage of the cotton trees sheltering and shading the bleached, skin-clad lodges of the red man, while in the midst of all murmured undisturbedly in its channel the little stream on whose banks the village was located, all combined to produce an artistic effect, as beautiful as it was interesting. But we were not there to study artistic effects. The next step was to determine whether we had captured an inhabited village, involving almost necessarily a fierce conflict with its savage occupants, or whether the red man had again proven too wily and crafty for his more civilized brothers.

Directing the entire line of troopers to remain mounted with carbines held at the " advance," I dismounted, and taking with me Gurrier, the half-breed, Dr. Coates, one of our medical staff, and Lieutenant Moylan, the adjutant, proceeded on our hands and knees toward the village. The prevailing opinion was that the Indians were still asleep. I desired to approach near enough to the lodges to enable the half-breed to hail the village in the Indian tongue, and if possible establish friendly relations at once. It became a question of prudence with us, which we discussed in whispers as we proceeded on our " Tramp, tramp, tramp, the boys are creeping," how far from our horses and how near to the village we dared to go. If so few of us were discovered entering the village in this questionable manner, it was more than probable that, like the returners of stolen property, we should be suitably rewarded and no questions asked. The opinions of Gurrier, the half-breed, were eagerly sought for and generally deferred to. His wife, a full-blooded Cheyenne, was a resident of the village. This with him was an additional reason for wishing a peaceful termination to our efforts. When we had passed over two-thirds of the distance between our horses and the village, it was deemed best to make our presence known. Thus far not a sound had been heard to disturb the stillness of the night.

Gurrier called out at the top of his voice in the Cheyenne tongue. The only response came from the throats of a score or more of Indian dogs which set up a fierce barking. At the same time one or two of our party asserted that they saw figures moving beneath the trees. Gurrier repeated his summons, but with no better result than before.

A hurried consultation ensued. The presence of so many dogs in the village was regarded by the half-breed as almost positive assurance that the Indians were still there. Yet it was difficult to account for their silence. Gurrier in a loud tone repeated who he was, and that our mission was a friendly one. Still no answer. He then gave it as his opinion that the Indians were on the alert, and were probably waiting in the shadow of the trees for us to approach nearer, when they would pounce upon us. This comforting opinion induced another conference. We must ascertain the truth of the matter; our party could do this as well as a large number, and to go back and send another party in our stead could not be thought of.

Forward was the verdict. Each one grasped his revolver, resolved to do his best, whether it was in running or fighting. I think most of us would have preferred to take our own chances at running. We had approached near enough to see that some of the lodges were detached some distance from the main encampment. Selecting the nearest of these, we directed our advance on it. While all of us were full of the spirit of adventure, and were further encouraged with the idea that we were in the discharge of our duty, there was scarcely one of us who would not have felt more comfortable if we could have got back to our horses without loss of pride. Yet nothing, under the circumstances, but a positive order would have induced any one to withdraw. The doctor, who was a great wag, even in moments of greatest danger, could not restrain his propensities in this direction. When everything before us was being weighed

and discussed in the most serious manner, he remarked:
" General, this recalls to my mind those beautiful lines:

'Backward, turn backward, O Time, in thy flight,
  Make me a child again just for tonight — '

this night of all others."

Cautiously approaching, on all fours, to within a few yards of the nearest lodge, occasionally halting and listening to discover evidence as to whether the village was deserted or not, we finally decided that the Indians had fled before the arrival of the cavalry, and that none but empty lodges were before us. This conclusion somewhat emboldened as well as accelerated our progress. Arriving at the first lodge, one of our party raised the curtain or mat which served as a door, and the doctor and myself entered. The interior of the lodge was dimly lighted by the decaying embers of a small fire built in the centre. All around us were to be seen the usual adornments and articles which constitute the household effects of an Indian family. Buffalo robes were spread like carpets over the floor; head-mats, used to recline upon, were arranged as if for the comfort of their owners; parflcches, a sort of Indian band-box, with their contents apparently undisturbed, were to be found carefully stowed away under the edges or borders of the lodge. These, with the door-mats, paint-bags, raw-hide ropes, and other articles of Indian equipment, were left as if the owners had only absented themselves for a brief period. To complete the picture of an Indian lodge, over the fire hung a camp-kettle, in which, by means of the dim light of the fire, we could see what had been intended for the supper of the late occupants of the lodge. The doctor, ever on the alert to discover additional items of knowledge, whether pertaining to history or science, snuffed the savory odors which arose from the dark recesses of the mysterious kettle. Casting about the lodge for some instrument to aid him in his pursuit of knowledge, he found a horn spoon, with which he began his investigation of the contents, finally succeeding in getting possession of a fragment which might have been the half of a duck or rabbit, judging merely from its size. " Ah! " said the doctor, in his most complacent manner, " here is the opportunity I have long been waiting for. I have often desired to test and taste of the Indian mode of cooking. What do you suppose this is?" holding up the dripping morsel. Unable to obtain the desired information, the doctor, whose naturally good appetite had been sensibly sharpened by his recent exercise *à la quadrupède,* set to with a will and ate heartily of the mysterious contents of the kettle. " What can this be?" again inquired the doctor. He was only satisfied on one point, that it was delicious — a dish fit for a king. Just then Gurrier, the half-breed, entered the lodge. He could solve the mystery, having spent years among the Indians. To him the doctor appealed for information. Fishing out a huge piece, and attacking it with the voracity of a hungry wolf, he was not long in determining what the doctor had supped so heartily upon. His first words settled the mystery: " Why, this is dog." I will not attempt to repeat the few but emphatic words uttered by the heartily disgusted member of the medical fraternity as he rushed from the lodge.

Other members of our small party had entered other lodges, only to find them, like the first, deserted. But little of the furniture belonging to the lodges had been taken, showing how urgent and hasty had been the flight of the owners. To aid in the examination of the village, reinforcements were added to our party, and an exploration of each lodge was determined upon. At the same time a messenger was despatched to General Hancock, informing him of the flight of the Indians. Some of the lodges were closed by having brush or timber piled up against the entrance, as if to preserve the contents. Others had huge pieces cut from their sides, these pieces evidently being carried away to furnish temporary shelter to the fugitives. In most of the lodges the fires were still burning. I had entered several without discovering anything important. Finally, in company with the doctor, I arrived at one, the interior of which was quite dark, the fire having almost died out. Procuring a lighted fagot, I prepared to explore it, as I had done the others; but no sooner had I entered the lodge than my fagot failed me, leaving me in total darkness. Handing it out to the doctor to be relighted, I began feeling my way about the interior of the lodge. I had almost made the circuit when my hand came in contact with a human foot; at the same time a voice unmistakably Indian, and which evidently came from the owner of the foot, convinced me that I was not alone. My first impression was that in their hasty flight the Indians had gone off leaving this one asleep. My next, very naturally, related to myself. I would have gladly placed myself on the outside of the lodge, and there matured plans for interviewing its occupant; but unfortunately to reach the entrance of the lodge I must either pass over or around the owner of the before-mentioned foot and voice. Could I have been convinced that among *its* other possessions there was neither tomahawk nor scalping-knife, pistol nor war-club, or any similar article of the noble red man's toilet, I would have risked an attempt to escape through the low narrow opening of the lodge; but who ever saw an Indian without one or all these interesting trinkets? Had I made the attempt, I should have expected to encounter either the keen edge of the scalping-knife or the blow of the tomahawk, and to have engaged in a questionable struggle for life. This would not do. I crouched in silence for a few moments, hoping the doctor would return with the lighted fagot. I need not say that each succeeding moment spent in the darkness of that lodge seemed like an age. I could hear a slight movement on the part of my unknown neighbor, which did not add to my comfort. Why does not the doctor return? At last I discovered the approach of a light on the outside. When it neared the entrance I called to the doctor and informed him that an Indian was in the lodge, and that he had better have his weapons ready for a conflict. I had, upon discovering the foot, drawn my hunting-knife from its scabbard, and now stood waiting the *dénouement*. With his lighted fagot in one hand and cocked revolver in the other, the doctor cautiously entered the lodge. And there, directly between us, wrapped in a buffalo robe, lay the cause of my anxiety — a little Indian girl, probably ten years old; not a full-blood, but a half-breed. She was terribly frightened at finding herself in our hands, with none of her people near. Why was she left behind in this manner? Gurrier, our half-breed interpreter, was called in. His inquiries were soon answered. The little girl, who at first was an object of our curiosity, became at once an object of pity. The Indians, an unusual thing for them to do toward their own blood, had wilfully deserted her; but this, alas! was the least of their injuries to her. After being shamefully abandoned by the entire village, a few of the young men of the tribe returned to the deserted lodge, and upon the person of this little girl committed outrages, the details of which are too sickening for these pages. She was carried to the fort and placed under the care of kind hands and warm hearts, where everything was done for her comfort that was possible. Other parties in exploring the deserted village found an old, decrepit Indian of the Sioux tribe, who also had been deserted, owing to his infirmities and inability to travel with the tribe. He also was kindly cared for by the authorities of the fort. Nothing was gleaned from our search of the village which might indicate the direction of the flight. General Hancock, on learning the situation of affairs, despatched some companies of infantry to the deserted village, with orders to replace the cavalry and protect the village and its contents from disturbance until its final disposition could be determined upon. Starting my command back to our camp near General Hancock's headquarters, I galloped on in advance to report the particulars to the General. It was then decided that with eight troops of cavalry I should start in pursuit of the Indians at early dawn on the following morning (April 15). There was no sleep for my command the remainder of the night, the time being fully occupied in preparation for the march, neither the extent nor direction of which was known.

Mess kits were overhauled, and fresh supplies of coffee, sugar, flour, and the other articles which go to supply the soldier's larder, were laid in. Blankets were carefully rolled so as to occupy as little space as possible; every useless pound of luggage was discarded, for in making a rapid pursuit after Indians, much of the success depends upon the lightness of the order of march. Saratoga trunks and their accompaniments are at a discount. Never was the old saying that in Rome one must do as Romans do more aptly illustrated than on an Indian campaign. The Indian, knowing that his safety either on offensive or defensive movements depends in a great measure upon the speed and endurance of his horse, takes advantage of every circumstance which will favor either the one or the other. To this end he divests himself of all superfluous dress and ornament when preparing for rapid movements. The white man, if he hopes for success, must adopt the same rule of action, and encumber his horse as little as possible. Something besides well-filled mess chests and carefully rolled blankets is necessary in preparing for an Indian campaign. Arms must be reëxamined, cartridge-boxes refilled, so that each man should carry about one hundred rounds of ammunition "on his person," while each troop commander must see that in the company wagon there are placed a few boxes of reserve ammunition. Then, when the equipment of the soldier has been attended to, his horse, without whose assistance he is helpless, must be looked after; loose shoes are tightened by the driving of an additional nail, and to accomplish this one may see the company blacksmith, a soldier, with the few simple tools of his kit on the ground beside him, hurriedly fastening the last shoe by the uncertain light of a candle held in the hands of the rider of the horse, their mutual labor being varied at times by queries as to " How long shall we be gone? " " I wonder if we will catch Mr. Lo? " " If we do, we'll make it lively for him." So energetic had everybody been that before daylight everything was in readiness for the start. In addition to the regularly organized companies of soldiers which made up the pursuing column, I had with me a detachment of white scouts or Plainsmen, and one of friendly Indians, the latter belonging to the tribe of Delawares, once so famous in Indian wars. Of the Indians one only could speak English; he acted as interpreter for the party. Among the white scouts were numbered some of the most noted of their class. The most prominent man among them was " Wild Bill," whose highly varied career was made the subject of an illustrated sketch in one of the popular monthly periodicals a few years ago. " Wild Bill " was a strange character, just the one which a novelist might gloat over. He was a Plainsman in every sense of the word, yet unlike any other of his class. In person he was about six feet one in height, straight as the straightest of the warriors whose implacable foe he was; broad shoulders, well-formed chest and limbs, and a face strikingly handsome; a sharp, clear, blue eye, which stared you straight in the face when in conversation; a finely-shaped nose, inclined to be aquiline; a well-turned mouth, with lips partially concealed by a handsome moustache. His hair and complexion were those of the perfect blond. The former was worn in uncut ringlets falling carelessly over his powerfully formed shoulders. Add to this figure a costume blending the immaculate neatness of the dandy with the extravagant taste and style of the frontiersman, and you have Wild Bill, then as now,

the most famous scout on the Plains. Whether on foot
or on horseback, he was one of the most perfect types of
physical manhood I ever saw. Of his courage there could
be no question; it had been brought to the test on too many
occasions to admit of a doubt. His skill in the use of the
rifle and pistol was unerring; while his deportment was
exactly the opposite of what might be expected from a man
of his surroundings. It was entirely free from all bluster
or bravado. He seldom spoke of himself unless requested
to do so. His conversation, strange to say, never bordered
either on the vulgar or blasphemous. His influence among
the frontiersmen was unbounded, his word was law; and
many are the personal quarrels and disturbances which he
has checked among his comrades by his simple announcement that "this has gone far enough," if need be followed
by the ominous warning that when persisted in or renewed
the quarreller "must settle it with me." "Wild Bill" is
anything but a quarrelsome man; yet no one but himself can
enumerate the many conflicts in which he has been engaged,
and which have almost invariably resulted in the death of
his adversary. I have a personal knowledge of at least
half a dozen men whom he has at various times killed,
one of these being at the time a member of my command.
Others have been severely wounded, yet he always escapes
unhurt. On the Plains every man openly carries his belt
with its invariable appendages, knife and revolver, often
two of the latter. Wild Bill always carried two handsome
ivory-handled revolvers of the large size; he was never seen
without them. Where this is the common custom, brawls
or personal difficulties are seldom if ever settled by blows.
The quarrel is not from a word to a blow, but from a word
to the revolver, and he who can draw and fire first is the
best man. No civil law reaches him; none is applied for.
In fact there is no law recognized beyond the frontier but
that of "might makes right." Should death result from
the quarrel, as it usually does, no coroner's jury is im-

panelled to learn the cause of death, and the survivor is not arrested. But instead of these old-fashioned proceedings, a meeting of citizens takes place, the survivor is *requested* to be present when the circumstances of the homicide are inquired into, and the unfailing verdict of " justifiable," " self-defence," etc., is pronounced and the law stands vindicated. That justice is often deprived of a victim there is not a doubt. Yet in all of the many affairs of this kind in which " Wild Bill " has performed a part, and which have come to my knowledge, there is not a single instance in which the verdict of twelve fair-minded men would not be pronounced in his favor. That the even tenor of his way continues to be disturbed by little events of this description may be inferred from an item which has been floating lately through the columns of the press, and which states that " the funeral of ' Jim Bludso,' who was killed the other day by ' Wild Bill,' took place to-day." It then adds: " The funeral expenses were borne by ' Wild Bill.' " What could be more thoughtful than this? Not only to send a fellow mortal out of the world, but to pay the expenses of the transit.

THE PONY EXPRESS

MARK TWAIN

In a little while all interest was taken up in stretching our necks and watching for the " pony-rider " — the fleet messenger who sped across the continent from St. Joe to Sacramento, carrying letters nineteen hundred miles in eight days! Think of that for perishable horse and human flesh and blood to do! The pony-rider was usually a little bit of a man, brimful of spirit and endurance. No matter what time of the day or night his watch came on, and no matter whether it was winter or summer, raining, snowing, hailing, or sleeting, or whether his " beat " was a level straight road or a crazy trail over mountain crags and precipices, or whether it led through peaceful regions or regions that swarmed with hostile Indians, he must be always ready to leap into the saddle and be off like the wind! There was no idling-time for a pony-rider on duty. He rode fifty miles without stopping, by daylight, moonlight, starlight, or through the blackness of darkness — just as it happened. He rode a splendid horse that was born for a racer and fed and lodged like a gentleman; kept him at his utmost speed for ten miles, and then, as he came crashing up to the station where stood two men holding fast a fresh, impatient steed, the transfer of rider and mail-bag was made in the twinkling of an eye, and away flew the eager pair and were out of sight before the spectator could get hardly the ghost of a look.   Both rider and horse went " flying light." The rider's dress was thin, and fitted close; he wore a " roundabout," and a skull-cap, and tucked his pantaloons into his boot-tops like a race-rider.   He carried no arms — he carried nothing that was not absolutely necessary, for even the postage on his literary freight was worth *five dollars a letter*.   He got but little frivolous correspondence to carry — his bag had business letters in it, mostly.   His horse was stripped of all unnecessary weight, too.   He wore a little wafer of a racing-saddle, and no visible blanket.   He wore light shoes, or none at all.   The little flat mail-pockets strapped under the rider's thighs would each hold about the bulk of a child's primer.   They held many and many an important business chapter and newspaper letter, but these were written on paper as airy and thin as gold-leaf, nearly, and thus bulk and weight were economized.   The stage-coach traveled about a hundred to a hundred and twenty-five miles a day (twenty-four hours), the pony-rider about two hundred and fifty.   There were about eighty pony-riders in the saddle all the time, night and day, stretching in a long, scattering procession from the Missouri to California, forty flying eastward, and forty toward the west, and among them making four hundred gallant horses earn a stirring livelihood and see a deal of scenery every single day in the year.

We had had a consuming desire, from the beginning, to see a pony-rider, but somehow or other all that passed us and all that met us managed to streak by in the night, and so we heard only a whiz and a hail, and the swift phantom of the desert was gone before we could get our heads out of the windows.   But now we were expecting one along every moment, and would see him in broad daylight. Presently the driver exclaims:

" Here he comes! "

Every neck is stretched further, and every eye strained

wider. Away across the endless dead level of the prairie a black speck appears against the sky, and it is plain that it moves. Well, I should think so! In a second or two it becomes a horse and rider, rising and falling, rising and falling — sweeping toward us nearer and nearer — growing more and more distinct, more and more sharply defined — nearer and still nearer, and the flutter of the hoofs comes faintly to the ear — another instant a whoop and a hurrah from our upper deck, a wave of the rider's hand, but no reply, and man and horse burst past our excited faces, and go winging away like a belated fragment of a storm!

So sudden is it all, and so like a flash of unreal fancy, that but for the flake of white foam left quivering and perishing on a mail-sack after the vision had flashed by and disappeared, we might have doubted whether we had seen any actual horse and man at all, maybe.

SLADE

From " Roughing It." By Mark Twain.

THERE was much magic in that name, SLADE! Day or night, now, I stood always ready to drop any subject in hand, to listen to something new about Slade and his ghastly exploits. Even before we got to Overland City, we had begun to hear about Slade and his " division " (for he was a " division-agent ") on the Overland; and from the hour we had left Overland City we had heard drivers and conductors talk about only three things — " Californy," the Nevada silver mines, and this desperado Slade. And a deal the most of the talk was about Slade. We had gradually come to have a realizing sense of the fact that Slade was a man whose heart and hands and soul were steeped in the blood of the offenders against his dignity; a man who awfully avenged all injuries, affronts, insults or slights, of whatever kind — on the spot if he could, years afterward if lack of earlier opportunity compelled it; a man whose hate tortured him day and night till vengeance appeased it — and not an ordinary vengeance either, but his enemy's absolute death — nothing less; a man whose face would light up with a terrible joy when he surprised a foe and had him at a disadvantage. A high and efficient servant of the Overland, an outlaw among outlaws and yet their relentless scourge, Slade was at once the most bloody, the most dangerous, and the most valuable citizen that inhabited the savage fastnesses of the mountains.

Really and truly, two-thirds of the talk of drivers and conductors had been about this man Slade, ever since the day before we reached Julesburg. In order that the Eastern reader may have a clear conception of what a Rocky Mountain desperado is, in his highest state of development, I will reduce all this mass of overland gossip to one straightforward narrative, and present it in the following shape:

Slade was born in Illinois, of good parentage. At about twenty-six years of age he killed a man in a quarrel and fled the country. At St. Joseph, Missouri, he joined one of the early California-bound emigrant trains, and was given the post of trainmaster. One day on the plains he had an angry dispute with one of his wagon-drivers, and both drew their revolvers. But the driver was the quicker artist, and had his weapon cocked first. So Slade said it was a pity to waste life on so small a matter, and proposed that the pistols be thrown on the ground and the quarrel settled by a fist-fight. The unsuspecting driver agreed, and threw down his pistol — whereupon Slade laughed at his simplicity, and shot him dead!

He made his escape, and lived a wild life for awhile, dividing his time between fighting Indians and avoiding an

Illinois Sheriff, who had been sent to arrest him for his first murder. It is said that in one Indian battle he killed three savages with his own hand, and afterward cut their ears off and sent them, with his compliments, to the chief of the tribe.

Slade soon gained a name for fearless resolution, and this was sufficient merit to procure for him the important post of overland division-agent at Julesburg, in place of Mr. Jules, removed. For some time previously, the company's horses had been frequently stolen, and the coaches delayed, by gangs of outlaws, who were wont to laugh at the idea of any man's having the temerity to resent such outrages. Slade resented them promptly. The outlaws soon found that the new agent was a man who did not fear anything that breathed the breath of life. He made short work of all offenders. The result was that delays ceased, the company's property was let alone, and, no matter what happened or who suffered, Slade's coaches went through, every time! True, in order to bring about this wholesome change, Slade had to kill several men — some say three, others say four, and others six — but the world was the richer for their loss. The first prominent difficulty he had was with the ex-agent Jules, who bore the reputation of being a reckless and desperate man himself. Jules hated Slade for supplanting him, and a good fair occasion for a fight was all he was waiting for. By and by Slade dared to employ a man whom Jules had once discharged. Next, Slade seized a team of stage-horses which he accused Jules of having driven off and hidden somewhere for his own use. War was declared, and for a day or two the two men walked warily about the streets, seeking each other, Jules armed with a double-barreled shot gun, and Slade with his history-creating revolver. Finally, as Slade stepped into a store, Jules poured the contents of his gun into him from behind the door. Slade was pluck, and Jules got several bad pistol wounds in return. Then both men fell, and were carried to their respective lodgings, both swearing that better aim should do deadlier work next time. Both were bed-ridden a long time, but Jules got on his feet first, and gathering his possessions together, packed them on a couple of mules, and fled to the Rocky Mountains to gather strength in safety against the day of reckoning. For many months he was not seen or heard of, and was gradually dropped out of the remembrance of all save Slade himself. But Slade was not the man to forget him. On the contrary, common report said that Slade kept a reward standing for his capture, dead or alive!

After awhile, seeing that Slade's energetic administration had restored peace and order to one of the worst divisions of the road, the Overland Stage Company transferred him to the Rocky Ridge division in the Rocky Mountains, to see if he could perform a like miracle there. It was the very paradise of outlaws and desperadoes. There was absolutely no semblance of law there. Violence was the rule. Force was the only recognized authority. The commonest misunderstandings were settled on the spot with the revolver or the knife. Murders were done in open day, and with sparkling frequency, and nobody thought of inquiring into them. It was considered that the parties who did the killing had their private reasons for it; for other people to meddle would have been looked upon as indelicate. After a murder, all the Rocky Mountain etiquette required of a spectator was, that he should help the gentleman bury his game — otherwise his churlishness would surely be remembered against him the first time he killed a man himself and needed a neighborly turn in interring him.

Slade took up his residence sweetly and peacefully in the midst of this hive of horse-thieves and assassins, and the very first time one of them aired his insolent swaggerings in his presence he shot him dead! He began a raid on the outlaws, and in a singularly short space of time he had completely stopped their depredations on the stage stock, recovered a large number of stolen horses, killed several of the worst desperadoes of the district, and gained such a dread ascendency over the rest that they respected him, admired him, feared him, obeyed him! He wrought the same marvelous change in the ways of the community that had marked his administration at Overland City. He captured two men who had stolen Overland stock, and with his own hands he hanged them. He was supreme judge in his district, and he was jury and executioner likewise — and not only in the case of offenses against his employers, but against passing emigrants as well. On one occasion some emigrants had their stock lost or stolen, and told Slade, who chanced to visit their camp. With a single companion he rode to a ranch, the owners of which he suspected, and, opening the door, commenced firing, killing three, and wounding the fourth.

From a bloodthirstily interesting little Montana book[1] I take this paragraph:

While on the road, Slade held absolute sway. He would ride down to a station, get into a quarrel, turn the house out of windows, and maltreat the occupants most cruelly. The unfortunates had no means of redress, and were compelled to recuperate as best they could. On one of these occasions, it is said he killed the father of the fine little half-breed boy Jemmy, whom he adopted, and who lived with his widow after his execution. Stories of Slade's hanging men, and of innumerable assaults, shootings, stabbings, and beatings, in which he was a principal actor, form part of the legends of the stage line. As for minor quarrels and shootings, it is absolutely certain that a minute history of Slade's life would be one long record of such practices.

Slade was a matchless marksman with a navy revolver. The legends say that one morning at Rocky Ridge, when he was feeling comfortable, he saw a man approaching who had offended him some days before — observe the fine memory he had for matters like that — and, " Gentlemen," said Slade, drawing, " it is a good twenty-yard shot — I'll clip the third button on his coat!" Which he did. The

---

[1] "The Vigilantes of Montana," by Prof. Thos. J. Dimsdale.

bystanders all admired it.   And they all attended the funeral, too.

On one occasion a man who kept a little whisky-shelf at the station did something which angered Slade — and went and made his will. A day or two afterward Slade came in and called for some brandy. The man reached under the counter (ostensibly to get a bottle — possibly to get something else), but Slade smiled upon him that peculiarly bland and satisfied smile of his which the neighbors had long ago learned to recognize as a death warrant in disguise, and told him to "none of that! — pass out the high-priced article." So the poor barkeeper had to turn his back and get the high-priced brandy from the shelf; and when he faced around again he was looking into the muzzle of Slade's pistol. "And the next instant," added my informant, impressively, "he was one of the deadest men that ever lived."

The stage drivers and conductors told us that sometimes Slade would leave a hated enemy wholly unmolested, unnoticed and unmentioned, for weeks together — had done it once or twice, at any rate. And some said they believed he did it in order to lull the victims into unwatchfulness, so that he could get the advantage of them, and others said they believed he saved up on enemy that way, just as a schoolboy saved up a cake, and made the pleasure go as far as it would by gloating over the anticipation. One of these cases was that of a Frenchman who had offended Slade. To the surprise of everybody Slade did not kill him on the spot, but let him alone for a considerable time. Finally, however, he went to the Frenchman's house very late one night, knocked, and when his enemy opened the door, shot him dead — pushed the corpse inside the door with his foot, set the house on fire and burned up the dead man, his widow and three children! I heard this story from several different people, and they evidently believed what they were saying.

It may be true, and it may not. "Give a dog a bad name," etc.

Slade was captured once, by a party of men who intended to lynch him. They disarmed him, and shut him up in a strong log-house, and placed a guard over him. He prevailed upon his captors to send for his wife, so that he might have a last interview with her. She was a brave, loving, spirited woman. She jumped on a horse and rode for life and death. When she arrived they let her in without searching her, and before the door could be closed she whipped out a couple of revolvers, and she and her lord marched forth defying the party. And then, under a brisk fire, they mounted double and galloped away unharmed!

In the fullness of time Slade's myrmidons captured his ancient enemy, Jules, whom they found in a well-chosen hiding-place in the remote fastnesses of the mountains, gaining a precarious livelihood with his rifle. They brought him to Rocky Ridge, bound hand and foot, and deposited him in the middle of the cattle-yard with his back against a post. It was said that the pleasure that lit Slade's face when he heard of it was something fearful to contemplate. He examined his enemy to see that he was securely tied and then went to bed, content to wait till morning before enjoying the luxury of killing him. Jules spent the night in the cattle-yard, and it is a region where warm nights are never known. In the morning Slade practised on him with his revolver, nipping the flesh here and there, and occasionally clipping off a finger, while Jules begged him to kill him outright and put him out of his misery. Finally Slade reloaded, and walking up close to his victim, made some characteristic remarks and then dispatched him. The body lay there half a day, nobody venturing to touch it without orders, and then Slade detailed a party and assisted at the burial himself. But he first cut off the dead man's ears and put them in his vest pocket, where he carried them for some time with great satisfaction. That is the story as I have frequently heard it told and seen it in print in California newspapers. It is doubtless correct in all essential particulars.

In due time we rattled up to a stage-station, and sat down to breakfast with a half-savage, half-civilized company of armed and bearded mountaineers, ranchmen and station employés. The most gentlemanly-appearing, quiet, and affable officer we had yet found along the road in the Overland Company's service was the person who sat at the head of the table, at my elbow. Never youth stared and shivered as I did when I heard them call him SLADE!

Here was romance, and I sitting face to face with it! — looking upon it — touching it — hobnobbing with it, as it were! Here, right by my side, was the actual ogre who, in fights and brawls and various ways, *had taken the lives of twenty-six human beings,* or all men lied about him! I suppose I was the proudest stripling that ever traveled to see strange lands and wonderful people.

He was so friendly and so gentle-spoken that I warmed to him in spite of his awful history. It was hardly possible to realize that this pleasant person was the pitiless scourge of the outlaws, the raw-head-and-bloody-bones the nursing mothers of the mountains terrified their children with. And to this day I can remember nothing remarkable about Slade except that his face was rather broad across the cheek bones, and that the cheek bones were low and the lips peculiarly thin and straight. But that was enough to leave something of an effect upon me, for since then I seldom see a face possessing these characteristics without fancying that the owner of it is a dangerous man.

The coffee ran out. At least it was reduced to one tin-cupful, and Slade was about to take it when he saw that my cup was empty. He politely offered to fill it, but although I wanted it, I politely declined. I was afraid he had not killed anybody that morning, and might be needing diversion. But still with firm politeness he insisted on filling my cup, and said I had traveled all night and better deserved it than he — and while he talked he placidly poured the fluid, to the last drop. I thanked him and drank it, but it gave me no comfort, for I could not feel sure that he would not be sorry, presently, that he had given it away, and proceed to kill me to distract his thoughts from the loss. But nothing of the kind occurred. We left him with only twenty-six dead people to account for, and I felt a tranquil satisfaction in the thought that in so judiciously taking care of No. 1 at that breakfast-table I had pleasantly escaped being No. 27. Slade came out to the coach and saw us off, first ordering certain rearrangements of the mailbags for our comfort, and then we took leave of him, satisfied that we should hear of him again, some day, and wondering in what connection.

* * * * * * *

And sure enough, two or three years afterward, we did hear of him again. News came to the Pacific coast that the Vigilance Committee in Montana (whither Slade had removed from Rocky Ridge) had hanged him. I find an account of the affair in the thrilling little book from which I have already quoted a paragraph — " The Vigilantes of Montana; being a Reliable Account of the Capture, Trial and Execution of Henry Plummer's Notorious Road Agent Band: By Prof. Thos. J. Dimsdale, Virginia City, N. T." Mr. Dimsdale's chapter is well worth reading, as a specimen of how the people of the frontier deal with criminals when the courts of law prove inefficient. Mr. Dimsdale makes two remarks about Slade, both of which are accurately descriptive, and one of which is exceedingly picturesque: " Those who saw him in his natural state only, would pronounce him to be a kind husband, a most hospitable host, and a courteous gentleman; on the contrary, those who met him when maddened with liquor and surrounded by a gang of armed roughs, would pronounce him a fiend incarnate." And this: "From Fort Kearney, west, he was feared *a great deal more than the Almighty.*" For compactness, simplicity, and vigor of expression, I will "back" that sentence against anything in literature. Mr. Dimsdale's narrative is as follows. In all places where italics occur they are mine:

After the execution of the five men on the 14th of January, the Vigilantes considered that their work was nearly ended. They had freed the country of highwaymen and murderers to a great extent, and they determined that in the absence of the regular civil authority they would establish a People's Court where all offenders should be tried by judge and jury. This was the nearest approach to social order that the circumstances permitted, and, though strict legal authority was wanting, yet the people were firmly determined to maintain its efficiency, and to enforce its decrees. It may here be mentioned that the overt act which was the last round on the fatal ladder leading to the scaffold on which Slade perished, *was the tearing in pieces and stamping upon a writ of this court, followed by his arrest of the Judge, Alex. Davis, by authority of a presented Derringer, and with his own hands.*

J. A. Slade was himself, we have been informed, a Vigilante; he openly boasted of it, and said he knew all that they knew. He was never accused, or even suspected, of either murder or robbery, committed in this Territory (the latter crime was never laid to his charge, in any place); but that he had killed several men in other localities was notorious, and his bad reputation in this respect was a most powerful argument in determining his fate, when he was finally arrested for the offense above mentioned. On returning from Milk River he became more and more addicted to drinking, until at last it was a common feat for him and his friends to "take the town." He and a couple of his dependents might often be seen on one horse, galloping through the streets, shouting and yelling, firing revolvers, etc. On many occasions he would ride his horse into stores, break up bars, toss the scales out of doors, and use most insulting language to parties present. Just previous to the day of his arrest, he had given a fearful beating to one of his followers; but such was his influence over them that the man wept bitterly at the gallows, and begged for his life with all his power. *It had become quite common, when Slade was on a spree, for the shopkeepers and citizens to close the stores and put out all the lights;* being fearful of some outrage at his hands. For his wanton destruction of goods and furniture, he was always ready to pay, when sober, if he had money; but there were not a few who regarded payment as small satisfaction for the outrage, and these men were his personal enemies.

From time to time Slade received warnings from men that he well knew would not deceive him, of the certain end of his conduct. There was not a moment, for weeks previous to his arrest, in which the public did not expect to hear of some bloody outrage. The dread of his very name, and the presence of the armed band of hangers-on who followed him alone prevented a resistance which must certainly have ended in the instant murder or mutilation of the opposing party.

Slade was frequently arrested by order of the court whose organization we have described, and had treated it with respect by paying one or two fines and promising to pay the rest when he had money; but in the transaction that occurred at this crisis, he forgot even this caution, and, goaded by passion and the hatred of restraint, he sprang into the embrace of death.

Slade had been drunk and "cutting-up" all night. He and his companions had made the town a perfect hell. In the morning, J. M. Fox, the sheriff, met him, arrested him, took him into court and commenced reading a warrant that he had for his arrest, by way of arraignment. He became uncontrollably furious, and *seizing the writ, he tore it up, threw it on the ground and stamped upon it.* The clicking of the locks of his companions' revolvers was instantly heard, and a crisis was expected. The sheriff did not attempt his retention; but being at least as prudent as he was valiant, he succumbed, leaving Slade the *master of the situation and the conqueror and ruler of the courts, law, and law-makers.* This was a declaration of war, and was so accepted. The Vigilance Committee now felt that the question of social order and the preponderance of the law-abiding citizens had then and there to be decided. They knew the character of Slade, and they were well aware that they must submit to his rule without murmur, or else that he must be dealt with in such fashion as would prevent his being able to wreak his vengeance on the committee, who could never have hoped to live in the Territory secure from outrage or death, and who could never leave it without encountering his friends, whom his victory would have emboldened and stimulated to a pitch that would have rendered them reckless of consequences. The day previous he had ridden into Doris's store, and, on being requested to leave, he drew his revolver and threatened to kill the gentleman who spoke to him. Another saloon he had led his horse into, and, buying a bottle of wine, he tried to make the animal drink it. This was not considered an uncommon performance, as he had often entered saloons and commenced firing at the lamps, causing a wild stampede.

A leading member of the committee met Slade, and informed him in the quiet, earnest manner of one who feels the importance of what he is saying: "Slade, get your horse at once, and go home, or there will be —— to pay." Slade started and took a long look, with his dark and piercing eyes, at the gentleman. "What do you mean?" said he. "You have no right to ask what I mean," was the quiet reply, "get your horse at once, and remember what I tell you." After a short pause he promised to do so, and actually got into the saddle; but, being still intoxicated, he began calling aloud to one after another of his friends, and at last seemed to have forgotten the warning he had received and became again uproarious, shouting the name of a well-known courtezan in company with those of two men whom he considered heads of the committee, as a sort of challenge; perhaps, however, as a simple act of bravado. It seems probable that the intimation of personal danger he had received had not been forgotten entirely; though, fatally for him, he took a foolish way of showing his remembrance of it. He sought out Alexander Davis, the Judge of the Court, and, drawing a cocked Derringer, he presented it at his head, and told him that he should hold him as a hostage for his own safety. As the judge stood perfectly quiet, and offered no resistance to his captor, no further outrage followed on this score. Previous to this, on account of the critical state of affairs, the committee had met, and at last resolved to arrest him. His execution had not been agreed upon, and, at that time, would have been negatived, most assuredly. A messenger rode down to Nevada to inform the leading men of what was on hand, as it was desirable to show that there was a feeling of unanimity on the subject, all along the gulch.

The miners turned out almost *en masse,* leaving their work and forming in solid column, about six hundred strong, armed to the teeth, they marched up to Virginia. The leader of the body well knew the temper of his men on the subject. He spurred on ahead of them, and, hastily calling a meeting of the executive, he told them plainly that the miners meant "business," and that, if they came up, they would not stand in the street to be shot down by Slade's friends; but that they would take him and hang him. The meeting was small, as the Virginia men were loath to act at all. This momentous announcement of the feeling of the Lower Town was made to a cluster of men, who were deliberating behind a wagon, at the rear of a store on Main street.

The committee were most unwilling to proceed to extremities. All the duty they had ever performed seemed as nothing to the task before them; but they had to decide, and that quickly. It was finally agreed that if the whole body of the miners were of the opinion that he should be hanged, that the committee left it in their hands to deal with him. Off, at hot speed, rode the leader of the Nevada men to join his command.

Slade had found out what was intended, and the news sobered him instantly. He went into P. S. Pfouts' store, where Davis was, and apologized for his conduct, saying that he would take it all back.

The head of the column now wheeled into Wallace street and marched up at quick time. Halting in front of the store, the executive officer of the committee stepped forward and arrested Slade, who was at once informed of his doom, and inquiry was made as to whether he had any business to settle. Several parties spoke to him on the subject; but to all such inquiries he turned a deaf ear, being entirely absorbed in the terrifying reflections on his own awful position. He never ceased his entreaties for life, and to see his dear wife. The unfortunate lady referred to, between whom and Slade there existed a warm affection, was at this time living at their ranch on the Madison. She was possessed of considerable personal attractions; tall, well-formed, of graceful carriage, pleasing manners, and was, withal, an accomplished horsewoman.

A messenger from Slade rode at full speed to inform her of her husband's arrest. In an instant she was in the saddle, and with all the energy that love and despair could lend to an ardent temperament and a strong physique, she urged her fleet charger over the twelve miles of rough and rocky ground that intervened between her and the object of her passionate devotion.

Meanwhile, a party of volunteers had made the necessary preparations for the execution, in the valley traversed by the branch. Beneath the site of Pfouts and Russell's stone building there was a corral, the gate-posts of which were strong and high. Across the top was laid a beam, to which the rope was fastened, and a dry-goods box served for the platform. To this place Slade was marched, surrounded by a guard, composing the best armed and most numerous force that has ever appeared in Montana Territory.

The doomed man had so exhausted himself by tears, prayers, and lamentations, that he had scarcely strength left to stand under the fatal beam. He repeatedly exclaimed, "My God! my God! must I die? Oh, my dear wife!"

On the return of the fatigue party, they encountered some friends of Slade, staunch and reliable citizens and members of the committee, but who were personally attached to the condemned. On hearing of his sentence, one of them, a stout-hearted man, pulled out his handkerchief and walked away, weeping like a child. Slade still begged to see his wife, most piteously, and it seemed hard to deny his request; but the bloody consequences that were sure to follow the inevitable attempt at a rescue, that her presence and entreaties would have certainly incited, forbade the granting of his request. Several gentlemen were sent for to see him, in his last moments, one of whom (Judge Davis) made a short address to the people; but in such low tones as to be inaudible, save to a few in his immediate vicinity. One of his friends, after exhausting his powers of entreaty, threw off his coat and declared that the prisoner could not be hanged until he himself was killed. A hundred guns were instantly leveled at him; whereupon he turned and fled; but, being brought back, he was compelled to resume his coat, and to give a promise of future peaceable demeanor.

Scarcely a leading man in Virginia could be found, though numbers of the citizens joined the ranks of the guard when the arrest was made. All lamented the stern necessity which dictated the execution.

Everything being ready, the command was given, "Men, do your duty," and the box being instantly slipped from beneath his feet, he died almost instantaneously.

The body was cut down and carried to the Virginia Hotel, where, in a darkened room, it was scarcely laid out, when the unfortunate and bereaved companion of the deceased arrived, at headlong speed, to find that all was over, and that she was a widow. Her grief and heart-piercing cries were terrible evidences of the depth of her attachment for her lost husband, and a considerable period elapsed before she could regain the command of her excited feelings.

There is something about the desperado-nature that is wholly unaccountable — at least it looks unaccountable. It is this. The true desperado is gifted with splendid courage, and yet he will take the most infamous advantage of his enemy; armed and free, he will stand up before a host and fight until he is shot all to pieces, and yet when he is under the gallows and helpless he will cry and plead like a child.

Words are cheap, and it is easy to call Slade a coward (all executed men who do not " die game " are promptly called cowards by unreflecting people), and when we read of Slade that he " had so exhausted himself by tears, prayers, and lamentations, that he had scarcely strength left to stand under the fatal beam," the disgraceful word suggests itself in a moment — yet in frequently defying and inviting the vengeance of banded Rocky Mountain cut-throats by shooting down their comrades and leaders, and never offering to hide or fly, Slade showed that he was a man of peerless bravery. No coward would dare that. Many a notorious coward, many a chicken-livered poltroon, coarse, brutal, degraded, has made his dying speech without a quaver in his voice and been swung into eternity with what looked like the calmest fortitude, and so we are justified in believing, from the low intellect of such a creature, that it was not *moral* courage that enabled him to do it. Then, if moral courage is not the requisite quality, what could it have been that this stout-hearted Slade lacked? — this bloody, desperate, kindly-mannered, urbane gentleman, who never hesitated to warn his most ruffianly enemies that he would kill them whenever or wherever he came across them next! I think it is a conundrum worth investigating.

GENERAL SHERIDAN HUNTS THE BUFFALO

DE B. R. KEIM

From "On the Border with Sheridan's Troopers." Reprinted by permission of the publishers, Claxton, Remsen & Heffinger, Philadelphia.[1]

To RELIEVE the monotony of inactivity the Commanding General, much to the pleasure of a number of the officers of the staff and garrison at Fort Hays, proposed a "genuine" buffalo hunt. The diversion was also in part out of compliment to Captain Merryman, of the U. S. revenue cutter M'Culloch, then on a visit to headquarters. A bright day in October was fixed for the sport. Accordingly at an early hour the horses were sent to the railroad and put on the cars. Leaving Hays City we ran up the track, a distance of thirty miles. Here, by means of a gangplank, the horses were led out of the cars and saddled by the orderlies. Leaving the guard the General had brought with him to protect the train, we mounted and "lit out," as rapid locomotion is called in that locality. Each person wore a brace of pistols for close work, and carried a breech-loading rifle to use at greater distance.

After a lively gallop of several miles, passing within the cordon of watchful sentinels, always found on the outskirts, we struck a herd numbering several thousand animals. Our approach had already been signalled and the herd was moving off at a rapid pace. There was no time to lose. Each one of the party singled out his animal, and putting spurs to his horse dashed after, striving to get abreast his

---

[1] Copyright, 1885, by David McKay.

game at a distance of a few paces, in order to deliver his fire.   The General led off in the charge followed by Merryman, who, accustomed to salt water navigation, swayed from side to side.   He, however, maintained a vigorous hold upon the pummel of the saddle, bounded into the air and returned emphatically, but not always gracefully, into his saddle with every leap of his horse.   The General, after considerable manœuvering, managed to separate a fine cow from her companions.   The chase was quite spirited for several hundred yards, but a well directed shot under the shoulder, which very summarily suspended the powers of locomotion on the part of the buffalo, put a termination to the race.   Several of the party soon became busily engaged on their own account in the exciting sport.   One young bull, of irate temper, finding himself selected as a target, undertook to show fight and turned upon his pursuer.   For some minutes the characters were reversed, and, judging from appearances, it might have been supposed that the buffalo was the hunter.   In the course of an hour five animals were killed.   Most of the horses, however, were perfectly " green," and consequently no use whatever, except to follow, giving the rider an opportunity to witness the sport without participating in it.

There is something majestic and formidable in the appearance of a buffalo.   It is therefore not surprising that but few horses will readily approach sufficiently near to enable the hunter to make a close shot.   Some horses rebel, notwithstanding every effort to allay their alarm.   Others, by a proper course of training, carry their riders, without any direction, into just the position desirable.   Such an animal is a treasure in the esteem of a plainsman.   He talks about his " buffalo horse " with more pride than he would of himself, had he accomplished a feat ever so wonderful.   It was interesting to watch the movements of the trained horse.   He approached the buffalo rapidly but cautiously.   His eyes were steadily fixed upon the animal and watched every motion.   Should the buffalo expedite his pace, the horse did likewise, regulating his increased rate of speed so as to get alongside without unnecessarily alarming the animal.   As the horse came abreast, the buffalo naturally swayed his course away to the right or left.   This was the dangerous part of the chase. Should the buffalo after moving away, the horse following, turn suddenly, a collision would be almost certain.   This the horse seemed to know so perfectly that he changed direction on a long turn.   After firing, should the animal fall, the horse kept up his speed, described a circle bringing him back to the carcass of the dead or wounded buffalo.

Timid horses and awkward riders run great risks of their lives by not knowing how to avoid any hostile demonstrations on the part of the buffalo.   The latter has the advantage, and by not keeping a close watch, fatal results are sure to occur.   An old hunter, mounted on a " buffalo horse," in every sense of the term, dashing fearlessly across the plain in pursuit of this truly magnificent game, presents a picture the very culmination of manly sport.

During our own attempts to make a fair show of knowledge of the subject, there were several very narrow escapes as regarded personal safety.   Two of our party being in pursuit of the same animal, there was quite a competition as to who would get the first shot.   The rider in the rear, in the excitement had his pistol go off out of time.   The ball passed within a very few inches of the front rider's head.   Both were alarmed, and the race terminated by the one apologizing, and the other feeling around to see whether he had been hurt.

While our own sport was going on, two Mexicans with us, were to be seen in the very midst of the herd following up the younger animals.   Each rider had his lariat, holding the coil in one hand and with the other swinging the loop above his head in order to get the proper momentum.   It was short work.   At the first attempt, each man had his noose over the head of a fine yearling. The horses gradually slackened their gait, while the terrified buffaloes made every effort to escape. One of the lariats, unfortunately, parted and off went the animal with it dangling at his heels. The other calf was secured and sent to the train.

After several hours occupied in the exciting amusement of the chase, we returned to the cars. The horses, much blown, were unsaddled and put aboard. A party of soldiers were sent out to bring in the meat.

On our homeward journey a fine herd of antelopes was discovered ahead, close to the track. By a little skillful calculation of time, distance, and velocity, the engineer brought us within three hundred yards. A perfect fusilade was opened out of the car windows, during which one of the beautiful little animals was seen to fall. The train stopped and the " meat " was brought in. This terminated the day's sport. At nine o'clock in the evening we reached Fort Hays.

I may, in this connection, make a few passing notes upon the resorts and habits of the American bison or buffalo, as he is popularly designated. With the savage nomad, he constitutes the actual and aboriginal occupant of the plains. The movements of the immense herds of buffaloes regulate the locations of the savage tribes. They constitute the commissariat of the Indian, and govern frequently his ability for war or control his desire for peace. Prior to the opening of the country to the settler, the buffalo roamed over the entire territory from the Missouri river to the Rocky mountains, and from the plains of western Texas to the head-waters of the Missouri in the north. To-day the buffalo is rarely seen south of the Red river, or within two hundred miles of the Missouri, at Kansas City. In numbers he is evidently rapidly diminishing, though the countless herds found during the summer along the railroads, would seem to indicate that the race is far from running out.

The buffalo is migratory in his habits and subject to two influences in his movements, the seasons, and the abundance or scarcity of pasturage. The migrations of the herds appear to be simultaneous. I have seen herd after herd stretching over a distance of eighty miles, all tending in the same direction. During the early spring months they are generally to be found in the regions south of the Canadian, as far as the Red. Here the winters are short and the grass shoots early. As the pasturage makes its appearance towards the north, the herds follow, moving across the Cimmaron, the Arkansas, the Smoky Hill, the Republican, and beyond the Platte. Cases frequently occur where small herds becoming detached from the main bodies, and particularly the old bulls and cows unable to travel, remain north of the Platte, and manage to eke out an existence through the coldest winters. Other small herds are found in different localities far south during the summer. These exceptions, to the general rule of their habits, are always the result of causes, such as inability to follow the main herd, or being detached and driven back.

In all his habits the buffalo displays an instinctive sense of organization and discipline which alone could accomplish the wise provisions of nature in subsisting such enormous masses of animal life. Not only does the great herd, as a mass, preserve a remarkable concert of action " on the move," but it is subdivided into smaller herds, which seem to be composed of animals having peculiar affinities. These small herds have each their leader, always a fine young or middle-aged bull, whose fighting qualities had won for him the ascendency over all other male competitors. In the black mass presented by the great herd a space, sometimes as limited as a hundred yards, can always be detected between the sub-divisions. Each herd always preserves its relative position to the others, and, in case of alarm, takes flight in a single mass. It also preserves the same relation in galloping to water.

As a precaution against surprise, each herd has its videttes, through which the alarm is given upon the appearance of danger. Approaching a herd, groups of buffaloes in fours and fives are first seen. These, taking the alarm, gallop towards the common centre. The ever-watchful and suspicious young males immediately on the outer edge of the herd receive the movements of the videttes as warnings. They sniff the air, and with piercing vision scan the plain. If the cause of alarm be discovered, the herd-leader, heading the way, sets out, followed by the cows and calves, while the males form a sort of rear guard and flankers. For the sake of protection, the females and the young occupy the centre of the herd. By a wise instinct, the young are thus secured from the ravenous wolf, and the natural timidity of the cow is guarded against sudden or unnecessary alarm.

The evening is the usual time for the herds to set out for water. When moving for this purpose, they may be seen in single-file, following their leaders, traveling at an ambling gait. Frequently they travel eight or ten miles to the nearest stream or pond. The passage of large numbers of buffalo in this way over the same ground soon marks out a well-beaten track, resembling a foot-path, and known to hunters as the " buffalo trail." On the banks of the streams running through the buffalo country these trails may be seen converging from all directions, some faintly marked, while some are worn eight and ten inches in depth. These trails not only follow the most direct course to a given point, but always lead to water or a water-course. The traveler on the plains is frequently obliged to take to the trail of the buffalo in order to reach water. In many places the " buffalo wallow " furnishes a supply of stagnant water which, though extremely unpalatable, has often saved life. The buffalo wallow is a circular, dish-shaped, hole in the earth, about twelve feet in diameter and a foot deep at its greatest concavity. During the warm season, immense clouds of dust are to be seen rising over a herd quietly grazing. Like other animals of his species, the buffalo frequently amuses himself by wallowing in the fine sand or plowing up the earth with his horns. The surface once broken, the place becomes a common resort, until the wallow assumes the shape above described. In the wet season, the rain fills up the wallow, and, unless consumed, standing water is to be found there far into summer.

Among the young buffalo bulls there seems to be a remarkable aspiration to secure the leadership of the herd. This question of rank is annually settled by a test of strength. Certain ambitious males set themselves up as competitors. The first opportunity that offers is accepted. The contests are stubborn and severe — frequently fatal. If the old leader gets the upper hand, he is doubly a hero, and his claims to pre-eminence are greater than ever. Next in rank to the herd-leader are a number of young buffalo, courtiers and gallants, who have free range of the herd so long as they do not come in contact with the leader, or trespass upon his privileges. Between the young and the old males there is an inveterate hostility. As the young grow in ability to cope with the fathers of the herd, a regular conflict takes place. If it terminates in favor of the former, the old buffaloes are unceremoniously driven out. Thus banished from their associations when strong and active, the old animals form a sort of hermit order on the outskirts of the herds, where they constitute the outer guard. These competitive encounters are constantly taking place. As one generation of males succeeds another, those driven out can never return, but live an exiled existence until age, the hunter's bullet, disease, or the ravenous wolf, finishes their days.

The females display, most remarkably, the attachments of maternity. In one instance, I remember, our party shot and badly wounded a fine calf about six months old. As the calf fell, the mother turned and looked upon it with an expression of absolute grief. Her offspring made repeated efforts to rise, but without avail. The mother, in perfect despair, ran around her young, uttering low moans. As we approached, the mother's nature was entirely changed. She stamped upon the ground as if to warn us to " keep off." Although she made no direct attack, she manifested a disposition to defend her young, which was only exceeded by the shouts and firing, which seemed to terrify her. To put the calf out of its suffering and relieve the distress of the mother, and insure our own safety, both animals were dispatched.

Always in the vicinity of the buffalo herd the hunter encounters that beautiful little animal, the antelope. Shy and timid, with an acute scent and far-reaching vision, it is difficult of approach. An old animal is killed now and then by a long-range rifle. Like other timid animals, the antelope has a remarkable development of that too-often fatal instinct, curiosity. By taking advantage of this failing, the experienced hunter succeeds in taking the game. The usual means resorted to is " still hunting." A red flannel flag, fastened to a short stick, is posted in a conspicuous place. The hunter then secretes himself and waits for an opportunity. This is always a slow process; but, with a proper degree of patience, if anywhere in the vicinity of antelopes so that the flag can be seen, he is sure " to bring a haul."

The wolves and the coyotes are the inveterate enemies of the antelope, and continually waylay its path. The fleetness of the animal, however, is its complete protection until weakened by age, or probably, it has been crippled. In times of danger, if possible, the antelope takes refuge within the lines of the nearest herd of buffaloes. Its excessive fright at these times often causes whole herds of the mighty beasts to take to their heels as if a battalion of hunters were on their tracks.

Probably one of the most perfect pictures of desertion and despair is the aged and enfeebled buffalo. Driven first from the herd as if it were a mortal offence to live beyond a certain period of summers, or his inability to follow its movements, he is left alone to wander feebly about, without companions, and an object of patient, sometimes decidedly impatient, watchfulness on the part of the wolf. When the buffalo has arrived at such an advanced age, he will be found near a constant stream where grass grows in abundance. Isolated, shy in his movements, and alarmed at the slightest indications of danger, he seems to lose his customary boldness, and becomes an easily terrified and suspicious animal. He loses his vigorous appearance, and literally becomes worn down and decrepit. The timidity of age grows upon him, and the solemn stillness and solitude which surrounds him is calculated to increase rather than diminish this instinctive terror. Few of these superannuated specimens come to a natural end. The starving wolf and his diminutive companion the coyote, are ever ready to take advantage of the first favorable opportunity of hastening the demise of the object of their solicitude and observation. Under the goading impulse of hunger, the wolf does not hesitate to attack any buffalo who may have strayed from the herd. As if tired of waiting for the natural course of the expiring fires of nature, his wolfship, with a few comrades, begins a regular series of battles until his victim is overpowered.

On one occasion while present with a small detachment of scouts, we suddenly drew to the summit of a " divide." In the valley below an old buffalo, and a pack of seven large gray wolves, were evidently in the act of engaging in a mortal fray. The old buffalo, as if realizing his situation, stood with his head down and confronting the wolves.

At times he threw his head up and down, dropped out his blackened tongue, and constantly uttered a low hoarse roar. We determined to witness the conflict, which was evidently at hand. We halted and lariated our animals. The buffalo, so much engrossed in his own safety, failed to discover our presence, though not more than several hundred yards off. The wolves saw us. This only sharpened their appetite, and seemed to hasten their desire to secure the feast which they had before them. The wolves were seated upon their haunches and formed a sort of semi-circle in front of the buffalo. They resembled so many wise men in council. The buffalo stood a few paces off, very careful to keep his moppy head towards his starving tormentors, and his hind-quarters in an opposite direction, free from any demonstration in the rear. By way of response to the fierce guttural effusions of the buffalo, the wolves at times set up a mournful chorus. No sooner did the wolves see us than they slyly deployed for action. Finding his rear thus in danger, the buffalo made a dive at the nearest wolf, tumbling him over and over. During this movement, however, the rest of the pack pounced upon the hind legs of the buffalo, snarling and snapping, and tearing at his hams. Their object, evidently, was to hamstring their antagonist. These attacks in the rear diverted the attention of the buffalo from the hapless victim of his first charge. The animal turned to attack in the opposite direction, but his tormentors were once more at his vulnerable point.

The contest after these opening performances grew lively and exciting. The buffalo evidently fully appreciated the situation, and the wolves were not to be robbed of their meal. The hind-quarters of the buffalo streamed with blood, and the animal showed signs of exhaustion. He did not dare to lie down for that would be fatal. The wolves had three of their number *hors du combat*. The noise of the contest had attracted quite an audience of coyotes, and a few interloper wolves, sitting at a distance, licking their chops, and impatiently awaiting the issue, evidently expecting an invitation to participate in the feast. The buffalo made several efforts at flight, but soon found that that was a useless manœuvre. The battle test had been going on more than an hour, and having no more time to devote to that sort of recreation, a well directed volley laid out several of their wolfish excellencies. The buffalo did not stop to thank us for our timely assistance, but took the first moment of relief to hobble off. The animal was evidently badly injured, and doubtless our interference was merely prolonging the burden of life, now doubly an encumbrance.

A wolf feast over the carcass of a buffalo is one of those sharp-toned entertainments, which could only be compared to an old fashioned tea-party, composed of snappish octogenarian, paralytic, and generally debilitated characters of both sexes, with a fair sprinkle of shriveled virginity, and a few used up celibates of the masculine gender. Each one guzzling to his heart's content, and growling, and finding fault with his neighbor.

The construction of railroads has developed a new and extensive field for pleasure seekers. The facilities of communication now opened with that strange and remote section, the plains, and, at the same time, the opportunity afforded of seeing the buffalo, that animal above all others associated from our earliest years with everything wild and daring, now invites visitors from all parts of the country. From the cities of Chicago, Cincinnati, St. Louis, and other less important points during the autumn of 1868, excursions were made up at low rates of fare.

The following announcement of an excursion I found at one of the railroad stations. I give a copy of it as one of the peculiar and progressive innovations made by the railways.

RAILWAY EXCURSION

AND

BUFFALO HUNT.

An excursion train will leave Leavenworth, at 8 a. m. and Lawrence, at 10 a. m. for

SHERIDAN,

On Tuesday, October 27, 1868, and return on Friday.
This train will stop at the principal stations both going and returning.
Ample time will be had for a grand Buffalo

HUNT ON THE PLAINS.

Buffaloes are so numerous along the road that they are shot from the cars nearly every day. On our last excursion our party killed twenty buffaloes in a hunt of six hours.

All passengers can have refreshments on the cars at reasonable prices.

Tickets of round trip from Leavenworth, $10.00.

The inducements, at these rates, to any one anxious to visit the plains, and see a live buffalo, and perhaps a " live injun," not so acceptable at that time, were certainly very tempting, as the full expense of the above trip, at the regular rate of fare, would not have been short of seventy dollars. A quarter of a century hence, the buffalo and the Indian will have entirely disappeared from the line of the railways. The few that still survive will have then been driven to the most remote, inaccessible, and uninhabitable sections, if not entirely exterminated.

AT TUCSON

CAPT. JOHN G. BOURKE

1870

It has been shown that Tucson had no hotels. She did not need any at the time of which I am writing, as her floating population found all the ease and comfort it desired in the flare and glare of the gambling hells, which were bright with the lustre of smoking oil lamps and gay with the varicolored raiment of moving crowds, and the music of harp and Pan's pipes. In them could be found nearly every man in the town at some hour of the day or night, and many used them as the Romans did their " Thermæ " — as a place of residence.

All nationalities, all races were represented, and nearly all conditions of life. There were cadaverous-faced Americans, and Americans whose faces were plump; men in shirt sleeves, and men who wore their coats as they would have done in other places; there were Mexicans wrapped in the red, yellow, and black striped cheap " serapes," smoking the inevitable cigarrito, made on the spot by rolling a pinch of tobacco in a piece of corn shuck; and there were other Mexicans more thoroughly Americanized, who were clad in the garb of the people of the North. Of Chinese and negroes there were only a few — but their place was occupied by civilized Indians, Opatas, Yaquis, and others, who had come up with " bull " teams and pack trains from

Sonora. The best of order prevailed, there being no noise save the hum of conversation or the click of the chips on the different tables. Tobacco smoke ascended from cigarritos, pipes, and the vilest of cigars, filling all the rooms with the foulest of odors. The bright light from the lamps did not equal the steely glint in the eyes of the " bankers," who ceaselessly and imperturbably dealt out the cards from faro boxes, or set in motion the balls in roulette.

There used to be in great favor among the Mexicans, and the Americans, too, for that matter, a modification of roulette called " chusas," which never failed to draw a cluster of earnest players, who would remain by the tables until the first suggestion of daylight. High above the squeak of Pan's pipes or the plinkety-plink-plunk of the harps sounded the voice of the " banker ": " Make yer little bets, gents; make yer little bets; all's set, the game's made, 'n th' ball's a-rollin'." When, for any reason, the " game " flagged in energy, there would be a tap upon the bell by the dealer's side, and " drinks all round " be ordered at the expense of the house.

It was a curious exhibit of one of the saddest passions of human nature, and a curious jumble of types which would never press against each other elsewhere. Over by the faro bank, in the corner, stood Bob Crandall, a faithful wooer of the fickle goddess Chance. He was one of the handsomest men in the Southwest, and really endowed with many fine qualities; he had drifted away from the restraints of home life years ago, and was then in Tucson making such a livelihood as he could pick up as a gambler, wasting brain and attainments which, if better applied, would have been a credit to himself and his country.

There was one poor wretch who could always be seen about the tables; he never played, never talked to any one, and seemed to take no particular interest in anything or anybody. What his name was no one knew or cared; all treated him kindly, and anything he wished for was supplied by the charity or the generosity of the frequenters of the gaming-tables. He was a trifle " off," but perfectly harmless; he had lost all the brain he ever had through fright in an Apache ambuscade, and had never recovered his right mind.

Then one was always sure to meet men like old Jack Dunn, who had wandered about in all parts of the world, and has since done such excellent work as a scout against the Chiricahua Apaches. I think that Jack is living yet, but am not certain. If he is, it will pay some enterprising journalist to hunt him up and get a few of his stories out of him; they'll make the best kind of reading for people who care to hear of the wildest days on the wildest of frontiers. And there were others — men who have passed away, men like James Toole, one of the first mayors of Tucson, who dropped in, much as I myself did, to see what was to be seen. Opposed as I am to gambling, no matter what protean guise it may assume, I should do the gamblers of Tucson the justice to say that they were as progressive an element as the town had. They always had plank floors, where every other place was content with the bare earth rammed hard, or with the curious mixture of river sand, bullock's blood, and cactus juice which hardened like cement and was used by some of the more opulent. But with the exception of the large wholesale firms, and there were not over half a dozen of them all told, the house of the governor, and a few — a very few — private residences of people like the Carillos, Sam Hughes, Hiram Stevens, and Aldrich, who desired comfort, there were no wooden floors to be seen in that country.

The gaming establishments were also well supplied with the latest newspapers from San Francisco, Sacramento, and New York, and to these all who entered, whether they played or not, were heartily welcome. Sometimes, but not very often, there would be served up about midnight a very acceptable lunch of " frijoles," coffee, or chocolate, " chile con carne," " enchiladas," and other dishes, all hot and savory, and all thoroughly Mexican. The flare of the lamps was undimmed, the plinkety-plunk of the harps was unchecked, and the voice of the dealer was abroad in the land from the setting of the sun until the rising of the same. Sunday or Monday, night or day, it made no difference — the game went on; one dealer taking the place of another with the regularity, the precision, and the stolidity of a sentinel.

" Isn't it ra-a-a-ther late for you to be open? " asked the tenderfoot arrival from the East, as he descended from the El Paso stage about four o'clock one morning, and dragged himself to the bar to get something to wash the dust out of his throat.

" Wa-a-al, it *is* kinder late fur th' night afore last," genially replied the bartender; " but's jest 'n th' shank o' th' evenin' fur t'-night."

It was often a matter of astonishment to me that there were so few troubles and rows in the gambling establishments of Tucson. They did occur from time to time, just as they might happen anywhere else, but not with sufficient frequency to make a feature of the life of the place.

Once what threatened to open up as a most serious affair had a very ridiculous termination. A wild-eyed youth, thoroughly saturated with " sheep-herder's delight " and other choice vintages of the country, made his appearance in the bar of " Congress Hall," and announcing himself as " Slap-Jack Billy, the Pride of the Pan-handle," went on to inform a doubting world that he could whip his weight in " b'ar-meat " —

> " Fur ber-lud's mee color,
> I kerries mee corfin on mee back,
> 'N' th' hummin' o' pistol-balls, bee jingo,
> Is me-e-e-u-u-sic in mee ears." (Blank, blank, blank.)

Thump! sounded the brawny fist of " Shorty " Henderson, and down went Ajax struck by the offended lightning. When he came to, the " Pride of the Pan-handle " had something of a job in rubbing down the lump about as big as a goose-egg which had suddenly and spontaneously grown under his left jaw; but he bore no malice and so expressed himself.

" Podners (blank, blank, blank), this 'ere's the most sociablest crowd I ever struck; let's all hev a drink."

If the reader do not care for such scenes, he can find others perhaps more to his liking in the various amusements which, under one pretext, or another, extracted all the loose change of the town. The first, in popular estimation, were the " maromas," or tight-rope walkers and general acrobats, who performed many feats well deserving of the praise lavished upon them by the audience. Ever since the days of Cortés the Mexicans have been noted for gymnastic dexterity; it is a matter of history that Cortés, upon returning to Europe, took with him several of the artists in this line, whose agility and cunning surprised those who saw them perform in Spain and Italy.

There were trained dogs and men who knew how to make a barrel roll up or down an inclined plane. All these received a due share of the homage of their fellow-citizens, but nothing to compare to the enthusiasm which greeted the advent of the genuine " teatro." That was *the* time when all Tucson turned out to do honor to the wearers of the buskin. If there was a man, woman, or child in the old pueblo who wasn't seated on one of the cottonwood saplings which, braced upon other saplings, did duty as benches in the corral near the quartermaster's, it was because that man, woman, or child was sick, or in jail. It is astonishing how much enjoyment can be gotten out of life when people set about the task in dead earnest.

There were gross violations of all the possibilities, of all the congruities, of all the unities, in the play, " Elena y

Jorge," presented to an appreciative public the first evening I saw the Mexican strolling heavy-tragedy company in its glory. But what cared we? The scene was lighted by bon-fires, by great torches of wood, and by the row of smoking foot-lights running along the front of the little stage.

The admission was regulated according to a peculiar plan: for Mexicans it was fifty cents, but for Americans, one dollar, because the Americans had more money. Another unique feature was the concentration of all the small boys in the first row, closest to the actors, and the clowns who were constantly running about, falling head over heels over the youngsters, and in other ways managing to keep the audience in the best of humor during the rather long intervals between the acts.

The old ladies who sat bunched up on the seats a little farther in rear seemed to be more deeply moved by the trials of the heroine than the men or boys, who continued placidly to puff cigarettes or munch sweet quinces, as their ages and tastes dictated. It was a most harrowing, sanguinary play, but it is all over at last.

Everybody would be very hungry by this time, and the old crones who made a living by selling hot suppers to theatre-goers reaped their harvest. The wrinkled dames whose faces had been all tears only a moment ago over the woes of Elena were calm, happy, and voracious. Plate after plate of steaming hot " enchiladas " would disappear down their throats, washed down by cups of boiling coffee or chocolate; or perhaps appetite demanded " tamales " and " tortillas," with plates of "frijoles " and " chile con carne."

The banquet may not have been any too grand, out in the open air, but the gratitude of the bright-eyed, sweet-voiced young señoritas who shared it made it taste delicious. Tucson etiquette in some things was ridiculously strict, and the occasions when young ladies could go, even in parties, with representatives of the opposite sex were few and far between — and all the more appreciated when they did come.

If ever there was created a disagreeable feature upon the fair face of nature, it was the Spanish dueña. All that were to be met in those days in southern Arizona seemed to be possessed of an unaccountable aversion to the mounted service. No flattery would put them in good humor, no cajolery would blind them, intimidation was thrown away. There they would sit, keeping strict, dragon-like watch over the dear little creatures who responded to the names of Anita, Victoria, Concepcion, Guadalupe, or Mercedes, and preventing conversation upon any subject excepting the weather, in which we became so expert that it is a wonder the science of meteorology hasn't made greater advances than it has during the past two decades.

The bull fight did not get farther west than El Paso. Tucson never had one that I have heard of, and very little in the way of out-door "sport" beyond chicken fights, which were often savage and bloody. The rapture with which the feminine heart welcomed the news that a "baile" was to be given in Tucson equalled the pleasure of the ladies of Murray Hill or Beacon Street upon the corresponding occasions in their localities. To be sure, the ceremony of the Tucson affairs was of the meagrest. The rooms were wanting in splendor, perhaps in comfort — but the music was on hand, and so were the ladies, young and old, and their cavaliers, and all hands would manage to have the best sort of a time. The ball-room was one long apartment, with earthen floor, having around its sides low benches, and upon its walls a few cheap mirrors and half a dozen candles stuck to the adobe by melted tallow, a bit of moist clay, or else held in tin sconces, from which they emitted the sickliest light upon the heads and forms of the highly colored saints whose pictures were to be seen in the most eligible places. If the weather happened to be chilly enough in the winter season, a petty fire would be allowed to blaze in one of the corners, but, as a general thing, this was not essential.

The moment you passed the threshold of the ball-room in Tucson you had broken over your head an egg-shell filled either with cologne of the most dubious reputation or else with finely cut gold and silver paper. This custom, preserved in this out-of-the-way place, dates back to the " Carnestolends " or Shrove-Tuesday pranks of Spain and Portugal, when the egg was really broken over the head of the unfortunate wight and the pasty mass covered over with flour.

Once within the ball-room there was no need of being presented to any one. The etiquette of the Spaniards is very elastic, and is based upon common sense. Every man who is good enough to be invited to enter the house of a Mexican gentleman is good enough to enter into conversation with all the company he may meet there.

Our American etiquette is based upon the etiquette of the English. Ever since King James, the mild-mannered lunatic, sold his orders of nobility to any cad who possessed the necessary six thousand pounds to pay for an entrance into good society, the aristocracy of England has been going down-hill, and what passes with it for manners is the code of the promoted plutocrat, whose ideas would find no place with the Spaniards, who believe in *" sangre azul "* or nothing. There was very little conversation between the ladies and the gentlemen, because the ladies preferred to cluster together and discuss the neighbors who hadn't been able to come, or explain the details of dresses just made or to be made.

Gentlemen invited whom they pleased to dance, and in the intervals between the figures there might be some very weak attempt at conversation, but that was all, except the marching of the gentle female up to the counter and buying her a handkerchief full of raisins or candies, which she carefully wrapped up and carried home with her, in accordance with a custom which obtained among the Aztecs and also among their Spanish conquerors, and really had a strong foothold in good old England itself, from which latter island it did not disappear until A.D. 1765.

While the language of conversation was entirely Spanish, the figures were called off in English, or what passed for English in those days in Arizona: " Ally man let 'n' all shassay "; " Bal'nce t' yer podners 'n' all han's roun' "; " Dozydozy-chaat 'n' swing."

What lovely times we used to have! What enchanting music from the Pan's pipes, the flute, the harp, the bass-drum, and the bull-fiddle all going at once! How lovely the young ladies were! How bright the rooms were with their greasy lamps or their candles flickering from the walls! It can hardly be possible that twenty years and more have passed away, yet there are the figures in the almanac which cannot lie.

After the " baile " was over, the rule was for the younger participants to take the music and march along the streets to the houses of the young ladies who had been prevented from attending, and there, under the window, or, rather, in front of the window — because all the houses were of one story, and a man could not get under the windows unless he crawled on hands and knees — pour forth their souls in a serenade.

The Spanish serenader, to judge him by his songs, is a curious blending of woe and despair, paying court to a damsel whose heart is colder than the crystalline ice that forms in the mountains. The worst of it all is, the young woman, whose charms of person are equalled by the charms of her mind, does not seem to care a rush what becomes of the despairing songster, who threatens to go away forever, to sail on unknown seas, to face the nameless perils of the desert, if his suit be not at once recognized by at least one frosty smile. But at the first indication of relenting on the part of the adored one, the suitor suddenly recollects that he cannot possibly stand the fervor of her glance, which rivals the splendor of the sun, and, accordingly, he begs her not to look upon him with those beautiful orbs, as he has concluded to depart forever and sing his woes in distant lands. Having discharged this sad duty at the windows of Doña Anita Fulana, the serenaders solemnly progress to the lattice of Doña Mercedes de Zutana, and there repeat the same heart-rending tale of disappointed affection.

It was always the same round of music, taken in the same series — "La Paloma," "Golondrina," and the rest. I made a collection of some twenty of these ditties or madrigals, and was impressed with the poetic fervor and the absolute lack of common sense shown in them all, which is the best evidence that as love songs they will bear comparison with any that have ever been written. The music in many cases was excellent, although the execution was with very primitive instruments. I do not remember a single instance where the fair one made the least sign of approval or pleasure on account of such serenades, and I suppose that the Mexican idea is that she should not, because if there is a polite creature in the world it is the Mexican woman, no matter of what degree.

But it is morning now, and the bells are clanging for first mass, and we had better go home and to bed. Did we so desire we could enter the church, but as there is much to be said in regard to the different feasts, which occurred at different seasons and most acceptably divided the year, we can leave that duty unfulfilled for the present and give a few brief sentences to the christening and funerals, which were celebrated under our observation.

The Mexicans used to attach a great deal of importance to the naming of their children, and when the day for the christening had arrived, invitations scattered far and near brought together all the relatives and friends of the family, who most lavishly eulogized the youngster, and then partook of a hearty collation, which was the main feature of the entertainment.

Funerals, especially of children, were generally without coffins, owing to the great scarcity of lumber, and nearly always with music at the head of the procession, which slowly wended its way to the church to the measure of plaintive melody.

Birthdays were not observed, but in their stead were kept the days of the saints of the same name. For example, all the young girls named Anita would observe Saint Ann's day, without regard to the date of their own birth, and so with the Guadalupes and Francescas and others.

I should not omit to state that there were whole blocks of houses in Tucson which did not have a single nail in them, but had been constructed entirely of adobes, with all parts of the wooden framework held together by strips of raw-hide.

Yet in these comfortless abodes, which did not possess ten dollars' worth of furniture, one met with charming courtesy from old and young. "Ah! happy the eyes that gaze upon thee," was the form of salutation to friends who had been absent for a space — "Dichosos los ojos que ven a V." "Go thou with God," was the gentle mode of saying farewell, to which the American guest would respond, as he shifted the revolvers on his hip and adjusted the quid of tobacco in his mouth: "Wa-al, I reckon I'll git." But the Mexican would arrange the folds of his serape, bow most politely, and say: "Ladies, I throw myself at your feet — À los pies de VV., señoritas."

Thus far there has been no mention of that great lever of public opinion — the newspaper. There was one of which I will now say a word, and a few months later, in the spring of 1870, the town saw a second established, of which a word shall be said in its turn. The *Weekly Arizonian* was a great public journal, an organ of public opinion, managed by Mr. P. W. Dooner, a very able editor.

It was the custom in those days to order the acts and resolutions of Congress to be published in the press of the remoter Territories, thus enabling the settlers on the frontier to keep abreast of legislation, especially such as more immediately affected their interests.

There may have been other matter in the *Weekly Arizonian* besides the copies of legislative and executive documents referred to, but if so I never was fortunate enough to see it, excepting possibly once, on the occasion of my first visit to the town, when I saw announced in bold black and white that " Colonel " Bourke was paying a brief visit to his friend, Señor So-and-so. If there is one weak spot in the armor of a recently-graduated lieutenant, it is the desire to be called colonel before he dies, and here was the ambition of my youth gratified almost before the first lustre had faded from my shoulder-straps. It would serve no good purpose to tell how many hundred copies of that week's issue found their way into the earliest outgoing mail, addressed to friends back in the States. I may be pardoned for alluding to the reckless profanity of the stage-driver upon observing the great bulk of the load his poor horses were to carry. The stage-drivers were an exceptionally profane set, and this one, Frank Francis, was an adept in the business. He has long since gone to his reward in the skies, killed, if I have not made a great mistake, by the Apaches in Sonora, in 1881. He was a good, " square " man, as I can aver from an acquaintance and friendship cemented in later days, when I had to take many and many a lonesome and dangerous ride with him in various sections and on various routes in that then savage-infested region. It was Frank's boast that no " Injuns " should ever get either him or the mail under his care. " All you've got to do with 'n Injun 's to be smarter nor he is. Now, f'r instance, 'n Injun 'll allers lie in wait 'longside the road, tryin' to ketch th' mail. Wa'al, I never don' go 'long no derned road, savey? I jest cut right 'cross lots, 'n' dern my skin ef all th' Injuns this side o' Bitter Creek kin tell whar to lay fur *me.*" This and similar bits of wisdom often served to soothe the frightened fancy of the weary "tenderfoot" making his first trip into that wild region, especially if the trip was to be by night, as it generally was.

Whipping up his team, Frank would take a shoot off to one side or the other of the road, and never return to it until the faint tinge of light in the east, or the gladsome crow of chanticleer announced that the dawn was at hand and Tucson in sight. How long they had both been in coming!

Through it all, however, Frank remained the same kind, entertaining host; he always seemed to consider it part of his duties to entertain each one who travelled with him, and there was no lack of conversation, such as it was.

The establishment of the rival paper, the *Citizen,* was the signal for a war of words, waxing in bitterness from week to week, and ceasing only with the death of the *Arizonian,* which took place not long after. One of the editors of the *Citizen* was Joe Wasson, a very capable journalist, with whom I was afterward associated intimately in the Black Hills and Yellowstone country during the troubles with the Sioux and Cheyennes. He was a well-informed man, who had travelled much and seen life in many phases. He was conscientious in his ideas of duty, and full of the energy and "snap" supposed to be typically American. He approached every duty with the alertness and earnestness of a Scotch terrier. The telegraph was still unknown to Arizona, and for that reason the *Citizen* contained an unusually large amount of editorial matter upon affairs purely local. Almost the very first columns of the paper demanded the sweeping away of garbage-piles, the lighting of the streets by night, the establishment of schools, and the imposition of a tax upon the gin-mills and gambling-saloons.

Devout Mexicans crossed themselves as they passed this fanatic, whom nothing would seem to satisfy but the subversion of every ancient institution. Even the more progressive among the Americans realized that Joe was going a trifle too far, and felt that it was time to put the brakes upon a visionary theorist whose war-cry was "Reform!" But no remonstrance availed, and editorial succeeded editorial, each more pungent and aggressive than its predecessors. What was that dead burro doing on the main street? Why did not the town authorities remove it?

"Valgame! What is the matter with the man? and why does he make such a fuss over Pablo Martinez's dead burro, which has been there for more than two months and nobody bothering about it? Why, it was only last week that Ramon Romualdo and I were talking about it, and we both agreed that it ought to be removed some time very soon. Bah! I will light another cigarette. These Americans make me sick — always in a hurry, as if the devil were after them."

In the face of such antagonism as this the feeble light of the *Arizonian* flickered out, and that great luminary was, after the lapse of a few years, succeeded by the *Star,* whose editor and owner arrived in the Territory in the latter part of the year 1873, after the Apaches had been subdued and placed upon reservations.

TOLD AT TRINIDAD

A. A. HAYES, JR.

1879

WE had driven over from El Moro only to find that the daily train for the South had started, and that we had a long night and day on our hands. We soon exhausted the sights of the town, and sat down on the hotel piazza in company with rather a motley group. We talked in a languid way about various subjects, and drifted after awhile to the old staging days; then a quiet New Yorker took his cigar out of his mouth, and said,

"Gentlemen, I should like to tell you a story. Those of you who saw the *New York Herald* of July —, 1876, may have noticed a rather unintelligible account of a crime committed by the scion of a wealthy and distinguished family long resident in the city. It was supposed to be a heavy forgery, but one soon saw that extraordinary measures and powerful influence had suppressed details and prevented further publicity, and the matter passed off as a nine days' wonder. When I myself first saw the item, I felt sure that I knew who the culprit was. James W —— and I were schoolmates at Geneva, and once great friends. He was the son of one of the finest gentlemen of the old school that I have ever seen — who had married rather late in life, and been a most affectionate and indulgent father. James

[1] Copyright, 1880, by Harper and Brothers.

was a boy of most attractive appearance, with very dark complexion, hair and eyes, and the figure of an athlete. There was apparently nothing in feature, expression, or manner, to cause suspicion that he was not a very fine fellow; and yet there came to me before long the positive conviction, first, that under that attractive exterior a desperate power of evil was at work; second (and I am no more able to explain this than those other spiritual mysteries which so many of us encounter in our lives), that it would be my fate to come into contact with him in after years when this power had developed itself.

" Through certain channels then open to me I easily ascertained that, after a career of deep dissipation, James W —— had committed a bold forgery; that in some way the money had been paid, and the affair quashed. Other things came to my ears, all strongly confirmatory of my expectations about him. About eighteen months later his mother died, and his father settled all his business and went to Europe; nearly every one supposing, in the mean time, that the son had suddenly started, when he was first missed from his accustomed haunts, on a journey to Central Asia, and that it would be months before he could hear this sad news.

" Later again, as the Union Pacific train, on which I was a passenger, stopped at the Green River station, I saw on the platform, evidently waiting to join us, a father and daughter. The former was a fine specimen of the better class of plainsmen — six feet two, and of powerful build — his eyes large and blue, his long hair and full beard light-colored, and his expression kindness itself. The young girl was about eighteen, slender and delicate, and altogether charming — one of those beautiful, tender, clinging young creatures sometimes found on the frontier, like the delicate wild flowers in the cañons. They were going to Chicago; and having been commended to Major G —— by some mutual acquaintances, I passed much time in his company, and we became excellent friends. He had been a widower for a number of years, and was deeply devoted to his pretty Anita, who in her turn seemed to adore him. I could not help thinking that she was ill-fitted to meet the cares of life, and that there was a look in her lovely eyes that suggested a rare capacity for suffering. She had never been east of the Missouri before, and the major told me that after a short stay in Chicago, they were going to live on a ranch which he had bought in the Wet Mountain Valley. He had been a noted hunter and Indian fighter in the West, and bore the scars of more than one struggle with wild beast and wilder man. I remained with them one day in Chicago, and remember Anita's childish delight in a bouquet of flowers which I gave her, when I called at the hotel to say good-bye, and her waving her handkerchief to me as I drove off to the station, and she stood on the balcony leaning on her father's shoulder.

"Chance brought me, within six or eight months, to the region south of the Arkansas, and I took a trip on the Wet Mountains with an old Mexican called Manuel. One day it occurred to me that we could not be far from my friend's location; so I asked Manuel if we could not cross the range and go down into the valley, and if he knew where Major G —— lived.

"'Oh si, señor!' he quickly replied, 'we easy come over the mountain and to the Rancho San José, where live the major. Oh, it is a place so beautiful! the valley which the señor will see when we pass the Sierra and go down the cañon.' 'And the major, and his daughter, are they well?' I asked. 'The major, yes,' said Manuel; 'but the señorita' —and his voice changed —'she is not well. The señor does not then know — but ah! how could he? — that she have so great trouble.'

"Much surprised and shocked, I gradually elicited from him a narration of what had occurred after the father and daughter took up their abode in the valley. It seemed that a young man, bound ostensibly on a hunting trip, once asked for a night's lodging at the ranch, and was evidently struck by the beauty of Anita; that he had returned again and again, and finally expressed his intention of taking up a homestead in the vicinity. Anita seemed attracted by him from the first. They were finally betrothed, and the major had the comfort of knowing that they would remain near him. He had apparently given his full confidence to the young man, and talked freely to him of his affairs; and notably, on one occasion, of his intention to keep quite a large sum of money in the house for two days, contrary to his usual custom, but for the purpose of paying for a mine which he had bought. The next morning the money was gone! The young man was never seen again.

"I heard this tale with great regret, and said to myself that the poor girl would never bear such a blow. When I asked Manuel about her condition, he broke into distressed and almost incoherent utterances about *la pobrecita* (the poor little one), for whom might the *Madre de Dios* intercede. I began to dread the visit to the ranch, and would have turned back but for a desire to offer my sympathies.

"When we entered the corral the sun was just sinking behind the Sangre de Cristo Range, and flooding the valley with light. The major came out when he heard our horses, and, recognizing me, at once bade us welcome. When I saw his poor daughter I was shocked beyond measure. She lay on a sofa looking at the western mountains. She knew me and gave me her poor little hand, so thin that it seemed almost transparent. Her face was pallid, and deep purple rings were under her eyes. I said a few commonplace words of sympathy, and then turned away. The major followed me into the house, and, coming up and taking my offered hand, said, ' They call it quick consumption. I know better than that — it is a broken heart!' His grasp tightened painfully on my hand. ' My God!' he cried, ' how can I bear it!' The scene was painful in the extreme. I found Manuel and told him that we must go on, and that he had best lead the horses outside of the corral, where I would join him. The major's life-long instincts of hospitality flashed out in a momentary protest at my departure, but he did not press me to stay. I knew that he had kind neighbors, and the ranch seemed no place for us. I went to say farewell to the dying girl, but finding her lying with closed eyes and folded hands, I dared not disturb her, although I knew that I saw her for the last time. Major G—— walked mechanically to the gate, and bade us good-bye. I saw the tears in old Manuel's eyes as we mounted and rode some distance in silence. Two weeks after this, coming from Fort Garland, I bought a Denver paper from the newsboy on the train, and saw that I had rightly judged of the poor child's inability to bear a rude shock, for I read that she had ' entered into rest.'

" Now, gentlemen, I am afraid that you will think I am spinning a sensational yarn, but it is only a few months since, just as we are sitting here, I was sitting with a party of gentlemen at the door of the fonda at the corner of the plaza in Santa Fe. We were admiring the gorgeous sunset, and listening to the band playing under the trees, when the ' buckboard ' of the Transportation Company arrived from the South. It was with a start that I rose to salute, in the only passenger, my poor friend Major G——. He had changed sadly; his hair had grown white, and his cheeks were sunken. Then he had a habit of pressing his hand to his forehead, which gave one a vivid impression of despair.

" He greeted me warmly, as of old, and mentioned that he had come from Mesilla, and was going on to Fort Garland in the morning, but he said little more at first, and I dreaded any recurrence to the past. In the evening I induced him to take a cigar, and to drink a little from my flask. Soon he seemed restored to a temporary animation, and after asking me if I proposed accompanying him on his journey, and expressing gratification at my willingness so to do, he went on as follows:

" ' I have heard something which leads me to think that the road agents are going to try to rob the stage, which will have some treasure freight. The only passengers besides us will be a couple of greasers, who can't help us if they would. You know the boys say that the agents always have things their own way. Now, as I feel at present, I'm not inclined to give up without a try. I don't want to ring you in unless you are for it; but, with all the trouble I've had, a bullet more or less is of no account to me; but I have a notion,' he continued, ' that I can block their game. It was done once by an old pard of mine, and, if you say so, I'll try it, and you just follow my lead. Will you take the chances?' I knew him to be a man of desperate courage and fertile in resource, and I assented. 'What kind of shooting-iron have you?' he asked. 'Navy Colt? No, that's good in its way; but I'll lend you a self-cocker like mine. Mind and take at least a strong cup of coffee before we start; and now you'd better turn in.'

" In the morning we took our places in the coach, the major sitting on the front seat, and left-hand side; I sat opposite, and each had a silent Mexican next him. We drove without incident to the place where the horses were first changed; but, before we started again, my friend said to me,

" ' I allow that we'll have our trouble, if at all, in the cañon four miles ahead. Now just put your blanket over your lap and hold your pistol under it. Keep a bright lookout, and if we strike 'em, just have your wits about you, and be ready to fire after I do.' Soon we rolled off again, and I saw him lean back for awhile and then sit upright, and keep his eye fixed on the road. The horses were good; we soon approached the cañon, and the suspense became almost unbearable. I could not help thinking about our chances in the case of attack. Just then — I remember that I was looking at a group of cedars — the stage stopped, and, as if conjured up by the hand of a magician, three men on horseback appeared on our side, two close to us, one behind. I seemed to comprehend the whole situation in the twinkling of an eye; the figures — the levelled barrels — the major sitting before me.

" ' *Throw up your hands,* —————— *you!* ' They were reckless enough to wear no masks — the speaker lowered his head to look in. Heavens! shall I ever forget that scene? On my part there was a startling recognition — on the major's there must have been the same, for never have I seen a human face so transformed, and it added an almost demoniacal force to the action, which all passed in a flash. The terror of the sudden start, the throwing out of the left arm, the frightened glare of the eyes, may have been the product of rare dramatic power; but there was something far more terribly real in his wild cry,

" '*Great God! who is that behind you?* ' The robbers instinctively turned their heads. Crack! — crack! The major's right arm, rigid as iron, held the smoking weapon, as two riderless horses galloped off, and I mechanically fired at the third man. Then my friend laid his revolver down, and put his hand to his forehead. We drove on a short distance, and then made one of the frightened Mexicans hold the horses, and the driver and I hurried back. It was with a sharp shudder, and a vivid realization that the forebodings of earlier days had come only too true, that I saw my old school-mate lying dead in the dusty road. And then I saw one of those strange phenomena of the occurrence of which there is ample scientific evidence. Gentlemen, I assure you that there *had* been mutual recognition, and the terror of it was in those dead eyes.

" We drove back to Santa Fe almost at a gallop, the major sitting like a statue in his seat, and never speaking. As we entered the plaza and stopped before the old palace a crowd gathered, and I whispered to an army officer to take my poor friend to head-quarters, while I attended to the needful formalities. I can see the scene before my eyes this moment: the motley gathering of Americans and Mexicans, with some uniforms among them; the driver eagerly talking — the hostlers taking the horses' heads. The United States Marshal and Commissioner came out of their offices, and I told them the story. The marshal stopped me for a moment after the first ten words, and sent for his two deputies and three horses. Then he lighted a cigar and offered me one as I went on with my brief narrative. The deputies came up, the marshal went to his office for his arms, and examined the percussion-caps as he asked me a few questions. Then they all three shook hands with me and galloped down the narrow street. They were fierce pursuers, and when I saw the chief deputy that evening, he told me that the third man was in the jail.

" 'I know 'em all well,' he added, ' and two more ungodly ruffians than the dead men never cheated the gallows. I've been after that black-haired one a long time for a matter in Wyoming '; and a wolfish look came for a moment over his pleasant face. ' I knew where to find the third man. He's a mean cur, and gave in without the show of a fight. To be sure, you plugged him pretty bad in the arm.'

" When the marshal had gone to his office the commissioner and I walked to head-quarters and found the major (whom the surgeon had induced to drink a composing draught) sitting in a chair, leaning his head upon his hand. He rose as we approached. ' Sam,' said he to the commissioner, ' the Lord delivered him into my hands! It was his will.'

" He started again the next morning, and as the stage turned the corner he waved his hand to me, and then put it to his head once again in that sad, weary way of his. Urged by the spirit of unrest which had seized upon him, he joined the prospectors at Leadville, exposed himself recklessly, and died of pneumonia in three weeks.

" Strangely enough, the news recently came that old Mr. W—— was never seen after taking a steamer at Vienna to go down the Danube.   That is the reason that I have felt at liberty to tell the story.   They say the way of the transgressor is hard; but in this case it seems to me that there is a good deal to be said about the ways of those against whom he transgressed.   Perhaps many of you have come across curious things in your lives, but nothing much stranger than what you have just heard."

And to this statement no one took exception.

SPECIMEN JONES

OWEN WISTER

From "Red Men and White." Reprinted by permission of the author and of Harper and Brothers, New York.[1]

EPHRAIM, the proprietor of Twenty Mile, had wasted his day in burying a man. He did not know the man. He had found him, or what the Apaches had left of him, sprawled among some charred sticks just outside the Cañon del Oro. It was a useful discovery in its way, for otherwise Ephraim might have gone on hunting his strayed horses near the cañon, and ended among charred sticks himself. Very likely the Indians were far away by this time, but he returned to Twenty Mile with the man tied to his saddle, and his pony nervously snorting. And now the day was done, and the man lay in the earth, and they had even built a fence round him; for the hole was pretty shallow, and coyotes have a way of smelling this sort of thing a long way off when they are hungry, and the man was not in a coffin. They were always short of coffins in Arizona.

Day was done at Twenty Mile, and the customary activity prevailed inside that flat-roofed cube of mud. Sounds of singing, shooting, dancing, and Mexican tunes on the concertina came out of the windows hand in hand, to widen and die among the hills. A limber, pretty boy, who might be nineteen, was dancing energetically, while a grave old gentleman, with tobacco running down his beard, pointed

[1] Copyright, 1895, by Harper and Brothers. Copyright, 1923, by Owen Wister.

a pistol at the boy's heels, and shot a hole in the earth now and then to show that the weapon was really loaded. Everybody was quite used to all of this — excepting the boy. He was an Eastern new-comer, passing his first evening at a place of entertainment.

Night in and night out every guest at Twenty Mile was either happy and full of whiskey, or else his friends were making arrangements for his funeral. There was water at Twenty Mile — the only water for twoscore of miles. Consequently it was an important station on the road between the southern country and Old Camp Grant, and the new mines north of the Mescal Range. The stunt, liquor-perfumed adobe cabin lay on the gray floor of the desert like an isolated slab of chocolate. A corral, two desolate stable-sheds, and the slowly turning windmill were all else. Here Ephraim and one or two helpers abode, armed against Indians, and selling whiskey. Variety in their vocation of drinking and killing was brought them by the travellers. These passed and passed through the glaring vacant months — some days only one ragged fortune-hunter, riding a pony; again by twos and threes, with high-loaded burros; and sometimes they came in companies, walking beside their clanking freight-wagons. Some were young, and some were old, and all drank whiskey, and wore knives and guns to keep each other civil. Most of them were bound for the mines, and some of them sometimes returned. No man trusted the next man, and their names, when they had any, would be O'Rafferty, Angus, Schwartzmeyer, José Maria, and Smith. All stopped for one night; some longer, remaining drunk and profitable to Ephraim; now and then one stayed permanently, and had a fence built round him. Whoever came, and whatever befell them, Twenty Mile was chronically hilarious after sundown — a dot of riot in the dumb Arizona night.

On this particular evening they had a tenderfoot. The boy, being new in Arizona, still trusted his neighbor. Such people turned up occasionally. This one had paid for everybody's drink several times, because he felt friendly, and never noticed that nobody ever paid for his. They had played cards with him, stolen his spurs, and now they were making him dance. It was an ancient pastime; yet two or three were glad to stand round and watch it, because it was some time since they had been to the opera. Now the tenderfoot had misunderstood these friends at the beginning, supposing himself to be among good fellows, and they therefore naturally set him down as a fool. But even while dancing you may learn much, and suddenly. The boy, besides being limber, had good tough black hair, and it was not in fear, but with a cold blue eye, that he looked at the old gentleman. The trouble had been that his own revolver had somehow hitched, so he could not pull it from the holster at the necessary moment.

"Tried to draw on me, did yer?" said the old gentleman. "Step higher! Step, now, or I'll crack open yer kneepans, ye robin's egg."

"Thinks he's having a bad time," remarked Ephraim. "Wonder how he'd like to have been that man the Injuns had sport with?"

"Weren't his ear funny?" said one who had helped bury the man.

"Ear?" said Ephraim. "You boys ought to been along when I found him, and seen the way they'd fixed up his mouth." Ephraim explained the details simply, and the listeners shivered. But Ephraim was a humorist. "Wonder how it feels," he continued, "to have — "

Here the boy sickened at his comments and the loud laughter. Yet a few hours earlier these same half-drunken jesters had laid the man to rest with decent humanity. The boy was taking his first dose of Arizona. By no means was everybody looking at his jig. They had seen tenderfeet so often. There was a Mexican game of cards; there was the concertina; and over in the corner sat Specimen Jones, with his back to the company, singing to himself. Nothing had been said or done that entertained him in the least. He had seen everything quite often.

"Higher! skip higher, you elegant calf," remarked the old gentleman to the tenderfoot. "High-yer!" And he placidly fired a fourth shot that scraped the boy's boot at the ankle and threw earth over the clock, so that you could not tell the minute from the hour hand.

"'Drink to me only with thine eyes,'" sang Specimen Jones, softly. They did not care much for his songs in Arizona. These lyrics were all, or nearly all, that he retained of the days when he was twenty, although he was but twenty-six now.

The boy was cutting pigeon-wings, the concertina played "Matamoras," Jones continued his lyric, when two Mexicans leaped at each other, and the concertina stopped with a quack.

"Quit it!" said Ephraim from behind the bar, covering the two with his weapon. "I don't want any greasers scrapping round here to-night. We've just got cleaned up."

It had been cards, but the Mexicans made peace, to the regret of Specimen Jones. He had looked round with some hopes of a crisis, and now for the first time he noticed the boy.

"Blamed if he ain't neat," he said. But interest faded from his eyes, and he turned again to the wall. "'Lieb Vaterland magst ruhig sein,'" he melodiously observed. His repertory was wide and refined. When he sang he was always grammatical.

"Ye kin stop, kid," said the old gentleman, not unkindly, and he shoved his pistol into his belt.

The boy ceased. He had been thinking matters over. Being lithe and strong, he was not tired nor much out of breath, but he was trembling with the plan and the prospect he had laid out for himself. "Set 'em up," he said to Ephraim. "Set 'em up again all round."

His voice caused Specimen Jones to turn and look once more, while the old gentleman, still benevolent, said, "Yer langwidge means pleasanter than it sounds, kid." He glanced at the boy's holster, and knew he need not keep a very sharp watch as to that. Its owner had bungled over it once already. All the old gentleman did was to place himself next the boy on the off side from the holster; any move the tenderfoot's hand might make for it would be green and unskilful, and easily anticipated. The company lined up along the bar, and the bottle slid from glass to glass. The boy and his tormentor stood together in the middle of the line, and the tormentor, always with half a thought for the holster, handled his drink on the wet counter, waiting till all should be filled and ready to swallow simultaneously, as befits good manners.

"Well, my regards," he said, seeing the boy raise his glass; and as the old gentleman's arm lifted in unison, exposing his waist, the boy reached down a lightning hand, caught the old gentleman's own pistol, and jammed it in his face.

"Now you'll dance," said he.

"Whoop!" exclaimed Specimen Jones, delighted. "*Blamed* if he ain't neat!" And Jones's handsome face lighted keenly.

"Hold on!" the boy sang out, for the amazed old gentleman was mechanically drinking his whiskey out of sheer fright. The rest had forgotten their drinks. "Not one swallow," the boy continued. "No, you'll not put it down either. You'll keep hold of it, and you'll dance all round this place. Around and around. And don't you spill any. And I'll be thinking what you'll do after that."

Specimen Jones eyed the boy with growing esteem. "Why, he ain't bigger than a pint of cider," said he.

"Prance away!" commanded the tenderfoot, and fired

a shot between the old gentleman's not widely straddled legs.

"You hev the floor, Mr. Adams," Jones observed, respectfully, at the old gentleman's agile leap. "I'll let no man here interrupt you." So the capering began, and the company stood back to make room. "I've saw juicy things in this Territory," continued Specimen Jones, aloud, to himself, "but this combination fills my bill."

He shook his head sagely, following the black-haired boy with his eye. That youth was steering Mr. Adams round the room with the pistol, proud as a ring-master. Yet not altogether. He was only nineteen, and though his heart beat stoutly, it was beating alone in a strange country. He had come straight to this from hunting squirrels along the Susquehanna, with his mother keeping supper warm for him in the stone farm-house among the trees. He had read books in which hardy heroes saw life, and always triumphed with precision on the last page, but he remembered no receipt for this particular situation. Being good game American blood, he did not think now about the Susquehanna, but he did long with all his might to know what he ought to do next to prove himself a man. His buoyant rage, being glutted with the old gentleman's fervent skipping, had cooled, a stress of reaction was falling hard on his brave young nerves. He imagined everybody against him. He had no notion that there was another American wanderer there, whose reserved and whimsical nature he had touched to the heart.

The fickle audience was with him, of course, for the moment, since he was upper dog and it was a good show; but one in that room was distinctly against him. The old gentleman was dancing with an ugly eye; he had glanced down to see just where his knife hung at his side, and he had made some calculations. He had fired four shots; the boy had fired once. "Four and one hez always made five," the old gentleman told himself with much secret pleasure, and pretended that he was going to stop his double-shuffle. It was an excellent trap, and the boy fell straight into it. He squandered his last precious bullet on the spittoon near which Mr. Adams happened to be at the moment, and the next moment Mr. Adams had him by the throat. They swayed and gulped for breath, rutting the earth with sharp heels; they rolled to the floor and floundered with legs tight tangled, the boy blindly striking at Mr. Adams with the pistol-butt, and the audience drawing closer to lose nothing, when the bright knife flashed suddenly. It poised, and flew across the room, harmless, for a foot had driven into Mr. Adams's arm, and he felt a cold ring grooving his temple. It was the smooth, chilly muzzle of Specimen Jones's six-shooter.

"That's enough," said Jones. "More than enough."

Mr. Adams, being mature in judgment, rose instantly, like a good old sheep, and put his knife back obedient to orders. But in the brain of the overstrained, bewildered boy universal destruction was whirling. With a face stricken lean with ferocity, he staggered to his feet, plucking at his obstinate holster, and glaring for a foe. His eye fell first on his deliverer, leaning easily against the bar watching him, while the more and more curious audience scattered, and held themselves ready to murder the boy if he should point his pistol their way. He was dragging at it clumsily, and at last it came. Specimen Jones sprang like a cat, and held the barrel vertical and gripped the boy's wrist.

"Go easy, son," said he. "I know how you're feelin'."

The boy had been wrenching to get a shot at Jones, and now the quietness of the man's voice reached his brain, and he looked at Specimen Jones. He felt a potent brotherhood in the eyes that were considering him, and he began to fear he had been a fool. There was his dwarf Eastern revolver, slack in his inefficient fist, and the singular person still holding its barrel and tapping one derisive finger over the end. careless of the risk to his first joint.

" Why, you little —— ——," said Specimen Jones, caressingly, to the hypnotized youth, " if you was to pop that squirt off at me, I'd turn you up and spank y'u. Set 'em up, Ephraim."

But the commercial Ephraim hesitated, and Jones remembered. His last cent was gone. It was his third day at Ephraim's. He had stopped, having a little money, on his way to Tucson, where a friend had a job for him, and was waiting. He was far too experienced a character ever to sell his horse or his saddle on these occasions, and go on drinking. He looked as if he might, but he never did; and this was what disappointed business men like Ephraim in Specimen Jones.

But now, here was this tenderfoot he had undertaken to see through, and Ephraim reminding him that he had no more of the wherewithal. " Why, so I haven't," he said, with a short laugh, and his face flushed. " I guess," he continued, hastily, " this is worth a dollar or two." He drew a chain up from below his flannel shirt-collar and over his head. He drew it a little slowly. It had not been taken off for a number of years — not, indeed, since it had been placed there originally. " It ain't brass," he added, lightly, and strewed it along the counter without looking at it. Ephraim did look at it, and, being satisfied, began to uncork a new bottle, while the punctual audience came up for its drink.

" Won't you please let me treat? " said the boy, unsteadily. " I ain't likely to meet you again, sir." Reaction was giving him trouble inside.

" Where are you bound, kid? "

" Oh, just a ways up the country," answered the boy, keeping a grip on his voice.

" Well, you *may* get there. Where did you pick up that — that thing? Your pistol, I mean."

" It's a present from a friend," replied the tenderfoot, with dignity.

" Farewell gift, wasn't it, kid? Yes; I thought so. Now

I'd hate to get an affair like that from a friend. It would start me wondering if he liked me as well as I'd always thought he did. Put up that money, kid. You're drinking with me. Say, what's yer name?"

" Cumnor — J. Cumnor."

" Well, J. Cumnor, I'm glad to know y'u. Ephraim, let me make you acquainted with Mr. Cumnor. Mr. Adams, if you're rested from your quadrille, you can shake hands with my friend. Step around, you Miguels and Serapios and Cristobals, whatever y'u claim your names are. This is Mr. J. Cumnor."

The Mexicans did not understand either the letter or the spirit of these American words, but they drank their drink, and the concertina resumed its acrid melody. The boy had taken himself off without being noticed.

" Say, Spec," said Ephraim to Jones, " I'm no hog. Here's yer chain. You'll be along again."

" Keep it till I'm along again," said the owner.

" Just as you say, Spec," answered Ephraim, smoothly, and he hung the pledge over an advertisement chromo of a nude cream-colored lady with bright straw hair holding out a bottle of somebody's champagne. Specimen Jones sang no more songs, but smoked, and leaned in silence on the bar. The company were talking of bed, and Ephraim plunged his glasses into a bucket to clean them for the morrow.

" Know anything about that kid? " inquired Jones, abruptly.

Ephraim shook his head as he washed.

" Travelling alone, ain't he? "

Ephraim nodded.

" Where did y'u say y'u found that fellow layin' the Injuns got? "

" Mile this side the cañon. 'Mong them sand-humps."

" How long had he been there, do y'u figure? "

" Three days, anyway."

Jones watched Ephraim finish his cleansing. " Your clock needs wiping," he remarked. " A man might suppose it was nine, to see that thing the way the dirt hides the hands. Look again in half an hour and it'll say three. That's the kind of clock gives a man the jams. Sends him crazy."

" Well, that ain't a bad thing to be in this country," said Ephraim, rubbing the glass case and restoring identity to the hands. " If that man had been crazy he'd been livin' right now. Injuns 'll never touch lunatics."

" That band have passed here and gone north," Jones said. " I saw a smoke among the foot-hills as I come along day before yesterday. I guess they're aiming to cross the Santa Catalina. Most likely they're that band from round the San Carlos that were reported as raiding down in Sonora."

" I seen well enough," said Ephraim, " when I found him that they wasn't going to trouble us any, or they'd have been around by then."

He was quite right, but Specimen Jones was thinking of something else. He went out to the corral, feeling disturbed and doubtful. He saw the tall white freight-wagon of the Mexicans, looming and silent, and a little way off the new fence where the man lay. An odd sound startled him, though he knew it was no Indians at this hour, and he looked down into a little dry ditch. It was the boy, hidden away flat on his stomach among the stones, sobbing.

" Oh, snakes! " whispered Specimen Jones, and stepped back. The Latin races embrace and weep, and all goes well; but among Saxons tears are a horrid event. Jones never knew what to do when it was a woman, but this was truly disgusting. He was well seasoned by the frontier, had tried a little of everything: town and country, ranches, saloons, stage-driving, marriage occasionally, and latterly mines. He had sundry claims staked out, and always carried pieces of stone in his pockets, discoursing upon their mineral-bearing capacity, which was apt to be very slight. That is why he was called Specimen Jones. He had exhausted all the important sensations, and did not care much for anything any more. Perfect health and strength kept him from discovering that he was a saddened, drifting man. He wished to kick the boy for his baby performance, and yet he stepped carefully away from the ditch so the boy should not suspect his presence. He found himself standing still, looking at the dim, broken desert.

"Why, hell," complained Specimen Jones, "he played the little man to start with. He did so. He scared that old horse-thief, Adams, just about dead. Then he went to kill me, that kep' him from bein' buried early to-morrow. I've been wild that way myself, and wantin' to shoot up the whole outfit." Jones looked at the place where his middle finger used to be, before a certain evening in Tombstone. "But I never —" He glanced towards the ditch, perplexed. "What's that mean? Why in the world does he git to cryin' for *now*, do you suppose?" Jones took to singing without knowing it. "'Ye shepherds, tell me, have you seen my Flora pass this way?'" he murmured. Then a thought struck him. "Hello, kid!" he called out. There was no answer. "Of course," said Jones. "Now he's ashamed to hev me see him come out of there." He walked with elaborate slowness round the corral and behind a shed. "Hello, you kid!" he called again.

"I was thinking of going to sleep," said the boy, appearing quite suddenly. "I — I'm not used to riding all day. I'll get used to it, you know," he hastened to add.

"'Ha-ve you seen my Flo' — Say, kid, where y'u bound, anyway?"

"San Carlos."

"San Carlos? Oh. Ah. 'Flo-ra pass this way?'"

"Is it far, sir?"

"Awful far, sometimes. It's always liable to be far through the Arivaypa Cañon."

"I didn't expect to make it between meals," remarked Cumnor.

"No. Sure. What made you come this route?"

"A man told me."

"A man? Oh. Well, it *is* kind o' difficult, I admit, for an Arizonan not to lie to a stranger. But I think I'd have told you to go by Tres Alamos and Point of Mountain. It's the road the man that told you would choose himself every time. Do you like Injuns, kid?"

Cumnor snapped eagerly.

"Of course y'u do. And you've never saw one in the whole minute-and-a-half you've been alive. I know all about it."

"I'm not afraid," said the boy.

"Not afraid? Of course y'u ain't. What's your idea in going to Carlos? Got town lots there?"

"No," said the literal youth, to the huge internal diversion of Jones. "There's a man there I used to know back home. He's in the cavalry. What sort of a town is it for sport?" asked Cumnor, in a gay Lothario tone.

"*Town?*" Specimen Jones caught hold of the top rail of the corral. "*Sport?* Now I'll tell y'u what sort of a town it is. There ain't no streets. There ain't no houses. There ain't any land and water in the usual meaning of them words. There's Mount Turnbull. It's pretty near a usual mountain, but y'u don't want to go there. The Creator didn't make San Carlos. It's a heap older than Him. When He got around to it after slickin' up Paradise and them fruit-trees, He just left it to be as He found it, as a sample of the way they done business before He come along. He 'ain't done any work around that spot at all, He 'ain't. Mix up a barrel of sand and ashes and thorns, and jam scorpions and rattlesnakes along in, and dump the outfit on stones, and heat yer stones red-hot, and set the United States army loose over the place chasin' Apaches, and you've got San Carlos."

Cumnor was silent for a moment. " I don't care," he said. " I want to chase Apaches."

" Did you see that man Ephraim found by the cañon? " Jones inquired.

" Didn't get here in time."

" Well, there was a hole in his chest made by an arrow. But there's no harm in that if you die at wunst. That chap didn't, y'u see. You heard Ephraim tell about it. They'd done a number of things to the man before he could die. Roastin' was only one of 'em. Now your road takes you through the mountains where these Injuns hev gone. Kid, come along to Tucson with me," urged Jones, suddenly.

Again Cumnor was silent. " Is my road different from other people's? " he said, finally.

" Not to Grant, it ain't. These Mexicans are hauling freight to Grant. But what's the matter with your coming to Tucson with me? "

" I started to go to San Carlos, and I'm going," said Cumnor.

" You're a poor chuckle-headed fool! " burst out Jones, in a rage. " And y'u can go, for all I care — you and your Christmas-tree pistol. Like as not you won't find your cavalry friend at San Carlos. They've killed a lot of them soldiers huntin' Injuns this season. Good-night."

Specimen Jones was gone. Cumnor walked to his blanket-roll, where his saddle was slung under the shed. The various doings of the evening had bruised his nerves. He spread his blankets among the dry cattle-dung, and sat down, taking off a few clothes slowly. He lumped his coat and overalls under his head for a pillow, and, putting the despised pistol alongside, lay between the blankets. No object showed in the night but the tall freight-wagon. The tenderfoot thought he had made altogether a fool of himself upon the first trial trip of his manhood, alone on the open sea of Arizona. No man, not even Jones now, was his friend. A stranger, who could have had nothing against him but his inexperience, had taken the trouble to direct him on the wrong road. He did not mind definite enemies. He had punched the heads of those in Pennsylvania, and would not object to shooting them here; but this impersonal, surrounding hostility of the unknown was new and bitter: the cruel, assassinating, cowardly Southwest, where prospered those jail-birds whom the vigilantes had driven from California. He thought of the nameless human carcass that lay near, buried that day, and of the jokes about its mutilations. Cumnor was not an innocent boy, either in principles or in practice, but this laughter about a dead body had burned into his young, unhardened soul. He lay watching with hot, dogged eyes the brilliant stars. A passing wind turned the windmill, which creaked a forlorn minute, and ceased. He must have gone to sleep and slept soundly, for the next he knew it was the cold air of dawn that made him open his eyes. A numb silence lay over all things, and the tenderfoot had that moment of curiosity as to where he was now which comes to those who have journeyed for many days. The Mexicans had already departed with their freight-wagon. It was not entirely light, and the embers where these early starters had cooked their breakfast lay glowing in the sand across the road. The boy remembered seeing a wagon where now he saw only chill, distant peaks, and while he lay quiet and warm, shunning full consciousness, there was a stir in the cabin, and at Ephraim's voice reality broke upon his drowsiness, and he recollected Arizona and the keen stress of shifting for himself. He noted the gray paling round the grave. Indians? He would catch up with the Mexicans, and travel in their company to Grant. Freighters made but fifteen miles in the day, and he could start after breakfast and be with them before they stopped to noon. Six men need not worry about Apaches, Cumnor thought. The voice of Specimen Jones came from the cabin, and sounds of lighting the stove, and the growling conversation of men getting up. Cumnor, lying in his blankets, tried to overhear what Jones was saying, for no better reason than that this was the only man he had met lately who had seemed to care whether he were alive or dead. There was the clink of Ephraim's whiskey-bottles, and the cheerful tones of old Mr. Adams, saying, " It's better 'n brushin' yer teeth "; and then further clinking, and an inquiry from Specimen Jones.

" Whose spurs? " said he.

" Mine."   This from Mr. Adams.

" How long have they been yourn? "

" Since I got 'em, I guess."

" Well, you've enjoyed them spurs long enough."   The voice of Specimen Jones now altered in quality.

" And you'll give 'em back to that kid."

Muttering followed that the boy could not catch.

" You'll give 'em back," repeated Jones.   " I seen y'u lift 'em from under that chair when I was in the corner."

" That's straight, Mr. Adams," said Ephraim.   " I noticed it myself, though I had no objections, of course.   But Mr. Jones has pointed out — "

" Since when have you growed so honest, Jones? " cackled Mr. Adams, seeing that he must lose his little booty.   " And why didn't you raise yer objections when you seen me do it? "

" I didn't know the kid," Jones explained.   "And if it don't strike you that game blood deserves respect, why it does strike me."

Hearing this, the tenderfoot, outside in his shed, thought better of mankind and life in general, arose from his nest, and began preening himself.   He had all the correct trappings for the frontier, and his toilet in the shed gave him pleasure.   The sun came up, and with a stroke struck the world to crystal.   The near sand-hills went into rose, the crabbed yucca and the mesquite turned transparent, with lances and pale films of green, like drapery graciously veiling the desert's face, and distant violet peaks and edges framed the vast enchantment beneath the liquid exhalations of the sky. The smell of bacon and coffee from open windows filled the heart with bravery and yearning, and Ephraim, putting his head round the corner, called to Cumnor that he had better come in and eat. Jones, already at table, gave him the briefest nod; but the spurs were there, replaced as Cumnor had left them under a chair in the corner. In Arizona they do not say much at any meal, and at breakfast nothing at all; and as Cumnor swallowed and meditated, he noticed the cream-colored lady and the chain, and he made up his mind he should assert his identity with regard to that business, though how and when was not clear to him. He was in no great haste to take up his journey. The society of the Mexicans whom he must sooner or later overtake did not tempt him. When breakfast was done he idled in the cabin, like the other guests, while Ephraim and his assistant busied about the premises. But the morning grew on, and the guests, after a season of smoking and tilted silence against the wall, shook themselves and their effects together, saddled, and were lost among the waste thorny hills. Twenty Mile became hot and torpid. Jones lay on three consecutive chairs, occasionally singing, and old Mr. Adams had not gone away either, but watched him, with more tobacco running down his beard.

"Well," said Cumnor, "I'll be going."

"Nobody's stopping y'u," remarked Jones.

"You're going to Tucson?" the boy said, with the chain problem still unsolved in his mind. "Good-bye, Mr. Jones. I hope I'll — we'll — "

"That'll do," said Jones; and the tenderfoot, thrown back by this severity, went to get his saddle-horse and his burro.

Presently Jones remarked to Mr. Adams that he wondered what Ephraim was doing, and went out. The old gentleman was left alone in the room, and he swiftly noticed that the belt and pistol of Specimen Jones were left alone with him. The accoutrement lay by the chair its owner had been lounging in. It is an easy thing to remove cartridges from the chambers of a revolver, and replace the weapon in its holster so that everything looks quite natural. The old gentleman was entertained with the notion that somewhere in Tucson Specimen Jones might have a surprise, and he did not take a minute to prepare this, drop the belt as it lay before, and saunter innocently out of the saloon. Ephraim and Jones were criticising the tenderfoot's property as he packed his burro.

"Do y'u make it a rule to travel with ice-cream?" Jones was inquiring.

"They're for water," Cumnor said. "They told me at Tucson I'd need to carry water for three days on some trails."

It was two good-sized milk-cans that he had, and they bounced about on the little burro's pack, giving him as much amazement as a jackass can feel. Jones and Ephraim were hilarious.

"Don't go without your spurs, Mr. Cumnor," said the voice of old Mr. Adams, as he approached the group. His tone was particularly civil.

The tenderfoot had, indeed, forgotten his spurs, and he ran back to get them. The cream-colored lady still had the chain hanging upon her, and Cumnor's problem was suddenly solved. He put the chain in his pocket, and laid the price of one round of drinks for last night's company on the shelf below the chromo. He returned with his spurs on, and went to his saddle that lay beside that of Specimen Jones under the shed. After a moment he came with his saddle to where the men stood talking by his pony, slung it on, and tightened the cinches; but the chain was now in the saddle-bag of Specimen Jones, mixed up with some tobacco, stale bread, a box of matches, and a hunk of fat bacon. The men at Twenty Mile said good-day to the tenderfoot, with monosyllables and indifference, and watched him depart into the heated desert. Wishing for a last look at Jones, he turned once, and saw the three standing, and the chocolate brick of the cabin, and the windmill white and idle in the sun.

"He'll be gutted by night," remarked Mr. Adams.

"I ain't buryin' him, then," said Ephraim.

"Nor I," said Specimen Jones. "Well, it's time I was getting to Tucson."

He went to the saloon, strapped on his pistol, saddled, and rode away. Ephraim and Mr. Adams returned to the cabin; and here is the final conclusion they came to after three hours of discussion as to who took the chain and who had it just then:

Ephraim. Jones, he hadn't no cash.

Mr. Adams. The kid, he hadn't no sense.

Ephraim. The kid, he lent the cash to Jones.

Mr. Adams. Jones, he goes off with his chain.

Both. What damn fools everybody is, anyway!

And they went to dinner. But Mr. Adams did not mention his relations with Jones's pistol. Let it be said, in extenuation of that performance, that Mr. Adams supposed Jones was going to Tucson, where he said he was going, and where a job and a salary were awaiting him. In Tucson an unloaded pistol in the holster of so handy a man on the drop as was Specimen would keep people civil, because they would not know, any more than the owner, that it was unloaded; and the mere possession of it would be sufficient in nine chances out of ten — though it was undoubtedly for the tenth that Mr. Adams had a sneaking hope. But Specimen Jones was not going to Tucson. A contention in his mind as to whether he would do what was good for himself, or what was good for another, had kept him sullen ever since he got up. Now it was settled, and Jones in serene humor again. Of course he had started on the Tucson road, for the benefit of Ephraim and Mr. Adams.

The tenderfoot rode along. The Arizona sun beat down

upon the deadly silence, and the world was no longer of crystal, but a mesa, dull and gray and hot. The pony's hoofs grated in the gravel, and after a time the road dived down and up among lumpy hills of stone and cactus, always nearer the fierce glaring Sierra Santa Catalina. It dipped so abruptly in and out of the shallow sudden ravines that, on coming up from one of these into sight of the country again, the tenderfoot's heart jumped at the close apparition of another rider quickly bearing in upon him from gullies where he had been moving unseen. But it was only Specimen Jones.

"Hello!" said he, joining Cumnor. "Hot, ain't it?"

"Where are you going?" inquired Cumnor.

"Up here a ways." And Jones jerked his finger generally towards the Sierra, where they were heading.

"Thought you had a job in Tucson."

"That's what I have."

Specimen Jones had no more to say, and they rode for a while, their ponies' hoofs always grating in the gravel, and the milk-cans lightly clanking on the burro's pack. The bunched blades of the yuccas bristled steel-stiff, and as far as you could see it was a gray waste of mounds and ridges sharp and blunt, up to the forbidding boundary walls of the Tortilita one way and the Santa Catalina the other. Cumnor wondered if Jones had found the chain. Jones was capable of not finding it for several weeks, or of finding it at once and saying nothing.

"You'll excuse my meddling with your business?" the boy hazarded.

Jones looked inquiring.

"Something's wrong with your saddle-pocket."

Specimen saw nothing apparently wrong with it, but perceiving Cumnor was grinning, unbuckled the pouch. He looked at the boy rapidly, and looked away again, and as he rode, still in silence, he put the chain back round his neck below the flannel shirt-collar.

" Say, kid," he remarked, after some time, " what does J stand for ? "

" J? Oh, my name ! Jock."

" Well, Jock, will y'u explain to me as a friend how y'u ever come to be such a fool as to leave yer home — wherever and whatever it was — in exchange for this here God-forsaken and iniquitous hole ? "

" If you'll explain to me," said the boy, greatly heartened, " how you come to be ridin' in the company of a fool, instead of goin' to your job at Tucson."

The explanation was furnished before Specimen Jones had framed his reply. A burning freight-wagon and five dismembered human stumps lay in the road. This was what had happened to the Miguels and Serapios and the concertina. Jones and Cumnor, in their dodging and struggles to exclude all expressions of growing mutual esteem from their speech, had forgotten their journey, and a sudden bend among the rocks where the road had now brought them revealed the blood and fire staring them in the face. The plundered wagon was three parts empty; its splintered, blazing boards slid down as they burned into the fiery heap on the ground; packages of soda and groceries and medicines slid with them, bursting into chemical spots of green and crimson flame; a wheel crushed in and sank, spilling more packages that flickered and hissed; the garbage of combat and murder littered the earth, and in the air hung an odor that Cumnor knew, though he had never smelled it before. Morsels of dropped booty up among the rocks showed where the Indians had gone, and one horse remained, groaning, with an accidental arrow in his belly.

" We'll just kill him," said Jones; and his pistol snapped idly, and snapped again, as his eye caught a motion — a something — two hundred yards up among the bowlders on the hill. He whirled round. The enemy was behind them also. There was no retreat. " Yourn's no good ! " yelled Jones, fiercely, for Cumnor was getting out his little, foolish revolver. "Oh, what a trick to play on a man! Drop off yer horse, kid; drop, and do like me. Shootin's no good here, even if I was loaded. *They* shot, and look at them now. God bless them ice-cream freezers of yourn, kid! Did y'u ever see a crazy man? If you 'ain't, *make it up as y'u go along!*"

More objects moved up among the bowlders. Specimen Jones ripped off the burro's pack, and the milk-cans rolled on the ground. The burro began grazing quietly, with now and then a step towards new patches of grass. The horses stood where their riders had left them, their reins over their heads, hanging and dragging. From two hundred yards on the hill the ambushed Apaches showed, their dark, scattered figures appearing cautiously one by one, watching with suspicion. Specimen Jones seized up one milk-can, and Cumnor obediently did the same.

"You kin dance, kid, and I kin sing, and we'll go to it," said Jones. He rambled in a wavering loop, and diving eccentrically at Cumnor, clashed the milk-cans together. " 'Es schallt ein Ruf wie Donnerhall,' " he bawled, beginning the song of "Die Wacht am Rhein." "Why don't you dance?" he shouted sternly. The boy saw the terrible earnestness of his face, and, clashing his milk-cans in turn, he shuffled a sort of jig. The two went over the sand in loops, toe and heel; the donkey continued his quiet grazing, and the flames rose hot and yellow from the freight-wagon. And all the while the stately German hymn pealed among the rocks, and the Apaches crept down nearer the bowing, scraping men. The sun shone bright, and their bodies poured with sweat. Jones flung off his shirt; his damp, matted hair was half in ridges and half glued to his forehead, and the delicate gold chain swung and struck his broad, naked breast. The Apaches drew nearer again, their bows and arrows held uncertainly. They came down the hill, fifteen or twenty, taking a long time, and stopping every few yards. The milk-cans clashed, and Jones thought he felt the boy's strokes weakening. " Die Wacht am Rhein " was finished, and now it was " ' Ha-ve you seen my Flora pass this way? ' "	" Y'u mustn't play out, kid," said Jones, very gently.	" Indeed y'u mustn't "; and he at once resumed his song.	The silent Apaches had now reached the bottom of the hill.	They stood some twenty yards away, and Cumnor had a good chance to see his first Indians.	He saw them move, and the color and slim shape of their bodies, their thin arms, and their long black hair.	It went through his mind that if he had no more clothes on than that, dancing would come easier.	His boots were growing heavy to lift, and his overalls seemed to wrap his sinews in wet, strangling thongs. He wondered how long he had been keeping this up.	The legs of the Apaches were free, with light moccasins only half-way to the thigh, slenderly held up by strings from the waist.	Cumnor envied their unencumbered steps as he saw them again walk nearer to where he was dancing.	It was long since he had eaten, and he noticed a singing dulness in his brain, and became frightened at his thoughts, which were running and melting into one fixed idea.	This idea was to take off his boots, and offer to trade them for a pair of moccasins.	It terrified him — this endless, molten rush of thoughts; he could see them coming in different shapes from different places in his head, but they all joined immediately, and always formed the same fixed idea.	He ground his teeth to master this encroaching inebriation of his will and judgment.	He clashed his can more loudly to wake him to reality, which he still could recognize and appreciate.	For a time he found it a good plan to listen to what Specimen Jones was singing, and tell himself the name of the song, if he knew it.	At present it was " Yankee Doodle," to which Jones was fitting words of his own.	These ran, " Now I'm going to try a bluff, And mind you do what I do "; and then again, over and over.	Cumnor waited for the word " bluff "; for it was hard and heavy, and fell into his thoughts, and stopped them for a moment.	The dance was so long now he had forgotten about that. A numbness had been spreading through his legs, and he was glad to feel a sharp pain in the sole of his foot. It was a piece of gravel that had somehow worked its way in, and was rubbing through the skin into the flesh. "That's good," he said, aloud. The pebble was eating the numbness away, and Cumnor drove it hard against the raw spot, and relished the tonic of its burning friction. The Apaches had drawn into a circle. Standing at some interval apart, they entirely surrounded the arena. Shrewd, half convinced, and yet with awe, they watched the dancers, who clashed their cans slowly now in rhythm to Jones's hoarse, parched singing. He was quite master of himself, and led the jig round the still blazing wreck of the wagon, and circled in figures of eight between the corpses of the Mexicans, clashing the milk-cans above each one. Then, knowing his strength was coming to an end, he approached an Indian whose splendid fillet and trappings denoted him of consequence; and Jones was near shouting with relief when the Indian shrank backward. Suddenly he saw Cumnor let his can drop, and without stopping to see why, he caught it up, and, slowly rattling both, approached each Indian in turn with tortuous steps. The circle that had never uttered a sound till now receded, chanting almost in a whisper some exorcising song which the man with the fillet had begun. They gathered round him, retreating always, and the strain, with its rapid muttered words, rose and fell softly among them. Jones had supposed the boy was overcome by faintness, and looked to see where he lay. But it was not faintness. Cumnor, with his boots off, came by and walked after the Indians in a trance. They saw him, and quickened their pace, often turning to be sure he was not overtaking them. He called to them unintelligibly, stumbling up the sharp hill, and pointing to the boots. Finally he sat down. They continued ascending the mountain, herding close round the man with the feathers, until the rocks and the filmy tangles screened them from sight; and like a wind that hums uncertainly in grass, their chanting died away.

The sun was half behind the western range when Jones next moved. He called, and, getting no answer, he crawled painfully to where the boy lay on the hill. Cumnor was sleeping heavily; his head was hot, and he moaned. So Jones crawled down, and fetched blankets and the canteen of water. He spread the blankets over the boy, wet a handkerchief and laid it on his forehead; then he lay down himself.

The earth was again magically smitten to crystal. Again the sharp cactus and the sand turned beautiful, and violet floated among the mountains, and rose-colored orange in the sky above them.

" Jock," said Specimen at length.

The boy opened his eyes.

" Your foot is awful, Jock. Can y'u eat? "

" Not with my foot."

" Ah, God bless y'u, Jock! Y'u ain't turruble sick. But *can* y'u eat? "

Cumnor shook his head.

" Eatin's what y'u need, though. Well, here." Specimen poured a judicious mixture of whiskey and water down the boy's throat, and wrapped the awful foot in his own flannel shirt. " They'll fix y'u over to Grant. It's maybe twelve miles through the cañon. It ain't a town any more than Carlos is, but the soldiers 'll be good to us. As soon as night comes you and me must somehow git out of this."

Somehow they did, Jones walking and leading his horse and the imperturbable little burro, and also holding Cumnor in the saddle. And when Cumnor was getting well in the military hospital at Grant, he listened to Jones recounting to all that chose to hear how useful a weapon an ice-cream freezer can be, and how if you'll only chase Apaches in your stocking feet they are sure to run away. And then Jones and Cumnor both enlisted; and I suppose Jones's friend is still expecting him in Tucson.

THE LAND OF THE STRADDLE-BUG

HAMLIN GARLAND

Dakota, 1883

From "The Moccasin Ranch." Reprinted by permission of the author and of Harper and Brothers, New York.[1]

I

EARLY in the gray and red dawn of a March morning in 1883, two wagons moved slowly out of Boomtown, the two-year-old "giant of the plains." As the teams drew past the last house, the strangeness of the scene appealed irresistibly to the newly arrived immigrants. The town lay behind them on the level, treeless plain like a handful of blocks pitched upon a russet robe. Its houses were mainly shanties of pine, one-story in height, while here and there actual tents gleamed in the half-light with infinite suggestion of America's restless pioneers.

The wind blew fresh and chill from the west. The sun rose swiftly, and the thin scarf of morning cloud melted away, leaving an illimitable sweep of sky arching an almost equally majestic plain. There was a poignant charm in the air — a smell of freshly uncovered sod, a width and splendor in the view which exalted the movers beyond words.

The prairie was ridged here and there with ice, and the swales were full of posh and water. Geese were slowly winging their way against the wind, and ducks were sitting here and there on the ice-rimmed ponds. The sod was

---

[1] Copyright, 1909, by Hamlin Garland.

burned black and bare, and so firm with frost that the wagon chuckled noisily as it passed over it. The whistle of the driver called afar, startling the ducks from their all-night resting-places.

One of the teams drew a load of material for a house, together with a few household utensils. The driver, a thin-faced, blue-eyed man of thirty, walked beside his horses. His eyes were full of wonder, but he walked in silence.

The second wagon was piled high with boxes and barrels of groceries and hardware, and was driven by a handsome young fellow with a large brown mustache. His name was Bailey, and he seemed to be pointing the way for his companion, whom he called Burke.

As the sun rose, a kind of transformation-scene took place. The whole level land lifted at the horizon till the teams seemed crawling forever at bottom of an enormous bowl. Mystical forms came into view — grotesquely elongated, unrecognizable. Hills twenty, thirty miles away rose like apparitions, astonishingly magnified. Willows became elms, a settler's shanty rose like a shot-tower — towns hitherto unseen swam and palpitated in the yellow flood of light like shaken banners low-hung on unseen flagstaffs.

Burke marched with uplifted face. He was like one suddenly wakened in a new world, where nothing was familiar. Not a tree or shrub was in sight. Not a mark of plough or harrow — everything was wild, and to him mystical and glorious. His eyes were like those of a man who sees a world at its birth.

Hour after hour they moved across the swelling land. Hour after hour, while the yellow sun rolled up the slope, putting to flight the morning shapes on the horizon — striking the plain into level prose again, and warming the air into genial March. Hour after hour the horses toiled on till the last cabin fell away to the east, like a sail at sea, till the road faded into a trail almost imperceptible on the firm sod.

And so at last they came to the land of " the straddle-bug " — the squatters' watch dog — three boards nailed together (like a stack of army muskets) to mark a claim. Burke resembled a man taking his first sea-voyage. His eyes searched the plain restlessly, and his brain dreamed. Bailey, an old settler — of two years' experience —whistled and sang and shouted lustily to his tired beasts.

It drew toward noon. Bailey's clear voice shouted back, " When we reach that swell we'll see the Western Coteaux." The Western Coteaux! To Burke, the man from Illinois, this was like discovering a new range of mountains.

" There they rise," Bailey called, a little later.

Burke looked away to the west. Low down on the horizon lay a long, blue bank, hardly more substantial than a line of cloud. " How far off are they? " he asked, in awe.

" About twenty-five miles. Our claims are just about in line with that gap." Bailey pointed with his whip. " And about twelve miles from here. We're on the unsurveyed land now."

Burke experienced a thrill of exultation as he looked around him. In the distance, other carriages were crawling like beetles. A couple of shanties, newly built on a near-by ridge, glittered like gold in the sun, and the piles of yellow lumber and the straddle-bugs increased in number as they left the surveyed land and emerged into the finer tract which lay as yet unmapped. At noon they stopped and fed their animals, eating their own food on the ground beside their wagons.

While they rested, Bailey kept his eyes on their backward trail, watching for his partner, Rivers. " It's about time Jim showed up," he said, once again.

Burke seemed anxious. " They won't get off the track, will they? "

Bailey laughed at his innocence. " Jim Rivers has located about seventy-five claims out here this spring. I guess he won't lose his bearings."

"I'm afraid Blanche 'll get nervous."

"Oh, Jim will take care of her. She won't be lonesome, either. He's a great favorite with the women, always gassin' — Well, this won't feed the baby," he ended, leaping to his feet.

They were about to start on when a swift team came into sight. The carriage was a platform-spring wagon, with a man and woman in the front seat, and in the rear a couple of alert young fellows sat holding rifles in their hands and eyeing the plain for game.

"Hello!" said the driver, in a pleasant shout. "How you getting on?"

"Pretty well," replied Bailey.

"Should say you were. I didn't know but we'd fail to overhaul you."

Burke went up to the wagon. "Well, Blanche, what do you think of it — far's you've got?"

"Not very much," replied his wife, candidly. She was a handsome woman, but looked tired and a little cross, at the moment. "I guess I'll get out and ride with you," she added.

"Why, no! What for?" asked Rivers, hastily. "Why not go right along out to the store with us?"

"Why, yes; that's the thing to do, Blanche. We'll be along soon," said Burke. "Stay where you are."

She sat down again, as if ashamed to give her reason for not going on with these strange men.

"I was just in the middle of a story, too," added Rivers, humorously. "Well, so long." And, cracking his whip, he started on. "We'll have supper ready when you arrive!" he shouted back.

Burke could not forget the look in his wife's eyes. She was right. It would have been pleasanter if she had stayed with him. They had been married several years, but his love for her had not grown less. Perhaps for the reason that she dominated him.

She was a fine, powerful girl, while he was a plain man, slightly stooping, with thin face and prominent larynx. She had brought a little property to him, which was unusual enough to give her a sense of importance in all business transactions of the firm.

She had consented to the sale of their farm in Illinois with great reluctance, and, as Burke rode along on his load of furniture, he recalled it all very vividly, and it made him anxious to know her impression of his claim. As he took her position for a moment, he got a sudden sense of the loneliness and rawness of this new land which he had not felt before. The woman's point of view was so different from that of the adventurous man.

Twice they were forced to partly unload in order to cross ravines where the frost had fallen out, and it was growing dark as they rose over the low swell, from which they could see a dim, red star, which Burke guessed to be the shanty light, even before Bailey called, exultantly:

" There she blows! "

The wind had grown chill and moist, the quacking ducks were thickening on the pools, and strange noises came from ghostly swells and hidden creeks. The tired horses moved forward with soundless feet upon the sod, which had softened during the day. They quickened their steps when they saw the lantern shine from the pole before the building.

The light of the lamp, and the sight of Blanche standing in the doorway of the cabin at the back of the store-room, was a beautiful sight to Burke. Set over against the wet, dark prairie, with its boundless sweep of unknown soil, the shanty seemed a radiant palace.

" Supper's all ready, Willard! " called Blanche, and the tired man's heart leaped with joy to hear the tender, familiar cadence of her voice. It was her happy voice, and when she used it men were her slaves.

Bailey came out with one of the land-seekers.

" Go in to supper, boys; we'll take care of the teams," was his hearty command.

The tired freighters gladly did as they were bid, and, scooping up some water from a near-by hollow on the sod, hurriedly washed their faces and sat down to a supper of chopped potatoes, bacon and eggs, and tea (which Blanche placed steaming hot upon the table), and in such joy as only the weary worker knows.

Mrs. Burke was in high spirits. The novelty of the trip, the rude shanty, with its litter of shavings, and its boxes for chairs, the bundles of hay for beds, gave her something like the same pleasure a picnic might have done. It appealed to the primeval in her. She forgot her homesickness and her vague regrets, and her smiles filled her husband with content.

Rivers and the others soon came in, and after supper there was a great deal of energetic talk. The young land-seekers were garrulous with delight over their claims, which they proudly exalted above the stumps and stones of the farms " back home."

" Why, it took three generations of my folks to clear off forty acres of land," said one of them. " They just wore themselves out on it. I told Hank he could have it, and I'd go West and see if there wasn't some land out there which wouldn't take a man's lifetime to grub out and smooth down. And I've found it."

Rivers had plainly won the friendship of Mrs. Burke, for they were having a jolly time together over by the table, where he was helping to wash the dishes. He had laughing, brown eyes, and a pleasant voice, and was one of the most popular of the lawyers and land-agents in Boom-town. There was a boyish quality in him which kept him giving and taking jocular remarks.

Bailey sometimes said: " Rivers would shine up to a seventy-year-old Sioux squaw if she was the only woman handy, but he don't mean anything by it — it's just his

way. He's one o' the best-hearted fellers that ever lived."
Others took a less favorable view of the land-agent, and
refused to trust him.

Bailey assumed command. "Now, fellers," he said,
" we'll vamoose the ranch while Mrs. Burke turns in." He
opened the way to the store-room, and the men filed out, all
but Burke, who remained to put up the calico curtain with
which his wife had planned to shield her bed.

Blanche was a little disturbed at the prospect of sleeping
behind such a thin barrier.

" Oh, it's no worse than the sleeping-car," her husband
argued.

A little later he stuck his head in at the store-room door.
" All ready, Bailey."

Bailey was to sleep on the rickety lounge, which served
as bedstead and chair, and the other men were to make
down as best they could in the grocery.

Bailey went out to the front of the shanty to look at the
lantern he had set up on a scantling. Rivers followed him.

" Going to leave that up there all night? "

" Yes. May keep some poor devil from wandering
around all night on the prairie."

Rivers said, with an abrupt change in his voice:

" Mrs. Burke is a hummer, isn't she? How'd his flat-
chested nibs manage to secure a ' queen ' like that? I must
get married, Bailey — no use."

Bailey took his friend's declaration more lightly than it
deserved. He laughed. " Wish you would, Jim, and relieve
me of the cookin'."

Blanche could hardly compose herself to sleep. " Isn't
it wonderful," she whispered. " It's all so strange, like
being out of the world, someway."

Burke heard the ducks quacking down in the " Moggason", and he, too, *felt* the silence and immensity of the
plain outside. It was enormous, incredible in its wildness.
" I believe we're going to like it out here, Blanche," he said.

Blanche Burke rose to a beautiful and busy day. The breakfast which she cooked in the early dawn was savory, and Rivers, who helped her by bringing water and building the fire, was full of life and humor. He seemed to have no other business than to " wait and tend " on her.

He called her out to see the sunrise. " Isn't this great! " he called, exultantly. Flights of geese were passing, and the noise of ducks came to them from every direction. He pointed out the distant hills, and called her attention to a solemn row of sand-hill cranes down by the swale, causing her to see the wonder and beauty of this new world.

" You're going to like it out here," he said, with conviction. " It is a glorious climate, and you'll soon have more neighbors than you want."

After breakfast Bailey and Burke left the " Moggason Ranch " — as Bailey called the store and shanty — to carry the lumber and furniture belonging to Burke on to his claim, two or three miles away. Rivers remained to work in the store, and to meet some other land-seekers, and Mrs. Burke agreed to stay and get dinner for them all.

During this long forenoon, Rivers exerted himself to prevent her from being lonely. He was busy about the store, but he found time to keep her fire going and to bring water and to tell her of his bachelor life with Bailey. She had never had anything like this swift and smiling service, and she felt very grateful to him. He encouraged her to make some pies and to prepare a " thumping dinner." " It will seem like being married again," he said, with a chuckle.

Burke and Bailey returned at noon to dinner.

" Mrs. Burke, you can sleep in your own ranch to-night," announced Bailey.

" I guess it will be a ranch."

"It'll be new, anyhow," her husband said, with a timid smile.

After dinner she straightened things up a little, and as

she got into the wagon she said: "Well, there, Mr. Rivers. *You'll* have to take care o' things now."

Rivers leered comically, sighed, and looked at his partner. "Bailey, I didn't know what we needed before; I know now. We need a woman."

Bailey smiled. "Go get one. Don't ask a clumsy old farmer like me to provide a cook."

"I'll get married to-morrow," said Rivers, with a droll inflection. They all laughed, and Burke clucked at the team. "Well, good-bye, boys; see you later."

After leaving the ranch they struck out over the prairie where no wagon-wheel but theirs had ever passed. Here were the buffalo trails, deep-worn ruts all running from northwest to southeast. Here lay the white bones of elk in shining crates, ghastly on the fire-blackened sod. Beside the shallow pools, buffalo horns, in testimony of the tragic past, lay scattered thickly. Everywhere could be seen the signs of the swarming herds of bison which once swept to and fro from north to south over the plain, all so silent and empty now.

A few antelope scurried away out of the path, and a wolf sitting on a height gravely watched the teams as if marvelling at their coming. The wind swept out of the west clear and cold. The sky held no shred of cloud. The air was like some all-powerful intoxicant, and when Bailey pointed out a row of little stakes and said, "There's the railroad," their imagination supplied the trains, the wheat, the houses, the towns which were to come.

At the claim Blanche sat on a box and watched the two men as they swiftly built the little cabin which was to be her home. Their hammers rang merrily, and soon she was permitted to go inside and look up at the great sky which roofed it in. This was an emotional moment to her. As she sat there listening to the voices of the men who were drawing this fragile shelter around her, a great awe fell upon her. It seemed as if she had drawn a little nearer to the Almighty Creator of the universe. Here, where no white man had ever set foot, she was watching the founding of her own house. Was it a home? Could it ever be a home?

Swiftly the roof closed over her head, and the floor crept under her feet. The stove came in, and the flour-barrel, and the few household articles which they had brought followed, and as the sun was setting they all sat down to supper in her new home.

The smell of the fresh pine was round them. Geese were flying over. Cranes were dancing down by the ponds, prairie-chickens were *booming*. The open doorway — doorless yet — looked out on the sea-like plain glorified by the red sun just sinking over the purple line of treeless hills to the west. It was the bare, raw materials of a State, and they were in at the beginning of it.

After Bailey left them the husband and wife sat in silence. When they spoke it was in low voices. It seemed as if God could hear what they said — that He was just there behind the glory of the western clouds.

II

Day by day the plain thickened with life. Each noon a crowd of land-seekers swarmed about the Moggason Ranch asking for food and shelter, and Blanche, responding to Rivers' entreaties, went down to cook, returning each night to her bed. Rivers professed to be very grateful for her aid.

All ages and sexes came to take claims. Old men, alone and feeble, school teachers from the East, young girls from the towns of the older counties, boys not yet of age — everywhere incoming claimants were setting stakes upon the green and beautiful sod.

Each day the grass grew more velvety green. Each day

the sky waxed warmer. The snow disappeared from the ravines. The ice broke up on the Moggason. The ponds disappeared. Plover flew over with wailing cry. Buffalo birds, prairie pigeons, larks, blackbirds, sparrows, joined their voices to those of the cranes and geese and ducks, and the prairie piped and twittered and clacked and chuckled with life. The gophers emerged from their winter-quarters, the foxes barked on the hills, the skunk hobbled along the ravines, and the badger raised mounds of fresh soil as if to aid the boomer by showing how deep the black loam was.

Everybody was in holiday mood. Men whistled and sang and shouted and toiled — toiled terribly — and yet it did not seem like toil! They sank wells and ploughed gardens and built barns and planted seeds, and yet the whole settlement continued to present the care-free manners of a great pleasure party. It seemed as if no one needed to work, and, therefore, those first months were months of gay and swift progress.

It was the most beautiful spring Blanche and Willard Burke had spent since their marriage nine years before. Blanche forgot to be petulant or moody. She was in superb health, and carried herself like a girl of eighteen. She appeared to have lost all her regrets.

She laughed heartily when Rivers came over one afternoon and boldly declared:

"Burke, I've c'me to borrow your wife. We've got a lot o' tenderfoots over there to-night, and I'm a little shy of Bailey's biscuits. I'm going to carry your cook away."

"All right; only bring her back."

Blanche was a little embarrassed when Rivers replied: "I don't like to agree to do that. Mebbe you'd better come over to make sure I do."

"All right. I'll come over in time for supper." Burke's simple, good face glowed with enjoyment of the fun. He smilingly went back to beating his ploughshare with hammer and wedge as Rivers drove away with Blanche. The clink of his steel rang through the golden light that flooded the prairie, keeping time to his whistled song.

In the months of April and May the world sent a skirmish-line into this echoless land to take possession of a belt of territory six hundred miles long and one hundred miles broad. The settlers came like locusts; they sang like larks. From Alsace and Lorraine, from the North Sea, from Russia, from the Alps, they came, and their faces shone as if they had happened upon the spring-time of the world. Tyranny was behind them, the majesty of God's wilderness before them, a mystic joy within them.

Under their hands the straddle-bug multiplied. He is short-lived, this prairie insect. He usually dies in thirty days — by courtesy alone he lives. He expresses the settlers' hope and sense of justice. In these spring days of good cheer he lived at times to sixty days — but only on stony ground or fire-scarred, peaty lowlands.

He withered — this strange, three-legged, voiceless insect — but in his stead arose a beetle. This beetle sheltered human beings, and was called a shack.

They were all alike, these shacks. They had roofs of one slant. They were built of rough lumber, and roofed with tarred paper, which made all food taste of tar.

They were dens but little higher than a man's head, and yet they sheltered the most joyous people that ever set foot to earth. In one cabin lived a girl and a canary-bird, all alone. In the next a man who cooked his own food when he did not share his rations with the girl, all in frank and honorable companionship. On the next claim were two school-teachers, busy as magpies, using the saw and hammer with deft accuracy. In the next was a bank-clerk out for his health — and these clean and self-contained people lived in free intercourse without slander and without fear. Only the Alsatians settled in groups, alien and unapproachable. All others met at odd times and places, breathing in the promiseful air of the clean sod, resolute to put the world of hopeless failure behind them.

Spring merged magnificently into summer. The grass upthrust. The water-fowl passed on to the northern lake-region. The morning symphony of the prairie-chickens died out, but the whistle of the larks, the chatter of the sparrows, and the wailing cry of the nestling plover came to take its place.

The gophers whistled and trilled, the foxes barked from the hills, and an occasional startled antelope or curious wolf passed through the line of settlement as if to see what lay behind this strange phalanx of ploughmen guarding their yellow shanties.

Week after week passed away, and the government surveyors did not appear. The Boomtown *Spike* told in each issue how the men of the chain and compass were pushing westward; but still they did not come, and the settlers' hopes of getting their claims filed before winter grew fainter. The mass of them had planned to take claims in the spring, live on them the required six months, " prove up," and return East for the winter.

In spite of these disappointments, all continued to be merry. No one took any part of it very seriously. The young men went out and ploughed when they pleased, and came in and sat on the door-step and talked with the women when they were weary. The shanties were hot and crowded, but no one minded that; by-and-by they were to build bigger.

And, then, all was so new and beautiful, and the sky was so clear. Oh, that marvellous, lofty sky with just clouds enough to make the blue more intense! Oh, the wonder of the wind from the wild, mysterious green sea to the west! With the change and sheen of the prairie, incessant and magical life was made marvellous and the winter put far away.

Merry parties drove here and there visiting. Formalities

counted for little, and yet with all this freedom of intercourse, this close companionship, no one pointed the finger of gossip toward any woman. The girls in their one-room huts received calls from their bachelor neighbors with the confidence that comes from purity of purpose, both felt and understood. Life was strangely idyllic during these spring days. Envy and hate and suspicion seemed exorcised from the world.

OLD EPHRAIM

THE GRIZZLY

THEODORE ROOSEVELT

From "Hunting-Trips of a Ranchman." Reprinted by permission of the publishers, G. P. Putnam's Sons, New York.[1]

BUT few bears are found in the immediate neighborhood of my ranch; and though I have once or twice seen their tracks in the Bad Lands, I have never had any experience with the animals themselves except during the elk-hunting trip on the Bighorn Mountains, described in the preceding chapter.

The grizzly bear undoubtedly comes in the category of dangerous game, and is, perhaps, the only animal in the United States that can be fairly so placed, unless we count the few jaguars found north of the Rio Grande. But the danger of hunting the grizzly has been greatly exaggerated, and the sport is certainly very much safer than it was at the beginning of this century. The first hunters who came into contact with this great bear were men belonging to that hardy and adventurous class of backwoodsmen which had filled the wild country between the Appalachian Mountains and the Mississippi. These men carried but one weapon: the long-barrelled, small-bored pea-rifle, whose bullets ran seventy to the pound, the amount of powder and lead being a little less than that contained in the cartridge of a thirty-two calibre Winchester. In the Eastern States almost all the hunting was done in the woodland; the shots were mostly obtained at short distance, and deer and black bear were

[1] Copyright, 1886 and 1914, by G. P. Putnam's Sons.

the largest game; moreover, the pea-rifles were marvellously accurate for close range, and their owners were famed the world over for their skill as marksmen. Thus these rifles had so far proved plenty good enough for the work they had to do, and indeed had done excellent service as military weapons in the ferocious wars that the men of the border carried on with their Indian neighbors, and even in conflict with more civilized foes, as at the battles of King's Mountain and New Orleans. But when the restless frontiersmen pressed out over the Western plains, they encountered in the grizzly a beast of far greater bulk and more savage temper than any of those found in the Eastern woods, and their small-bore rifles were utterly inadequate weapons with which to cope with him. It is small wonder that he was considered by them to be almost invulnerable, and extraordinarily tenacious of life. He would be a most unpleasant antagonist now to a man armed only with a thirty-two calibre rifle, that carried but a single shot and was loaded at the muzzle. A rifle, to be of use in this sport, should carry a ball weighing from half an ounce to an ounce. With the old pea-rifles the shot had to be in the eye or heart; and accidents to the hunter were very common. But the introduction of heavy breech-loading repeaters has greatly lessened the danger, even in the very few and far-off places where the grizzlies are as ferocious as formerly. For nowadays these great bears are undoubtedly much better aware of the death-dealing power of men, and, as a consequence, much less fierce, than was the case with their forefathers, who so unhesitatingly attacked the early Western travellers and explorers. Constant contact with rifle-carrying hunters, for a period extending over many generations of bear-life, has taught the grizzly by bitter experience that man is his undoubted overlord, as far as fighting goes; and this knowledge has become an hereditary characteristic. No grizzly will assail a man now unprovoked, and one will almost always rather run than fight; though if he is wounded or thinks himself cornered he will attack his foes with a headlong, reckless fury that renders him one of the most dangerous of wild beasts. The ferocity of all wild animals depends largely upon the amount of resistance they are accustomed to meet with, and the quantity of molestation to which they are subjected.

The change in the grizzly's character during the last half century has been precisely paralleled by the change in the characters of his northern cousin, the polar bear, and of the South African lion. When the Dutch and Scandinavian sailors first penetrated the Arctic seas, they were kept in constant dread of the white bear, who regarded a man as simply an erect variety of seal, quite as good eating as the common kind. The records of these early explorers are filled with examples of the ferocious and man-eating propensities of the polar bears; but in the accounts of most of the later Arctic expeditions they are portrayed as having learned wisdom, and being now most anxious to keep out of the way of the hunters. A number of my sporting friends have killed white bears, and none of them were ever even charged. And in South Africa the English sportsmen and Dutch Boers have taught the lion to be a very different creature from what it was when the first white man reached that continent. If the Indian tiger had been a native of the United States, it would now be one of the most shy of beasts. Of late years our estimate of the grizzly's ferocity has been lowered; and we no longer accept the tales of uneducated hunters as being proper authority by which to judge it. But we should make a parallel reduction in the cases of many foreign animals and their describers. Take, for example, that purely melodramatic beast, the North African lion, as portrayed by Jules Gérard, who bombastically describes himself as " le tueur des lions." Gérard's accounts are self-evidently in large part fictitious, while if true they would prove less for the bravery of the lion than for the phenomenal cowardice, incapacity, and bad

marksmanship of the Algerian Arabs. Doubtless Gérard
was a great hunter; but so is many a Western plainsman,
whose account of the grizzlies he has killed would be wholly
untrustworthy. Take for instance the following from page
223 of "La Chasse au Lion": "The inhabitants had assembled one day to the number of two or three hundred
with the object of killing (the lion) or driving it out of
the country. The attack took place at sunrise; at mid-day
five hundred cartridges had been expended; the Arabs carried off one of their number dead and six wounded, and the
lion remained master of the field of battle." Now if three
hundred men could fire five hundred shots at a lion without
hurting him, it merely shows that they were wholly in-
capable of hurting any thing, or else that M. Gérard was
more expert with the long-bow than with the rifle. Gérard's
whole book is filled with equally preposterous nonsense; yet
a great many people seriously accept this same book as trustworthy authority for the manners and ferocity of the North
African lion. It would be quite as sensible to accept M.
Jules Verne's stories as being valuable contributions to science. A good deal of the lion's reputation is built upon
just such stuff.

How the prowess of the grizzly compares with that of
the lion or tiger would be hard to say; I have never shot
either of the latter myself, and my brother, who has killed
tigers in India, has never had a chance at a grizzly. Any
one of the big bears we killed on the mountains would, I
should think, have been able to make short work of either
a lion or a tiger; for the grizzly is greatly superior in bulk
and muscular power to either of the great cats, and its
teeth are as large as theirs, while its claws, though blunter,
are much longer; nevertheless, I believe that a lion or a
tiger would be fully as dangerous to a hunter or other
human being, on account of the superior speed of its charge,
the lightning-like rapidity of its movements, and its apparently sharper senses. Still, after all is said, the man should

have a thoroughly trustworthy weapon and a fairly cool head, who would follow into his own haunts and slay grim Old Ephraim.

A grizzly will only fight if wounded or cornered, or, at least, if he thinks himself cornered. If a man by accident stumbles on to one close up, he is almost certain to be attacked really more from fear than from any other motive; exactly the same reason that makes a rattlesnake strike at a passer-by. I have personally known of but one instance of a grizzly turning on a hunter before being wounded. This happened to a friend of mine, a Californian ranchman, who, with two or three of his men, was following a bear that had carried off one of his sheep. They got the bear into a cleft in the mountain from which there was no escape, and he suddenly charged back through the line of his pursuers, struck down one of the horsemen, seized the arm of the man in his jaws and broke it as if it had been a pipe-stem, and was only killed after a most lively fight, in which, by repeated charges, he at one time drove every one of his assailants off the field.

But two instances have come to my personal knowledge where a man has been killed by a grizzly. One was that of a hunter at the foot of the Bighorn Mountains who had chased a large bear and finally wounded him. The animal turned at once and came straight at the man, whose second shot missed. The bear then closed and passed on, after striking only a single blow; yet that one blow, given with all the power of its thick, immensely muscular forearm, armed with nails as strong as so many hooked steel spikes, tore out the man's collar-bone and snapped through three or four ribs. He never recovered from the shock, and died that night.

The other instance occurred to a neighbor of mine — who has a small ranch on the Little Missouri — two or three years ago. He was out on a mining trip, and was prospecting with two other men near the head-water of the Little

Missouri, in the Black Hills country. They were walking down along the river, and came to a point of land, thrust out into it, which was densely covered with brush and fallen timber. Two of the party walked round by the edge of the stream; but the third, a German, and a very powerful fellow, followed a well-beaten game trail, leading through the bushy point. When they were some forty yards apart the two men heard an agonized shout from the German, and at the same time the loud coughing growl, or roar, of a bear. They turned just in time to see their companion struck a terrible blow on the head by a grizzly, which must have been roused from its lair by his almost stepping on it; so close was it that he had no time to fire his rifle, but merely held it up over his head as a guard. Of course it was struck down, the claws of the great brute at the same time shattering his skull like an egg-shell. Yet the man staggered on some ten feet before he fell; but when he did he never spoke or moved again. The two others killed the bear after a short, brisk struggle, as he was in the midst of a most determined charge.

In 1872, near Fort Wingate, New Mexico, two soldiers of a cavalry regiment came to their death at the claws of a grizzly bear. The army surgeon who attended them told me the particulars, as far as they were known. The men were mail carriers, and one day did not come in at the appointed time. Next day, a relief party was sent out to look for them, and after some search found the bodies of both, as well as that of one of the horses. One of the men still showed signs of life; he came to his senses before dying, and told the story. They had seen a grizzly and pursued it on horseback, with their Spencer rifles. On coming close, one had fired into its side, when it turned with marvellous quickness for so large and unwieldy an animal, and struck down the horse, at the same time inflicting a ghastly wound on the rider. The other man dismounted and came up to the rescue of his companion. The bear then left the latter and attacked the other. Although hit by the bullet, it charged home and threw the man down, and then lay on him and deliberately bit him to death, while his groans and cries were frightful to hear. Afterward it walked off into the bushes without again offering to molest the already mortally wounded victim of its first assault.

At certain times the grizzly works a good deal of havoc among the herds of the stockmen. A friend of mine, a ranchman in Montana, told me that one fall bears became very plenty around his ranches, and caused him severe loss, killing with ease even full-grown beef-steers. But one of them once found his intended quarry too much for him. My friend had a stocky, rather vicious range stallion, which had been grazing one day near a small thicket of bushes, and, towards evening, came galloping in with three or four gashes in his haunch, that looked as if they had been cut with a dull axe. The cowboys knew at once that he had been assailed by a bear, and rode off to the thicket near which he had been feeding. Sure enough a bear, evidently in a very bad temper, sallied out as soon as the thicket was surrounded, and, after a spirited fight and a succession of charges, was killed. On examination, it was found that his under jaw was broken, and part of his face smashed in, evidently by the stallion's hoofs. The horse had been feeding when the bear leaped out at him but failed to kill at the first stroke; then the horse lashed out behind, and not only freed himself, but also severely damaged his opponent.

Doubtless, the grizzly could be hunted to advantage with dogs, which would not, of course, be expected to seize him, but simply to find and bay him, and distract his attention by barking and nipping. Occasionally a bear can be caught in the open and killed with the aid of horses. But nine times out of ten the only way to get one is to put on moccasins and still-hunt it in its own haunts, shooting it at close quarters. Either its tracks should be followed until the bed wherein it lies during the day is found, or a given locality in which it is known to exist should be carefully beaten through, or else a bait should be left out and a watch kept on it to catch the bear when he has come to visit it.

For some days after our arrival on the Bighorn range we did not come across any grizzly.

Although it was still early in September, the weather was cool and pleasant, the nights being frosty; and every two or three days there was a flurry of light snow, which rendered the labor of tracking much more easy. Indeed, throughout our stay on the mountains, the peaks were snow-capped almost all the time. Our fare was excellent, consisting of elk venison, mountain grouse, and small trout; the last caught in one of the beautiful little lakes that lay almost up by timber line. To us, who had for weeks been accustomed to make small fires from dried brush, or from sage-brush roots, which we dug out of the ground, it was a treat to sit at night before the roaring and crackling pine logs; as the old teamster quaintly put it, we had at last come to a land " where the wood grew on trees." There were plenty of black-tail deer in the woods, and we came across a number of bands of cow and calf elk, or of young bulls; but after several days' hunting, we were still without any head worth taking home, and had seen no sign of grizzly, which was the game we were especially anxious to kill; for neither Merrifield nor I had ever seen a wild bear alive.

Sometimes we hunted in company; sometimes each of us went out alone; the teamster, of course, remaining in to guard camp and cook. One day we had separated; I reached camp early in the afternoon, and waited a couple of hours before Merrifield put in an appearance.

At last I heard a shout — the familiar long-drawn *Ei-koh-h-h* of the cattle-men, — and he came in sight galloping at speed down an open glade, and waving his hat, evidently having had good luck; and when he reined in his small, wiry, cow-pony, we saw that he had packed behind his saddle the fine, glossy pelt of a black bear. Better still, he announced that he had been off about ten miles to a perfect tangle of ravines and valleys where bear sign was very thick; and not of black bear either but of grizzly. The black bear (the only one we got on the mountains) he had run across by accident, while riding up a valley in which there was a patch of dead timber grown up with berry bushes. He noticed a black object which he first took to be a stump; for during the past few days we had each of us made one or two clever stalks up to charred logs which our imagination converted into bears. On coming near, however, the object suddenly took to its heels; he followed over frightful ground at the pony's best pace, until it stumbled and fell down. By this time he was close on the bear, which had just reached the edge of the wood. Picking himself up, he rushed after it, hearing it growling ahead of him; after running some fifty yards the sounds stopped, and he stood still listening. He saw and heard nothing, until he happened to cast his eyes upwards, and there was the bear, almost overhead, and about twenty-five feet up a tree; and in as many seconds afterwards it came down to the ground with a bounce, stone dead. It was a young bear, in its second year, and had probably never before seen a man, which accounted for the ease with which it was treed and taken. One minor result of the encounter was to convince Merrifield — the list of whose faults did not include lack of self-confidence — that he could run down any bear; in consequence of which idea we on more than one subsequent occasion went through a good deal of violent exertion.

Merrifield's tale made me decide to shift camp at once, and go over to the spot where the bear-tracks were so plenty. Next morning we were off, and by noon pitched camp by a clear brook, in a valley with steep, wooded sides, but with good feed for the horses in the open bottom. We rigged the canvas wagon sheet into a small tent, sheltered by the trees from the wind, and piled great pine logs near by where we wished to place the fire; for a night camp in the sharp fall weather is cold and dreary unless there is a roaring blaze of flame in front of the tent.

That afternoon we again went out, and I shot a fine bull elk. I came home alone toward nightfall, walking through a reach of burnt forest, where there was nothing but charred tree-trunks and black mould. When nearly through it I came across the huge, half-human footprints of a great grizzly, which must have passed by within a few minutes. It gave me rather an eerie feeling in the silent, lonely woods, to see for the first time the unmistakable proofs that I was in the home of the mighty lord of the wilderness. I followed the tracks in the fading twilight until it became too dark to see them any longer, and then shouldered my rifle and walked back to camp.

That evening we almost had a visit from one of the animals we were after. Several times we had heard at night the musical calling of the bull elk — a sound to which no writer has as yet done justice. This particular night, when we were in bed and the fire was smouldering, we were roused by a ruder noise — a kind of grunting or roaring whine, answered by the frightened snorts of the ponies. It was a bear which had evidently not seen the fire, as it came from behind the bank, and had probably been attracted by the smell of the horses. After it made out what we were it stayed round a short while, again uttered its peculiar roaring grunt, and went off; we had seized our rifles and had run out into the woods, but in the darkness could see nothing; indeed it was rather lucky we did not stumble across the bear, as he could have made short work of us when we were at such a disadvantage.

Next day we went off on a long tramp through the woods and along the sides of the canyons. There were plenty of berry bushes growing in clusters; and all around these there were fresh tracks of bear. But the grizzly is also a flesh-eater, and has a great liking for carrion. On visiting the place where Merrifield had killed the black bear, we found that the grizzlies had been there before us, and had utterly devoured the carcass, with cannibal relish. Hardly a scrap was left, and we turned our steps toward where lay the bull elk I had killed. It was quite late in the afternoon when we reached the place. A grizzly had evidently been at the carcass during the preceding night, for his great footprints were in the ground all around it, and the carcass itself was gnawed and torn, and partially covered with earth and leaves — for the grizzly has a curious habit of burying all of his prey that he does not at the moment need. A great many ravens had been feeding on the body, and they wheeled about over the tree tops above us, uttering their barking croaks.

The forest was composed mainly of what are called ridge-pole pines, which grow close together, and do not branch out until the stems are thirty or forty feet from the ground. Beneath these trees were walked over a carpet of pine needles, upon which our moccasined feet made no sound. The woods seemed vast and lonely, and their silence was broken now and then by the strange noises always to be heard in the great forests, and which seem to mark the sad and everlasting unrest of the wilderness. We climbed up along the trunk of a dead tree which had toppled over until its upper branches struck in the limb crotch of another, that thus supported it at an angle halfway in its fall. When above the ground far enough to prevent the bear's smelling us, we sat still to wait for his approach; until, in the gathering gloom, we could no longer see the sights of our rifles, and could but dimly make out the carcass of the great elk. It was useless to wait longer; and we clambered down and stole out to the edge of the woods. The forest here covered one side of a steep, almost canyon-like ravine, whose other side was bare except of rock and sage-brush. Once out from under the trees there was still plenty of light, although the sun had set, and we crossed over some fifty yards to the opposite hill-side, and crouched down under a bush to see if perchance some animal might not also leave the cover. To our right the ravine sloped downward toward the valley of the Bighorn River, and far on its other side we could catch a glimpse of the great main chain of the Rockies, their snow peaks glinting crimson in the light of the set sun. Again we waited quietly in the growing dusk until the pine trees in our front blended into one dark, frowning mass. We saw nothing; but the wild creatures of the forest had begun to stir abroad. The owls hooted dismally from the tops of the tall trees, and two or three times a harsh wailing cry, probably the voice of some lynx or wolverine, arose from the depths of the woods. At last, as we were rising to leave, we heard the sound of the breaking of a dead stick, from the spot where we knew the carcass lay. It was a sharp, sudden noise, perfectly distinct from the natural creaking and snapping of the branches; just such a sound as would be made by the tread of some heavy creature. " Old Ephraim " had come back to the carcass. A minute afterward, listening with strained ears, we heard him brush by some dry twigs. It was entirely too dark to go in after him; but we made up our minds that on the morrow he should be ours.

Early next morning we were over at the elk carcass, and, as we expected, found that the bear had eaten his fill at it during the night. His tracks showed him to be an immense fellow, and were so fresh that we doubted if he had left long before we arrived; and we made up our minds to follow him up and try to find his lair. The bears that lived on these mountains had evidently been little disturbed; indeed, the Indians and most of the white hunters are rather chary of meddling with " Old Ephraim," as the mountain men style the grizzly, unless they get him at a disadvantage; for the sport is fraught with some danger and but small profit. The bears thus seemed to have very little fear of harm, and we thought it likely that the bed of the one who had fed on the elk would not be far away.

My companion was a skilful tracker, and we took up the trail at once. For some distance it led over the soft, yielding carpet of moss and pine needles, and the foot-prints were quite easily made out, although we could follow them but slowly; for we had, of course, to keep a sharp look-out ahead and around us as we walked noiselessly on in the sombre half-light always prevailing under the great pine trees, through whose thickly interlacing branches stray but few beams of light, no matter how bright the sun may be outside. We made no sound ourselves, and every little sudden noise sent a thrill through me as I peered about with each sense on the alert. Two or three of the ravens that we had scared from the carcass flew overhead, croaking hoarsely; and the pine tops moaned and sighed in the slight breeze — for pine trees seem to be ever in motion, no matter how light the wind.

After going a few hundred yards the tracks turned off on a well-beaten path made by the elk; the woods were in many places cut up by these game trails, which had often become as distinct as ordinary foot-paths. The beast's footprints were perfectly plain in the dust, and he had lumbered along up the path until near the middle of the hill-side, where the ground broke away and there were hollows and boulders. Here there had been a windfall, and the dead trees lay among the living, piled across one another in all directions; while between and around them sprouted up a thick growth of young spruces and other evergreens. The trail turned off into the tangled thicket, within which it was almost certain we would find our quarry. We could still follow the tracks, by the slight scrapes of the claws on the bark, or by the bent and broken twigs; and we advanced with noiseless caution, slowly climbing over the dead tree trunks and upturned stumps, and not letting a branch rustle or catch on our clothes. When in the middle of the thicket we crossed what was almost a breastwork of fallen logs, and Merrifield, who was leading, passed by the upright stem of a great pine. As soon as he was by it he sank suddenly on one knee, turning half round, his face fairly aflame with excitement; and as I strode past him, with my rifle at the ready, there, not ten steps off, was the great bear, slowly rising from his bed among the young spruces. He had heard us, but apparently hardly knew exactly where or what we were, for he reared up on his haunches sideways to us. Then he saw us and dropped down again on all fours, the shaggy hair on his neck and shoulders seeming to bristle as he turned toward us. As he sank down on his forefeet I had raised the rifle; his head was bent slightly down, and when I saw the top of the white bead fairly between his small, glittering, evil eyes, I pulled trigger. Half-rising up, the huge beast fell over on his side in the death throes, the ball having gone into his brain, striking as fairly between the eyes as if the distance had been measured by a carpenter's rule.

The whole thing was over in twenty seconds from the time I caught sight of the game; indeed, it was over so quickly that the grizzly did not have time to show fight at all or come a step toward us. It was the first I had ever seen, and I felt not a little proud, as I stood over the great brindled bulk, which lay stretched out at length in the cool shade of the evergreens. He was a monstrous fellow, much larger than any I have seen since, whether alive or brought in dead by the hunters. As near as we could estimate (for of course we had nothing with which to weigh more than very small portions) he must have weighed about twelve hundred pounds, and though this is not as large as some of his kind are said to grow in California, it is yet a very unusual size for a bear. He was a good deal heavier than any of our horses; and it was with the greatest difficulty that we were able to skin him. He must have been very old, his teeth and claws being all worn down and blunted; but nevertheless he had been living in plenty, for he was as fat as a prize hog, the layers on his back being a finger's length in thickness. He was still in the summer coat, his hair being short, and in color a curious brindled brown, somewhat like that of certain bull-dogs; while all the bears we shot afterward had the long thick winter fur, cinnamon or yellowish brown. By the way, the name of this bear has reference to its character and not to its color, and should, I suppose, be properly spelt grisly — in the sense of horrible, exactly as we speak of a " grisly spectre " — and not grizzly; but perhaps the latter way of spelling it is too well established to be now changed.

In killing dangerous game steadiness is more needed than good shooting. No game is dangerous unless a man is close up, for nowadays hardly any wild beast will charge from a distance of a hundred yards, but will rather try to run off; and if a man is close it is easy enough for him to shoot straight if he does not lose his head. A bear's brain is about the size of a pint bottle; and any one can hit a pint bottle off-hand at thirty or forty feet. I have had two shots at bears at close quarters, and each time I fired into the brain, the bullet in one case striking fairly between the eyes, as told above, and in the other going in between the eye and ear. A novice at this kind of sport will find it best and safest to keep in mind the old Norse viking's advice in reference to a long sword. "If you go in close enough your sword will be long enough." If a poor shot goes in close enough he will find that he shoots straight enough.

I was very proud over my first bear; but Merrifield's chief feeling seemed to be disappointment that the animal had not had time to show fight. He was rather a reckless fellow, and very confident in his own skill with the rifle; and he really did not seem to have any more fear of the grizzlies than if they had been so many jack-rabbits. I did not at all share his feelings, having a hearty respect for my foes' prowess, and in following and attacking them always took all possible care to get the chances on my side. Merrifield was sincerely sorry that we never had to stand a regular charge; while on this trip we killed five grizzlies with seven bullets, and except in the case of the she and cub, spoken of further on, each was shot about as quickly as it got sight of us. The last one we got was an old male, which was feeding on an elk carcass. We crept up to within about sixty feet, and as Merrifield had not yet killed a grizzly purely to his own gun, and I had killed three, I told him to take the shot. He at once whispered gleefully: "I 'll break his leg, and we 'll see what he 'll do!" Having no ambition to be a participator in the antics of a three-legged bear, I hastily interposed a most emphatic veto; and with a rather injured air he fired, the bullet going through the neck just back of the head. The bear fell to the shot, and could not get up from the ground, dying in a few minutes; but first he seized his left wrist in his teeth and bit clean through it, completely separating the bones of the paw and arm. Although a smaller bear than the big one I first shot, he would probably have proved a much more ugly foe, for he was less unwieldy, and had much longer and sharper teeth and claws. I think that if my companion had merely broken the beast's leg he would have had his curiosity as to its probable conduct more than gratified.

We tried eating the grizzly's flesh but it was not good, being coarse and not well flavored; and besides, we could not get over the feeling that it had belonged to a carrion feeder. The flesh of the little black bear, on the other hand, was excellent; it tasted like that of a young pig. Doubtless, if a young grizzly, which had fed merely upon fruits, berries, and acorns, was killed, its flesh would prove good eating; but even then, it would probably not be equal to a black bear.

A day or two after the death of the big bear, we went out one afternoon on horseback, intending merely to ride down to see a great canyon lying some six miles west of our camp; indeed, we went more to look at the scenery than for any other reason, though, of course, neither of us ever stirred out of camp without his rifle. We rode down the valley in which we had camped, through alternate pine groves and open glades, until we reached the canyon, and then skirted its brink for a mile or so. It was a great chasm, many miles in length, as if the table-land had been rent asunder by some terrible and unknown force; its sides were sheer walls of rock, rising three or four hundred feet straight up in the air, and worn by the weather till they looked like the towers and battlements of some vast fortress. Between them at the bottom was a space, in some places nearly a quarter of a mile wide, in others very narrow, through whose middle foamed a deep, rapid torrent of which the sources lay far back among the snow-topped mountains around Cloud Peak. In this valley, dark-green, sombre pines stood in groups, stiff and erect; and here and there among them were groves of poplar and cotton-wood, with slender branches and trembling leaves, their bright green already changing to yellow in the sharp fall weather. We went down to where the mouth of the canyon opened out, and rode our horses to the end of a great jutting promontory of rock, thrust out into the plain; and in the cold, clear air we looked far over the broad valley of the Bighorn as it lay at our very feet, walled in on the other side by the distant chain of the Rocky Mountains.

Turning our horses, we rode back along the edge of another canyon-like valley, with a brook flowing down its centre, and its rocky sides covered with an uninterrupted pine forest — the place of all others in whose inaccessible wildness and ruggedness a bear would find a safe retreat. After some time we came to where other valleys, with steep, grass-grown sides, covered with sage-brush, branched out from it, and we followed one of these out. There was plenty of elk sign about, and we saw several black-tail deer. These last were very common on the mountains, but we had not hunted them at all, as we were in no need of meat. But this afternoon we came across a buck with remarkably fine antlers, and accordingly I shot it, and we stopped to cut off and skin out the horns, throwing the reins over the heads of the horses and leaving them to graze by themselves. The body lay near the crest of one side of a deep valley, or ravine, which headed up on the plateau a mile to our left. Except for scattered trees and bushes the valley was bare; but there was heavy timber along the crests of the hills on its opposite side. It took some time to fix the head properly, and we were just ending when Merrifield sprang to his feet and exclaimed: "Look at the bears!" pointing down into the valley below us. Sure enough there were two bears (which afterwards proved to be an old she and a nearly full-grown cub) travelling up the bottom of the valley, much too far off for us to shoot. Grasping our rifles and throwing off our hats we started off as hard as we could run, diagonally down the hill-side, so as to cut them off. It was some little time before they saw us, when they made off at a lumbering gallop up the valley. It would seem impossible to run into two grizzlies in the open, but they were going up hill and we down, and moreover the old one kept stopping. The cub would forge ahead and could probably have escaped us, but the mother now and then stopped to sit up on her haunches and look around at us when the cub would run back to her. The upshot was that we got ahead of them, when they turned and went straight up one hill-side as we ran straight down the other behind them. By this time I was pretty nearly done out, for running along the steep ground through the sage-brush was most exhausting work; and Merrifield kept gaining on me and was well in front. Just as he disappeared over a bank, almost at the bottom of the valley, I tripped over a bush and fell full-length. When I got up

I knew I could never make up the ground I had lost, and besides, could hardly run any longer; Merrifield was out of sight below, and the bears were laboring up the steep hillside directly opposite and about three hundred yards off, so I sat down and began to shoot over Merrifield's head, aiming at the big bear. She was going very steadily and in a straight line, and each bullet sent up a puff of dust where it struck the dry soil, so that I could keep correcting my aim; and the fourth ball crashed into the old bear's flank. She lurched heavily forward, but recovered herself and reached the timber, while Merrifield, who had put on a spurt, was not far behind.

I toiled up the hill at a sort of trot, fairly gasping and sobbing for breath; but before I got to the top I heard a couple of shots and a shout. The old bear had turned as soon as she was in the timber, and came towards Merrifield, but he gave her the death wound by firing into her chest, and then shot at the young one, knocking it over. When I came up he was just walking towards the latter to finish it with the revolver, but it suddenly jumped up as lively as ever and made off at a great pace — for it was nearly full-grown. It was impossible to fire where the tree trunks were so thick, but there was a small opening across which it would have to pass, and collecting all my energies I made a last run, got into position, and covered the opening with my rifle. The instant the bear appeared I fired, and it turned a dozen somersaults down-hill, rolling over and over; the ball had struck it near the tail and had ranged forward through the hollow of the body. Each of us had thus given the fatal wound to the bear in which the other had fired the first bullet. The run, though short, had been very sharp, and over such awful country that we were completely fagged out, and could hardly speak for lack of breath. The sun had already set, and it was too late to skin the animals; so we merely dressed them, caught the ponies — with some trouble, for they were frightened at the smell of the bear's blood on our hands, — and rode home through the darkening woods. Next day we brought the teamster and two of the steadiest pack-horses to the carcasses, and took the skins into camp.

The feed for the horses was excellent in the valley in which we were camped, and the rest after their long journey across the plains did them good. They had picked up wonderfully in condition during our stay on the mountains; but they were apt to wander very far during the night, for there were so many bears and other wild beasts around that they kept getting frightened and running off. We were very loath to leave our hunting grounds, but time was pressing, and we had already many more trophies than we could carry; so one cool morning, when the branches of the evergreens were laden with the feathery snow that had fallen overnight, we struck camp and started out of the mountains, each of us taking his own bedding behind his saddle, while the pack-ponies were loaded down with bear-skins, elk and deer antlers, and the hides and furs of other game. In single file we moved through the woods, and across the canyons to the edge of the great table-land, and then slowly down the steep slope to its foot, where we found our canvas-topped wagon; and next day saw us setting out on our long journey homewards, across the three hundred weary miles of treeless and barren-looking plains country.

Last spring, since the above was written, a bear killed a man not very far from my ranch. It was at the time of the floods. Two hunters came down the river, by our ranch, on a raft, stopping to take dinner. A score or so of miles below, as we afterwards heard from the survivor, they landed, and found a bear in a small patch of brush-wood. After waiting in vain for it to come out, one of the men rashly attempted to enter the thicket, and was instantly struck down by the beast, before he could so much as fire his rifle. It broke in his skull with a blow of its great paw, and then seized his arm in its jaws, biting it through and through in three places, but leaving the body and retreating into the bushes as soon as the unfortunate man's companion approached. We did not hear of the accident until too late to go after the bear, as we were just about starting to join the spring round-up.

THE VANISHED SCENE

HAL G. EVARTS

From "The Passing of the Old West." Reprinted by permission of the publishers, Little, Brown, and Company.[1]

WHEREVER men fared, no matter how secluded the pocket of the hills to which they penetrated, they found evidence that some solitary wanderer had been before them. His horses had grazed in hidden meadows and they found the ashes of his camp fires on the shores of unmapped lakes. It was said that the range that rimmed the new land in on the east was impenetrable, that no man could cross through its wild passes; but in the dead of winter, long after the Crow tribe had taken to winter quarters in the lower valleys, some white man's lone trail was often seen leading down out of these peaks which others shunned even in the warmth of summer. He was even welcome in the wigwams of the Crows and frequently he tarried for a few days in their villages, but his restlessness always drove him forth to leave his tracks in the secluded fastnesses of the winter hills. When a party of explorers pressed westward up the valley of the Stinking Water to determine if an entrance might be effected from the east, they found the trails of horses leading up a tributary stream which broke in from the west where the main river flared back in a wide sweeping curve to the north and east. These tracks led up an elk trail, threaded the mazes of a frowning gorge, crossed the lower extremities of late-melting snow banks and came out at last upon the Yellowstone Slope.

[1] Copyright, 1921, by Little, Brown, and Company.

The news of the segregation of these hills and valleys he loved had brought to Mart Woodson another of those rare moments of exaltation. The invariable theme of his childhood tales had dealt with the near-serfdom of the inhabitants of far countries and had built up in his mind the belief that the people of other lands were chattels. Now, as if in direct refutation of those ancient policies which decreed that the land was God-given for the benefit and pleasure of the few, his country had set aside the wonder-spot of the world for the enjoyment of the many. This vast reservation, more than three thousand square miles of it, belonged to the people as a whole, a joint estate to descend to unborn generations for a thousand years to come. Never a foot of it could come into the possession of individuals or concerns.

What more could a man ask than to live his life upon his own estate comprising hundreds of square miles? This belonged to him. A thousand might share it, or ten thousand, but his own rights would ever remain the same. He could make his night fire on the shores of some stream, leave it the next morning and never look upon it again till the last day of his life, but always with the certain knowledge that on that day he could return and say, " Here is my camp," and no man could wave him off. But a man should know his own property, — so Mart Woodson set forth to explore every nook of this vast estate which had so unexpectedly been willed to him.

His wants were few. He killed his meat as he needed it and when he felt the necessity of gaining a few dollars with which to buy supplies he worked with the construction gang that had been sent here to hew out a primitive road system through the People's Park while the nearest railroad point was yet five hundred miles away; but mostly he roamed the hills and whenever seen was mounted on a bay mare that mothered a mare colt. He scoured the hills for gold in summers and panned the streams from the Flathead to the Green, prospected the ledges for quartz from Big Wing River to the Gallatin. When a party of explorers verified the existence of the stream which flowed to both seas and heralded to the world their find of Two Ocean Pass, they found also a low mound of earth surmounted by a headboard slabbed out with an ax and rudely carved with the words " Tom North," testimony that in this spot men had lived and died before they came.

Jim Bridger's tale of the mountain of black glass had roused a shriek of derision that echoed round the earth, yet in time others found it as he had said they would, and as they gazed upon the obsidian cliff they found the tracks of a mare and colt along its base. Homeric mirth had rocked the world at Bridger's assertion that he had caught fish in the icy waters of a lake and cooked them in boiling springs without rising from his seat or removing his prey from the hook. When explorers reached this spot they found the bones of fish upon the rocks. The lone wanderer had once more preceded them and cooked his meal of trout a month before they came.

And it was Woodson himself who now came in for a share of ridicule and met general disbelief when he told men of the petrified forest he had found. It stood on a steep side-hill cut away by the action of water. Tier upon tier it rose, succeeding layers exposed to view, fifteen periods of forestation one above the other. Near the base were stumps more than a dozen feet in diameter, relics of the ages past, when tropical vegetation flourished here. Above these ancient ones, in successive accumulation, was the evidence of the gradual cooling of the earth on down to date, the top strata containing vegetation of the present age. Here were not merely crumbling fragments of bygone periods but exact reproductions, the preserved record of the whole; bark and twigs intact, ferns and shrubbery, even to the buds, held in delicate tracery of stone and sprouting from the outcroppings to the cliff. But in Woodson's case the disbelief was not so widespread. Men were beginning to believe all things possible of this wondrous corner of the earth. It was decided that he should lead a party to the spot, but when they sought for him the wanderer was gone. Years later he led men to the ledges and they found it as he had said, the most complete record of its kind in the world.

Woodson had moved on in search of new lands and for months he traveled into the west, moving by easy stages with his little pack string, sampling the ledges and panning the streams en route. Everywhere there was food in plenty and he lived off the country as he roamed. He came at last into a land whose natural wealth staggered his imagination, the giant forests of the northwest coast. There were stretches where he might travel for weeks without once leaving the timber; and such timber! Fir, spruce and cedar side by side, each monster capable of furnishing from within its own mighty trunk the lumber for a small village. They stood ten to eighteen feet through at the butts, rising with barely perceptible lessening of dimension, towering three hundred feet aloft, two thirds of their height without a limb. From these a man might cut beams six feet through by a hundred feet in length as easily as eight-inch board stuff is cut from the average tree. Week after week he wandered through this king of forests, the ferns growing to his saddle skirts. There was one stretch of a hundred miles each way, covered with a solid stand of the finest timber known to man. He lingered in this tract for a solid year. Here, in this one stretch, he estimated, was enough lumber to rebuild the world, lumber that was clear, straight-grained and without a knot.

He was a man of the open, attuned to Nature's varying moods; he had felt the different spells exerted by mountain, lake and plain and thought that he knew them all; yet here was something new. There was a hush in the dim aisles of this mightiest of all forests, a reverent silence rarely broken. It was so completely roofed over by the tufted tops as to almost exclude the light. Even the night sounds were subdued as if the wild things hesitated to raise their voices above the softest croon and cheep necessary for communication among themselves. Woodson some way disliked to shatter the silence with his voice and when he spoke to his horses it was in the modulated tones one uses in some ancient cathedral freighted with reverent memories.

After a year the call of the Yellowstone drew him on the back trail. As he traveled he sometimes pondered about that mark he would make for himself in the world. Yet there was no hurry. There was undreamed plenty of everything in this land of his. One had but to choose his course, dip in and help himself from the storehouse that was inexhaustible, — Nature's storehouse that replenished itself without help. He reflected that ever since history began, this natural reservoir had been refilled more rapidly than it could possibly be depleted by man. A world of plenty; leather for all the world from the buffalo of the plains; hardwood timber without end to the eastward; free grass for fifty million cows; meat for the nation from the antelope of the plains and the elk and mule deer of the hills; wealth untold for those who would seek for it and burrow in the ground for gold; and in this great untouched forest of the northwest coast was enough lumber to roof the earth. He smiled and slapped the brown mare on the neck as a whimsical thought crossed his mind.

" She didn't forget a thing," he said. "She didn't leave one thing out. There's enough of everything to go round and a lot to spare. Back in the Yellowstone, where we're headed for, there's enough natural and unnatural wonders to entertain the people of the world. She didn't even leave that out — plenty of everything for us all."

As he traveled eastward his desire to look again upon this best land of all increased and he made longer packs. Soon it was rumored that the lone wanderer, for so long a part of the Park, had returned to roam once more in the hills of the Yellowstone. He knew the valleys of warm springs where his horses might winter while others were forced to drive their stock to the lower country. He prospected far and wide in summer but always he came back to winter within the limits of his own estate.

After a lapse of perhaps fifteen years since Woodson and Old Tom had quit the plains, a little pack train was seen winding down the east slope of the hills. The man rode a bay mare that mothered a mare colt. In the rear of the string still another bay mare, ancient and decrepit, pensioned for long service and unburdened by a pack, trailed stiffly after the rest. The man told those he met along the trails that he was headed for the lower country to join a hide outfit for one last buffalo hunt on the plains. Men smiled at the naïve plans of this Rip Van Winkle who had been asleep in the hills; for the buffalo was gone.

Woodson knew that the men from his old outfit — Hanson, Cleve, McCann and all the rest — would be wherever the most of the shaggy beasts had congregated for the southward drift of fall. But when he made inquiry he found that their names were unknown to the present-day dwellers of the foothills. Men told him that the buffalo was no more. That the last of them had been killed off to make room for the settler's cows. As he traveled east he experienced a series of surprises. Stockmen's cabins showed at every water hole where, but a few years past, there had been no human habitation within two hundred miles. All this was as it should be, he reflected; a wild country tamed and made habitable for man. It was clear that the buffalo had to go to make room for the cows. But the job had certainly been sweeping and thorough. He crossed vast stretches where domestic stock had not yet arrived but the way had been paved for them years in advance of their coming, for not a single buffalo track could he find. Little towns had sprung up with amazing rapidity. Out in the long desolate stretch between Lander and Rawlins he covered fortytwo miles unmarked by a water hole, an arid region where domestic stock could not live but where the buffalo might have ranged in thousands; but here too they had been wiped out to the last hoof. It came to him that he knew of enough waste areas, as yet untouched by cows, to support a half-million head of buffalo. They would have constituted a source of revenue for many years to come. Men spoke vaguely of the " lost herd " that lived in some unknown spot and would one day repopulate these waste stretches with buffalo. Woodson could see that all this development was for the best; there were now homes where no homes stood before. But a vague uneasiness assailed him, a sense of something gone amiss with a popular idol. Some way it seemed that he had been warned of this. Some forgotten prophecy welled up out of the past to clamor for expression at the threshold of his consciousness. It troubled him that he should not quite place the thing and he attempted to shake it off.

He left his horses with a cowman and held on to the east. The old trails where once the prairie schooners and the ox-bows had wound interminably to the far horizon were no longer traveled. Steel rails stretched away in their stead; and the creak of wheels and leather and the bawls of plodding oxen, — all these were replaced by the rattle and roar of freight cars and the screech of the locomotives' whistles; city streets wound where there had been naught but dog towns on blistering flats.

Truly development was wonderful and he rejoiced with the rest over this sweeping transformation, the swiftest and most complete reclamation in the history of the world. But again the still small voice assailed him from within and whispered that a good and worthy job had been just a trifle too well done.

A cold fall storm was driving down from the north and overtook him in the salt-marsh country of Western Kansas. The water fowl scurried ahead of it. Every pond and slough, each broad prairie lake and marshy bottom was covered with members of the feathered horde en route to the winter quarters on the Gulf. Flock followed flock in an endless procession, streaking the sky. The prairies were covered with feeding geese. Great white cranes stalked majestically in the open flats, traveling in bands of hundreds, and at night the wild whoops of overhead squadrons almost drowned the clamor of oncoming hordes of geese. This evidence of abundance cheered him. He estimated that he saw over a million birds a day; and he reflected that everywhere east and west of him this great migration was going on; the east coast and the west, the Mississippi flyway and the course of every inland river; all were experiencing this same deluge of birds headed into the south. Nowhere had he seen so much bird life except during the pigeon flights in the hardwood country of his boyhood home. There he had seen the skies blackened with wild pigeons, had seen limbs broken from the trees by the sheer weight of thousands of roosting birds. The shock of finding the buffalo gone from the plains in a few short years was counteracted by this fresh evidence of plenty.

It was in Dodge that his trail crossed that of Hanson, a man from his old outfit. Hanson, with a younger man named Rice, was hunting antelope for the hides. The two spoke of old friends. Cleve had gone to the lumber camps of the northwest coast, Hanson informed, and McCann to the hardwood belt to the east. They had quit the hunting. Antelope were fleet and it was difficult to stalk them in the flats. Hanson had known the time when all hands might kill and skin an average of twenty buffalo to the man each day. He now lamented the necessity of hunting the wary pronghorn for less than a dollar a hide. A man was doing well to average four a day.

" The old days are gone," he said. " Things are different now. It's hard pickings for a man to make a living in times like these."

But Rice looked forth on the world with the optimism

of youth. It was a land of plenty in which he lived. He had planned a hunt in the hills of Western Colorado and urged Woodson to throw in with them.

" There's millions of deer up there," he said. " They're paying three dollars apiece for venison saddles at the mines. I've seen ten thousand mule deer boiling through the passes, all in sight at once, when they gathered from the Gore Range and the Rabbit Ear to drift down to the Oak Hills for the winter. There's deer without end. I hunted up there last year. We loaded thirty four-horse freight wagons with deer saddles, high as we could lash 'em on, all from a two-day kill in one pass as they came streaming down, a thousand to the band. There's good money in meat-hunting for the mines. You better throw in with us, Mart, and come along."

They urged their case but Woodson would not join. The rapidity with which old conditions had slipped past him filled him with a sense of bewilderment. He could not get his start, as he had intended, by hide-hunting on the plains. That day had gone, and some way he could see no future in hunting deer to supply Denver and the Colorado mining towns with meat. Perhaps he would better go to the lumber camps, either east or west, and take up that end. There was more permanency to that. He could not make up his mind and decided at last to go back to the quiet hills of the Yellowstone for one final look around while making his decision.